SEVEN COMEDIES
BY
MARIVAUX

Other Books by Oscar Mandel

A Definition of Tragedy (1961)
The Theatre of Don Juan (1963)
Chi Po and the Sorcerer: A Chinese Tale for Children and Philosophers (1964)
Gobble-Up Stories (1966)
The Fatal French Dentist: A Comedy in One Act (1967)

marianne

Pierre Carlet de Chamblain
DE MARIVAUX,
de l'Académie Françoise,
né en 1688.   mort en 1763.

Le paysan
parvenu

Théâtre
de
Marivaux

From an engraving based on a now lost painting of Marivaux by
Pougin de Saint-Aubin. The engraved portrait appears in the 1781
edition of Marivaux's *Oeuvres complètes*.

SEVEN COMEDIES

BY

MARIVAUX

SELECTED AND EDITED BY

OSCAR MANDEL

ENGLISH VERSIONS BY

OSCAR AND ADRIENNE S. MANDEL

CORNELL UNIVERSITY PRESS

Ithaca, New York

First published 1968

Library of Congress Catalog Card Number: 68–16386

PRINTED IN THE UNITED STATES OF AMERICA
KINGSPORT PRESS, INC.

Vive mon joli jardin, soir et matin
J'y ris, j'y chante, j'y badine:
Ah! le favorable terrain,
La rose y croît sans épines.

Arlequin

Preface

Of the thirty-odd plays which Marivaux wrote from 1720 to
1757, I have selected four full-length and three one-act plays.
Four of these seven plays have never been published in English
at all; and the remaining three are presented in new versions.
Marivaux's two standard works, Le Jeu de l'amour et du
hasard and Les Fausses confidences, are given as a matter of
course. In my opinion, however, they have achieved their pre-
eminence by accident. They had lucky starts, and accumulated
performances, editions, and commentaries, according to the law
(as valid in literature as in the market place) that the rich become more rich. Since the English world of letters is unencum-
bered by tradition in this respect, I hope that several other plays,
which the French themselves are beginning to re-evaluate, will
eventually be raised to the same rank as the two consecrated
classics. Jean Vilar's productions at the Théâtre National Populaire of L'Heureux stratagème and Le Triomphe de
l'amour in 1962 proved that Marivaux, like so many artists in
the true classical vein, worked at a fairly uniform level. He does
not undergo the cataclysmic ups and downs of Romantic or of
modern authors, and there is in consequence no good reason why
one of his works should be revered and another forgotten.

Those who know their Marivaux will undoubtedly ask why I
have not translated either of the plays entitled La Suprise de
l'amour. I answer simply that for all their fame I believe them
to be a degree or two inferior to La Double inconstance and

L'Heureux stratagème, and to several other neglected plays as well, the utterly delightful La Dispute among them.[1] Marivaux wrote few stage directions for his plays, but gestures, inflections of the voice, and even facial expressions are all of extreme importance in them. "The gestures no less than the words," writes Claude Roy, "the silences no less than the replies, the movements no less than the cries, the entrances and exits, the stops, the hesitations marked by commas, the sidelong glances and the sighs—all are absolutely necessary for a full revelation of the text." Nevertheless, I have not encumbered these translations with officious suggestions: the texts are kept as bare as in the French. All I would whisper to the director is that the spirit of a bagatelle by Couperin ought to prevail beyond as well as within the words of the text.

It will be noticed that in the translations printed here, English names replace the French ones of Marivaux. This is done on the theory that a translation ought to go as far as possible in making what is familiar in the original equally familiar in the other language. Names like Orgon and Dorante, which are familiar to the French, are irremediably foreign to our ears, and usually pronounced with woeful distortions. Why then not find substitutes which approximate the effect on a French audience? Needless to say, this process of "naturalization," which pushes translation to its logical limit, is possible only where the locality is not emphasized or essential to the action, and where the characters have not become household names.

An additional incentive to renaming Marivaux's characters was that some of them are given only their titles in the originals. Now the English do not call each other Countess, Baron, or Knight, but Lady, Lord, and Sir So-and-So. Since, therefore, it became necessary to invent names, it seemed natural to make the inventions English rather than French. Those, however, who take the view that a transmutation of names amounts to adap-

[1] Le Triomphe de plutus is included in this volume as a bit of fluff which even the French theatres have not as yet "discovered." I am pleased that Professor E. J. H. Greene, in his excellent recent study of Marivaux, has a kind word to say about this playlet.

tation rather than naturalization will find the original names
listed in an appendix.

The case of Arlequin presented a different problem, since his
is a household name, and since he could easily have become
Harlequin. We decided to call him Robin or Puff for several
reasons. The first is that Harlequin is a foreigner to us even if
he does have an equivalent English name. The second is that,
with the exception of two early plays—ARLEQUIN POLI PAR
L'AMOUR and LA DOUBLE INCONSTANCE—Marivaux retained
the name of the traditional clown as a mere gesture toward the
Théâtre Italien. In actuality he converted the character into the
usual clever or doltish French servant—the very same who went
under the names of Lubin and Frontin in the plays he addressed
to the Comédie-Française; for—with the exceptions just noted
—he deprived the zany of all the visual capers which made the
true Arlecchino what he was. And third, so clearly is Arlequin
a fish out of water in most of Marivaux's comedies that in many
French productions he is stripped of his traditional motley and
clothed in the livery of a French servant.

The idea of naturalizing Marivaux's plays into English has
presided over all the translations in this volume. Because we feel
that these comedies can and should be staged in the English-
speaking world, we have labored to avoid the kind of literally
accurate "translatese" which makes an appearance, for example,
in one of the versions of Marivaux currently in print: "It is your
silence that I require in order to extricate myself from my present
absurd predicament, into which I have been precipitated by no
one but you." However, our desire for stageworthy speech has
not led us into reconceiving or adapting Marivaux. True, we
have ranged at will among English words, idioms, phrases,
similes, rhetorical and syntactical constructions, in order to obtain a tonal equivalence for Marivaux's lines which literal translation can never achieve; but our freedom has been circumscribed
by the principle of general conceptual equivalence—the principle that the theme of every given semantic unit must be preserved at any cost. In short, we have been free tenants of
Marivaux's words, but slaves to his ideas.

Our own words are drawn from the large stock of general English which a modern audience will find compatible with eighteenth-century staging, even if narrow inquiry would disclose that many of our expressions were not current in 1740. We have rigorously excluded all archaic words, expressions, and constructions. Better an occasional touch of the twentieth century, particularly in highly comic or exuberant passages, than a pedantic reconstruction of dead English.

Finally, in line with the overriding principle of naturalization, we have proscribed all vestiges of French—the *Monsieurs, Mademoiselles, pardis,* and *vertuchoux* which adorn so many translations of Molière. If an English or American translator can make a character say, "Parbleu! you speak like the wise man that you are," might not a Frenchman have Hamlet exclaim, "By heaven! je ferai un fantôme de celui qui me retient"? No translation is altogether successful until the reader forgets that an original exists in a foreign language.

My thanks go to the California Institute of Technology, which gave me a leave of absence to complete this work; to the Old Dominion Foundation, which helped with a grant; to the Bibliothèque de l'Arsenal, where I was able to leaf at will in the abundant dramatic literature of Marivaux's time; and to several friends and colleagues who gave me their generous advice in the course of my work: Mrs. Shirley Clement and Professors Marcel Bolomet, George P. Mayhew, and Richard P. Lillard.

O. M.

Amalfi, 1965, and Los Angeles, 1967

Contents

APPENDIXES

SEVEN COMEDIES

BY

MARIVAUX

Introduction

"Marivaux comes after Molière and Racine as Menander follows Aristophanes and Euripides." Thus Lucien Dubech in his classic *Histoire générale illustrée du théâtre*. At the Comédie-Française, where the thousandth performance of LE JEU DE L'AMOUR ET DU HASARD was celebrated in 1948, Marivaux is now the most frequently performed comic playwright after Molière. Since the Second World War, directors like Barrault, Vilar, and Planchon have mounted highly acclaimed productions at the Odéon, the Vieux Colombier, and the Théâtre National Populaire. Quite regularly, the dust is blown off a half-forgotten piece and a "new" work by Marivaux is staged, whether in Paris or in the provinces. Even the working classes are treated to these patrician follies: in the spring of 1965 I saw LA SURPRISE DE L'AMOUR shiver in a tent in Nanterre, an industrial suburb of Paris.

In their tours outside of France, French theatrical companies often present the best-known of Marivaux's comedies. We might note the highly successful production of LES FAUSSES CONFIDENCES by the Renaud-Barrault troupe in New York in 1952, and of LE JEU DE L'AMOUR ET DU HASARD by the Comédie-Française in London in 1967. But there is scarcely a country, from Latin America to the Soviet Union, in which a French company has not performed one or another of Marivaux's plays.

In France itself, to cite precise figures, nineteen of Marivaux's comedies have been produced at the Comédie-Française between

1901 and 1963, some many times and some only a few. Seven more have been staged in other French theatres in the same period; so that of the thirty comedies which Marivaux wrote for performance, twenty-six can be called "living theatre"—no mean achievement for any writer.[1] Beyond this, the plays continue to be reprinted in all forms, from cheap single school-text editions to luxurious book club collections. And a vast scholarly and critical literature concerning Marivaux keeps pace with editions and productions.

But in spite of occasional visits by French companies, very little of this interest has crossed either the Channel or the Atlantic. In over two centuries, only five of Marivaux's plays have been translated into English. The translations which do exist have all appeared singly; it has never been possible for a British or American reader who knows no French to browse through a volume of these standard plays. He has had to look for them one by one, now in an obscure eighteenth-century tome, now in a defunct magazine, now in a collection alongside other authors. And with one minor exception in 1761, it would seem that Marivaux has not been professionally performed in the English language at all—at least until the summer of 1965, when LA DOUBLE INCONSTANCE was given in English at the Pitlochry Festival in Scotland.

As for the literature concerning Marivaux, the first English book ever written about him—a specialized study of his novels—was published in 1941, one hundred and seventy-eight years after his death. The first English work dealing with his plays was a handbook published in 1958. It is fair to say therefore that while a rudimentary path to this classic has been beaten, Marivaux is still, for us, the most unavailable of all the great French playwrights.

The young man who chose to make his way in the worlds of literature and fashion as Monsieur de Marivaux was born in 1688 plain Pierre Carlet, the son of a finance official in Riom, a

---

[1] With a long overdue revival of L'HÉRITIER DE VILLAGE in Sartrouville, near Paris, in 1967, the number now stands at twenty-eight.

small town in the Auvergne. Nothing precise is known of Marivaux's early experiences, or even of his whereabouts, but in 1710 we find him in Paris, ostensibly to study law, actually to establish himself as a writer. Presently he contrived to be at home among authors like Fontenelle and la Motte, and to be received in several of the best salons; but when and how this son of the provincial bourgeoisie made his useful contacts we again do not know. Before long, however, he was breaking into print, battling at the side of his friends for the Moderns in that famous quarrel, and writing a parody of Homer which did nothing to advance the good cause. He was more successful with fashionable "letters," essays, and stories. To read these is to understand that Marivaux is from the start a man at ease in his times; he breathes and exhales the lucid air of Regency France; he enjoys—he loves—the salons where, according to a witness, he watches for his turn to toss off the aphorism he has been grooming in his mind.

We do not hear of any period of callow apprenticeship which he had to serve at the gatherings of Mme de Lambert or Mme de Tencin. It is as though he had been born full-grown in these drawing rooms; and his work was to remain a perfect formulation of their ideas. We can speak here of "natural elegance" as though the expression were not self-contradictory. Questions of love, the arts, justice, government, politics, religion; observations on mankind; news of the world—every concern was brought to these assemblies, where the rich, the intelligent, and the merely well-connected met. Everything could be said or at least suggested here, provided it was said or suggested with grace. To put it most broadly, this was a society in which a finish of beauty was placed on every activity of man for the last time in the history of the West. Whatever was spoken, conceived, and manufactured was spoken, conceived, and manufactured as beautifully as possible: down to the very weapons which killed other men.

Marivaux had taken his place in this world more as a man of talent than as a man of means. He had, however, means enough to dress well, and a judicious marriage—whether it was also a marriage of love we do not know—brought him a dowry. But

Marivaux was affable and careless; a friend persuaded him to invest his funds in Law's enterprises; and he was nearly ruined in the debacle of 1720. As it happens, he had begun his theatrical career a few months before the disaster; but there is no evidence that he ever sought to make money through his plays: they brought him little, and he wrote nothing to make them bring more.

Marivaux had made the acquaintance of a hack writer named Rustaing de Saint-Jory, with whom he collaborated on a comedy for the Théâtre Italien in March of 1720. The play promptly failed, but we can surmise that it gave Marivaux the introduction he needed. The Italians had reappeared in Paris in 1716 after an enforced exile of nineteen years. They were still newcomers; in serious financial trouble; and casting about for advice, help, and new plays in French. Half a year after his first failure, Marivaux gave them his most Italianate work, ARLEQUIN POLI PAR L'AMOUR, a genuine offspring of the *commedia dell'arte*. The public applauded. Marivaux and the Italians were undoubtedly pleased with each other. For twenty years, from 1720 to 1740, Marivaux was to supply them with his best work, eighteen comedies in all. But in 1742 the Academy made him a fellow-Immortal, and this uncomic honor all but closed his career. Unlike Molière, Marivaux had never become a professional man of the theatre. He never acted, never directed, and never produced a play. Novelist and essayist as much as dramatist, and man of the world as much as any of these, he clearly did not dream at any time in his life of becoming a trouper.

Ten of his plays, including his one tragedy, went to the Comédie-Française, but only one of them, LE PRÉJUGÉ VAINCU, was really well received by the public. The lightness of his prose, and his unusual talent for shades of feeling, half-differences, and tenuous gradations seem to have been too much—or too little!—for the French actors, who liked alexandrines, oratory, bold effects, and idiosyncratic characters. Though he kept trying to establish himself at the more respectable Théâtre Français, Marivaux had found his true home at the Hôtel de Bourgogne among the Italians, whose gracefulness matched his own; and in Gio-

vanna Benozzi a Sylvia so excellent that many of his contemporaries thought she would take his plays to the grave with her.

As it turned out, the Italians were enriched more in reputation
than hard cash during the twenty years in which they faithfully
produced Marivaux's plays. The comedies sometimes gave a good
account of themselves, but even at best they could not compete
with the ballets, fireworks, and musicals to which the Italians
had to resort in order to survive. And as often as not, the players
performed to nearly empty houses. Marivaux was not a bad
commercial risk, but he broke no records and made no impresario
rich.

So it was, too, with his literary standing. True, his reputation
should not be underrated, as it often is, for romantic effect. He
had many devoted admirers who made no noise, his plays were
performed by noble amateurs in several French chateaux, the
Italian and French companies took his new work year after year,
and he lived to see four collected editions of his plays through
the presses. This was a substantial accomplishment, and it would
be absurd to think of Marivaux as a neglected author because he
was not singled out as the greatest of his time. Still, when the
Mercure Galant calls him as late as 1747 "a famous Academician, accustomed to deserve the applause [*les suffrages*] of the
public," we hardly know whether we should rejoice over his
fame, or ruefully observe that he was accustomed to *deserve*, not
to *obtain,* his due.

Voltaire and a crowd of lesser wits were hostile to him. They
objected to what was immediately and has ever since been called
"marivaudage," that is to say a delicate and exquisite banter
about details of feeling. Voltaire accused Marivaux of "weighing
flies' eggs in scales of gossamer." The great man was obviously
put out by a writer who trifled full-time without participating in
the epic battles of the day. Pedants, on the other hand, were
appalled by audacities and impurities in Marivaux's language
which the modern ear is unable to detect. The Academician
whose duty it was to welcome the new member in 1743 insulted
him instead. Another was heard to say, "Our task at the Academy is to build up the language, while that of M. de Marivaux is

to tear it down." In sum, Marivaux was what is called a name, but there is no record of anyone pointing a finger at him to prophesy his permanence.

From a small bundle of anecdotes, from post-mortem *Eloges* and reports, and from the negative evidence of his own reticences, we gather that Marivaux was a quiet, witty, dapper, pleasant, and obliging man, rather more fastidious than most, not victimized by passions, not given to roaring, unwilling to quarrel with the world, and quite unable to beat his own drum. He was not indifferent to criticism—several stories concur as to his touchiness—but his response was to withdraw, not to counterattack, and then to forgive and forget at the first explanation. He wrote only one Preface for a play—a miracle of restraint for his times (or ours)—and engaged in no personal controversies. Nor was he a learned man. And despite his sympathy for the social views of the *philosophes,* he disliked their attacks on Christianity, a religion he respected and perhaps practiced to the end, though he did not allow it to interfere in his work.

He remained poor all his life. His wife had died in 1723, leaving him a daughter who eventually took the veil. As Marivaux could not pay for her annuity, the Duke of Orleans supplied the required funds. From the 1740's to his death in 1763, Marivaux cohabited with a certain Mlle de Saint-Jean, who was a little less poor than he, who supported him, and with whom we can suppose that he lived in quiet concord. There is little enough material for a life of Marivaux even in his best years. He was not the sort of man whose words are set down by eager Boswells, or over whom ladies gossip in their letters. For the autumnal years we have almost nothing. We get an impression of solitude without unhappiness; a corner kept for him in the salons; a tell-tale preoccupation with minor Academic duties. At his death (which was hardly noticed) he left an uncommon amount of fine linen.

The plays showed every sign of falling to dust. And yet in the years of the Revolution, of all times, Marivaux was rediscovered. The Comédie-Française inherited the plays which had been written for the now vanished Italians. And the nineteenth century gave him the absolute renown which had eluded him by a hair's breadth in his own lifetime. As a classic he was allowed to badger students at examinations, while in the theatres he simply managed to keep being amusing and interesting in ways which could neither be imitated nor superseded. Voltaire, it turned out, had chosen to forget that flies' eggs are worth weighing too, that weighing them is no easy matter, and that few artists are dextrous enough to make scales, or anything else, of gossamer. While Voltaire's own plays are shelved, while the tough Regnard is eclipsed, and while even Beaumarchais must be propped up by Mozart and Rossini, Marivaux seems as firmly settled in the French pantheon, a place of no easy admission, as Molière himself. This is, with a vengeance, the Triumph of Gossamer.

Who are the people in Marivaux's typical plays? One or two pairs of lovers at cross-purposes with each other; an occasional rival who leaves empty-handed; the servants, busy with their own love-knots while they are tying or untying their masters'; a father, a mother, an uncle, or a brother; and now and then a loquacious farmer.

Sometimes the principals are nameless; they are called simply la Comtesse, la Marquise, le Chevalier, le Comte: a broad hint that Marivaux is not primarily concerned with the delineation of peculiar characters. He is not, as he himself insisted, and as all critics agree, in Molière's school. Early in life he had determined to be original, by which he meant that he would not be overwhelmed by the presence of Molière. He preferred, says d'Alembert, to sit in the last rank of original writers than in the first row of imitators.

Now the tradition of comedy which Molière had bequeathed required the strong picture of a specific folly or vice. This was comedy of "humour" laced with social satire. Molière painted the miser, the misanthrope, the social climber, the hypochondriac, the religious hypocrite, even the atheist. His followers added the gambler, the married philosopher, the backbiter, the babbler, the stubborn man, the impertinent, the ambitious, the distracted man, and so on. The Comédie-Française looked upon itself as the temple of this drama of types.

In contrast to this genre, the *commedia dell'arte* was non-psychological and non-polemical. It drew on a small set of permanent types—the romantic lovers, the comic servants, the mean father, the dotty rival—and proceeded to embroil them in the most extravagant adventures, from robbed cradles to the revealing mark on the left ankle, through mistaken identities, meetings with monsters or pirates, shipwrecks, visits of the gods, disguises, duels, and other afflictions, all interrupted by the farcical capers—the *lazzi*—of Arlecchino, Brighella, Pedrolino, or any of the other zany servants. The world of the *commedia* was a madcap world of boisterous whimsy. The scenarios (it will be remembered that the actors usually relied on sketches of the action rather than written plays) had no philosophical, moral, or social pretensions of any kind. True, the comedians shot satirical gags in every direction—against lawyers, doctors, pedants, and especially loose wives and cuckolded husbands—but this was satire by the way, and uncontroversial satire at that. These gags peppered the plays; the plays were not acted out for their sake.

While his claim to originality was well-founded, Marivaux nevertheless shared with Molière a deep indebtedness to the *commedia*. The two men merely developed different sides of the Italian drama. Molière took as his province the old men of the *commedia*: the types of the Dottore and Pantalone. He gave them a character and an obsession. They were still grouchy fathers or tottering wooers, but now they were also misers or social climbers, and their activities in character (say the miser ordering a miserly dinner) overshadowed their role as fathers, and even relegated to the margin the intrigue by which the lovers had to be married.

Marivaux, perhaps because of his experience of the salons and his early intention of becoming a novelist, took up what Molière had neglected, and brought the lovers to the fore. The older men and women with their follies and vices recede or even disappear. Before us stand the young romantic principals, whom we immediately recognize as the lovers of the *commedia*. But Marivaux does not treat them in the Moliéresque manner; he does not give them "humours," peculiarities, obsessions—they are not gamblers or liars or prudes or slanderers who parade these short-comings before us. Marivaux is interested in the normal emotion of love itself (which the *commedia* had accepted as a simple fact requiring no analysis); he watches it appearing in a corner of the mind, then hiding, sometimes vanishing, aroused again, piqued, irritated, held back, offered to the wrong person, and finally settled where it belongs. He tells us how any normal girl feels when she believes she has fallen in love with a social inferior, or how she reacts when she learns by accident that an attractive man is insanely in love with her.

Usually, we might add, his young ladies are more sprightly, more attractive, and better observed than their suitors. Now we see a girl waiting and trembling for a declaration; now a coquette who jilts a man, only to long for him again when he neglects her; now a young widow resolved never to marry again, who struggles against her growing inclination to fall in love; now a flirtatious thing who swears fidelity to one man only to fall in love with another; now a girl so embarrassed by her own emotion that she "represses" it into unconsciousness; and now a girl who avenges herself on a fickle suitor. Marivaux observes his young men, too, but here he tends to repeat himself, and his markedly feminine genius cannot impart the toughness or the vigor we want in them. They do not swoon or weep, thank heaven, but they do sigh and implore too ardently, bashfulness makes them blind and deaf to the most obvious advances, and they have no sense of humor.[2] Sometimes, I am afraid, we feel like kicking them. If all must be said, even Marivaux's young women come in second-best to Molière's, whenever the master applies his mind to them. Marivaux has nothing quite so good as Célimène or Agnès, because he is too reticent, almost too hesitant. Molière is roast beef to his lemon soufflé. He is a miniaturist of genius; and nothing more, but also nothing less, should be claimed for him.

While Molière gave a new dimension to the characters of Pantalone and "il Dottore," and Marivaux explored the romantic

---

[2] ARLEQUIN POLI PAR L'AMOUR and LA DOUBLE INCONSTANCE, two early plays translated in this volume, provide notable exceptions.

lovers of the *commedia,* both joyously adopted Arlecchino and
Colombina. These servants—and their French siblings—lead
their masters' game, but they also divert us with troubles and
wisdom of their own. They make an earthy rejoinder to the lofty
sentiments of their superiors. In his plays of social commentary,
Marivaux sometimes uses them to convey his cautiously egalitar-
ian views.[3] Elsewhere, with the traditional freedom of the king's
fool, they comment acidulously on the mismanaged affairs of
society. Marivaux obviously delighted in the speech and the
attitudes of the "lower orders." These inferiors are usually the
most intelligent characters in the plays. At the same time, along
with Arlequin, Lisette, Trivelin, Frontin, and Spinette, Marivaux put shrewd or naïve farmers on stage—Blaise, Claudine,
Dimas, and others, probably derived from Molière and the
French tradition of popular comedy, and all of them as lovable as
Shakespeare's best clods.

Critics of Molière and Marivaux usually fall into the error of
giving these servants their secondary attention, because they
seem to play secondary roles. Of Marivaux, at any rate, it must
be said that he is never more gay and more brilliant than in the
so-called subordinate episodes in which his little people appear.
In LA DOUBLE INCONSTANCE, fortunately, they are full-fledged
protagonists, a fact which makes this the most effervescent of all
his longer plays.

Now and then a rather wicked person makes an appearance
on Marivaux's stage, but wicked persons somehow get themselves forgiven (or forgotten) before the curtain falls. Marivaux
does not hoot and hound them off the scene as the cruel Shakespeare does with Malvolio and the indignant Molière with Tar-
tuffe. Besides, when all is said and done, they are not so wicked
after all. Next to the cynical ferocity of Lesage, Regnard, Dan-
court, and other wits of his day (or that of the Restoration
dramatists of England), Marivaux's amiability and indulgence

---

[3] These little thesis-plays—L'ILE DES ESCLAVES, L'ILE DE LA RAISON,
and LA COLONIE—are of great historical interest, and they have been
staged in France in our time because of their "significance." This significance, however, does not extend to their aesthetic merit.

are altogether startling. In the work of his contemporaries, all the comic characters are irredeemable scoundrels, down to the ingé-nue; in his, none. And yet, by a miracle, he remains free of "larmoyance" and "attendrissement," if we accept one or two mediocre attempts in the new bourgeois genre.[4] For while his plays have no real villains, his slyness toward his heroes and heroines keeps our eyes—like their own—thoroughly dry.

Marivaux's success owes much to his control of the half-tone and the trembling uncertainty. Having few characters on stage, and only a short journey to go with them—say, from the birth to the declaration of love—Marivaux is able to *stay with them*, minute step by minute step. He is, in a word, an intimate writer. And in this he breaks with the past, for up to his time both French and Italian comedy had always bustled with activity: a mad criss-cross of thwarted lovers, a rich gallery of characters, or a fantastic whirl of events. There had been no time in these plays for psychological details. Marivaux was the first playwright of Western Europe to reduce a comic action to a Racinian minimum in order to make time for the close inspection of love.

When we say "close inspection of love," however, certain limitations must be understood. Marivaux is happier with his "escrime de sentiments" (the phrase belongs to Xavier de Cour-ville) than with expressions of passion or scenes of intimate tenderness. His genius may be feminine, but it is also cool. In fact, it resembles nothing so much as the genius of Jane Austen. As soon as love has been confessed, in Marivaux as in Austen, the story is over; and it declares itself in a single sentence, or even by a gesture.

There are many other points of resemblance between Mari-vaux and Austen. Among them is their essential concern, not so much with love in general, as with the specific matter of love's relation to vanity—*amour-propre*—the ego's self-esteem. Mari-vaux is as preoccupied with the ego as La Rochefoucauld had been. This above all is what keeps his plays from sentimentality.

[4] E.g., LA MÈRE CONFIDENTE (1735), a sad piece of false senti-mentality, which was one of Marivaux's most successful plays throughout the eighteenth century.

Through the flattered or wounded ego Arlequin is won in LA DOUBLE INCONSTANCE, the Comtesse in L'HEUREUX STRATAGÈME, Sylvia in LES FAUSSES CONFIDENCES, and Lucidor in L'ÉPREUVE. A shattered ego prevents Sylvia in LE JEU DE L'AMOUR ET DU HASARD from acknowledging to herself and others that she is in love with a servant. Not to mention Marivaux's other plays, including the two SURPRISE DE L'AMOUR, in which the satisfaction of the ego is represented again and again as the necessary prelude to love. The critical coolness of this view is complemented by Marivaux's easy tolerance of vanity. He smiles at this human weakness; he is not appalled by it. He seems to feel that satisfied vanity, like a sound income, is a natural ingredient in marriage.

It is not easy to decide how "French" or how "Italian" Marivaux really is. A play like ARLEQUIN POLI PAR L'AMOUR is obviously in the Italian spirit. But it is his first work of any note, and he did not do another similar fairy tale until he wrote LA DISPUTE, twenty-four years later—for the Comédie-Française! A few other plays show unmistakable Italian tendencies: thus the fanciful and "romantic" settings of LA DOUBLE INCONSTANCE, LE PRINCE TRAVESTI, and LE TRIOMPHE DE L'AMOUR. The marriage plot is of course common property of the French and the Italian traditions. So is the ubiquitous trick. Or the use of prose. Undoubtedly, the naïve characters whom Marivaux draws so well have a distinctly Italian flavor. And in writing comedies without sharp "humours" Marivaux was again tending toward the Italian rather than the French method. But he is perhaps most distinctly Italian in his use of travesty. Travesty was not unknown at the Comédie-Française; Molière had been fond of it; but it remained a distinctly un-French device. Thus, while Marivaux uses physical disguise in thirteen of his plays, not one of them was meant for the Théâtre Français.

But if Marivaux owed much to the Italian tradition, he continued and accelerated the gallicizing of the Italians. His language and its allusions are of a perfect purity which contrasts with the Italian repertory even of his own day. While Autreau could still write in 1720, "Long live a bright lover and a stupid husband," or call a girl "a skittish and capricious chicken out to get a dumb husband," and have a wedding performed by a notary named Cornelio Cornetto; and while Deportes could refer in 1721 to the scarf that hides a girl's breasts, and write, "One might as well not have . . . something, as not be proud of them"—license, in short, without coarseness of expression—Marivaux excluded every indecorous reference, to say nothing of coarse and indelicate words, from the comedies he wrote after 1720. His indulgent cynicism was untouched, but it was expressed in a language of extraordinary refinement, a pole away from the rough old *commedia.*

Marivaux is unmistakably French in other ways. He obeys the unities of time, place, and action with the rigor of a man determined from his cradle to take his place in the Academy. Far more important, he suppresses every trace of the visual gag, remorselessly snuffing out the *lazzi* and verbalizing his Arlequin, at any rate after his two early successes, ARLEQUIN POLI PAR L'AMOUR and LA DOUBLE INCONSTANCE. He uses no machines, no spectacle, no music, no songs (except in ARLEQUIN POLI PAR L'AMOUR). He throws out the entire romantic baggage of the *commedia,* banishing apparitions, shipwrecks, kidnapings, duels, corsairs, changelings, and all the other adventures beloved of the *commedia.* He psychologizes and internalizes the action, so that, even though the plays abound in trickery, our awareness is focused on the real persons rather than on the artificial tricks. And he radically simplifies and unifies the intrigue. In sum, favorable as the terrain was to Marivaux at the Hôtel de Bourgogne (where the Italians performed), and much as he learned from the *commedia,* our playwright's gossamer remained firmly French.

"To give us light is only to embrace half of what we are, and indeed the half toward which we are more indifferent; we are much less concerned to know than to enjoy; and the soul enjoys when it feels." Marivaux wrote this in 1755, but the cult of feeling had begun to spread in Europe before 1720, when Marivaux was beginning his career, and even then he did not remain aloof from it. His novels are full of sensibility; the plays are at least touched by it. I have mentioned a "comédie larmoyante" which Marivaux committed to the stage. But in most of his comedies, this new emotionalism manifests itself only as a mellow kindliness, an amiable tolerance which stops short of effusiveness—stops short, that is, of ruining his work. Marivaux's outlook on life is that of an Epicurean, willing to allow men, and especially women, the weaknesses from which he himself is not exempt. As he does not make the mistake of worshiping Man, he does not sit in ashes when people misbehave. Sensibility, in short, leads him to forgiveness, not to "larmoyance" or to false optimism. He sheds no tears over virtue.

In a word, he stays tough; his gossamer is made of steel. He gives us, though never in anger, representations of spite, vanity, cunning, envy , trickery, betrayal, ruthlessness, avarice, social climbing and snobbery, alongside his pictures of tenderness, affability, generosity, and intelligence. Nor are these vices reserved for his antagonists; he shows, and sometimes accepts them in his principals. What happens when sensibility meets cynicism head-on, and neither will yield its place? The two wed, and what is born of them is the Marivaldian quality I have mentioned before: slyness. Slyness is compatible with benevolence, and it is compatible with cynicism. But it precludes passion of any sort—torment or ecstasy. Marivaux's slyness is equidistant from the brutality of Lesage and Regnard and the sentimentality of Nivelle de la Chaussée and Diderot. Larroumet sums up Marivaux's equilibrium when he speaks of "this irony tempered by goodness, amiable and caressing even in its chaffing, this mild gayness, . . . this orderly, self-controlled verve, this flower of elegance and courtesy."

I look upon Marivaux as the literary master of the rococo,[5] or decorative classicism. I have not seen this term applied to Marivaux's art, perhaps because it carries injurious connotations for

---

[5] This word was first used in the late eighteenth century; the first mention in a dictionary occurs in 1842.

us. But rococo art, which is the *idealized* expression of the last great patrician epoch of Europe, is also the last art which frankly makes what Thomas Mann calls "pretense and play" out of human experience. These are the last years in which serious artists will be able to look upon their work as decoration, diversion, the high sport of the intellect, rather than as revelation, commination, and prophecy. When I suggest for Marivaux the title of literary master of the rococo, I do so with nostalgic respect and admiration.

Marivaux is rococo in his transparence and mobility (a mobility without violence); in the come-and-go of moods, actions, decisions, which we can take as the literary equivalents of curls and garlands; in his sanity, his gayety, his unbelievable happiness, his light roses and blues which only a darker rose and blue can threaten; in his unfaltering grace.

For gracefulness is his overriding law, just as wit is the absolute law of Restoration comedy. Marivaux will be witty too, but only as far as gracefulness allows; he will be satirical, but only as far as gracefulness allows; realistic, moralizing, philosophical, tender, or sensual, but only as far as gracefulness allows. This is making a world that never was out of the world that is. In the mirror which Marivaux holds up to us, we do recognize ourselves (otherwise we would lose interest), but radiant and light as we could wish to be in a dream of ourselves. Considering how subversively mild Marivaux is, and how violent and "uncompromising" (dreaded word) we expect even our comedies to be nowadays, one cannot easily say that Marivaux is "our contemporary." But one can utter a prayer, preferably to the accompaniment of a minuet, that a corner may be preserved in our lives, and possibly even enlarged, for a literature which takes gracefulness to heart.

Robin, Bachelor of Love
(Arlequin poli par l'amour)

Presented for the first time at
the Théâtre Italien on October 17, 1720

CHARACTERS

LUCINDA, *a charming witch*
TRIVET, *her servant*
ROBIN, *a youth abducted by the witch*
SYLVIA, *a shepherdess*
A SHEPHERDESS, *cousin to Sylvia*
A SHEPHERD, *in love with Sylvia*
A DANCING MASTER
ELVES, DEVILS, SINGERS, AND DANCERS

SCENE ONE

Lucinda's garden.
(*Enter Lucinda and Trivet.*)

TRIVET (*to Lucinda, who is sighing*). You're sighing, madam; and, unfortunately for yourself, you are likely to go on sighing for a long time to come, unless your reason takes a hand in the matter. May I speak openly?

LUCINDA. You may.

TRIVET. The young man you spirited away from his parents is as dark and handsome a lad as anyone could ask for. When you found him dozing in a wood, he seemed to you like Cupid himself in his sleep. I am not surprised that you took a sudden fancy to him.

LUCINDA. Isn't it natural to love what is lovable?

TRIVET. Quite natural. And yet, before all this happened, you were, I believe, more or less devoted to Merlin, the great sorcerer.

LUCINDA. Well! One man has made me forget the other. Very natural too.

TRIVET. Pure nature, I agree. One more small observation, however; namely, that you chose to abduct your young man a matter of days before your marriage to this same Merlin. Now *that* is a serious business. Perhaps—between you and me—you are being a shade *too* natural. Still, let this pass too. The worst that can happen is that you'll be unfaithful. This would be wicked in a man, but in a woman it's not quite so deplorable. True, the world

19

admires a faithful woman; but some women are so modest, they don't care to be admired. You're one of them. Less honor, but more pleasure. Very good.

LUCINDA. Honor indeed! In my position! I'd be a fool to let such a trifle stand in my way.

TRIVET. Well said. But let me continue. You carry the young man into your palace, still fast asleep, and stand guard over him, waiting for him to wake up. You are dressed for conquest in a fashion which proves your generous contempt for honor. You are sure the young man will be startled into a desperate passion the moment he catches sight of you. At last he wakes up. He greets you with the most perfectly stupid look a clod ever wore on his face. You draw nearer to him. He yawns at you vigorously two or three times, stretches, turns over, and falls asleep again. So ends the awakening which was to make history. You leave the room a little disappointed, perhaps; perhaps, too, driven away by a deep and well-fed snore. An hour goes by. Our lad wakes up once more, sees no one near, and bellows: "Hey!" This amorous cry brings you back to his bedside. "What can I do for you, my handsome youth?" you ask. "Bring me something to eat," he answers. "Aren't you surprised to see me?" "Oh?" says he; "I suppose so." That was two weeks ago. And such, ever since, has been the tenor of his conversation. But still you persist in your passion. Worse, you allow Merlin to believe that *he* will have you for his wife, while your real purpose is to marry young Robin. Marry them both if you like, but a woman who takes two husbands usually finds that one of them gets in the way of the other.

LUCINDA. I'll answer you in two words, Trivet. I am passionately in love with the young man in question, though when I abducted him I was not aware of his—limitations. But his dullness doesn't repel me. I am in love not only with his present charms, but also with those he will acquire once his mind is cultivated. Oh I shiver when I think of him, in all his beauty, flinging himself at my feet, and crying "I love you, Lucinda!" Already he is handsome beyond words, but when love retouches his mouth, his eyes, and all his features, he'll be divine. Leave him to me, Trivet! Have you noticed how often he looks my way? Every day the moment draws nearer when he'll become aware of me and aware of himself. And when he does, I'll marry him within the hour. As my husband, of course, he will be safe from Merlin; but until then, I must be cautious. Merlin's power equals my own, and I am forced to delude him as long as I can.

TRIVET. But supposing our young man refuses to fall in love, or to acquire an education, will you bestow yourself on Merlin?

LUCINDA. No; because even if I married the one, I could never relinquish the other; and if Robin ever came to love me—married or not—the truth is, I couldn't trust myself.

TRIVET. That goes without saying. Tempt a woman, win a woman, it's all one. Well, here comes our handsome blockhead, along with his dancing master.
(*Enter Robin, his mouth open, followed by the Dancing Master.*)

LUCINDA. My lovely boy, you look unhappy; has something happened to upset you?

ROBIN. Oh, I couldn't say.
(*Trivet laughs.*)

LUCINDA (*to Trivet*). Please don't laugh, you're offending me. I love him; therefore you must respect him. (*Robin is busy catching flies.*) Are you ready for your lesson, dear Robin?

ROBIN. Uh?

LUCINDA. Will you take your lesson for love of me, Robin?

ROBIN. No.

LUCINDA. What? You refuse, even though I'm so very fond of you? (*Robin notices a large ring she is wearing. He takes her hand, stares at the ring, and laughs.*) Shall I give you my ring?

ROBIN. Oh, yes!
(*She holds out the ring and he tries to snatch it.*)

LUCINDA. Robin! When a handsome lad like you receives a present from a lady, he has to kiss fingers for it. (*Robin smacks Lucinda's fingers.*) He doesn't understand, but I like his mistake. Your own fingers, silly boy. (*Robin puts his fingers into his mouth.*) Oh, well. Here's the ring, but now in return you must take your lesson.

(*The Dancing Master teaches Robin how to make a proper bow. A great deal of fooling accompanies this.*) [1]

ROBIN (*suddenly*). I'm bored.

LUCINDA. Don't worry; we'll try to entertain you another way.

ROBIN (*laughing and clapping his hands*). Good! Good! Good! (*Enter a company of singers and dancers. Lucinda makes Robin sit next to her. During the dance, Robin whistles in the air.*)

BOY SINGER (*to Robin*). Love is calling, pretty boy!

ROBIN (*getting up*). Where? Where? I can't hear him.

BOY SINGER. Love is calling, pretty boy!

ROBIN. Why doesn't he call louder?

BOY SINGER (*pointing to Lucinda*).

> A goddess sits beside you;
> Eager for love's ardent joy,
> Her flashing eyes invite you—
> Love is calling, pretty boy!

ROBIN (*staring at Lucinda's eyes*). Isn't this odd! Ha!

GIRL SINGER. Love's a game all men can learn.

ROBIN. I'm ready, why don't you teach me?

GIRL SINGER.

> Oh how I pity you, sweet dunce!
> My Daphnis knows how lovers burn:
> I kissed away his ignorance!

---

[1] This stage direction, and others like it, are traditional openings for the clown's *lazzi* and the general tomfoolery, spiced with appropriate ad libs, of the *commedia dell'arte*. [Tr.]

LUCINDA. Well, Robin, haven't these sweet songs inspired you the least little bit? What do you feel?

ROBIN. I feel a great appetite.

TRIVET. He means he wants his dinner. However, here's a villager who is going to do a country dance for you. We'll dine after he has finished.
(*While the man dances, Robin falls asleep. Afterwards, Lucinda pulls him by the arm.*)

LUCINDA. Wake up! What on earth can we do to entertain you?

ROBIN (*bawling*). I want my mother and father! Where are they?

LUCINDA (*to Trivet*). Take him away. His dinner may cheer him up again. As for myself, I must be gone for a little while. Let Robin stroll wherever he pleases after his meal.
(*All leave.*)

SCENE TWO

A meadow. Sheep grazing.
(*Enter Sylvia with a crook in her hand, and a Shepherd.*)

SHEPHERD. Are you avoiding me, beautiful Sylvia?

SYLVIA. What else can I do? Always babbling about love! I'm bored to tears with love!

SHEPHERD. I'm only expressing what I feel, Sylvia.

SYLVIA. Well, *I* don't feel a thing, so there.

SHEPHERD. That's why I'm so miserable.

SYLVIA. I can't help that, can I? I know that every shepherdess has a swain who never leaves her side. They all tell me they're in love; they sigh and sigh; and all that sighing makes them happy. Think how unfortunate I am. From the moment you said you were pining away for me, I tried my best to do a little sighing too, because I'd like to be as happy as the others, and yet nothing happened. If I knew the secret, I'd oblige you at once, because I'm very kind-hearted, you know.

SHEPHERD. Alas, the only secret I know is that I love you.

SYLVIA. There ought to be a better secret, because this one won't do. I'd like it to work—I'm really very sorry. How did you happen to fall in love with me?

SHEPHERD. I looked at you; and that was all.

SYLVIA. You see the difference! For me, the more I look at you, the less I care for you. Never mind—it may come to me at last. But for the moment you mustn't disturb me. For instance, just now, I'd hate you if you stayed any longer.

SHEPHERD. I'll go away to please you. But—only to relieve my distress—let me give you a tiny kiss.

SYLVIA. Oh no! That would be giving in, and giving in isn't proper. I know it isn't, because the other girls hide when they do it.

SHEPHERD. Nobody can see us here.

SYLVIA. True. But I won't do anything improper unless it's going to be enjoyable.

SHEPHERD. Well, I see I must leave you, fair Sylvia. Think of me now and then.

SYLVIA. I will, I will.
(*The Shepherd leaves.*)

SYLVIA. This shepherd's chatter about love is the most tedious thing. Every time he talks to me, he spoils my mood. (*She sees Robin.*) Who is that? Heavenly days, what a handsome boy!
(*Enter Robin, batting a shuttlecock. He drops it near Sylvia, and as he bends down to pick it up, he sees her. He remains bent but looks at her in surprise. He straightens himself bit by bit, keeping his eyes on her. Sylvia is embarrassed and pretends to withdraw. Robin stops her.*)

ROBIN. Don't go!

SYLVIA. I'm leaving, because I don't know who you are.

ROBIN. Don't know who I am? What a shame. Why don't we get acquainted?

SYLVIA (*still embarrassed*). I don't mind . . .

ROBIN (*chuckling*). You're the prettiest thing.

SYLVIA. Thank you, sir.

ROBIN. Oh, I'm telling you the truth.

SYLVIA (*tittering*). You're very pretty yourself.

ROBIN. So much the better. Where do you live? I'll pay you a visit.

SYLVIA. I live very close by. But you mustn't come there. We'd better always meet right here, because of a shepherd who is in love with me; if he saw you he'd become jealous and follow us about.

ROBIN. A shepherd who's in love with you!

SYLVIA. Yes.

ROBIN. How dare he! I'll show the rascal. But what about you? Do you love him too?

SYLVIA. I tried to, but I didn't succeed.

ROBIN. That's as it should be. The only people you ought to love are you and me. Do you think you can manage it?

SYLVIA. Indeed I can; nothing is easier.

ROBIN. Really and truly?

SYLVIA. Yes; I never lie. But tell me, where do *you* live?

ROBIN. Over there, in that big house.

SYLVIA. In the witch's palace?

ROBIN. Yes.

SYLVIA (*sadly*). I've always been unlucky.

ROBIN (*also sadly*). What's the matter, my sweet?

SYLVIA. The matter is that this witch is more beautiful than I. Our friendship won't last, I'm afraid.

ROBIN. I'll die if it doesn't! (*Tenderly*) Here, here, don't be upset, my pretty dear.

SYLVIA. But will you love me forever?

ROBIN. As long as I live.

SYLVIA. It would be very wrong of you to deceive me; I'm such a simple creature! Oh, my sheep are wandering off! I'd be scolded if any of them got lost. I'll have to go now. When will you return?

ROBIN. These sheep are a miserable nuisance!

SYLVIA. Yes, they are, but what can I do? Will you come this evening?

ROBIN. Without fail. (*He takes her hand and kisses it.*) Look at the darling little fingers. They taste better than any candy I ever ate.

SYLVIA (*laughs*). Good-bye, good-bye . . . (*Aside*) Here I am sighing, and nobody had to tell me the secret for it. (*She drops her kerchief.*)

ROBIN. My love!

SYLVIA. What is it, my own? Oh, you've got my kerchief! Give it to me.

ROBIN (*holds it out, then takes it back again*). No; I want to keep it, so I won't be lonely without you. What do you do with it?

SYLVIA. I dry my face with it after washing.

ROBIN (*unfolding it*). Where? What place do you use, so I can kiss the spot?

SYLVIA. I use it all. But I can't stay—I've lost sight of my sheep. Good-bye, till tonight.
(*Robin waves, and both leave.*)

SCENE THREE

Lucinda's garden.
(*Enter Lucinda and Trivet.*)

LUCINDA. Well! Has Robin dined?

TRIVET. Like four men. Nobody can beat him there.

LUCINDA. Where is he now?

TRIVET. I think he's romping in the meadows. But I have news for you.

LUCINDA. What is it?

TRIVET. Merlin has been here to see you.

LUCINDA. I'm glad I was away. I hate to sham love for a man who no longer interests me.

TRIVET. Still, I'm sorry your little simpleton has driven Merlin out of your heart. The great enchanter is bubbling over with joy; he believes you're about to marry him. A while ago I caught him looking at your portrait. "Have you ever set eyes on anything so beautiful?" he asked me. "Oh, Trivet, think of the pleasures that await me!" Poor man, little does he know! The only pleasures that await him are those of the imagination. He's not destined to lay hands on the fair shape of reality. But he'll be coming back, madam; how do you propose to settle with him?

LUCINDA. For the time being I must throw more dust in his eyes.

TRIVET. What about your conscience? Doesn't it ache a little?

LUCINDA. Oh, I've more important things on my mind than badgering my conscience.

TRIVET (*aside*). Here's the complete woman for you.

LUCINDA. I feel so dreary without Robin. I'm going to look for him. Wait, here he comes. Look, Trivet! Don't you think he is carrying himself better than usual?
(*Enter Robin. He is softly stroking his face with Sylvia's kerchief.*)

LUCINDA (*to Trivet*). I wonder what he'll do by himself. Stand next to me. I'll twist the ring that will make us invisible.
(*Robin jumps with joy as he contemplates the kerchief. Happily he puts it into his bosom, lies down, and gaily rolls over it.*)

LUCINDA. What's the meaning of this? How very strange. Where could he have found that kerchief? Is it one of mine, I wonder? Ah, Trivet, if it were, these postures would be most promising.

TRIVET. He probably found a scented undershirt somewhere.

LUCINDA. Nonsense. I want to question him. But let's withdraw a little and pretend we're just arriving.
(*They leave. Robin sings and saunters about.*)

ROBIN. Tra la la.
(*Re-enter Lucinda and Trivet.*)

LUCINDA. Good day, Robin.

ROBIN (*bowing, and hiding the kerchief*). I'm your very humble servant.

LUCINDA (*aside to Trivet*). What manners! And never before has he spoken a whole sentence to me.

ROBIN. Madam, would you be good enough to tell me how one feels when one is in love with a certain person?

LUCINDA (*delighted, to Trivet*). Did you hear that, Trivet? (*To Robin*) The person who loves, dear Robin, longs to be with his beloved day and night. He can't bear to part from her; he grieves when he loses sight of her; he is on fire, impatient, full of desire.

ROBIN (*joyfully, half-aside*). That's me!

LUCINDA. Do you feel all the things I mentioned?

ROBIN (*affecting indifference*). Oh, no. I was only curious.

TRIVET. Don't believe it.

LUCINDA. I don't; but I am dissatisfied with his answer. Dear Robin, weren't you thinking of me when you asked your question?

ROBIN. Ha ha, I'm no fool, I'm not telling what I think.

LUCINDA (*furious*). What do you mean by that? And where did you find this kerchief?

ROBIN (*frightened*). On the ground.

LUCINDA. Whose is it?

ROBIN. It belongs to . . . I don't know.

LUCINDA. There's some dreadful mystery behind this. Give it to me! (*She tears the kerchief from Robin and looks at it aside.*) It's not mine; and he was kissing it! But gently. Let me conceal my suspicion. I mustn't intimidate him, otherwise he won't tell me anything at all.

ROBIN (*humbly, doffing his hat*). Please may I beg to have the kerchief again?

LUCINDA (*sighing*). Here, Robin; since you're so fond of it, I won't take it away from you.
(*Robin takes the kerchief, kisses Lucinda's hand, and bows.*)

LUCINDA. You're leaving me! Where are you going?

ROBIN. I'm going to take a nap under a tree.

LUCINDA (*softly*). Go, go.
(*Robin leaves.*)

LUCINDA. Trivet, I'm undone!

TRIVET. I confess I'm open-mouthed myself, madam. What has come over our little pest?

LUCINDA (*desperate*). He has become clever, Trivet, clever! —but not for *my* benefit! And instead of coming to my senses,

I'm wilder about him than ever! What a blow! Ungrateful, adorable villain! Did you mark how changed he is? Did you notice the polish of his manners as he addressed me? His very features are more refined! But someone else has brought him out, not I! He displays delicate feelings; he shows discretion; he dares not tell me whose kerchief it was; he guesses that I would be jealous. Ah, he must be far gone in love to have become so shrewd. Unhappy Lucinda! Another woman will hear him utter the "I love you" I have longed for; he will be adored by someone else; and worst of all, he will deserve it! I can't bear it. Come, Trivet. My rival must be found; I'll follow Robin and search all the places where they can meet; you, look on the other side; and hurry; I'm breathing my last.

SCENE FOUR

A meadow.
(*Enter Sylvia and her cousin.*)

SYLVIA. Dear cousin, I'll tell you my whole story, and then you can give me your advice. Here is where I was standing when he came. The moment I saw him, a small voice whispered inside me that I loved him. Isn't it extraordinary? And then he came close and spoke to me. Guess what he said. That he loved me too! I was as happy as if somebody had made me a present of all the sheep in the village. Now I understand why our girls are always glad to be in love. He is so charming, I wish I had been in love from the day I was born. But that's not all. He'll be here again soon. He has kissed my hand already, and I know he'll want to kiss it again. Tell me—you've had so many suitors—should I let him?

COUSIN. By no means, cousin. Be as cold to him as possible. That's what keeps a lover attentive.

SYLVIA. Isn't there an easier way to keep him attentive?

COUSIN. No, there isn't. Another thing: don't keep telling him that you love him.

SYLVIA. But how can I help it? I'm too young to tie up my tongue.

COUSIN. Well, do as you like. Excuse me, but somebody is waiting for me, and I can't stay. Good-bye, cousin. (*She leaves.*)

SYLVIA (*alone*). Now I'm worried. Rather than be cold, I'd choose not to care for anyone at all. And yet she tells me that coldness keeps a lover attentive. How strange! They ought to change this tiresome rule. Whoever invented it wasn't in love as much as I. Oh! Here he is again. How on earth am I going to be cold?
(*Enter Robin. He joyously capers around Sylvia, strokes her with his hat, to which he has attached the kerchief, kisses the latter and then pets Sylvia.*)

ROBIN. Here you are, my sweet.

SYLVIA. Yes, here I am.

ROBIN. Are you happy to see me?

SYLVIA. Pretty happy.

ROBIN. Pretty happy! That's not happy enough.

SYLVIA. Oh yes it is; there's no need for more.

ROBIN. I don't want you to say that.
(*He tries to kiss her hand, but she takes it away.*)

SYLVIA. No. You can't kiss my hand.

ROBIN. Again! go away; I can't trust you any more! (*He cries.*)

SYLVIA (*tenderly, chucking his chin*). Please don't cry, my dear.

ROBIN (*groaning*). You promised to be my love.

SYLVIA. But I am.

ROBIN. No you're not. If you love someone, you don't forbid him to kiss your hand, do you? Look, here's mine; see if I behave like you.

SYLVIA (*aside*). I can't bear it, cousin or no cousin. (*To Robin*) Don't cry, my little lover, here, kiss my hand, kiss it as often as you like. But don't ask me how much I love you, because I'll never tell you more than half the truth. Of course I am all yours, but if I admitted it, you'd become indifferent to me; or so I've been told.

ROBIN (*plaintively*). Whoever told you that is a liar and a chatterbox who knows nothing about our case. My heart beats twice as fast when I kiss you and when you say that you care for me; which goes to show that my love grows when you're kind.

SYLVIA. Maybe so, because mine does too. But since it's supposed to be dangerous, let's try to avoid an accident. Every time you ask me whether I like you very much, I'll say "Oh, not very much," but it won't be true; and when you ask permission to kiss me, I'll refuse, and yet I'll want you to.

ROBIN. Very good, ha ha ha! Let's do it. But first, I'll kiss your hand for half an hour or so outside the rules.

SYLVIA. Fair enough. Here's my hand.

ROBIN (*kisses her hand for a while, then changes his mind*). A thought just occurred to me. Suppose the bargain gets in our way?

SYLVIA. What of it? We'll change it. Aren't we the masters here?

ROBIN. That's true. Well, shall we try it out?

SYLVIA. Let's.

ROBIN. I can't keep a straight face. Let's see now. Do you love me very much?

SYLVIA. No, not very much.

ROBIN (*seriously*). I hope this is part of the joke, otherwise . . .

SYLVIA (*laughing*). Silly! Of course it's part of the joke!

ROBIN (*laughs*). Very good. Now give me your hand, my sweet.

SYLVIA. I don't want to.

ROBIN. Oh but I know that actually you do.

SYLVIA. Even more than you; but I'm not saying it.

ROBIN. Let me kiss it, or else I'll get angry.

SYLVIA. You're fooling, my love.

ROBIN. No, I'm serious.

SYLVIA. Really now?

ROBIN. Really.

SYLVIA (gives him her hand). Here it is.
(Enter Lucinda.)

LUCINDA (aside). Just what I dreaded! I'll make myself invisible.
(She turns her ring.)

ROBIN (after kissing Sylvia's hand). I was joking. Ha ha ha!

SYLVIA. You caught me this time—but I'm glad you did.

ROBIN (holding her hand). And I'm glad that you tell me you're
glad.

LUCINDA (aside). Merciful heavens! Listen to him. Now I'll
show myself. (She turns her ring again.)

SYLVIA and ROBIN. Ah! Oh!

LUCINDA (to Robin). You seem to have learned the ways of the
world.

ROBIN (embarrassed). Hm—not enough to see you in time . . .

LUCINDA. Ingrate! (She touches him with her wand.) Follow
me. (She touches Sylvia too.)

SYLVIA. No, no!
(Lucinda leaves, followed in silence by Robin, marching like a
robot.)

SYLVIA. Wicked woman! I'm trembling with fear. Is she going to
kill my darling? She'll never forgive him for loving me. But I
know what to do. I'll call all the shepherds together and lead

them to her palace. Oh! What's the matter with me? I can't move. The witch has cast a spell on my legs! (*Several elves appear.*) Help! Help! Gentlemen, have mercy on me! Oh help!

ELF. Away, away!

SYLVIA. Don't take me away! Let me go home!

ELF. Away, away!
(*They carry her off.*)

SCENE FIVE

Lucinda's garden.
(*Enter Lucinda and Robin, the latter still walking like a robot, until Lucinda touches him again with her wand.*)

LUCINDA. Shame on you! I've showered you with attentions and smothered you in tenderness without obtaining a word of affection in return, but no sooner does a miserable peasant girl come along than you turn into a Lancelot. What is so lovable about that girl? Answer me, villain; speak up.

ROBIN (*pretending to be a simpleton again*). Eh? What was that?

LUCINDA. It's no use pretending to be stupid now. Be yourself or I'll stab that good-for-nothing love of yours through the heart.

ROBIN. Don't! I promise to be as intelligent as you wish.

LUCINDA. You want to protect her.

ROBIN. Oh, no. But I don't like to see people die, that's all.

LUCINDA (*more gently*). You'll see me die if you refuse to love me.

ROBIN (*coaxing*). Please don't be angry with us.

LUCINDA. Oh, Robin, look at me; repent of your wickedness to me. I'll forget how this change came over you. But since you *have* acquired so much understanding, you should recognize the advantages that I offer you.

ROBIN. True. I'm beginning to see my error. You're a hundred times better, and prettier too. Oh, I'm furious.

LUCINDA. Why?

ROBIN. Because I allowed myself to be inveigled by a little minx whose beauty is nothing compared to yours.

LUCINDA. Robin, are you going to love a girl who deceives you—a flirt—a coquette who doesn't care a straw for you?

ROBIN. You're mistaken there; she adores me.

LUCINDA. She's abusing you, Robin. Don't I know it? She is pledged to a shepherd in the village who is her lover. If you wish, I'll send for her, and she'll confirm what I tell you.

ROBIN. Oh, oh, ah, oh! My heart! Your words are killing me! Let me know everything! Quickly! If she's a cheat, I'll make love to you, I'll marry you before her very eyes to punish her!

LUCINDA. Good; I'll go send for her.

ROBIN. Wait. You're very clever. If you're here when she speaks to me, you'll give her a sour look and she'll be afraid to tell me her true feelings.

LUCINDA. I'll step out of the way.

ROBIN. The devil you will! You're a witch, and you'll play us the same trick as before. Sylvia will think so too. You know how to stand in the middle of a crowd unbeknownst to anybody. No hocus-pocus this time, if you please. Swear that you won't be there in secret.

LUCINDA. I swear, word of a witch.

ROBIN. I'm not sure that's a solid oath. But I remember another, I've heard it in stories where people swear, wait, by the Six, the Tix—the Styx.

LUCINDA. It's all the same, my boy.

ROBIN. Never mind. Swear anyway. Ha! I see you're afraid, it must be a good oath.

LUCINDA. Very well, I swear by Styx that I won't be present, and now I'll send for the girl.

ROBIN. And I, meantime, will go and moan in the garden. (*He leaves.*)

LUCINDA (*alone*). I'm bound by my oath, but I've a way of frightening this shepherdess without being present. After that, I'll give Trivet my ring, have him listen to their conversation unseen, and then make him repeat it to me. Trivet! Come here! (*Enter Trivet.*)

TRIVET. Madam?

LUCINDA. Tell the shepherdess to come to me, Trivet; I want to see her. And take my ring. As soon as I leave the girl alone, you are to dispatch Robin to her, and to follow him discreetly in order to overhear their conversation. Turn the ring and make yourself invisible to them. The moment they're done, come back to me with your report. I'm counting on you, Trivet.

TRIVET. Yes, madam. (*He leaves.*)

LUCINDA (*alone*). Wretched Lucinda! Unhappy passion! The more I love, the more I suffer. And yet some hope remains to me. Here comes my rival. (*Severely, as Sylvia enters*) Come here! Stand before me!

SYLVIA. Must I stay here against my will, madam? Am I guilty because Robin has fallen in love with me? He thinks I am beautiful, but, madam, what can a girl do about *that*?

LUCINDA (*aside*). Ha—if I weren't afraid of spoiling everything, I'd tear her to pieces. (*Aloud*) Listen to me, young lady; a thousand torments await you if you disobey me.

SYLVIA (*trembling*). Heaven help me. What do you want me to do?

LUCINDA. Robin will be here in a moment. You are to inform him that you were merely trifling with him; that you don't love him; and that you're about to be married to a shepherd. You'll not see me during your conversation, but I shall be near you all the same. If you fail to obey my commands down to the last syllable, if you allow him to suspect through a single word of yours that I am forcing you to speak as you do, you'll be stretched on the rack before the hour is over.

SYLVIA. What, I'm to tell him I was only teasing? It's hopeless, madam. He'll start crying, and then I'll break down. You know very well it's bound to happen that way.

LUCINDA. How dare you talk back to me! Infernal spirits, appear, bind her in chains, and torment her without mercy!
(*Enter infernal spirits.*)

SYLVIA (*crying*). I can't do what you're asking me! Have you no pity?

LUCINDA (*to the devils*). That's not all. Go find the rogue she loves, and kill him in her presence.

SYLVIA. Kill him? No, bring him to me, madam, I'll swear that I hate him, and I promise not to cry; I love him too much to cry.

LUCINDA. If you shed a single tear or breathe one sigh, Robin is lost, and so are you. (*To the devils*) Unbind her. (*To Sylvia*) After you've spoken with him—and if I am satisfied with you—I'll have you safely sent home. Now wait for him. (*She leaves with her devils.*)

SYLVIA (*alone*). I must stop crying right away, so that my darling won't know I love him. Oh my poor dear boy, if I cry, I'll be the cause of his death. Horrid witch! Here he comes. I'll dry my tears. (*Enter Robin, very dejected. At first he doesn't say anything and only looks at Sylvia. Trivet enters, invisible to both.*)

ROBIN. Sylvia . . . ?

SYLVIA (*casually*). Yes—what do you want?

ROBIN. Look at me.

SYLVIA. Why should I? They told me to come here to answer your questions. But I'm in a hurry. What is it?

ROBIN (*tenderly*). Is it true you were only pretending with me?

SYLVIA. Oh yes. I did it all for a lark.

ROBIN (*still tenderly, and coming closer*). My pretty Sylvia, you can speak openly; that trollop of a witch swore she'd stay out of earshot. There, there, now, my sweet, my love, tell me, did you really lie to me? Are you going to marry some clown of a shepherd?

SYLVIA. Yes and yes again. It's all true.
(*Robin breaks into sobs.*)

SYLVIA (*aside*). My courage is failing.
(*Still crying, Robin searches his pocket. He finds a small knife which he sharpens on his sleeve.*)

SYLVIA. What are you doing?
(*Robin extends his arm as if to take a wider swing with his knife, and opens his coat a little.*)

SYLVIA. He's going to kill himself! Stop, stop! I was forced to lie to you! (*Looking about*) Oh, mighty witch, forgive me, wherever you are, you see I couldn't help myself.

ROBIN. Ha, ha, ha, now I'm happy! Bear me up, hold me. I'm dizzy with joy! (*Sylvia embraces him. Trivet appears.*)

SYLVIA. The witch!

TRIVET. No, my dear children, not the witch; it's only Trivet. Lucinda gave me her ring and ordered me to spy on you. But I'd be sorry to betray two tender pigeons like you to her vengeance. Besides, she doesn't deserve a servant's loyalty. She has been unfaithful to the most generous sorcerer alive, who has earned my complete devotion. Calm yourselves, I'm going to make you happy. Robin, you must make believe that you are disillusioned with Sylvia, and Sylvia, you must pretend to leave Robin with a taunt on your lips. I'll call Lucinda, tell her you've obeyed all her orders, and make her witness your parting words. Now, Robin, as soon as you're alone with Lucinda, tell her you're done with Sylvia and swear that your heart is now all hers. Then, between this and that, and coaxing her and prattling about love, catch hold of her magic wand. As soon as you have it, Lucinda will be powerless. Touch her with it, and she's your slave. And then you'll be able to leave this place and go where you will.

SYLVIA. May heaven reward you, kind sir.

ROBIN. Honest fellow, once I've got the magic wand, I'll fill your hat with money.

TRIVET. Get ready now. I'm going to call Lucinda. (*He leaves.*)

ROBIN. Oh, I'm so happy, my happiness is running up and down my body. Sylvia, my dear, I must kiss you—come, there's plenty of time.

SYLVIA. No—not now, sweet Robin, no kisses now, so that we can kiss to our heart's content the rest of our lives. The witch is coming. Tell me all the mean things you can think of, so you can take her wand away from her.
(*Enter Lucinda and Trivet.*)

ROBIN. My eyes are unsealed, you hussy!

TRIVET (*to Lucinda*). I believe this will warm your heart, dear lady.

ROBIN. Away, you tramp. Have you no shame? Devils in hell—get out of here!

SYLVIA. Ha ha ha, I never laughed so hard. Farewell! I'm off to marry my lover. Next time, little man, don't believe everything you're told. (*Aside to Lucinda*) Shall I go now, madam?

LUCINDA (*to Trivet*). Take her out.
(*Trivet and Sylvia leave.*)

LUCINDA. You see, Robin, I told you the truth about her.

ROBIN. Pah! I don't care. Ugly brat! I've finally learned to appreciate you. What a fool I was. Let her go. We'll teach her a lesson, once we're husband and wife.

LUCINDA. Oh Robin, are you going to love me after all?

ROBIN. Who else should I love? My eyes must have been in my pocket. I admit I was put out at first, but now I wouldn't give a bent pin for all the shepherd girls of the realm. (*Softly*) Still—perhaps you've grown tired of me, now that I've been such a fool.

LUCINDA (*delighted*). Robin of my soul, I'm making you my lord and husband; I am marrying you, giving you my heart, my fortune, and my power. Does that satisfy you?

ROBIN. You're an angel! (*He takes her hand.*) As for me—I give you—my own person—my hat—my stick.[2] (*Jestingly, he places his stick at her side, and takes the wand out of her hand.*) And I'll gird on your wand in its place.

LUCINDA (*alarmed*). Wait! Give it to me again! You'll break it.

ROBIN (*avoiding her, and walking about the stage*). Gently, gently.

LUCINDA. Give it to me at once! I need it!

ROBIN (*manages to touch her with the wand*). Now, now, sit down and behave.

LUCINDA (*sitting*). Treason! I'm ruined.

ROBIN (*laughing*). Victory! Ha ha ha! You were scolding me not so long ago for being a simpleton—but who's the simpleton now? (*He jumps, laughs, dances, whistles, and circles around Lucinda, pointing the wand at her.*) Better behave, lady witch; do you see this stick? (*Calling out*) Here, everybody! Bring in my true love! Trivet! My servants! And the devils too! Faster! I'm in command, my word is law—faster—or else, by thunder— (*All the actors appear.*)

[2] The original stage direction refers to "his sword." But Arlequin (our Robin) always carried a stick, and besides we hardly expect him to be wielding a deadly weapon here. [Tr.]

ROBIN (*to Sylvia*). Look at me, Sylvia, I'm the magician now. Here, take the wand—take it—try a little witchcraft too.

SYLVIA (*taking the wand and leaping with joy*). Sweet Robin, we're safe from envy now.

A DEVIL. You are our mistress now. Command us.

SYLVIA. Oh, those ugly brutes again! I'm frightened.

ROBIN. Wait, I'll teach them to mind their manners. Give me the wand, I'll thrash them with it. (*He beats everybody, including Trivet.*)

SYLVIA. That's enough, Robin. (*Robin keeps threatening everybody, even Lucinda. Now Sylvia approaches the latter and bows to her.*) Good afternoon, madam; how do you feel? A little less wicked, I hope? (*Lucinda glares.*) Look how furious she is.

ROBIN (*to Lucinda*). Is she really! I'm the master here. Give us a pleasant smile. At once!

SYLVIA. Leave her alone, my dear; let's be generous; the most beautiful thing in the world is compassion.

ROBIN. I'll forgive her. But I order everybody to sing and dance; and when that's over, we'll use our wand and help ourselves to a kingdom.

THE END

Double Infidelity
(La Double inconstance)

Presented for the first time at
the Théâtre Italien on May 3, 1722

CHARACTERS

THE PRINCE
LORD LUMLEY
FLAMINIA, *daughter of one of the Prince's gentlemen*
LISA, *her sister*
SYLVIA
ROBIN
TRIVET, *the Prince's factotum*
LACKEYS AND CHAMBERMAIDS

The action takes place in the Prince's palace.

ACT ONE

(Enter Sylvia, Trivet, and several girls waiting on Sylvia. Sylvia is angry.)

TRIVET. Won't you listen to me, madam?

SYLVIA. Don't bother me.

TRIVET. Shouldn't a person be reasonable?

SYLVIA. No, a person shouldn't, and I won't.

TRIVET. And yet—

SYLVIA. And yet I don't want to be reasonable. You can repeat "and yet" fifty times if you wish. I'll still refuse to be reasonable. And what will you do about it?

TRIVET. You took such a light supper last night, madam, you'll become ill unless you breakfast this morning.

SYLVIA. I despise health and I'm glad to be sick; so there. Don't trouble yourself, send everything back, because I'll have neither breakfast, nor lunch, nor dinner today; nor tomorrow either. You took me away from Robin, and now all I care to do is to be furious and to hate you one and all until I've seen him again. Those are my resolutions, and if you want to drive me insane, keep telling me to be reasonable and you'll soon have done it.

TRIVET. God help me, I don't intend to try; I can see you'll keep your word. And yet if I dared—

SYLVIA *(angrier)*. Another "and yet"!

45

TRIVET. Oh, I beg your pardon, this one was a slip, but it's the last one; I stand corrected. Only I should like you to consider . . .

SYLVIA. I thought you stood corrected! I don't want your considerations!

TRIVET (*continuing*). . . . That the man who loves you is your prince.

SYLVIA. I can't keep him from loving me; he's the master; but am I compelled to love him in return? No, I am not; and why not? Because I can't. What could be simpler? A child would see it, but apparently you don't.

TRIVET. Consider that you are the bride he has chosen among his subjects, as he must by law.

SYLVIA. Who told him to choose me? Did he ask my opinion? If he had asked me, "Do you want me, Sylvia?" I would have answered, "No, my lord, an honest woman must love her husband, and I couldn't love you." *That* is reason for you. But not at all. He falls in love with me, bang, he carries me off, and never asks how *I* feel about him.

TRIVET. He carries you off only to offer you his hand in marriage.

SYLVIA. Well, what does he want me to do with his hand, now that I don't feel like putting mine into it? Do you force people to take presents in spite of themselves?

TRIVET. But do consider, madam, how he has treated you in the two days you've been here. Aren't you waited on as though you were already his wife? Look at the tokens of respect offered to you, the number of women in your retinue, the entertainment you've enjoyed at his command. What is this Robin next to a Prince who showers you with delicate attentions—a Prince who will not even appear before you until you are inclined to see him? What is he next to a Prince who is young, considerate, and full of love? For heaven's sake, madam, open your eyes to your good luck, and take advantage of his kindnesses.

SYLVIA. Tell me—you, and all the women who are giving me advice— are you being paid to irritate me with your babble?

TRIVET. I do what I can; that's the sum of my wisdom.

SYLVIA. Your wisdom has accomplished precious little.

TRIVET. But will you at least tell me where I am wrong?

SYLVIA. Yes, I'll tell you, yes—

TRIVET. Gently! I didn't mean to provoke you.

SYLVIA. In that case you're a bungler.

TRIVET. Your servant.

SYLVIA. My servant! Well, my servant, instead of singing the praises of this place, tell me why these four or five geese are spying on me day and night. My love is taken away from me, I'm given these women to replace him, and now I'm expected to be happy! And what's all this music to me, all these singers and these dancers? Robin used to sing better than any of them, and as for dancing, let me tell you I'd rather dance myself than watch others doing it. A simple girl happy in her village is better off than a princess weeping in a palace. Is the Prince in love with me? That's not my fault. I didn't look for him, and he needn't have looked for me. Is he young and attractive? So much the better for him; I'm glad. Let him keep himself for his equals, and let him leave me my poor Robin, who is no more the fancy gentleman than I am the fancy lady; who is no richer, no vainer, and no better lodged than I am; who loves me without frills, whom I love the same way, and for whom I'll die of grief if I don't see him again. Poor boy! What have they done to him? What has become of him? Wherever he is, he's sunk in despair, I know it, because he's so kind, so good! Maybe he's being mistreated. . . . Oh, I'm beside myself! Look here, Mr. Trivet, do you really want to please me? Take yourself away, I can't bear the sight of you. Leave me alone with my grief.

TRIVET. This is blunt and clear. But set your mind at rest, madam.

SYLVIA. Not another word.

TRIVET. I repeat, set your mind at rest. You want to see Robin, and Robin will stand before you in a minute.

SYLVIA. I'll see Robin?

TRIVET. And talk to him, too.

SYLVIA. Very well; I'll go wait for him. But if this is a trick, I don't want to see or hear anyone ever again.
(*She leaves. From the other side, the Prince and Flaminia have entered and watched her go out.*)

PRINCE (*to Trivet*). Well? Is there any hope? What does she say?

TRIVET. What she says is not worth repeating, my lord; nothing has happened yet to deserve your curiosity.

PRINCE. No matter; tell me anyway.

TRIVET. No, my lord; these trifles can only bore you. Tenderness for Robin, impatience to see him again, no wish to make your acquaintance, violent desire not to set eyes on you, and plentiful hatred for us all: such, in short, are her feelings. As you can see, there's nothing pleasant to report, and frankly, if I may express my thoughts, I would suggest putting her back where we found her.
(*The Prince looks gloomy.*)

FLAMINIA. I've suggested the same thing already, but it's no use. We'll have to proceed. The love which Sylvia and Robin bear each other must be destroyed.

TRIVET. My own view is that there's something uncanny about that girl. It isn't natural for a woman to reject luxuries. This creature belongs to a species unknown to us. No mere woman would give us all that trouble. There's a warning here; we're dealing with a prodigy. Let's stop right now.

PRINCE. All this only fans my love for her.

FLAMINIA (*laughing*). Don't listen to his prodigy, my lord; he's been reading fairy tales. I know my sex: the only prodigious thing about us is our vanity. Sylvia is not ambitious, true; but she has a heart; therefore she is vain; and that's all I need to bring her down to where we women live. But when shall we see Robin?

TRIVET. He'll be here right away.

PRINCE. I'm afraid we're taking a great risk, Flaminia. If she sees Robin, she will dote on him more than ever.

TRIVET. True; but if she doesn't see him, she'll go mad; she promised it herself.

FLAMINIA. My lord, we need Robin.

PRINCE. Very well, keep him here as long as you can. Tell him I'll lavish gold and titles on him if he'll kindly marry somebody else.

TRIVET. And if he refuses, we'll crush him.

PRINCE. No, Trivet. The same law which demands that I marry one of my subjects forbids me to use force on them.

FLAMINIA. You are right, my lord. And I hope all can be settled in a friendly spirit. Doesn't Sylvia know you already, without realizing that you are the Prince?

PRINCE. Yes, she does. While hunting one day, you may recall, I was separated from my companions. I met Sylvia not far from her house. I was thirsty, and she gave me water to drink. Her beauty and her simplicity carried me away. I told her so. And since that day I have seen her five or six times, pretending to be an official of the palace. But though she has treated me with wonderful sweetness, I have been unable to supplant Robin, who, by the way, discovered me with her on two occasions.

FLAMINIA. We'll put her ignorance of your rank to good use, my lord. She knows that for the time being she is not to see you. Follow my directions, and I'll take care of the rest.

PRINCE. I'll do whatever you say; and if you win Sylvia's heart for me, you'll find me grateful beyond all your wishes. (*He leaves.*)

FLAMINIA. Trivet, call my sister.

TRIVET. No need, here she is. I'll go meet Robin. (*He leaves.*) (*Enter Lisa.*)

LISA. What are my orders, Flaminia?

FLAMINIA. Come closer; let me inspect you.

LISA. Here, inspect away.

FLAMINIA. Hm. You're looking pretty today, no doubt about it.

LISA (*laughing*). I know I am. What's that to you?

FLAMINIA. Off with your rouge! [1]

LISA. Impossible. My mirror insists on it.

FLAMINIA. Off with it, I say.

LISA (*wiping her rouge with the aid of a mirror*). This is rape! Why are you persecuting me?

FLAMINIA. I have my reasons. Now then, Lisa: you're tall and well proportioned.

LISA. Many people think so.

FLAMINIA. You like to attract men.

LISA. It's a weakness of mine.

FLAMINIA. Could you put on a sweet and innocent look for a man, pretend you were attracted to him, and make him love you in a good cause?

LISA. An expedition of that kind requires rouge.

FLAMINIA. Aren't you ever going to forget your rouge? I tell you rouge won't do. We've got a simple lad on our hands, an inexpe-

[1] In the French text, the little quarrel is over a patch which Lisa is wearing on her cheek. Patches were the fashion in upper circles in the seventeenth and eighteenth centuries. [Tr.]

rienced rustic who thinks that our women ought to be as modest as the milkmaids of his village. Remember, these girls have their own notions about modesty, and they'd be shocked by some of the liberties we allow ourselves. In short, no cosmetics; improve your behavior instead; behavior is what I'm concerned about. But will you know how to act? What will you say to him?

LISA. I'll say to him . . . What would *you* say to him?

FLAMINIA. All right, listen to me. First, no flirtatious airs. For instance, I read a determination in your little face to attract men: erase it. In your gestures you affect something vivacious and giddy; now you're nonchalant, now you're tender, now you're mincing; your eyes decide to be naughty, they want to melt, to kill; they perform a thousand antics. You're light-headed, you walk with your nose in the air; you try for a young, seductive, dissipated expression. You talk to people, I don't know, with a special tone, a special kind of language spiced with quips and nonsense. I don't deny that these tricks make a pretty show in good society; everybody agrees that they are charming; men adore them. But in the present case you must, if you please, get rid of all these frills. Our little man wouldn't approve of them; they'd be too strong for his taste. Here: imagine a man who has never drunk anything but clear fresh water; you know he'd make a face over wine or brandy.

LISA. Somehow, the way you describe my charms, they don't sound as lovely as you say they are.

FLAMINIA. I was analyzing them; that's why they look ridiculous. But with men you're safe.

LISA. And what do I substitute for these tricks of mine?

FLAMINIA. Nothing whatever. Let your eyes go where they would go if you weren't a coquette. Hold your head as you would hold it if it weren't empty. And let your face be what it is when nobody is looking at you. Why don't we try? Give me a sample—for instance, a candid look.

LISA. How is this?

FLAMINIA. Hm. It needs a little more work.

LISA. It's no use. You're only a woman, you don't inspire me. Forget the test. You'll ruin my best effects. All this is meant for Robin, isn't it?

FLAMINIA. That's right.

LISA. Poor boy! And what about my scruples? If I don't truly fall in love with him, I'll feel dishonest. Don't forget I'm a respectable girl.

FLAMINIA. If he happens to fall in love with you, you'll marry him and come into a fortune. Does that relieve your scruples? Remember what we are—the daughters of a minor official; obey me, and you'll become a lady.

LISA. So much for my conscience. Naturally, as a lady, I won't be required to love my husband. Well, I'm going now. Tell me when it's time to begin.

FLAMINIA. Here's Robin—I'm coming with you.
(*Enter Trivet and Robin, the latter looking about with astonishment.*)

TRIVET. Well, Master Robin, how do you like it here? (*Robin doesn't answer.*) Isn't it a handsome house?

ROBIN. What in blazes have I got to do with this house? And who are you? What do you want of me? Where are we going?

TRIVET. I am an honest man and your servant as of today; I'm entirely at your disposal; and we're going right where we are.

ROBIN. Honest man or rogue, I don't need you either way. You're dismissed and I'm going home.

TRIVET (*stopping him*). Just a moment!

ROBIN. What's that? Hey, isn't it rude to stop your master? Hey?

TRIVET. A greater master than you has made me your servant.

ROBIN. And who's the freak who gives me servants I don't want?

TRIVET. When you come to know him, you'll change your tune. Meantime let the two of us come to an understanding.

ROBIN. Why? Have we got anything to tell one another?

TRIVET. We have. About Sylvia.

ROBIN. Ah, Sylvia, ah me! I beg your forgiveness. It comes to me now that I've wanted to talk to you all along.

TRIVET. You lost her two days ago, didn't you?

ROBIN. That's right. She was stolen by a pack of thieves.

TRIVET. They weren't thieves.

ROBIN. If they weren't thieves, they were robbers.

TRIVET. I know where she is.

ROBIN. You know where she is, my friend, my valet, my master, my anything you like? Oh, what a pity I'm not rich, I'd give you all my income for wages. Tell me which way I should turn, my true-hearted friend—to the right, to the left, or straight ahead?

TRIVET. You'll meet her right here.

ROBIN. How good and kind you must be to have brought me here! Oh, Sylvia, sweetest child of my heart, I'm crying for joy!

TRIVET (*aside*). This fool's prelude bodes no good. (*Aloud*) Wait—I've something else to tell you.

ROBIN. First I want to see Sylvia; take pity on me, I can't wait.

TRIVET. I told you that you'll be seeing her; but before you do I must have a talk with you. Do you remember a gentleman who called on Sylvia five or six times, and whom you saw with her?

ROBIN (*sadly*). Yes. He looked like a hypocrite.

TRIVET. This person found your sweetheart very attractive.

ROBIN. He found nothing new, by God.

TRIVET. And he told the Prince about her, and the Prince was impressed with his story.

ROBIN. The gossip!

TRIVET. His lordship wanted to see her, and gave orders to have her brought here.

ROBIN. But he'll return her to me, surely, as is right?

TRIVET. Hm. There's a small difficulty. He's fallen in love with her and would like to be loved by her in turn.

ROBIN. His turn can't come, because it's me she loves.

TRIVET. You're missing the point; listen to the end.

ROBIN (*a little louder*). You've reached the end already. Is somebody trying to swindle me out of my rights?

TRIVET. Do you know that the Prince has to choose a wife among his people?

ROBIN. No, I don't know. What's that to me?

TRIVET. I'm trying to inform you.

ROBIN. I don't want to be informed.

TRIVET. Before he marries her, the Prince would like to have Sylvia fall in love with him. Naturally, her love for you stands a little in his way.

ROBIN. Let him make love elsewhere, otherwise he'd have the wife, I'd have her heart, we'd both be short something, and we'd all three be miserable.

TRIVET. You're right; but don't you grasp that if you were to marry Sylvia, the Prince would be unhappy?

ROBIN. Well now, he'd be a little depressed at the beginning; but thinking he'd done his duty like a decent man would cheer him up. Instead of which, if he marries Sylvia, he'll cause the poor child to cry; I'll be crying too, of course; only the Prince will be left laughing; but to laugh by oneself is no pleasure.

TRIVET. Still, Master Robin, take my advice and do your Prince a favor. He can't bring himself to let Sylvia go. I'll even tell you that the odd way he became acquainted with the girl was foretold to him, and it was predicted that she would be his wife. It's bound to happen; it's all written down in heaven.

ROBIN. In heaven they don't write down such drivel. Just to show you: supposing it was foretold that I would knock you down and stab you in the back, would it make you happy if I fulfilled the prediction?

TRIVET. Certainly not! One should never hurt anybody.

ROBIN. Well! Your prediction is going to be the death of me, so it's a foul prediction and you'd better hang the astrologer.

TRIVET. But damn it all, who's hurting you? The palace is full of pretty girls. Marry one of them; you won't regret it.

ROBIN. Thank you! So I'm to marry another girl, make Sylvia angry, and have her fling herself at somebody else! What have they paid you, I wonder, to set this trap for me? But you're an ass, my good friend. Keep your pretty girls. I'm not dealing with you, you're too expensive for me.

TRIVET. Do you realize that the match I'm suggesting to you will earn you the Prince's friendship?

ROBIN. The friendship of somebody I don't even know!

TRIVET. What about the wealth this friendship will bring you?

ROBIN. That's a bauble of no use to a man who has his health, a sound appetite, and a job.

TRIVET. You don't know what you're refusing!

ROBIN. That's why it's no loss to me.

TRIVET. Town house, country house . . .

ROBIN. Wonderful! The only point that worries me is, who'll be living in my town house while I'm in my country house?

TRIVET. Your servants, of course!

ROBIN. My servants? I'm to get rich so those ruffians can enjoy themselves at my expense! But wait a minute: could I live in both houses at the same time?

TRIVET (*laughing*). I suppose not; you can't be in two places at once, you know.

ROBIN. Well then, you simpleton, what's the use of two houses?

TRIVET. Whenever you like, you'll go from the one to the other.

ROBIN. So I'm to give up my Sylvia for the pleasure of moving every month?

TRIVET. Doesn't anything tempt you? Very strange. Anybody else would jump at these mansions, these servants—

ROBIN. All I need is one room; I don't like to support idlers; and I'll never find a servant more faithful to me and keener to serve me than I myself.

TRIVET. I admit you've got an attendant there you won't want to dismiss. But wouldn't you enjoy riding in a fine carriage drawn by the best horses, or being surrounded by luxurious furniture?

ROBIN. You are a great fool, my friend, to be comparing Sylvia with furniture, a carriage, and the horses that pull it. What more can you do in a house than sit down, eat, and sleep? Give me a good bed, a solid table, a dozen straw-bottom chairs, and I'm as furnished and as comfortable as I want to be. Ah, but I haven't got a carriage! Well then, I won't tip over. (*Pointing to his legs*) And isn't this a team my mother gave me? Aren't they sound legs? As God is my witness, this carriage of mine ought to be good enough for you too. Away, you loafers! Turn your horses over to honest farmers who need them. We'll all have bread on our tables, you'll walk, and the gout won't get you.

TRIVET. Sharp! sharp! If you had your way, there wouldn't be shoes enough to supply the world.

ROBIN. Let the world wear clogs. I've had enough of your chatter. You promised to produce Sylvia, and an honest man keeps his word.

TRIVET. Just a moment. You don't care for honors, riches, handsome houses, luxury, reputation, carriages—

ROBIN. All frippery.

TRIVET. But what about good food? Would that tempt you? Would you enjoy a cellar full of the best wines? Would you rejoice in a chef who prepared expert and plentiful dinners for you? Picture to yourself, if you please, the most savory meats and seafood: they're yours, and for a lifetime . . . You're not answering me.

ROBIN. What you're talking about now sounds better than all the rest, because I admit I'm a glutton, but all the same my heart is bigger than my stomach.

TRIVET. Come, come, Sir Robin, be a happy man, leave one girl and take another.

ROBIN. No. I'll stick to plain beef and home-bottled wine.

TRIVET. Oh, the wines you would have drunk, the morsels you would have tasted!

ROBIN. I'm sorry, but that's how it is. The best morsel is Sylvia's heart. Are you or are you not going to show her to me?

TRIVET. I am, don't worry. Only it's a bit early yet in the morning.
(*Enter Lisa.*)

LISA. Oh, there you are, Mr. Trivet. The Prince is asking for you.

TRIVET. The Prince? I'm off. Why don't you keep Sir Robin company while I'm gone?

ROBIN. There's no need; I'm pretty good company to myself when I'm alone.

TRIVET. Oh no, you might get bored. I'll be right back. (*He leaves.*)

ROBIN (*in a corner*). Here's a little minx who's going to throw herself at me. Let her try!

LISA (*softly*). Sir, are you Miss Sylvia's suitor?

ROBIN (*coldly*). I am.

LISA. She's very pretty.

ROBIN (*as before*). She is.

LISA. Everybody loves her.

ROBIN (*brusque*). Everybody shouldn't.

LISA. Why not, if she deserves it?

ROBIN (*as before*). Because the only one *she's* going to love is myself.

LISA. I don't doubt it and I forgive her for being attached to you.

ROBIN. And what's the point of your forgiveness?

LISA. I mean I'm no longer as surprised as I was when I first heard about her stubborn love for you.

ROBIN. And why were you surprised?

LISA. Because she was snubbing a most attractive Prince.

ROBIN. And suppose he's attractive, does that prevent me from being attractive too?

LISA (*softly*). No, but he *is* a Prince, after all.

ROBIN. What of it? As far as girls are concerned, the Prince hasn't got a thing I haven't got.

LISA (*as before*). That's true. I only meant that he rules over subjects and land, and that, attractive as you are, you do *not* rule over subjects and land.

ROBIN. How you carry on about subjects and land! I grant you I have no subjects. But it follows I'm not responsible for anyone. If all goes well, I'm glad; if things go wrong, I'm not to blame. As for land, a landowner doesn't take up more room than I do, and land never improved a man's looks. In short, there was no reason for you to be surprised.

LISA (*aside*). What a little beast! I compliment him and he snaps at me.

ROBIN. What was that?

LISA. I'm unfortunate in everything I say. And yet, looking at you, I had hoped for gentler words.

ROBIN. That goes to show how a face can fool you.

LISA. Yes, I've been deceived by yours. One's often so wrong to have a prejudice in favor of a person.

ROBIN. Oh, terribly wrong. But what can I do? I didn't choose my face.

LISA. I look at you and I'm amazed.

ROBIN. And yet here I am; there's no remedy, I'll never change.

LISA. I know it now.

ROBIN. Luckily, it doesn't matter to you, does it?

LISA. Why do you ask?

ROBIN. In order to find out.

LISA. I'd be a fool to tell you the truth; a girl mustn't be the first to speak.

ROBIN (*aside*). Listen to her! (*Aloud*) You know, it's really a pity you're a coquette.

LISA. Me?

ROBIN. Yes, you.

LISA. Are you aware that this is no way for a man to speak to a woman? You're insulting me.

ROBIN. Why? There's no harm in seeing what's pointed out to you. I'm not to blame for telling you that you're a coquette; blame yourself for being one.

LISA. But why do you think I'm a coquette?

ROBIN. Because there's too much sugar in your words, because you keep hinting that I've turned your head. Well, if I have, say good-bye at once so you can recover; because I'm spoken for, you know, and besides I don't want a girl to make advances to me, I want to make them myself. But if you're only playing with me—then I say shame, young lady, shame!

LISA. This is too absurd for words!

ROBIN. How can young men stand these airs at court? God, but a woman's ugly when she's a flirt!

LISA. My poor man, you're raving.

ROBIN. You talk about Sylvia. There's charm for you! If I told you about our love, you'd be amazed to hear how shy she is. You should have seen how she avoided me the first days; and then how she avoided me a tiny bit less; and then, little by little, how she stopped avoiding me at all; and next how she gave me shy looks; and then how she was ashamed when I caught her doing it; and how I was happy as a king to see her shame; and then how I snatched her hand, and how she allowed me to hold it; and then how she blushed; and how I talked to her; and how she wouldn't say a word, though I could see she was thinking; and then how she gave me looks instead of words, and then words she let go without knowing what happened, because her heart went faster than herself. I was delirious; there was something magical about it all. I had met a girl, a rare girl, someone very unlike yourself.

LISA. You're very amusing. I'm laughing.

ROBIN. I don't want you to laugh at my expense. Good-bye; and if everybody were like me, you'd catch a white crow before finding a lover.
(*Enter Trivet.*)

TRIVET. Are you leaving?

ROBIN. I am. This lady wants me to fall in love with her, but I won't.

TRIVET. Come on, let's go for a walk before lunch; it'll distract you.
(*They leave. Enter the Prince and Flaminia.*)

FLAMINIA. Well, are we making progress? What's the news about Robin's heart?

LISA. Grim news for me.

FLAMINIA. Was he rude to you?

LISA. "Shame, young lady, you are a coquette"; that's his style.

PRINCE. I'm sorry to hear this, Lisa; but don't be chagrined; you've lost nothing in my eyes.

LISA. I confess, my lord, that if I were vain I'd have grounds for concern. I have proof now that I can be disliked. It's the kind of proof we women prefer to live without.

FLAMINIA. I see it's my turn to try now.

PRINCE. Since Robin can't be won over, Sylvia will never be mine.

FLAMINIA. Listen to me, my lord. I have seen Robin, and I like him. I have put it into my head to make you happy. I have promised you that happy you shall be. And I mean to keep my promise. Consider it all settled. You don't know me, my lord. Do you think for a minute that Robin and Sylvia can hold out against me? That I am incapable of regulating hearts like theirs? My lord, I have undertaken a task; I am stubborn; I am, to sum it all up, a woman. The race of women would disown me if I gave up now. Make the arrangements for your wedding, my lord; Sylvia must consent, you shall have her heart and her hand. Wait, I hear a voice; it's Sylvia's; she is saying "I love you, my Prince." I see the wedding—there—you're man and wife. Robin marries me. You honor us with generous rewards. And the story ends.

LISA. The story ends? It hasn't even begun!

FLAMINIA. Silence, heretic.

PRINCE. You encourage my hope, but frankly I fail to see any great likelihood of success.

FLAMINIA. I have means of making the likelihood come true. My first step is to call Sylvia; it's time for her to see Robin.

LISA. Your means will fall apart the moment they see each other again.

PRINCE. I think so too.

FLAMINIA. Splendid: we differ only over yes or no; nothing worth mentioning. Meantime, I've decided they'll see each other as often as they please. This is the first of several traps I intend to set for their love.

PRINCE. Well, do as you like.

FLAMINIA. Let's all be off! Here's Robin. (*They leave.*)
(*Enter Robin, Trivet, and servants.*)

ROBIN. Incidentally, will you tell me one thing? I've been trying to decide for over an hour why those tall clowns are following me about. I can't lift a finger without being watched.

TRIVET. This is our Prince's way of showing his regard for you. He wants these men to follow you in your honor.

ROBIN. Oh, you mean it's an honor to be followed?

TRIVET. Absolutely.

ROBIN. And tell me, who follows the men who are following me?

TRIVET. Nobody.

ROBIN. And you don't have anybody following you either?

TRIVET. No, I don't.

ROBIN. You mean you people are not honored?

TRIVET. We don't deserve to be.

ROBIN (*shaking his stick*). If that's the case, clear out! The whole crew! Away!

TRIVET. Why? What do you mean?

ROBIN. Get out! I don't like dishonorable people who don't deserve to be honored.

TRIVET. You don't understand me!

ROBIN (*beating him*). I'll talk more clearly.

TRIVET. Stop, stop, what are you doing?
(*The servants run away, and Trivet takes refuge in the wings.*)

ROBIN. Scum! I don't seem to be able to discharge them. Is this how they honor a good man, by making a gang of rascals dog his footsteps? Who do they take me for? (*He sees Trivet again.*) Haven't I made myself clear yet, my friend?

TRIVET (*from a distance*). Let me speak, Sir Robin. You've beaten me black and blue, but I'll forgive you. You're not unreasonable, are you?

ROBIN. Of course not.

TRIVET (*as before*). I told you we don't deserve to have servants, but it's not because we're dishonorable; it's because only the rich and the powerful are honored in this particular way. If it were enough to be a good man, I myself, as I live and breathe, would have an army of underlings trailing after me.

ROBIN (*putting his stick away*). Oh, well, now I understand you. Why the devil don't you talk plainer? I wouldn't have dislocated my arm, and your back would be in better shape too.

TRIVET. I still feel that whacking of yours.

ROBIN. I meant you to. Luckily it was all a misunderstanding, and you ought to be glad that you took your beating as an innocent man. I see now that powerful people are honored around here, and a good man gets nothing.

TRIVET. That's it exactly.

ROBIN (*disgusted*). In short, you can be honored without being honorable.

TRIVET. True, but one might also be honored and honorable at the same time.

ROBIN. Still and all, please leave me without an escort. Those who'll see me walking by myself will understand that I'm a good man, which I like as well as being taken for a lord.

TRIVET. But our orders are to stay with you.

ROBIN. Well then, take me to Sylvia.

TRIVET. You'll have your wish, she's coming. In fact—that's right—here she is. I'll leave you to yourselves. (*He leaves.*) (*Enter Sylvia and Flaminia.*)

SYLVIA (*running joyfully to Robin*). There he is! Oh, dearest, sweetest Robin, it's you! I'm seeing you again! My poor boy! Oh, I'm so happy!

ROBIN (*breathless*). And so am I. Oh, oh, oh, I'm dying, I'm too happy.

SYLVIA. There, there, my love, gently. How much he loves me; how wonderful to be loved like this.

FLAMINIA. My dear children, I'm overjoyed to see you so faithful to one another. (*Aside*) And I'm ruined if anybody hears me. But I can't help myself, my heart goes out to them.

SYLVIA (*answering her*). You're very kind, that's why. Oh, Robin, how wretched I've been.

ROBIN. Do you still love me?

SYLVIA. Do I still love you! Is that a question you should ask?

FLAMINIA. Oh, I'll bear witness to her love. I've seen her in despair, wailing over your absence. I almost cried with her. I couldn't wait to see you together; and here you are. Good-bye, my friends; I'm leaving you, because you bring tears to my eyes. Alas, you remind me of my love for someone—someone who died. . . . He had something of Robin's expression. I'll never forget him. Good-bye, Sylvia; I've been assigned to keep watch over you, but you can count on me. Love Robin, he deserves it. And you, Robin, whatever happens, look on me as a friend, a person who wishes to be of use to you.

ROBIN. You're a dear, and I'm your friend too. I'm so sorry your sweetheart is dead. I see you're unhappy, and so are we. (*Flaminia leaves.*)

SYLVIA (*plaintively*). Well, Robin, my love?

ROBIN. Well, Sylvia, my soul?

SYLVIA. How unhappy we are!

ROBIN. Let us love each other always; that will help us to be patient.

SYLVIA. Yes, but what is going to happen to our love? I'm so worried.

ROBIN. I don't know, I tell you to be patient, but I'm no braver than you are. My poor lovely treasure, three days have gone by without my seeing your beautiful eyes. You must gaze at me forever to compensate me.

SYLVIA. Oh, I've so many things to tell you. I'm afraid of losing you; I'm afraid of somebody hurting you in a fit of jealousy; I'm afraid of your being away from me for a long time, and getting used to it.

ROBIN. My dove, would I get used to being miserable?

SYLVIA. I don't want you to forget me, but neither do I want you to suffer because of me; I can't tell you what I want, I love you too much, I'm in a daze, everything makes me unhappy.

ROBIN (*crying*). Ay ay ay ay!

SYLVIA. Now I'm going to cry, too.

ROBIN. How can I stop crying when I see you so anxious? You wouldn't be shedding these tears if you pitied me.

SYLVIA. Hush; I won't tell you any more that I'm unhappy.

ROBIN. But I'll guess the truth. Please promise to be cheerful.

SYLVIA. I promise. But you must promise to love me forever.

ROBIN. I'll love you, and nothing will shake my love, as long as there's a breath left in my body. I'm yours and you're mine, do you hear? Shall I take an oath? Tell me what to say.

SYLVIA. I don't know any oaths, and I trust you without them. And you can trust me too. All my love is yours. Who else should have any particle of it? You're the prettiest boy in the whole world, and there isn't a girl anywhere who could love you as much as I do. Isn't that all we need? Let's remain just as we are, and forget all about oaths.

ROBIN. In a hundred years we'll be the same as now.

SYLVIA. The very same.

ROBIN. Then there's nothing to be afraid of, and we might as well be happy.

SYLVIA. We'll suffer a bit, that's all.

ROBIN. Who cares? After a little misery, pleasure tastes all the better.

SYLVIA. And yet I could manage to be happy without any misery at all.

ROBIN. Let's simply not think about our misery.

SYLVIA. Dearest boy! What would I do without your encouragement?

ROBIN. I think only of you.

SYLVIA. And where have you learned to say all these lovely things? There's only one of you in this world, and only one of me to love you.

ROBIN. Oh, the honey of your words!
(*Enter Trivet and Flaminia.*)

TRIVET. It breaks my heart to interrupt you, young lady, but your mother has arrived and wishes to see you right away.

SYLVIA. Don't leave me, Robin. I have no secrets from you.

ROBIN (*taking her arm*). Let's go, my love.

FLAMINIA. Don't be afraid, my children. Go meet your mother by yourself, dear Sylvia, it's more proper that way. Trust me— you're both free to see each other as much as you like. I wouldn't lie to you.

ROBIN. I know, you're on our side.

SYLVIA. Very well, I'll go alone. Wait for me, my dear. (*She leaves with Trivet.*)

ROBIN (*stopping Flaminia, who is pretending to go*). Why don't you stay and distract me a little while Sylvia's gone? You're the only person I can stand to be with in this house.

FLAMINIA (*as though confidentially*). My dear Robin, I enjoy your company too, but I'm afraid somebody might notice how much I like you.
(*Re-enter Trivet.*)

TRIVET. Sir Robin, lunch is being served.

ROBIN (*gloomily*). I'm not hungry.

FLAMINIA. You must eat, I want you to, you need it.

ROBIN. Do you think so?

FLAMINIA. I do.

ROBIN. But I couldn't. (*To Trivet*) Is the soup good?

TRIVET. Exquisite.

ROBIN. Hm. We'd better wait for Sylvia. She's fond of soup.

FLAMINIA. I think she'll eat with her mother. You're the master, of course, but I advise you to leave them together, and to see her after lunch.

ROBIN. If you say so; but my appetite isn't ready yet.

TRIVET. The wine has been cooled, and the roast is on the table.

ROBIN. I'm so depressed . . . Does the roast look tasty?

TRIVET. Tasty is hardly the word!

ROBIN. So much grief . . . Well, let's go. Meat shouldn't be eaten cold.

FLAMINIA. Don't forget to drink to my health.

ROBIN. Come along and drink to mine for old friendship's sake.

FLAMINIA. Gladly. I can give you half an hour.

ROBIN. You're a dear.

ACT TWO

(Enter Sylvia and Flaminia.)

SYLVIA. Yes, I believe you. I think you do wish me well. That's why you're the only person I can endure in the palace; all the others I look on as my enemies. But where is Robin?

FLAMINIA. He'll soon be here; he's still at lunch.

SYLVIA. What a miserable place this is! Never have I seen such polite ladies and gentlemen. Oh, the sweet manners, the bowing and curtsying, the compliments, the promises! You'd think they were the kindest people in the world. But not a bit! Because there isn't a single one who fails to whisper into my ear, "Miss Sylvia, believe me, you ought to give up Robin and marry the Prince." And all this, mind you, without shame, in the most natural manner, as though they were urging me to do a good deed. "But I'm pledged to Robin," say I; "where's constancy, integrity, good faith?" That they don't understand; it's Greek to them; they laugh in my face, they tell me that I'm behaving like a baby, that a grown-up girl ought to show more sense. Pretty, isn't it? To be mean, to deceive your neighbor, to break your word, to be a liar, those are the duties of the great in this horrid place. Who are these people? Where do they come from? What clay are they made of?

FLAMINIA. Of the same clay as everybody, my dear Sylvia. Don't let it surprise you; they fancy you'd be happy with the Prince.

SYLVIA. But shouldn't I be faithful? Could I be happy without doing my duty? More than that, isn't my faithfulness one of my charms? And yet, these fine people have the cheek to tell me, "There, be wicked, reap misery, forfeit your happiness and your good faith," and because I won't, they think I'm a prude.

FLAMINIA. What do you expect? They reason in their own way, they want the Prince to be happy.

SYLVIA. Why doesn't the Prince take a girl who wants him? Such a silly whim—to court a girl who isn't interested. How odd can a man be? All this waste of concerts and plays, these dinners as lavish as wedding feasts, these jewels he keeps sending me; they must cost him huge sums, it's an abyss, he's ruining himself; and I ask you, what does he gain? If he gave me a whole dress shop, I wouldn't be as happy as with a ball of yarn I got from Robin.

FLAMINIA. I know. That's love for you. I've been in love too, and I see myself in that ball of yarn.

SYLVIA. If I'd really had to exchange Robin for somebody else, it would have been for a gentleman I met five or six times and who is as handsome as a man can be. I'd like to see whether the Prince is worth his little finger! Ah, what a pity I couldn't let myself fall in love with him. Believe me, I'm sorrier for that gentleman than I am for the Prince.

FLAMINIA. Oh, I assure you you'll feel just as sorry for the Prince once you get to know him.

SYLVIA. Well, let him try to forget me; let him send me away and spend his time on other girls. I've met several ladies here who are engaged just as I am, but that doesn't keep them from carrying on with everybody else. It's nothing to them, but it's a thing I can't do for the life of me.

FLAMINIA. The trouble is, do we have anyone here as good as you?

SYLVIA (*modestly*). Oh, yes! There are prettier girls. And even when they're only half as pretty, they're still better off than I am with all my good looks. Why, I've seen real hags that do such things to their faces that one's quite taken in by them.

FLAMINIA. Yes, but yours is charming precisely because you do nothing with it.

SYLVIA. Good. I'm all of one piece. I stay as I am, I don't come and go. Whereas they pretend to be gay, their eyes flutter at everybody, they put on bold shameless airs—and this makes them more attractive than a bashful thing like myself that doesn't dare look at people and that blushes if somebody says she's pretty.

FLAMINIA. Well—this is exactly what impresses the Prince, this is what he values—innocence, simple beauty, natural grace. Believe me, Sylvia, don't lavish your praise on our women here, because they're miles away from praising you.

SYLVIA. Oh? What do they say?

FLAMINIA. They're simply impertinent. Or jealous. They ridicule you, they taunt the Prince, they ask him how is his rustic beauty. "Have you ever seen such a common face?" I heard one of them say the other day, "or such a clumsy gait?" Then somebody criticized your eyes, somebody else your mouth, and even a few of the men found fault with your appearance. I was beside myself!

SYLVIA (*angry*). Oh, the horrible men, who tell lies to please those fools!

FLAMINIA. So it goes.

SYLVIA. And how I despise these women! But if I'm so very ugly, why is the Prince in love with me instead of them?

FLAMINIA. Oh, they're sure he won't love you long; they say it's a passing whim he'll be the first to laugh at.

SYLVIA. Ha! It's lucky for them I'm in love with Robin; otherwise I'd show up these chatterboxes.

FLAMINIA. And wouldn't they deserve it! I've told them: "You're doing all you can to get Sylvia dismissed and to attract the Prince; but if she were so inclined, he wouldn't condescend even to look at you."

SYLVIA. At least you know the truth; I could crush them if I wanted to.

FLAMINIA. Hush—here's somebody coming.

SYLVIA. Oh, that's the very gentleman I was telling you about. Yes, that's the one! Look at him, isn't he handsome, though!
(*Enter the Prince as a gentleman, and Lisa as a lady-in-waiting. The Prince bows humbly to Sylvia.*)

SYLVIA. I see it's you again. You knew I was here.

PRINCE. Yes, Miss Sylvia, I knew it. But since you told me once to stay away from you, I wouldn't have dared to come if this lady hadn't asked me to escort her. She has obtained the Prince's permission to pay her respects to you.
(*Lisa and Flaminia exchange winks.*)

SYLVIA (*gently*). I'm not unhappy to see you again, though I'm in low spirits just now. As for this lady, I'm obliged to her for wishing to pay her respects to me. I don't deserve them, but if she wants to curtsy to me, let her go about it and I'll return the compliment as best I can; she'll excuse me if I do it badly.

LISA. Yes, my dear, I'll excuse you with all my heart; I don't ask for what's impossible.

SYLVIA (*aside*). I don't ask for what's impossible! Indeed! (*She curtsies.*)

LISA. How old are you, my child?

SYLVIA. I've forgotten, mother.

FLAMINIA (*to Sylvia*). Good.

LISA. Is she angry, by any chance?

PRINCE. What do you mean? My dear lady, under pretext of paying a respectful call, you're abusing Miss Sylvia.

LISA. That wasn't my intention, I assure you. I was only anxious to see the little girl who has turned you-know-whose head. Perhaps I can find the secret of her charm. I'm told she's naïve, and I suppose this creates an amusing pastoral effect. Will you ask her to give us a few strokes of naïveté? Let's see her wit.

SYLVIA. Don't trouble yourself, madam; my wit isn't as comical as yours.

LISA (*laughing*). Ha, ha, there's naïveté for you.

PRINCE (*to Lisa*). You'd better leave us, madam.

SYLVIA. The sooner the better. If she doesn't go away, I'll really lose my temper.

PRINCE (*to Lisa*). The Prince will be offended.

LISA. I'm going. To know that this is the creature he chose to love is satisfaction enough for me. (*She leaves.*)

FLAMINIA. What gall!

SYLVIA. I'm furious! Was I carried off to be exposed to these women? I hope I'm as good as any of them. Believe me, I wouldn't care to trade places with them, not for the world.

FLAMINIA. Oh, well. Insults from her kind should be taken as compliments.

PRINCE. My beautiful Sylvia, this woman has misled both the Prince and myself. Believe me when I say that her behavior has shocked me. You know my feelings for you; you know how deeply I respect you. I was coming here to look once again at a person dearer to me than I can say, and to acknowledge in you our future sovereign. But I shouldn't let myself go. Flaminia is listening. And I mustn't be a burden to you.

FLAMINIA. No harm done! Don't I know a person can't see her without loving her?

SYLVIA. All the same, I'd rather he didn't love me, because I'm sorry I can't reciprocate. You see he's not like all the others. One can say anything to *them*. But he's always so sweet, I can't be mean to him.

PRINCE. How kind you are, Sylvia! How can I be worthy of you, except by loving you forever?

SYLVIA. Well, I give you permission to love me, that's settled. And I'll enjoy it too, provided you promise to take your grief patiently; because that's the best I can do for you. Robin was first, you know; nothing else stands in your way. If I'd guessed you were coming after him, I would have waited for you. But you're unlucky, and I'm none too happy myself.

PRINCE. You be the judge, Flaminia. How can a man stop loving her? So tender, so generous! I had rather be pitied by Sylvia than adored by any other woman.

SYLVIA. I'll let you judge too, Flaminia. What should a girl do with a man who thanks her no matter what she says?

FLAMINIA. I can't blame him. You're such a lovely girl, if I were a man I would say and do the very same things as he.

SYLVIA. Don't make it worse for him. He needn't be told that I'm lovely; poor man, he believes it already. (*To the Prince*) Do try to love me peacefully, will you—and help me get even with that woman.

PRINCE. I'll do it at once, my dear Sylvia. As for me, I don't care how you treat me, my mind is made up, and I'll have the pleasure at least of loving you as long as I live.

SYLVIA. Oh, I'm sure you will. I know you.

FLAMINIA. Go now, my dear sir; inform the Prince against the lady in question. Let everybody know the respect we owe our Sylvia.

PRINCE. You'll hear from me presently. (*He leaves.*)

FLAMINIA. And I'll go look for Robin, whom somebody must be keeping at table. In the meantime, why don't you try the dress that was made for you? I can't wait to see it on you.

SYLVIA. I'm sure it will fit me; and it's a lovely material. But I'd rather not take these dresses. The Prince wants me in exchange, and that's a bargain I'll never agree to.

FLAMINIA. You're wrong there. Even if he left you, everything would be yours. Really, you don't know him.

SYLVIA. If you say so . . . But I hope he doesn't ask me afterwards, "Why did you take my presents?"

FLAMINIA. He'll ask you, "Why didn't you take more of them?"

SYLVIA. Very well: I'll help myself to as many presents as he likes; that way he won't be able to blame me.

FLAMINIA. Carry on. I'll answer for everything.
(*Sylvia leaves.*)

FLAMINIA. Things are beginning to fall into place. Here's Robin. Really, I don't know; but if the little man were to fall in love with me, I wouldn't half mind.
(*Enter Robin, laughing, with Trivet.*)

ROBIN. Ha, ha, ha! Hello, Flaminia.

FLAMINIA. Hello, Robin. Tell me why you're laughing, so I can laugh too.

ROBIN. It's Trivet, he's been showing me about the house. He's my lackey, you know, and he serves me for nothing. Well, you should see how people go dashing from room to room as though they were in the street. And all the chatter—worse than in our market place. All that time there's the master of the house who doesn't seem to mind a bit. People come in without saying how d'you do, they watch him eat, and he goes on without asking anybody, "How about a drink, you there?" Well, I was still laughing at these freaks when, on my way back, I noticed a tall rascal lifting a lady's dress from behind. Now here's a prank, says I to myself, and I tell him straight off, "Stop it, you low scamp; this trifling is indecent." But the lady overhears me. She turns around and says, "Can't you see he's carrying my train?" "You mean he's carrying your tail," says I. That's when the rascal started to laugh, then the lady fell to laughing, Trivet laughed, everybody was laughing; so to keep 'em company I decided to laugh too. But now I want to ask you, what were we all laughing about?

FLAMINIA. About nothing. You don't happen to know that what this lackey was doing was done according to custom.

ROBIN. You mean it was another honor?

FLAMINIA. That's right.

ROBIN. Well, I'm glad I laughed. It's a funny honor, by God, and a cheap one, too.

FLAMINIA. You're in a good mood. That's how I like to see you. How was your meal?

ROBIN. God love me! I wish you had seen the tasty concoctions! And the cook's fricassee! There's no fighting that cook. I drank so many healths to Sylvia and you, it won't be my fault if you ever get sick.

FLAMINIA. What? Did you think of me at all?

ROBIN. Once I've given my friendship to a person, I never forget it, especially at table. But what about Sylvia, is she still with her mother?

TRIVET. Oh, Sir Robin, still thinking about Sylvia?

ROBIN. Hold your tongue when I speak.

FLAMINIA. You're in the wrong, Trivet.

TRIVET. I, in the wrong?

FLAMINIA. That's right. Why do you try to keep him from talking about what he loves?

TRIVET. I'm beginning to see how much you care for the Prince's interests.

FLAMINIA (as though frightened). Robin, that man is going to make trouble for me on your account.

ROBIN (angry). No, my sweet, he won't. (To Trivet) Look here, I'm your master, you said so yourself, I didn't know a thing about it. Well, you loafer, if I catch you tattling, and if they so much as say boo to this fine girl, you'll be short two ears; I'll have them in my pocket.

TRIVET. I'll live without ears, and do my duty.

ROBIN. Two ears! Do I make myself clear? And now get out.

TRIVET. I forgive you everything, because I have to; but as for you, Flaminia, you'll be paying the fiddler.
(*Robin threatens him, Flaminia stops Robin, and Trivet leaves.*)

ROBIN. This is too much. No sooner do I find a sensible person in this house than some busybody takes issue with our conversation. My dear Flaminia, let's talk about Sylvia now as much as we like. It's only when I'm with you that I can bear to be without her.

FLAMINIA. I'm not ungrateful—there's nothing I wouldn't do to make both of you happy. Besides, you're so wonderful, Robin, that when I see anybody upsetting you, I suffer as much as you do.

ROBIN. Dear, dear girl! I feel calmer when you pity me. Already I'm only half as sorry to be miserable as I was before.

FLAMINIA. Who wouldn't pity you? Who wouldn't be interested in your fate? You don't realize what you're worth, Robin.

ROBIN. That's possible, you know. I've never taken that close a look.

FLAMINIA. It's terrible to be so powerless! If you could read into my heart!

ROBIN. What a shame; I can't read; but you'll explain it to me. I swear to God, I'd like to be rid of my grief, if only out of consideration for the way you worry about it; but everything will be settled by and by, you'll see.

FLAMINIA (*in a sad voice*). No, I'll never be a witness to your happiness; it's all over. Trivet is going to talk, I'll be taken away from you; who knows where they'll put me? Perhaps I'm speaking to you for the last time, Robin, and there'll be no pleasure left for me in this world.

ROBIN. For the last time! Oh, I was born under a wicked star! I had one only love, they took her away, and now are they going to take you too? Where will I get the strength to bear all this trouble? Do these people think my heart is made of brass? Have they decided to kill me? Are they savages?

FLAMINIA. Whatever happens, I hope you won't forget Flaminia, who wanted nothing so much as your happiness.

ROBIN. My dear good girl, you've won my heart. Advise me in my distress; let's put our heads together; what do you propose? I'm not very bright when I'm angry. I must love Sylvia, but I must keep you too. My love shouldn't suffer because of our friendship, nor our friendship because of my love; and here I am all tangled up.

FLAMINIA. And here *I* am all unhappy! From the time I lost the man I loved, I've been at peace only in your company; with you I've revived a little. You're so much like him, sometimes I think he is speaking again. I've never liked anyone except him and you.

ROBIN. Poor girl! How inconvenient that I'm in love with Sylvia; otherwise I'd gladly offer you your love's likeness. I take it he was a handsome young man?

FLAMINIA. Didn't I tell you he was just like you? You're his living portrait.

ROBIN. And you loved him very much?

FLAMINIA. Look at yourself, Robin; see how much you deserve to be loved, and you'll understand how much I loved him.

ROBIN. Can a body answer more sweetly? Every word you say is friendly. I'd never have guessed I was that good-looking; but since you loved the copy of me so well, I've got to believe that the original is pretty fair, too.

FLAMINIA. I think I would have liked you even better. But I wouldn't have been beautiful enough for you.

ROBIN (*with fire*). God strike me! That thought of yours makes you a beauty in itself!

FLAMINIA. I'm so troubled, I'd better leave you. It's hard, God knows, to tear myself away from you, but where would it all lead? Farewell, Robin; I'll remain at your side if I'm allowed. I don't know where I am.

ROBIN. Neither do I.

FLAMINIA. Seeing you gives me too much pleasure.

ROBIN. I haven't refused to give you that pleasure, have I? Look at me as long as you wish, I'll give you look for look.

FLAMINIA. I don't dare. Adieu. (*She leaves.*)

ROBIN (*gazing after her*). She's too good for this place. If I had to lose Sylvia by some accident, I think I'd take refuge with her in my despair.
(*Enter Trivet, and behind him Lord Lumley.*)

TRIVET. Sir Robin, can a man take a chance on showing himself without compromising his shoulders? I ask because you handle your wooden sword like a professional.

ROBIN. I'll be good if you are.

TRIVET. Here's a gentleman who wants to speak with you.
(*Lord Lumley approaches with many bows, which Robin returns.*)

ROBIN (*aside*). I've seen this man somewhere.

LORD LUMLEY. I have come to beg a favor of you, Mr. Robin; but perhaps I am disturbing you.

ROBIN. No, sir. You're doing me no good, and you're doing me no harm. (*Lord Lumley covers himself.*) Just let me know whether I ought to put my hat back on too.

LORD LUMLEY. Whatever you do, I shall feel honored.

ROBIN (*covering his head*). If you say so. What does your lordliness desire of me? But you might as well drop the ceremony; you'd waste your time, because I don't know the rules.

LORD LUMLEY. These are not ceremonies, but tokens of esteem.

ROBIN. Balderdash. I have seen your face before, sir. Somewhere at the hunt, where you were blowing a bugle. I took off my hat as you were passing by, and that's a doffing you still owe me.

LORD LUMLEY. What! Did I fail to return your salute?

ROBIN. You couldn't have failed more.

LORD LUMLEY. I must have missed the fact that you were a gentleman.

ROBIN. No, you didn't. But as you had no favor to ask me just then, I didn't catch your eye.

LORD LUMLEY. I simply don't recognize myself in this.

ROBIN. That's no loss. Well, what do you want?

LORD LUMLEY. I am throwing myself upon your kindness. I had the misfortune to speak lightly of you in the Prince's presence.

ROBIN. Just don't recognize yourself in this either.

LORD LUMLEY. Yes, but the Prince became angry.

ROBIN. Maybe he dislikes slanderers.

LORD LUMLEY. So it appears.

ROBIN. Good. He's an honest man; I'm glad. If he weren't keeping my Sylvia from me, I'd be friends with him. Well, what did he say to you? That you were a boor?

LORD LUMLEY. Yes.

ROBIN. He was right. What are you complaining about?

LORD LUMLEY. That wasn't all. "Robin," said the Prince, "is a man of honor. As I value him, I desire him to be respected. The frankness and simplicity of his character are qualities I should wish to find in all of you. I stand in the way of his love, and it grieves me to the soul that my passion compels me to injure his."

ROBIN (*overcome*). Bless my heart, I'm beginning to take a fancy to him, and I'm not half as angry with him as I thought I was.

LORD LUMLEY. Then he ordered me to withdraw. Whereupon my friends tried to placate him on my behalf.

ROBIN. If your friends wanted to withdraw along with you, they'd be doing the world a favor. Birds of a feather flock together.

LORD LUMLEY. As a matter of fact, he also grew angry with them.

ROBIN. God bless him as a proper man. Look at the bad lot he shook out of his house.

LORD LUMLEY. Only if you plead for us can we ever reappear before him.

ROBIN. Gentlemen, bon voyage to you.

LORD LUMLEY. How is that? You refuse to intercede for me? Oh, if you don't I am a ruined man. Now that I can no longer show myself to the Prince, what shall I do at court? I shall have to retire to my estates like an exile.

ROBIN. You mean being exiled is nothing but to be sent to your own house to eat up your own goods?

LORD LUMLEY. That's what it is.

ROBIN. And you'll live peacefully and comfortably; you'll have your four meals a day as usual?

LORD LUMLEY. Of course. What's so strange about that?

ROBIN. You're not fooling me now? You're sure a man is exiled when he slanders somebody?

LORD LUMLEY. It happens often enough.

ROBIN (*joyfully*). That settles it; I'm going to slander the first person I meet, and tell Flaminia and Sylvia to do it too.

LORD LUMLEY. But why?

ROBIN. Because I want to go into exile too, that's why. The way people are treated here, a man is better off punished than rewarded.

LORD LUMLEY. However that may be, I beg you to save me from this particular punishment. Besides, what I said about you was insignificant.

ROBIN. What was it?

LORD LUMLEY. Nothing at all.

ROBIN. Let's hear it anyway.

LORD LUMLEY. I said you had a candid innocent air, and you seemed to mean no harm.

ROBIN (*laughing*). I look like a simpleton, in short. But what does it matter? I look like a simpleton, you look like a genius; which proves that looks shouldn't be trusted. Come on, is that all you said?

LORD LUMLEY. I only added that you entertain all the people you talk to.

ROBIN. Well, I have to give them a chance to get even with me. Was that all?

LORD LUMLEY. Yes.

ROBIN. That's ridiculous. You don't deserve to go into exile; you've been rewarded for nothing.

LORD LUMLEY. And yet I am asking you to help me remain where I am. A man in my position can't live anywhere except at court. All my influence, all my ability to injure my enemies would vanish if I were living far from the Prince, and if I couldn't cultivate the friendship of those in power.

ROBIN. I'd sooner cultivate a good field. Rain or shine, it's bound to yield something, while your kind of friends must be hard to find and harder to keep.

LORD LUMLEY. You're quite right. Powerful men are unpredictable, but what's to be done? We can't resent them, we must smile and bend, because we could never hit our enemies without their help.

ROBIN. What a life! You take a thrashing on one side in order to give one on the other. Funny kind of vanity. You're humble and you're arrogant at the same time.

LORD LUMLEY. That's how we are raised. But listen to me. You could easily obtain my pardon, because you know Flaminia, don't you?

ROBIN. She's my intimate friend.

LORD LUMLEY. The Prince has a great deal of affection for her. She is the daughter of one of his trusted men. Now I am willing to make her fortune by marrying her off to a rich cousin of mine in the country. Inform the Prince of my design; and he'll take me into his favor again.

ROBIN. Maybe so; but I won't take you into mine, damn it. I don't want anybody marrying my friends. Hang your cousin!

LORD LUMLEY. I thought . . .

ROBIN. Stop thinking.

LORD LUMLEY. I give up my project.

ROBIN. Be sure you do. I'll promise to intercede for you provided you keep the cousin out.

LORD LUMLEY. I am deeply obliged to you, and I shall await the results of your promise. Good day, Mr. Robin.

ROBIN. Your servant. (*Lord Lumley leaves*) Well! I'm a man of consequence now, everybody obeys me. I'd better not breathe a word to Flaminia about the cousin.
(*Enter Flaminia.*)

FLAMINIA. My dear boy, I've brought Sylvia back to you. She's coming right away.

ROBIN. Why didn't you come sooner to tell me? We could have chatted while waiting for her.
(*Enter Sylvia.*)

SYLVIA. Hello, Robin dear. I've just been trying on the most beautiful dress! How pretty I looked in it! Ask Flaminia. If I chose to wear any of these dresses, we'd see who was clumsy here. But I'll say this—they have the cleverest seamstresses.

ROBIN. My love, they're not as clever as you're shapely.

SYLVIA. If I'm shapely, Robin, you're very gallant to say so.

FLAMINIA. I'm glad to see you both a little happier now.

SYLVIA. Why not? As long as no one bothers us, I'd as soon be here as any other place. What's the difference, here or there? You can make love anywhere.

ROBIN. I'd like to see anybody bother us! They're sending people in to me on their knees because they made some flip remark about me.

SYLVIA (*gaily*). To me too. I'm waiting right now for a lady who is to repent before my eyes for saying I wasn't beautiful.

FLAMINIA. If anybody vexes you from now on, let me know.

ROBIN. Oh yes, Flaminia loves us both like a sister. (*To Flaminia*) And it's tit for tat as far as we're concerned.

SYLVIA. Oh, that reminds me; guess who I met here? The handsome man who used to come after me—remember?—and who was in love with me. I want you to be friends, because he's very kind too.

ROBIN. Oh, by all means.

SYLVIA. After all, what harm is there in his liking me? When all's said and done, the people who love us are better company than those who don't.

FLAMINIA. Quite right.

ROBIN (*gaily*). Let's add Flaminia, in that case; she cares for us; and that'll make a foursome.

FLAMINIA. It's a friendly thought I'll never forget, Robin.

ROBIN. Well, since we're all together, let's have a snack to cheer us up.

SYLVIA. You go, Robin. Now that we can meet as much as we like, we needn't be in each other's way. Don't worry about me. (*Robin gestures to Flaminia to come with him.*)

FLAMINIA. I'll join you, especially as somebody is coming who'll keep Sylvia company. (*She leaves.*)
(*Enter Lisa, accompanied by several ladies. She makes a number of ceremonious curtsies to Sylvia.*)

SYLVIA. Not quite so many curtsies, madam, so I won't be obliged to return them. You fancy me too awkward to perform them, I know.

LISA (*in a sad voice*). Your merits have spoken here.

SYLVIA. Not for long, I'm sure, because I'm not putting myself out to impress anyone. I'm rather sorry to be as good-looking as I am, and I'm sorry you're not quite pretty enough.

LISA. Ah, what a situation!

SYLVIA. Here you are sighing because of a little village girl. You're taking your time now—where have you left your tongue, madam? Do you lose your gift for prattling when it comes to making amends?

LISA. I can't begin to speak.

SYLVIA. Then don't. Because you can moan until tomorrow morning, but you won't change my looks; beautiful or ugly, my face will remain what it is. But what brings you here? Haven't you scolded me enough? Well then, finish me off, help yourself!

LISA. Spare me, Miss Sylvia; my outburst has brought trouble on my whole family. The Prince compels me to apologize to you, and I am begging you to accept my excuses without taunting me.

SYLVIA. It's all over, I won't mock you anymore. I know that gentleness doesn't win friends in your world, but neither does spite. I'm sorry for you and I forgive you. But why did you provoke me before?

LISA. I thought the Prince had an inclination for me, and I believed I was not unworthy of it. But I see now that true charm doesn't always gain the upper hand.

SYLVIA. While ugly faces and bad figures do, because the upper hand is mine! Oh, the twisted minds of these jealous women!

LISA. Very well, I admit I'm jealous. But since you don't love the Prince, why not help me regain his affection? I know I had caught his eye. If you were willing, I could cure him of his weakness for you.

SYLVIA. Believe me, you'll never cure him; it's beyond any remedy of yours.

LISA. And yet I think it could be done. After all, I'm not as unappealing as all that.

SYLVIA. Let's talk about something else. Your fine qualities bore me.

LISA. Be that as it may, we'll soon see whether I have really so little power over him.

SYLVIA. We'll see fiddlesticks! Watch out! I'll speak to the Prince. He hasn't dared come near me as yet, because I'm cross with him; but I'll let him know he can be a little bolder, just to see.

LISA. And I'm going. Each one of us will do the best she can. For the rest, I have done as I was told with regard to you, and I ask you to forget what has taken place between us.

SYLVIA (*sharply*). Go your way, I don't even know you're alive. (*Lisa leaves by one way, while Flaminia enters by another.*)

FLAMINIA. What's the matter, Sylvia? You seem upset.

SYLVIA. I'm simply boiling. That impudent woman who was here before came again to apologize; and I don't know how the hussy went about it, but she managed to infuriate me again, saying that it was my ugliness which had won the Prince, that she was more charming and skillful than I, that she'd set to work taking the Prince's love away from me, that I would see, and on and on, I don't know what-all she threw in my face! Can you blame me for being angry?

FLAMINIA. Listen to me; if you don't silence these people, you'll have to hide your head for the rest of your life.

SYLVIA. Don't I want to silence them? But how can I, with Robin in the way?

FLAMINIA. I understand you. Your love is the very worst impediment.

SYLVIA. I've always been unlucky with these impediments.

FLAMINIA. On the other hand, if Robin sees you leaving the court despised by all, do you think he'll be happy?

SYLVIA. You mean he'd love me less?

FLAMINIA. I'm afraid so.

SYLVIA. You remind me of something. Don't you think he's been neglecting me a little since he arrived? Just now he left me for a snack. A fine excuse!

FLAMINIA. Yes, I noticed it too; but please don't repeat my words. We're talking among girls now; tell me the truth, do you really love that boy so much?

SYLVIA. Oh yes, I do; I have to, you know.

FLAMINIA. Shall I tell you what I think? You don't seem to be made for one another. You, Sylvia, have taste, intelligence, an air of refinement and distinction; while he displays to one and all his coarse looks and his gross manners. The two simply don't go together, and I can't understand how you came to fall in love with him. I'll go so far as to say that you're injuring yourself.

SYLVIA. Put yourself in my place. He was the most likable boy of the district; and he was my neighbor in the village; he's sometimes funny, and I'm good-natured, so he made me laugh now and then. He followed me about because he was in love with me;

and as I was used to seeing him day after day, I began to love him too, for lack of anyone better; but I always knew he was given to drink and gluttony.

FLAMINIA. Drink and gluttony! Lovely qualities in the suitor of our charming and tender Sylvia! Come now, what have you decided to do?

SYLVIA. I don't know what to say; so many yesses and noes are going through my head, which should I listen to? On the one side, Robin is a gadabout who thinks only of his dinner; on the other side, if I'm sent away, these arrogant women will spread the word that I was told, "Go away, you're not pretty enough." And on still another side, the gentleman I met again—

FLAMINIA. Yes?

SYLVIA. This is in strict confidence. I don't know what's happened to me since I saw him again; but he seems so sweet, he tells me such tender things, he talks about his love so politely, so humbly, that I'm full of pity for him, and this pity keeps me from thinking as straight as I should.

FLAMINIA. Do you love him?

SYLVIA. I don't think so, because I'm supposed to love Robin.

FLAMINIA. He's an excellent gentleman.

SYLVIA. I know.

FLAMINIA. If you forgot your revenge in order to marry him, I'd forgive you, and that's the truth.

SYLVIA. I wouldn't mind, provided Robin wanted to marry another girl. I'd have the right to tell him, "You left me, I'm leaving you, we're even." But there's no chance of that. Who'd want to marry Robin here—the little boor.

FLAMINIA. No one's fighting over him, between you and me. But I'll tell you what: I've always intended to spend my life in the country. Robin is a coarse fellow; I don't care for him, but I don't hate him either; and the way I feel, if he were willing, I'd rid you of him as a favor.

SYLVIA. Yes, but is that what I want? Do I want this, do I want that? I'm still searching.

FLAMINIA. You'll see the Prince today. Meantime, here's the gentleman you like. Try to make up your mind—we'll meet again in a while. (*She leaves.*)
(*Enter the Prince.*)

SYLVIA. Here you are. You'll tell me again that you care for me, and make me unhappier than before.

PRINCE. No—I came to see whether the lady who offended you had done her duty as commanded. As for myself, beautiful Sylvia, whenever my love wearies you, whenever I myself displease you, order me to hold my tongue or to withdraw; I'll be still, I'll go wherever you send me, and I'll suffer without complaint, resolved as I am to obey you in all things.

SYLVIA. Just listen to him! Wasn't I right? How am I ever to send you away? If I please, you'll be still; if I please, you'll leave me; you won't dare complain, you'll obey me in everything. A fine way you've chosen to make me give you orders!

PRINCE. Can I do better than make you the mistress of my destiny?

SYLVIA. What's the use? Could I bring myself to make you unhappy? If I told you to go away, you'd believe I hate you; if I told you to be still, you'd believe I was cold; and all these beliefs would be untrue; I'd be distressing you without making myself a bit happier.

PRINCE. Well then, beautiful Sylvia, what do you want me to do?

SYLVIA. What I want! I'm waiting for somebody to tell me; I know even less than you about it. Robin loves me; the Prince courts me; you deserve me; there are women here who insult me and whom I'd like to punish; I'll be shamed if I don't marry the

Prince; Robin worries me; you trouble my mind because you love me too much. Oh, I wish I had never met you; all this turmoil in my brain is making me miserable.

PRINCE. Your words affect me very deeply, Sylvia. My sorrow has touched you more than it deserves. You are unhappy because you are unable to love me, and this makes me guilty of your unhappiness.

SYLVIA. I could love you, though. It wouldn't be hard, *if* I wanted to.

PRINCE. Allow me, then, to suffer as long as I live.

SYLVIA (*impatient*). I warn you, I can't bear to see you so fond of me. I swear you're doing it on purpose. Is this reasonable? Oh God, it would be easier to love you altogether than to worry so. The conclusion will be that I'll drop everything, and then where will you be?

PRINCE. Dearest Sylvia, I don't want to be a burden to you. You wish me to leave you. Such is your will, and I obey you. Farewell, Sylvia.

SYLVIA (*quickly*). Farewell, Sylvia? I'll really scold you now. Where are you going? Stay here: *that's* my will. I hope I know my own will better than you do.

PRINCE. I only wanted to oblige you.

SYLVIA. Where is all this taking us? What shall I do with Robin? If only you were the Prince!

PRINCE. What if I were?

SYLVIA. I'd tell Robin you were the master, and it couldn't be helped. But I'd want to use that pretext only for you.

PRINCE (*aside*). Isn't she lovely? I ought to reveal myself now.

SYLVIA. What's the matter with you? Are you angry? It's not because of his possessions I'd want you to be the Prince, but because of yourself. I wish you were the Prince so that Robin would think I'd been forced to submit. He wouldn't know it was love. No, I suppose I'm glad you're not the master after all; I'd be too tempted. And even if you were, I couldn't choose to be unfaithful; and that's my conclusion.

PRINCE (*aside*). Let's wait a little longer. (*Aloud*) All I ask, Sylvia, is that you continue to think kindly of me. The Prince has prepared an entertainment in your honor. Allow me to escort you to it, and let me be with you as much as possible. You are to meet the Prince after the feast; and I am instructed to tell you that you will be free to go if you remain indifferent to him.

SYLVIA. Oh, I'll remain indifferent, and I'm as good as gone already. But once I'm home, you'll visit me again. Who knows what will happen then? Perhaps you'll win me. Let's leave. Robin might come!

ACT THREE

(The Prince and Flaminia in conversation.)

FLAMINIA. Yes, my lord, you did well to keep your identity concealed, in spite of Sylvia's tender response. This delay doesn't spoil anything, and gives her time to be confirmed in her inclination for you. Thank God, you've nearly reached your goal.

PRINCE. Ah, Flaminia, how lovely she is.

FLAMINIA. Infinitely.

PRINCE. I know no one like her in high society. It is pleasant, of course, to have a passionate mistress tell one distinctly, "I love you." And yet, Flaminia, this pleasure is pale and insipid compared to my joy when I listen to Sylvia, though she doesn't say "I love you" at all.

FLAMINIA. Dare I ask you to repeat something of what she does say?

PRINCE. Impossible. I'm delighted, I'm bewitched; but that's all I can report.

FLAMINIA. The report is unusual but promising.

PRINCE. If you knew, says she, if you knew how wretched I am because I may not love you, because I must be faithful to Robin, and because I see you grief-stricken! One moment more, and she would have cried, "Love me no more, I beg you, or else I shall fall into your arms!"

FLAMINIA. Well, that's even better than a declaration.

PRINCE. I repeat, Sylvia's is the only love which deserves that name. Other women use their cultivated minds, their education, their polished manners when they love, all of which falsify nature. But here the heart speaks in all its purity; as its emotions rise, it shows them; candor is its only art, bashfulness its only decorum. Confess, Flaminia, that nothing could be more charming. All that restrains her now is her reluctance to love me without Robin's consent. Hurry, Flaminia, hurry. Will you conquer him soon? You know I may not and will not use force against him. What does he say?

FLAMINIA. To tell you the truth, my lord, I think I have got him in love with me, only he doesn't know it yet. By calling me his dear friend, he is living at ease with his conscience, and enjoying his love gratis.

PRINCE. Excellent.

FLAMINIA. In my next conversation with him, I mean to let him know the true nature of his little intimacies with me. And between his weakness for me, which will not remain incognito for long, and your own gentle words to him, we'll be putting an end to your worries and completing my labors, from which, my lord, I will emerge victorious and defeated.

PRINCE. In what way?

FLAMINIA. Oh, it's a detail of small importance; namely that I've taken a fancy to Robin—only to put spice in my plot, of course. But let's leave this room, my lord. Go find Sylvia. Here's Robin, and he mustn't see you yet.
(Both leave. Enter Trivet and Robin, the latter looking gloomy.)

TRIVET. Well, what am I supposed to do with this writing-desk and paper?

ROBIN. Silence, underling; give me time to think.

TRIVET. As much as you wish.

ROBIN. Tell me, who provides my board in this place?

TRIVET. The Prince does.

ROBIN. Deuce take it! All this good food is beginning to worry me.

TRIVET. Why?

ROBIN. I'm afraid of being charged without my knowing it. (*Trivet laughs.*) What are you laughing at, you oaf?

TRIVET. I'm laughing at your funny notions. Go on, Sir Robin, eat and drink without fear.

ROBIN. I'm enjoying my meals in good faith, and I'm hanged if I want to be handed a bill when I go; but I'll take your word for it. Tell me, though, what's the title of the man in charge of the Prince's official business?

TRIVET. You mean his Secretary of State?

ROBIN. That's right; I intend to send him a letter. I'll ask him to advise the Prince that I'm collecting dust here and that I want matters settled once and for all, as my father is at home all by himself.

TRIVET. So?

ROBIN. So, if they want to keep me here, they must send him a cart and make him come too.

TRIVET. Say the word, and the cart will be sent.

ROBIN. And after that, me and Sylvia must be married; and the door of the house has to be opened to me, because I'm used to running about without a leash. And after that we'll set up housekeeping here along with Flaminia, who likes us and wants to stay with us. And after that, if the Prince still feels like paying the bill, I'll enjoy the food with a clear conscience.

TRIVET. That's all very well, Sir Robin, but you don't really need Flaminia, do you?

ROBIN. Yes, I do.

TRIVET (*grumbles*). Hmm.

ROBIN (*imitating him*). Hmm! The low-grade flunkeys I get! Go on, dip your pen, and scribble my message.

TRIVET. I'm listening.

ROBIN. "Sir."

TRIVET. Stop! The correct way is "My lord."

ROBIN. Put both and let him choose.

TRIVET. If you say so.

ROBIN. "This is to inform you that my name is Robin."

TRIVET. Gently! The formula is, "This is to inform your Grace."

ROBIN. Your Grace, your Grace! Is this Secretary of State a dancer?

TRIVET. No, but it's required anyway.

ROBIN. Damn this gibberish! Since when is it the custom to talk about the figure of a man you're doing business with?

TRIVET. Anything you say. "This is to inform you that my name is Robin." What next?

ROBIN. "And that I am courting a girl whose name is Sylvia, and who is a respectable girl from my village."

TRIVET. Excellent!

ROBIN. "And also that I have recently made friends with a girl who can't live without us, nor us without her; wherefore, upon receipt of same—"

TRIVET (*stopping as though grief-stricken*). Flaminia can't live without you? Ay, the pen drops out of my hand.

ROBIN. And what's this insolent swooning all about?

TRIVET. For two years, Sir Robin, for two years I've sighed in secret for Flaminia.

ROBIN (*producing a stick*). I'm heartbroken, my dear boy; but before we let her know, I'll give you a few thanks on her behalf.

TRIVET. Thanks, with a stick? I'll manage without your courtesy. Suppose I'm in love with her? What's that to you? You like her, that's all, and when you like somebody you don't feel jealous.

ROBIN. You're mistaken, my liking behaves exactly as if it were loving; and I'm going to prove it to you. (*Beats him.*)

TRIVET. The devil take your liking! (*He runs away.*)
(*Enter Flaminia*)

FLAMINIA. What's going on? What's the matter, Robin?

ROBIN. The rascal was telling me that he's loved you these two years.

FLAMINIA. That's possible.

ROBIN. And you, my dear, what do you say?

FLAMINIA. That it's too bad for him.

ROBIN. Really? Really?

FLAMINIA. Really. But would you mind if somebody were in love with me?

ROBIN. Well—you're your own mistress; but if you had a suitor, maybe you'd fall in love with him; and that would spoil our friendship, because my share would be smaller. And I don't want to lose any part of it.

FLAMINIA (*gently*). Robin, do you realize that you're quite ruthless with my heart?

ROBIN. Me? What harm am I doing?

FLAMINIA. If you don't stop speaking to me the way you do, soon I won't be able to tell what kind of feeling I have for you. The truth is, I'm afraid to examine myself on this matter. I might find more than I wish.

ROBIN. Well then, don't ever examine, Flaminia. Just let things be. And don't look for a man. I have a girl and I'm keeping her; but if I didn't have one, I wouldn't go looking. What would I do with her as long as you were about? She'd be in my way.

FLAMINIA. She'd be in your way! After that, how can I be a mere friend to you?

ROBIN. Well, what *will* you be?

FLAMINIA. Don't ask me, I don't want to know. The only thing I'm sure of is that in the whole wide world I like no one better than you. That's more than you can say. Sylvia comes first in your heart, as of course she should.

ROBIN. Hush! You're side by side in my heart.

FLAMINIA. I'll send her to you if I find her. Will that make you happy?

ROBIN. As you wish. But don't send her; both of you come.

FLAMINIA. I can't. The Prince has asked for me, and I must see what he wants. Good-bye, Robin, I'll be back soon. (*As she leaves, she smiles at Lord Lumley, who is coming in.*)

ROBIN. Here's the man I met before. Sir Slander—I don't know your other name—I've said nothing about you to the Prince, for the simple reason that I haven't seen him.

LORD LUMLEY. Thank you for your good will, Sir Robin; but I have won the Prince's favor again simply by saying that you would be speaking to him in my defense. I hope I can count on you.

ROBIN. Oh yes. I may look like a simpleton, but I'm the soul of honor.

LORD LUMLEY. To promote our reconciliation I am bringing you the greatest gift it is possible to bestow.

ROBIN. You mean Sylvia?

LORD LUMLEY. No, the gift I am referring to is in my pocket; namely, a patent of nobility for being related to Sylvia. It appears that you two *are* somewhat related.

ROBIN. Not a bit. Take it back; I don't want to cheat anybody.

LORD LUMLEY. What does it matter? Accept it anyway. The Prince would be delighted. Surely you must have the same ambition as any man with blood in his veins.

ROBIN. Well, I know there's blood in my veins; and as for ambition, I've heard of it, though I've never met the thing. Maybe I have it unbeknownst to me.

LORD LUMLEY. If you haven't, this document will give it to you.

ROBIN. What is ambition, anyway?

LORD LUMLEY (*aside*). Ye gods! (*Aloud*) Ambition is a noble pride in rising above others.

ROBIN. A noble pride! You people like to give flowery names to every piece of nonsense.

LORD LUMLEY. You don't understand. This pride signifies a desire for reputation.

ROBIN. Your signification is no improvement. It's six of one to half a dozen of the other.

LORD LUMLEY. Come, come, take it, I say. Wouldn't you like to be a lord?

ROBIN. Oh, I don't know; it depends.

LORD LUMLEY. You'll find a title useful. Your neighbors will respect and fear you.

ROBIN. But it will keep them from liking me; because when I respect and fear people, I'm not half as fond of them as I ought to be. It's too much to handle all at the same time.

LORD LUMLEY. You amaze me.

ROBIN. That's the way I am. You see, I'm a decent sort and wouldn't hurt a fly, but even if I wanted to, I haven't got the power. Well, if I did have the power, if I were a gentleman, I'm damned if I could promise always to be friendly. Now and then I'd act like the nobleman of our village, who doesn't spare the stick, because nobody dares give it back to him.

LORD LUMLEY. But supposing the stick fell on your back, wouldn't you like to be in a position to return the blows?

ROBIN. Yes, I would, and on the spot.

LORD LUMLEY. Well then, as men are occasionally wicked, place yourself in a position to do evil so that evil will not be done to you; and to accomplish this, take your patent of nobility.

ROBIN (*takes the parchment*). By thunder, you're right and I'm an ass. Well, here I go; I've got a title. The only thing left to fear is the rats that could nibble away at my nobility; but I'll see to them. I thank you, and the Prince too, who is very obliging when you come right down to it.

LORD LUMLEY. I'm pleased to see you happy. Farewell.

ROBIN. Your servant. (*Lord Lumley goes.*) Wait, wait!

LORD LUMLEY (*returning*). What can I do for you?

ROBIN. There must be obligations when you're a nobleman.

LORD LUMLEY. The only obligation is to be upright.

ROBIN. They must have given you a special exemption when you were slandering me.

LORD LUMLEY. Please forget that incident. A nobleman is always generous.

ROBIN. Upright and generous. By heaven, those are good obligations. They're even nobler than my patent of nobility. And if one doesn't carry out these obligations, is one still a nobleman?

LORD LUMLEY. By no means.

ROBIN. Oh, oh! There must be plenty of lords digging in the fields.

LORD LUMLEY. I really don't know how many.

ROBIN. And is that all? No other duty?

LORD LUMLEY. No. Of course, in your particular case, as you seem to be the Prince's favorite, you will have an additional obligation: that of deserving this favor by a more perfect submission and obedience. For the rest, as I told you, be virtuous, love honor better than life, and all will be well.

ROBIN. Gently there. These last duties don't sound as good as the others. In the first place, please explain, what is this honor one's supposed to love better than life?

LORD LUMLEY. To love honor, you'll be happy to hear, means that a man must avenge any injury done to him, or die rather than endure it.

ROBIN. Then all you told me before was a cock-and-bull story. If I'm supposed to be generous, I have to forgive people; if I'm supposed to be mean, I have to knock them down. How do I go about murdering people and letting them live at the same time?

LORD LUMLEY. You'll be kind and generous as long as you're not insulted.

ROBIN. I understand. I'm forbidden to be better than anybody else. If I return good for evil, I'll lose my honor. God almighty! Wickedness isn't so uncommon that you've got to recommend it as a special duty. I'll tell you what; let's strike a bargain: if somebody insults me, I'll insult him back—provided I'm the stronger of the two. Can I keep your goods on those terms? Give me your final word.

LORD LUMLEY. To answer insult with insult is not enough. An insult can be washed away only in the blood of your enemy, or in your own.

ROBIN. Thank you, I'll keep the stain! You talk about blood as though it were water in a pail. Here's your patent of nobility. My honor has too much common sense to be noble. Good-bye to you.

LORD LUMLEY. You don't mean it.

ROBIN. I do. Take it back.

LORD LUMLEY. No, no. Keep it, and talk it over with the Prince. We won't be so demanding in your case.

ROBIN (*takes back the patent*). He'll have to sign a contract and exempt me from getting myself killed, and what for? To make a man repent of his insolence to me.

LORD LUMLEY. Excellent. You'll stipulate whatever you like. Farewell, I am your servant.

ROBIN. And I am yours.
(*Lord Lumley leaves. Enter the Prince.*)

ROBIN. Who the devil is coming now? Ha, the man who's responsible for kidnaping Sylvia. So it's you, Sir Babble, who spread tales about people's beautiful sweethearts, till I was swindled out of mine!

PRINCE. No insults, Robin.

ROBIN. Say, are you a gentleman?

PRINCE. Certainly.

ROBIN. Gad, you're lucky; otherwise I'd tell you what I think of you. And then your honor might do its duty, and I'd have to kill you in order to avenge you against me.

PRINCE. Calm down a little, Robin. The Prince has ordered me to talk to you.

ROBIN. You're free to talk, but nobody ordered me to listen.

PRINCE. I see that, in order to curb you, I must tell you who I am. Know then that I am not an official of the palace, as both you and Sylvia believe; I am the Prince himself.

ROBIN. Is this true?

PRINCE. You must believe me.

ROBIN. My lord, forgive me for talking like an impertinent fool.

PRINCE. Gladly; you are forgiven.

ROBIN (*sadly*). Since you bear me no grudge, my lord, won't you take care that I bear none against you? I'm not worthy of being angry with a Prince, I'm too unimportant for that. If you hurt me, I'll cry my heart out, that's all; and you should pity me, being so powerful, because I know you don't want to rule over the land for your own well-being alone.

PRINCE. I've really given you cause to complain, haven't I, Robin?

ROBIN. What shall I say, my lord? I have only one girl to love me; as for you, your house is full of them, and yet you take mine away. Suppose I'm a poor man, and that all my property amounts to a penny. You come along, worth a silver mine; you fling yourself on my poverty and you tear the penny out of my hand. Isn't that a sorry thing to do?

PRINCE (*aside*). He is right, and I am touched by his grief.

ROBIN. I know you're a kindly Prince, everybody says so; I'm the only one who won't be able to say it like the others.

PRINCE. I am depriving you of Sylvia, so much is true; but ask me anything you like in exchange. Take whatever you want from me, but leave me the one person I love.

ROBIN. No. You're asking for the best of the bargain. Tell me the honest truth: if another man had taken her away, wouldn't you force him to return her to me? Well, the only person who has taken her is yourself. Show us now that justice is for everybody.

PRINCE (*aside*). How can I answer him?

ROBIN. Come, my lord, ask yourself: "Shall I harm this simple fellow because I have the power to do so? Isn't it up to me, his master, to protect him? Shall I be unjust to him now and repent of it later? Who will fill the office of Prince if I don't? No, I shall order Sylvia to be restored to him."

PRINCE. Always the same idea! Remember that I'm not obliged to listen to you. I could keep Sylvia once and for all and send you home. Instead, though I am in love with her, though you are obstinate, and though you have shown me scant respect, I take an interest in your grief and try to alleviate it by granting you many favors. I lower myself to the point of begging you to let Sylvia go of your own free will. Everybody blames you and urges you by word and example to yield to me. And still you resist. You say I am your Prince; confirm it by submitting to me.

ROBIN. The people who tell you that you are right are deceiving you, my lord, even though you trust them. Without them you wouldn't be scolding me now; you wouldn't say I'm lacking in respect simply because I'm asking for my due. You are my Prince, and I'm devoted to you; but as I am your subject, I ought to be considered too.

PRINCE. You're driving me to distraction.

ROBIN. Oh, the trouble I'm in!

PRINCE. Will I have to renounce Sylvia? How will she ever love me, if you won't help? Robin, I've wounded you, I know; but you've wounded me more cruelly still.

ROBIN. Find some consolation, my lord; go on a journey; your grief will vanish on the roads.

PRINCE. No, my boy. I hoped for something more from you, but instead you have done me all the harm you can. No matter; I had intended rich rewards for you, and, hard as you are, they are still yours.

ROBIN. Ay, life is so difficult!

PRINCE. I confess that I have been unjust to you, but see, you are avenged to your heart's content.

ROBIN. I'd better leave. You're so upset about being wrong, I'm in danger of telling you that you're right.

PRINCE. No; you've every right to be happy, Robin. You wanted justice; be satisfied; but my own peace of mind is gone forever.

ROBIN. You're so kind to me, I ought to be kind to you too.

PRINCE (sadly). Don't trouble yourself about me.

ROBIN. Look how miserable he is! Oh, what shall I do?

PRINCE (*embracing Robin*). Thank you for your sympathy. Farewell, Robin; in spite of your refusal, I think highly of you. (*He takes a few steps.*)

ROBIN. My lord!

PRINCE. What is it? Do you want to request something?

ROBIN. No. I'm only wondering whether I'll end up giving her to you.

PRINCE. You have a kind heart, Robin.

ROBIN. So have you. That's why I'm losing my grip. How weak good people are!

PRINCE. That's a beautiful thought.

ROBIN. And yet I can't promise anything; I'm too confused right now. But just in case—if I gave you Sylvia, would I become your favorite?

PRINCE. You would.

ROBIN. I ask because I've been told that you're used to flattery. And I'm used to speaking the truth. Good habits don't agree with bad ones; I'm afraid your love won't be strong enough for mine.

PRINCE. We'll quarrel if you fail to tell me all your thoughts, Robin. But now, all I ask you to remember is that I am your friend.

ROBIN. Will Flaminia be free to do as she likes?

PRINCE. Don't talk to me about Flaminia! She's responsible for all the grief you're causing me.

ROBIN. No, she isn't; she's a fine girl; you mustn't be angry with her.
(*But the Prince has left.*)

ROBIN. I think that louse of a servant of mine has been spreading tales about Flaminia. I'd better go find her. But what am I going to do now? Am I going to give up Sylvia? Is it possible? Could I?

Certainly not. I acted like a boob with the Prince because I hate to see anybody cry; but the Prince has a soft heart too, and he won't press the point. (*Enter Flaminia, looking unhappy.*) Oh, Flaminia, I was going to look for you.

FLAMINIA. Adieu, Robin.

ROBIN. What do you mean—adieu?

FLAMINIA. Trivet has betrayed us; the Prince knows about our understanding and has ordered me to leave the palace and never to see you again. But I couldn't leave without another word with you. After that I'll go I don't know where to avoid his anger.

ROBIN. I'm stunned!

FLAMINIA. And I'm in despair. To be parted from you forever, you who are dearer to me than anything in the world! Our time is short, I am compelled to leave you, but before I go I must open my heart to you.

ROBIN. What's the matter, my sweet? What's the matter with your heart?

FLAMINIA. What I felt for you wasn't friendship, Robin; I was mistaken.

ROBIN (*breathless*). It was love?

FLAMINIA. The tenderest there is. Good-bye.

ROBIN. Wait! Maybe I was mistaken about myself too.

FLAMINIA. What! Can it be? Do you love me, and shall we never see each other again? Oh don't say another word, Robin, let me fly. (*She takes a couple of steps.*)

ROBIN. Stay.

FLAMINIA. Let me go; what can we do?

ROBIN. Let's talk sensibly.

FLAMINIA. What can I say?

ROBIN. My friendship has run away as far as yours; it's out of sight; I love you—there, that settles it, and I don't know what I'm saying. Uff!

FLAMINIA. What a predicament!

ROBIN. I'm not married, fortunately.

FLAMINIA. That's true.

ROBIN. Sylvia will marry the Prince and he'll be satisfied.

FLAMINIA. Absolutely.

ROBIN. After which, since we miscalculated and we love each other by mistake, we'll reach an understanding and somehow make the best of it.

FLAMINIA (*softly*). I see; you mean you and I will get married.

ROBIN. Well—yes. Is it my fault? Why didn't you warn me that you were going to turn my head?

FLAMINIA. And you—did you send out a warning that you would captivate me?

ROBIN. How the deuce could I guess it?

FLAMINIA. You were attractive enough to suspect it might happen.

ROBIN. Let's not blame each other. If it's a question of being attractive, you were guiltier than me.

FLAMINIA. Well then, marry me, I consent. But we'd better not waste any time; I'm afraid I'll be ordered away any moment.

ROBIN (*sighing*). I'd better have a talk with the Prince. Don't tell Sylvia I love you. She'll think I'm guilty of something, when it's obvious that I'm innocent. I'll pretend I'm giving her up for her own sake, so she can make her way in the world.

FLAMINIA. I was about to give you the same idea.

ROBIN. Wait—let me kiss your hand . . . Who would have thought this would give me so much pleasure? I don't know whether I'm coming or going. (*He leaves.*)

FLAMINIA (*aside*). The Prince was right: these little persons make love in the most irresistible way. Here's the other one now. (*Enter Sylvia.*) What are you dreaming about, fair Sylvia?

SYLVIA. About something I don't understand—myself.

FLAMINIA. What's so incomprehensible about yourself?

SYLVIA. You remember how I wanted to be avenged on these women? Well, that's all over.

FLAMINIA. You're not vindictive, you see.

SYLVIA. And I loved Robin, didn't I?

FLAMINIA. So it seemed to me.

SYLVIA. Well, I think I don't any more.

FLAMINIA. That's not such a calamity.

SYLVIA. And if it were a calamity, what could I do about it? When love came along, I loved him; now that it's going away, I don't. It came without my bidding, and it leaves on its own; I don't think I'm to blame.

FLAMINIA (*aside*). I'll needle her a bit. (*Aloud*) I agree with you more or less.

SYLVIA. What do you call "more or less"? I order you to agree with me without afterthought. Really! The women they send after me, telling me yes one time and no another!

FLAMINIA. Why are you losing your temper?

SYLVIA. For a very good reason. I come to you for advice like a simple soul, and you start quibbling with your more-or-lesses.

FLAMINIA. I was only joking, Sylvia. I truly believe you're not to blame in the least. But who is it you're in love with? Is it that gentleman?

SYLVIA. Could it be anyone else? Mind you, I haven't yet agreed to love him. But it'll have to come to that in the end; because to be saying no forever to a man who keeps asking me to say yes, to see him pining away, and groaning all the time, and always to be comforting him for the sorrows I bring on him—oh dear, it's a wearisome business. Better to stop his sorrows altogether.

FLAMINIA. Wonderful! He'll die of joy when he hears the news.

SYLVIA. Otherwise he'd die of grief, and that's worse.

FLAMINIA. Oh, beyond comparison.

SYLVIA. I'm waiting for him now. We just spent two hours together, and he's going to come back with the Prince himself. But now and then I worry about Robin—will I be making him very miserable? What's your opinion? But don't go putting a lot of scruples into my head.

FLAMINIA. Don't worry, it won't be hard to console him.

SYLVIA. Thank you! To listen to you, it doesn't take much to forget me. Don't tell me he's found someone else here!

FLAMINIA. Nonsense. I don't know what I was saying. Forget you? You'll be lucky if he doesn't go mad with despair.

SYLVIA. Now why did you say that to me? You and your mad with despair! You've made me hesitate again.

FLAMINIA. Suppose he no longer loves you. What would you say to that?

SYLVIA. If he no longer loves me . . . keep the news to yourself.

FLAMINIA. But you're annoyed because he *does* love you! What do you really want?

SYLVIA. You can laugh, but I'd like to see you in my place.

FLAMINIA. Here's your admirer; take my advice—settle with him and don't worry about the rest. (*She leaves.*)
(*Enter the Prince.*)

PRINCE. Sylvia—won't you look at me? Your face becomes overcast every time I come near you. It always distresses me to think I might be imposing on you.

SYLVIA. Imposing! And I who was talking about you just now!

PRINCE. About me? What were you saying, beautiful Sylvia?

SYLVIA. Oh, I was saying quite a few things; for instance, that you don't yet know what I really think.

PRINCE. I know you've decided to refuse me your heart; isn't that knowing what you think?

SYLVIA. Don't boast; you're not as wise as all that. Tell me, though: you're a man of principle, and I'm sure you'll speak the truth. You know how I stand with Robin. Now suppose I felt like being in love with you. If I gave way to my feelings, would I be acting right? or wrong? There now, give me your honest advice.

PRINCE. Since a person is not in control of his own emotions, it follows that if you feel like being in love with me, you have the right to satisfy yourself. That is my opinion.

SYLVIA. Are you speaking as a friend?

PRINCE. Yes, Sylvia, and in all sincerity.

SYLVIA. Well, I happen to agree with you. I think we're both right; and so I'll love you if I please and I won't let him reproach me.

PRINCE. But as it doesn't please you, I haven't gained a thing.

SYLVIA. Don't try to guess—you're a bad mind-reader. But where is this Prince? If I have to see him, let him come at once; but he needn't bother as far as I'm concerned.

PRINCE. He'll come only too soon. Perhaps when you see him, you'll turn away from me.

SYLVIA. Courage! Here you are trembling again. You've sworn never to have a carefree moment.

PRINCE. I admit I'm afraid.

SYLVIA. What a man! I'll make you happy. Here: I won't ever love the Prince, and I solemnly swear—

PRINCE. Stop, Sylvia, I beg you, don't complete your oath.

SYLVIA. Why shouldn't I swear? Really!

PRINCE. Shall I let you swear against myself?

SYLVIA. Against yourself? Are you the Prince?

PRINCE. Yes, Sylvia, I am. I concealed my rank up to this moment, so that I should owe your love only to my own. But now that you know me, you are free to accept my heart and my hand, or to refuse them both. Speak, Sylvia.

SYLVIA. Oh, my Prince, what an oath I was about to take! You sought the pleasure of being loved for yourself, and you have found it. My happiness is that you know I am speaking the truth.

PRINCE. These words seal our marriage.
(*Enter Robin and Flaminia.*)

ROBIN. I overheard you, Sylvia.

SYLVIA. Well then, I won't have to tell you what happened. Console yourself as best you can, Robin. The Prince will talk to you. I am too troubled. Please come to an understanding, because I'm beyond thinking—and that's the truth. What would you tell me? That I've left you. What would I answer? That I know it. Let's pretend that you've said it and that I've answered, and then you can leave and the story ends.

PRINCE. Flaminia, I place Robin in your hands. I love him and intend to make him a man of means. Robin, take Flaminia, marry her, and enjoy the good will of your Prince forever. Now, fair Sylvia, I have given commands for a festival in your honor. With your permission, I will take that happy opportunity to proclaim you the future sovereign of our people.

ROBIN (*to Flaminia*). As for us, our friendship fooled us, but I don't care; we're about to play it a trick of our own.

THE END

Money Makes the World Go Round
(Le Triomphe de Plutus)

Presented for the first time at
the Théâtre Italien on April 22, 1728

CHARACTERS

APOLLO, *under the name of Dulcimer*
PLUTUS, *under the name of Richard*
MR. GRANGEWELL, *Lydia's uncle*
LYDIA, *wooed by Apollo and Plutus*
PUFF, *Dulcimer's servant*
SPINETTA, *Lydia's maid*
SINGERS AND DANCERS

The action takes place in front of Mr. Grangewell's house.

PLUTUS (*alone*). There goes Apollo. He's come down to court a new flame of his. The other day I happened to say I wanted to make a conquest too. Mr. Curlyhead laughed in my face, informed me that no girl could love me, and treated me like an imbecile. So now I've landed here to swindle him out of his girl. Feathers are going to fly, though he doesn't know it yet. Just think of that shiftless dog of a god trying to tangle with Plutus, lord of riches! Shush—here he comes. Let's look innocent.
(*Enter Apollo.*)

APOLLO. Look who's here! Plutus disguised as a banker. Let me shake your hand.

PLUTUS. How d'you do, Master Apollo.

APOLLO. May I ask what brings you below?

PLUTUS. I've come to make love to a girl.

APOLLO. Please speak more decently. You mean you wish to make your addresses to her.

PLUTUS. Make love, make addresses—what's the difference?

APOLLO. I suppose you were stung by our little altercation the other day. You want to show that you can be a success too. Excellent idea. But tell me, is the girl attractive?

PLUTUS. I could eat her up. I saw her not long ago when I was flying over the land, and I decided to come down and give her a hug.

APOLLO. Listen to me, friend Plutus; if the lady happens to be blessed with refined tastes, I shall advise you not to exhibit these blunt expressions of yours: *I could eat her up; give her a hug.* Your vulgar style is bound to repel her.

PLUTUS. All right—keep your precious style to yourself. I use plain talk, thank you; and what's more I've got ducats here whose style is as good as literature. Do I make myself clear?

APOLLO. I hadn't thought of your ducats. I admit they are great orators.

PLUTUS. Who'll spare me a cartful of rhetorical flowers.

APOLLO. And yet I know women whom gold cannot persuade. Indeed, I have come here to call on a pretty person who would, I suspect, think little of me, had I only your means at my command. Perhaps your lady will feel as she does.

PLUTUS. Let her feel as she likes, I couldn't care less. Here's money on my body, and that's all I need. But what about your pretty person? Is she a widow? A virgin?

APOLLO. A virgin.

PLUTUS. So is mine.

APOLLO. Mine is the ward of an uncle who wishes to marry her off. As she is quite well-to-do, he is looking for a suitable match for her.

PLUTUS. Well! That's exactly how it stands with my little brunette. She lives with an uncle too. His name is Grangewell.

APOLLO. The same man! Don't tell me we're rivals!

PLUTUS. I'm really sorry for you. (*Apollo laughs*) Go on, laugh at me, you madrigal-monger, you aromatic dandy! Mock me with your wit and your golden curls, go on!

APOLLO. Frankly, my friend, you're not equipped to contend with me over a woman's heart.

PLUTUS. No, because I'm equipped to carry it straight off.

APOLLO. That remains to be seen. Perhaps I should tell you a little detail—namely that I have met your sweetheart already, I have spoken with her, and, I say it in all modesty, she has shown a certain disposition in my favor.

PLUTUS. What's disposition to me? I'm carrying a box full of jewels that stick their tongues out at your dispositions. Just wait and see.

APOLLO. I am not afraid of you, my dear rival. But here we are in front of Mr. Grangewell's house. My charmer's maid is coming out, and disguised as I am, I'm going to have a few words with her. Stay if you wish, and speak with her too. You see how good-natured I can be when I see no danger.

PLUTUS. Talk to her, my friend; I'll work my way, you work your own.
(*Enter Spinetta.*)

APOLLO. Dear Spinetta, how do you do? Is your mistress in good health?

SPINETTA. I'm pleased to see you back with us, Mr. Dulcimer. While you were gone I carried out a hundred little maneuvers in your behalf.

APOLLO. And you will not find me ungrateful for them.

SPINETTA. Couldn't you be not ungrateful right now?

PLUTUS. Come on, give her a madrigal or two.

APOLLO. Be patient for a while, Spinetta; you won't regret it. I was born munificent.

SPINETTA. So you've been telling me. Are you taking this gentleman with you to see Miss Lydia?

APOLLO. Yes. He is a friend of mine, and I should like him to meet Lydia's uncle, Mr. Grangewell.

PLUTUS. I've been told he's a fair, honest man, and I'm the kind that loves honest people.

SPINETTA. Very good, sir. (*To Apollo*) Your friend seems a little thick.

APOLLO. Seems and is. Enough for now, Spinetta. My impatience urges me on, I must see Lydia. Come, sir, follow me in.

PLUTUS. I'll tell you what. Go in and announce me. I'd like to exchange a word or two with this lovely child. You'll find me here.

APOLLO. As you wish. (*He leaves.*)

SPINETTA. Might I ask you, sir, what it is you wish of me?

PLUTUS. I wish you a prosperous life.

SPINETTA. Everybody wishes me a prosperous life, but nobody gives it to me.

PLUTUS. I'm different. My name isn't Dulcimer, you know; it's Richard, and here's proof that the name fits me. (*He gives her a purse.*)

SPINETTA. Oh! Such clear proof! The proof is so powerful I'm almost stunned.

PLUTUS. Take it, take it. And if one proof isn't enough, I'll give you two or even three more.

SPINETTA. Prove on. If a doubt is all that's required, I'll doubt till nightfall.

PLUTUS. Here's something for the doubt that just attacked you. (*He gives her a ring.*)

SPINETTA. Be sure to provide for the doubt I feel coming on.

PLUTUS. Just let me know, and don't worry. The only condition I set is that you must be my friend.

SPINETTA (*aside*). Who is this man? (*Aloud*) Your friend, sir—what do you understand by your friend? A little lovemaking perhaps? I wouldn't enjoy that at all, I'm a virtuous girl.

PLUTUS. Keep your virtue; that's not what I'm after.

SPINETTA. You must be aiming high. Well, what *are* you after?

PLUTUS. I've fallen in love with your mistress. I'm a rich trader —extremely rich, in fact—silver and gold don't cost me anything, and I don't like to love all by myself.

SPINETTA. And why should you? Your love deserves the best company. But what you're asking isn't so easy. The point is, my mistress is a virtuous girl too.

PLUTUS. Does virtue prevent a body from being in love?

SPINETTA. No, not if the love in question has honorable intentions. But yours doesn't look all that respectable to me. Now if your design was to marry her, rich as you are, and the salt of the earth besides—I can see that for myself—your chances would be excellent, provided I gave the business my attention, and the proofs kept up their good work when they were needed.

PLUTUS. You can count on the proofs.

SPINETTA (aside). What a man! (Aloud) Do you mean you'd marry my mistress?

PLUTUS. Absolutely. I'll do anything anybody wants of me.

SPINETTA. That settles it, I'm on your side. But your friend is in love with Miss Lydia too, and I've reason to believe that she is fond of him. He too speaks of marriage. He is rather handsome. He is very bright. You'll have all that to fight against.

PLUTUS. Pooh! I'm rich, and that's more than anything he can show. Let me tell you that all he owns is his good looks.

SPINETTA. I'm inclined to believe you, because all *he* has proved to me is his talent for promises. However, Miss Lydia likes him; but on the other hand Mr. Grangewell knows where his interest lies, and your money will dazzle him. Meantime, Mr. Dulcimer tells us he's a gentleman in easy circumstances, and as such he's made his way as best he could into my mistress' heart. She listens to him because she dabbles in culture, and he's an intellectual.

PLUTUS. Does she like to spend money?

SPINETTA. And how.

PLUTUS. We've got her, Spinetta, set your mind at ease. You praise me to her all you can, and I'll make her presents; everything she longs for is hers. As for myself, why, I don't think I'm all that repulsive. I've a kind of way with things, and there's worse faces than mine. Tell her I'm a plain-spoken straightforward man. And tell her about the beauty of my silver and gold. Gold and silver don't wrinkle. A golden coin eighty years old is as beautiful as one that was minted today. It's no mean achievement to be young on the cash register side.

SPINETTA. Right! Oh sweet tinkling youth! It's all agreed, I'll pave your way. True, when I first saw you I thought there was something a bit common about your face, and the manners, I thought, went with the face. But now that I know you better, you've changed, you're almost tolerable, and tomorrow you'll be charming. Of course, it all depends on you.

PLUTUS. Don't worry, I'll be charming all right. I'll make your fortune, and a fortune that eats three meals a day to boot. Wait and see.

SPINETTA. I swear, if this goes on, you'll be an Adonis.

PLUTUS. Here's somebody coming toward us. Who is it?

SPINETTA. It's Puff, Mr. Dulcimer's valet.
(*Enter Puff.*)

PUFF. Hello, Spinetta, how are you? I'm glad to see you again. Did my master arrive before me?

SPINETTA. Yes. He's in the house.

PLUTUS. How are you, my boy?

PUFF. God bless you, sir. Here's a nice man who asks me how are you without even knowing me.

SPINETTA. He is the nicest man in the world, believe me.

PLUTUS. Are you Dulcimer's servant, my boy?

PUFF. Yes, worse luck. I serve him out of friendship, to tell you the truth, and not for the millions that's in it.

PLUTUS. Haven't you grown fat waiting on him?

PUFF. Fat? I'm as skinny as when I began.

PLUTUS. Good wages?

PUFF. I couldn't tell you, I haven't seen them yet. And yet I keep asking him for a sample. I'll tell you frankly, I don't believe he's got either a sample or the goods itself.

SPINETTA. I agree.

PLUTUS. Do you need money, by any chance?

PUFF. Need money? Since I was born, I've never needed anything else.

PLUTUS. I'm sorry for you. Come on, I like your face. Go drink to my health.

PUFF. Am I awake? Oh, sir, I'm dumbfounded. Ten crowns to drink your health? Spinetta, is the sun up or am I dreaming?

SPINETTA. This kind gentleman has already made me dream the same way as you.

PUFF. My dream is going to take me to the nearest bar.

PLUTUS. I want you to be my friend too.

PUFF. I couldn't be your enemy if I tried.

PLUTUS. Listen my boy, I love the same girl as your master.

PUFF. Miss Lydia?

PLUTUS. That's right. Spinetta has promised me her help, and I want yours too.

PUFF. Don't worry.

PLUTUS. If Dulcimer doesn't pay your wages, I will.

PUFF. Hm. You might settle my first three months in advance, which he's been promising to do.

SPINETTA. You don't beat about the bush, do you?

PUFF. That wouldn't be fair to him. He's so kind.

PLUTUS. Never mind, I won't haggle over pennies with you. Here, I'm paying you on my scale.

PUFF. And I don't even look, I'm that sure of you. My dear sir, you are an honest gentleman, and your manners are perfect.

SPINETTA. Gently. Here comes Miss Lydia's uncle. Speak to him, Mr. Richard.
(*Enter Grangewell.*)

GRANGEWELL. Oh, there you are, Puff my boy. Has your master arrived?

PUFF. I hear that he has, Mr. Grangewell, but I only came this minute. I stopped in a village to refresh myself. As it's hot today, you'll allow me to do the same in your kitchen.

GRANGEWELL. Help yourself. (*Exit Puff.*)

PLUTUS. Sir, I've been told by Spinetta that your name is Mr. Grangewell.

GRANGEWELL. So it is. What can I do for you?

PLUTUS. If you could find your advantage in my friendship, yours would suit me very nicely.

GRANGEWELL. Sir, you flatter me. (*Aside*) Here's a funny opening.

PLUTUS. I'm a blunt sort of fellow, as you can see, but frankness is better than etiquette, I always say.

GRANGEWELL. Sir, I owe my friendship to all honest persons, and as soon as I have had the pleasure of making your acquaintance—

SPINETTA. Never mind, I've known thousands of fine people who get muddled in formalities, and I bet this gentleman is one of them. Here's how it is: he's a friend of Mr. Dulcimer— they've just arrived together. And now I'll leave you both. Mr. Dulcimer is in the house. (*She leaves.*)

PLUTUS. I was asking the dear child for news of you while waiting.

GRANGEWELL. Sir, as a friend of Mr. Dulcimer, whom I esteem, you are welcome here. Forgive me for not returning sooner, but I was detained on business.

PLUTUS. Business, eh? Come, let me know what it is. Business is my specialty.

GRANGEWELL. Well, sir, it's all about a piece of land at some distance from here which doesn't suit me and which I'm trying to sell. You see, I'm marrying off my niece, and plan to give her the revenue from this sale. The land is worth twenty thousand crowns, but the person I am negotiating with won't offer more than fifteen. No agreement in sight, I'm afraid.

PLUTUS. Shake here, Mr. Grangewell.

GRANGEWELL. I beg your pardon?

PLUTUS. Shake here.

GRANGEWELL. What do you mean?

PLUTUS. The estate is mine, and the money is yours. I'll pay you on the spot.

GRANGEWELL. But—sir—how can I do this? You haven't seen it, you may not like its location—

PLUTUS. Forget it. I like any location. Isn't it always trees and meadows all over the place?

GRANGEWELL. Let me show you the map at least.

PLUTUS. I can't read maps. Enough. It's an estate. I haven't seen it, but I see you; you've got an honest face, and so your land is bound to suit me.

GRANGEWELL. Well, if you insist—

PLUTUS. Do you recognize the signature on this note?

GRANGEWELL. Oh, excellent. I owe you a thousand thanks.

PLUTUS. If tomorrow you change your mind, I'll resell you the land, and on credit too so it'll be no burden to you.

GRANGEWELL. I don't know how to express my gratitude.

PLUTUS. Oh yes, you do. You could express it if you wanted to.

GRANGEWELL. Tell me how.

PLUTUS. You have an attractive niece, Mr. Grangewell.

GRANGEWELL. Yes?

PLUTUS. Let's swap. Take back your land gratis, and I'll take your niece at the same price.

GRANGEWELL. You've seen my niece, sir?

PLUTUS. Yes, I have. A few months ago, traveling this way, I saw half a face that really appealed to me. When I inquired whose it was, they told me it belonged to Miss Lydia, niece of a man of means, Mr. Grangewell. Damn, says I to myself, I'm bound to like the whole face if I can make it mine. My friend Dulcimer told me a few days later he was coming here, and I followed, meaning to change places with him. He's in love with your niece too, but if you and me come to terms I don't care. True, he's my friend, but love and friendship don't mix. Besides, I'm too plain a man to be scrupulous.

GRANGEWELL. It is true, however, that Mr. Dulcimer seems to be wooing my niece.

PLUTUS. Poor girl. She's won quite a prize.

GRANGEWELL. Mr. Dulcimer speaks of himself as a man of quality, rather well off and determined to settle here. And I must say he seems well-bred.

PLUTUS. Well-bred, him? He's penniless.

GRANGEWELL. If he is, it's a great defect in him. Thank you for your warning. But I'd like to ask you, sir—what is your profession?

PLUTUS. Me? I've got millions, passed along from father to son. That's my main business. In addition, I trade here and there and make a few killings to distract myself. The profits will supply pin money for my wife. I'll prove it all to you in black and white. That's what I call being a good prospect in body and soul. Not that I'm so bad in either anyway. If you were a marriageable girl, would you snub me on account of my figure? Everybody can see I eat properly. My bulk speaks for the qualities of my cook. Take it from me, if I marry Miss Lydia, Ill put flesh on you. I'll triple that chin, by God, and as for that belly, just leave it to me!

GRANGEWELL. I like your disposition.

PLUTUS. It's as good as my bank account.

GRANGEWELL. I'll speak to my niece, I promise you. I assure you she'll conform to my wishes.

PLUTUS. A man like me is a treasure, you know.

GRANGEWELL. She's coming. Here's what I suggest. Exchange a couple of words with her, then leave me alone with her for a few minutes. Meantime you can go into the house for refreshments. (*Enter Lydia and Spinetta.*)

GRANGEWELL. Niece, where is Mr. Dulcimer?

LYDIA. He has locked himself in to compose a musical entertainment for me.

PLUTUS. Oh well, as far as music is concerned, madam, he'll instruct you so well in it that you'll be able to teach it yourself.

LYDIA. That is not what I wish to do with it. Uncle, isn't this the gentleman Dulcimer brought with him? He fits the description I've just been hearing.

GRANGEWELL. Yes, my dear niece, and a well-bred gentleman he is. Brief as our acquaintance has been, he has already obtained my particular esteem.

PLUTUS. Nonsense! I'm only a good plain fellow. But I've sharp eyes, I know beauty when I see it, and I tell you flatly that your niece is a winner. That's all the compliments in my stock, ma'am, I don't know where to look for phrases. You're as beautiful as a star, and that's the unvarnished truth.

LYDIA. The simile is strong, though common.

PLUTUS. I gave it to you as it came.

GRANGEWELL. Enough of this. My dear Lydia, do me the favor of looking on Mr. Richard as my friend, and even as the best friend I've found so far.

LYDIA. I will obey you, my dear uncle.

SPINETTA. Come, come; as soon as Miss Lydia gets to know the real Mr. Richard, you won't have to recommend him any more.

PLUTUS. It's a fact; all those who know me love me. Miss Lydia didn't relish my simile. Next time I'll find a better one. What's to prevent me, for instance, from comparing you to Venus? Is that better? Take your pick. And yet, I wouldn't be easy in my mind if you resembled her in every way. The dear creature has a husband I don't care to take after.

GRANGEWELL. Sir, my niece—

PLUTUS. Only a joke. Now I think of it, Dulcimer is busy composing verses in your praise, and I'd better dream up something for you too. Allow me to go muse a little. Uncle Grangewell, I leave the rest to you; no loafing on the job. (*Exit Plutus.*)

LYDIA. Will you tell me, sir, why you've grown so fond of that man, and all in fifteen minutes? In my opinion he is so ridiculous as to be downright original.

SPINETTA. Original is right. I don't believe there's a copy of him to be had anywhere.

GRANGEWELL. Niece, you may think the man ridiculous, but let me tell you again that I can't praise him too highly.

SPINETTA. Here's the whole story. He saw you one time when he was traveling this way; he fell in love with you; and now he's come back to see you again. Shall I tell you how he won me over to his interests? Take a look. How do you like my new ring?

LYDIA. Fancy that! Very pretty indeed. Where does it come from?

GRANGEWELL. I'll bet he gave it to you.

SPINETTA. With the sweetest smile in the world.

LYDIA. On this evidence I confess one can't dispute his generosity.

GRANGEWELL. Do you realize, my dear niece, that Mr. Richard is a businessman whose income simply astonishes me? And guess what he means to do with this income.

LYDIA. Build?

GRANGEWELL. No; give you pin money.

LYDIA. I suppose you're making up fairy tales for me.

GRANGEWELL. The girl doesn't know! I've sold the land which was supposed to give you your dowry.

LYDIA. Have you changed your mind, dear uncle?

GRANGEWELL. She won't understand! The land was bought by Mr. Richard, sight unseen, on the strength of my word, without a second thought, and at my price. Here, says he, I want to pay you on the spot. Look at this note.

LYDIA. What a pity a man with such a brilliant fortune is a rustic.

GRANGEWELL. A rustic?

SPINETTA. Mr. Richard? A rustic?

LYDIA. You'll agree at least that he's far from being a wit, and that he is very stout.

SPINETTA. But it's a stoutness that comes of being plump.

GRANGEWELL. Come, come, Dulcimer is a nobody in comparison. Not to mention that there's a great deal of claptrap in him.

LYDIA. But dearest uncle, you are giving him a rather coarse rival. I believe I can boast of a certain delicacy, and coarseness appals me.

SPINETTA. Coarseness! Heaven and earth, I tell you he has as sharp a mind as anybody; it so happens he wants to use it only when he feels like it.
(*Enter Puff.*)

GRANGEWELL. What's the news, Puff my boy?

PUFF. By your leave, sir, I've come on a little errand for Miss Lydia.

LYDIA. Well, what is it?

PUFF. I don't dare open my mouth because of Mr. Grangewell here; and yet I'm no coward either, and if you gave me the sign, I'd soon have it all said.

GRANGEWELL. Speak up. What's all the mystery about?

PUFF. Well, I've got this gold in my pocket to which I promised I'd recommend Mr. Richard to you, ma'am.

SPINETTA. What do you say to that! Even with Puff the man is open-handed.

PUFF. He asked me for the privilege of my influence with you, Miss Lydia, and I must say he paid me pretty well for what it's worth.

GRANGEWELL. Amazing.

PUFF. And he gave me the wages that Mr. Dulcimer owes me. I think that was very decent of him.

SPINETTA. He's telling you the truth. I was there.

PUFF. I'm going to marry him too, that's all.

GRANGEWELL. What do you mean, you're going to marry him too?

PUFF. I'm all his. He's already given me the wedding present.

GRANGEWELL. Niece, that man must not escape.

PUFF. He loves you like a soul in pain. And is he ever droll to listen to; nothing but jokes. And then he always says, "Go on, take," and never "Come on, give." He has a face like a holiday. Here he comes! Just look at him. But I'm off on another mission for him. (*Exit Puff.*)

PLUTUS. Well, are you smiling at the world, my queen? How do you do it? You're even more beautiful than you were when I left you. Meantime, Dulcimer is upstairs versifying. Each man to his own poetry. Here's mine. (*He offers her a bracelet.*)

SPINETTA. It's a poem that could use a rhyme.

PLUTUS. We'll rhyme, don't worry. I've got a rhyme here in my pocket.

LYDIA. Now, Mr. Richard, one can accept a poem, a song—but a bracelet as magnificent as this one is something else again.

PLUTUS. Poems are read and bracelets are worn—that's the only difference. Give me your arm, my goddess.

LYDIA. Really, sir, I can hardly—

GRANGEWELL. I allow you to accept, Lydia.

PLUTUS. You're the best uncle I've ever met. Here, I've given my heart away, and when the heart's gone, it doesn't cost anything to send the rest packing after it. I love you. Nobody can love like me, and I'm going to love you more and more all the time. It feels wonderful! You should take a nibble at it too, my beauty. I'm the life of the party already, but I'll learn to write songs and sketches and vaudevilles. I've got a solid mind, you know, only I hate to bother it. The only part of me I let go is my heart. It's gone to you now. Take it, my charmer, but in the meantime put on this little bracelet.

SPINETTA. Can a man speak with a better will?

LYDIA. Really, sir, you are very persistent—

PLUTUS. There, tell me what you think of me.

LYDIA. Why—I think—I think well of you.

PLUTUS. Ho ho, I rather thought so. And maybe you love me a little too? Do you like my character? You can twist me around your little finger. You'll be so happy and you'll have such good times, you won't know where to begin. Come now, is it settled? I'm in a hurry—your eyes are rushing me. Uncle Grangewell, let's call it settled. I'm on my knees. Spinetta, to the rescue!

GRANGEWELL. Give in, dear niece. You couldn't find a better man.

SPINETTA. Dear Miss Lydia, dear, dear Miss Lydia, have a heart for this lovely man.

PLUTUS. We implore you, me and the hundred thousand crowns I have on me as a sample from my strongbox. Take them, here, examine them yourself.

SPINETTA. This is the purest incense.

LYDIA. You overwhelm me. (*Aside*) Let me die on the spot if I know how to refuse him. There's something about him—I don't know what—that sweeps me off my feet. (*Aloud*) Different men have different qualities, sir, and you have yours. But what would become of Dulcimer?

PLUTUS. He'll leave, and I'll pay for his trip.

GRANGEWELL. Here he comes with his serenade.

SPINETTA. Those are *his* millions, poor fellow.

GRANGEWELL. The devil take his music. That's all we need! (*Enter Apollo with singers and dancers.*)

APOLLO. Tra la la, tra la la. A prelude, madam. The singers and dancers are here to perform my little creation. Mr. Grangewell, I promise you will enjoy it. I think the piece is a success, though not as amusing as Mr. Richard's conversation, of course; but let that pass.

SPINETTA. Mr. Richard's conversation is wonderful.

GRANGEWELL. And soundly backed from beginning to end.

PLUTUS. Thank you, Uncle Grangewell, and I'll keep backing it as before. What do you say, my queen? Do you agree with them?

LYDIA. Certainly.

APOLLO (aside to Lydia). I'm sure he has strained your patience. I've come just in time.

LYDIA. Is the music ready?

APOLLO. Gentlemen, strike up.

Song

God of lovers, fear no more
To see the bold escape thy yoke.
A maid appears all shall adore,
And, wooing her, thy power invoke.

Thy triumph, blissful god, to hers
That reigns among us shall be due;
And will thy glory be the worse
For rising from herself to you?

APOLLO. I'm afraid you were not too happy with this, Mr. Grangewell.

GRANGEWELL. Oh, don't pay any attention to me. I'm deaf to music.

SPINETTA. I was falling asleep.

APOLLO. And you, madam, were you disappointed too?

LYDIA. The music was elegant enough, but the performance seemed a little chilly to me.

PLUTUS. That's because the singers are hoarse. A little greasing of throats is what's needed.

APOLLO. Gently! You needn't pay my performers.

A SINGER. What? The gentleman makes us a present—why should you care? It won't prevent you from paying us. In fact, the sooner the better.

PLUTUS. Well said. Satisfy them if you can. As for me, I'm going to offer you the kind of music you can measure by the yard. I'm waiting for the dancers.
(*Enter Puff.*)

PUFF. Sir—

APOLLO. What is it? Anything new?

PUFF. Yes, sir, but it has nothing to do with you. I've come to tell Mr. Richard that his musicians will be here in a minute.

APOLLO. I'd like to know why you're sticking your nose into his business.

PLUTUS. You're going to hear a funny sort of music, Mr. Grangewell.

GRANGEWELL. I'm sure it will be interesting.

PLUTUS. Rich sounds, a marvelous harmony that makes the whole world dance, music to which nobody is deaf.

GRANGEWELL. Now I'm really curious.

SPINETTA. And I can't wait to hear it.

THE SINGER. Sir, I hope you'll let us do a little show later too in your honor.

PLUTUS. Why not? You won't spoil anything, and you can join my dancers—here they are, in fact.
(*Enter four peddlers with their packs. They exhibit silks and trinkets.*)

GRANGEWELL. I admit I've never heard a concert of this kind before.

PLUTUS. What's so convenient about it is that it can be performed without rehearsal.

PUFF. Here's a tune for me, and good-bye all.

PLUTUS. Take all this music into the house. Well, Miss Lydia, what do you think?

APOLLO. Are these tunes to your taste too, madam?

GRANGEWELL. She'd be pretty particular if they weren't.

APOLLO. You don't answer. Oh, I see only too clearly what this silence portends. Ungrateful girl, who would have thought that such was your character?

PLUTUS. Oho, you're angry now.

LYDIA. Ungrateful? Really, you're a fine one to insult me. What do you call ungrateful?

APOLLO. False, false girl! I see how you reward all my attentions. You never deserved my love.

PLUTUS. Let's you and me dance off to his singing, my queen.

GRANGEWELL. Yes, Lydia, follow me. This is too much entertainment.

PLUTUS. Come on, you two, part good friends and never see each other again. Remember, always obey the rules of propriety. Take it from me, Dulcimer, and vent your anger in a sonnet. Or write an opera. It might bring in something.
(*All leave except Apollo and Grangewell.*)

APOLLO (*detaining Grangewell*). One moment, Mr. Grangewell! Are you a party to this affront? Do you approve of your niece's action?

GRANGEWELL. Well now—as you know—she's quite a reasonable girl.

APOLLO. And yet, you had given me grounds for hope.

GRANGEWELL. Hope? When was that? I don't remember a thing.

APOLLO. Do I hear what I hear? And is this your last word?

GRANGEWELL. Listen to me—you're in a bad mood today. Since you're not leaving tonight, we'll have a chance to see each other again. Good-bye for now.
(*Enter Spinetta.*)

SPINETTA. We're all waiting for you, sir.

GRANGEWELL. I'm coming. (*To Apollo*) Your humble servant. (*He leaves.*)

APOLLO. Spinetta, one word with you, if I may.

SPINETTA. I'm in a hurry.

APOLLO. Is this what we've come to? Are you abandoning me too? You who gave me so many proofs of your kindness!

SPINETTA. I hope they make you rich. Oh, I think they're calling me. Excuse me.

APOLLO. Stop! You're going to tell me the reason for everything I see here.

SPINETTA. What do you see that's so exceptional?

APOLLO. I see that the object of my passion flies from me. I see that the whole world forsakes me.

SPINETTA. I don't know of any remedy for that.

APOLLO. So Mr. Richard has won the battle.

SPINETTA. What battle? I don't understand you.

APOLLO. You don't understand me? You don't know that your mistress and I have formed an attachment?

SPINETTA. Oh well, I'm wasting my time here. Dinner is ready. Aren't you joining us? What a pity. Farewell, Mr. Dulcimer, remember me kindly.
(*Enter Puff.*)

PUFF. Dinner, Spinetta. (*She leaves.*)

APOLLO. Puff, my poor Puff, come here. I'm heart-broken.

PUFF. And I'm hungry.

APOLLO. What's your opinion of all these events?

PUFF. What events? I haven't noticed any events.

APOLLO. Are you trying to play dumb with me?

PUFF. Who are you angry at? Hurry up, because my master is waiting.

APOLLO. Your master? I am your master, and nobody else.

PUFF. *Were* my master.

APOLLO. You dog, with whom did you come here?

PUFF. With you. We kept each other company on the way.

APOLLO. Even my servant disowns me!

PUFF. Wait! I've got a dim recollection, it was long ago, yes, I was in the service of a Mr. Dill—Dull—Dill—Dulcimer—that's it, Dulcimer.

APOLLO. Villain!

PUFF. No, he wasn't a villain. He was a very honest man who didn't pay his servants. Well, that's all been changed. I traded him for a certain Mr. Richard, who dresses me well and pays me even better. Quite an improvement over Mr. Dulcimer. Good-bye. If you run across him, by the way, give him my regards. Poor man!
(*He leaves.*)

APOLLO. The insolence!
(*Enter a musician and Spinetta.*)

MUSICIAN. Excuse me, is Mr. Richard in the house?

APOLLO. Oh, it's you; I'm glad you came. I had ordered a little entertainment for tonight, but it's all off and you're discharged.

MUSICIAN. That's all right, we weren't even thinking about you, we're busy with another engagement. Mr. Richard wants us to perform, and we're looking for him.

APOLLO. That was the final blow. I am convinced at last that gold is the only divinity men worship.
(*Knocking within.*)

SPINETTA. What's that?

MUSICIAN. It must be our divertimento beginning.

SPINETTA. Here's the whole family.

APOLLO (*aside*). Now that they're all assembled, the time has come to show them how shameful their choice has been.
(*Enter all the actors.*)

APOLLO. Plutus, you have defeated Apollo. But I am not jealous of your victory. It is no disgrace to the god who stands for excellence that he is valued less in the human heart than the god of vice.

PLUTUS (*laughing*). Listen to the boy with his excellence!

GRANGEWELL. What does all this mean?

PLUTUS. It means that Dulcimer is Apollo, and that I am Plutus, who robbed him of his girl. Don't be upset; you may keep my presents. Well, I'm leaving now. I've a feeling you'll manage to survive without me. I love you all, you've made me win my bet, and I'm going to entertain Olympus with my story. Forward! Enjoy yourselves! The musicians are paid; on with the dance!

Divertimento[1]

A FOLLOWER OF PLUTUS.
Great is your glory, lord of gold,
 The earth is at your feet.
 Say freeze, our cheeks grow cold,
 Say burn, we die of heat;
 You speak, the word is peace,
The god of war rolls back the nations;
 Love itself cannot increase
 Without your helpful allocations.

[1] The original "vaudeville" for this play was written by a certain Panard. It is typical of the song-and-dance routines which concluded most performances in the Italian Theatre of Paris. While I have kept the "message" of Panard's stanzas, it will be obvious that what follows is an extremely free rendition. [Tr.]

Song

1.

Down the river you'll be sold
Unless your god's the god of gold.
  The gravest sage
  Of all the age
  Without good cash
  Is less than trash,
For that's the way the game is played.
But when your banknotes are displayed
  You are a wit,
  Our eyes are lit,
  Your least remark
  Sets off a spark,
We pour your drink, we light your pipe,
We love your views, you're just our type.

For long as June shall follow May,
Lord Plutus, coin in hand, will sway.

2.

Time was, although I don't know when,
Pure maidens said to soulful men:
  "Your profit?
  I don't love it.
  Your credit?
  I can't pet it.
That's not the way my game is played."
Today, alas new rules are made:
  "Pimple-nosed,
  Varicosed,
  Undersized
  Or paralyzed,
You'll be my love," our beauties say,
"As long, my dear, as you can pay."

For long as June shall follow May,
Lord Plutus, coin in hand, will sway.

3.

When Rosamond was prosperous
Her beaux were soft and amorous.
   "Teach me," they'd cry,
   "Or else I'll die,
   To shoot my dart
   Deep in your heart,
Tell me the way your game is played."
But when her dividends decayed—
   "I've work to do
   In Timbuctoo;
   Next month, maybe,
   I'll try, we'll see."
For Love will any shock endure
Except the crime of being poor.

And long as June shall follow May,
Lord Plutus, coin in hand, will sway.

4.

When playwrights, with experienced tact,
Put clever lines in every act,
   You pay them well,
   For you can tell
   With judgment smart
   What is good art,
And how the actors should have played.
But when routines are old and frayed,
   You yawn, you grieve,
   You groan, you leave,
   And we're to blame,
   Ours is the shame.

The audience, we admit, knows best.
Have we, we wonder, passed the test?

If so, as June must follow May,
Tomorrow Plutus once again will play.

THE END

❦

The Game of Love and Chance
(Le Jeu de l'amour et du hasard)

Presented for the first time at
the Théâtre Italien on January 23, 1730

CHARACTERS

Mr. Humphrey
Thomas Humphrey
Sylvia
Dorian
Lisa
Trivet
A Servant

The action takes place in Mr. Humphrey's house.

ACT ONE

SYLVIA. Tell me once more, what business is this of yours? Why answer for my feelings?

LISA. Because I thought your feelings would be the same as anyone else's this time. Your father asks me whether you're glad he is marrying you off. I tell him yes, of course. And you must be the only girl alive for whom that yes of mine doesn't hold true. And yet no is simply abnormal.

SYLVIA. No is abnormal! You're a goose. Does marriage attract you that much?

LISA. Well—yes again.

SYLVIA. Hold your tongue and save your impertinence for somebody else. And learn not to judge my heart by yours.

LISA. My heart is like everybody else's. Why should yours be different?

SYLVIA. I suppose you'll tell me I'm eccentric.

LISA. I might if I were your equal.

SYLVIA. Lisa, you're determined to make me angry.

LISA. Not in the least. But really now, is there any harm in telling Mr. Humphrey that you are happy to be given away in marriage?

SYLVIA. First of all, what you told him isn't true. I'm not bored with single life.

LISA. Another novelty!

SYLVIA. I don't see why my father should think I'm overjoyed at the prospect of marriage. It might lead him to a rash decision.

LISA. You mean you won't marry the man he has chosen for you?

SYLVIA. I don't know. What worries me is that I may not find him suitable.

LISA. I hear that your future husband is one of the most respectable men in the world, handsome, pleasant, witty, good-natured—in short, a gentleman. What more could you ask? Can you imagine a sweeter marriage, a more delicious union?

SYLVIA. Delicious! What a silly way of talking!

LISA. Really, Miss Sylvia, you're a lucky girl. Usually a man of his kind is not interested in the formalities; and other girls might be willing to skip the ceremony for his sake, if he insisted. Amiable and handsome: so much for making love; sociable and witty: so much for entertainment in society. Heavenly gods! The useful and the agreeable are combined in him, the man's a paragon.

SYLVIA. Yes, but only in the picture you're drawing of him. And though other people praise him too, still it only amounts to hearsay. Besides, I have my own way of seeing things. For instance, they say he's a handsome man, which I think is almost a pity.

LISA. A pity! A pity! There's a weird thought!

SYLVIA. But it makes good sense. Usually a handsome man is conceited. I've noticed it.

LISA. He's wrong to be conceited. But he's right to be handsome.

SYLVIA. They also say he's well built. I won't quarrel with that!

LISA. Good, let's forgive him.

SYLVIA. But as for good looks and fine features, I can live without them. Those are superfluous charms.

LISA. Merciful God, if I ever marry, what's superfluous to you is going to be necessary to me.

SYLVIA. You don't know what you're saying. In marriage, it's better to deal with a sensible man than with a charmer. In other words, all I ask is a good disposition. And that's more difficult to find than most people think. Everybody praises his disposition, to be sure, but who has lived with him? A clever man doesn't reveal his character. I have seen men behaving in company as if they were sweetness, good nature, and common sense personified. Their goodness is written all over their faces. Take Mr. Wellworth. People kept saying about him, "He's a true gentleman, mild and sensible." And everybody agreed, I among them. "His face doesn't lie." But oh, beware of that sweet and engaging face! Presently it becomes sullen, brutal, and savage, it terrifies the entire household. Mr. Wellworth found a wife. And this is the only expression known to her, to his children, and to his servant. But everywhere else he parades the sweet face he puts on like a mask whenever he leaves his house.

LISA. A freak with two faces!

SYLVIA. And aren't we all happy when we see Mr. Wiseman? Well, here is a man who doesn't utter a word at home, doesn't laugh, doesn't even snarl. He is icy, solitary and inaccessible. His wife hardly knows him. She is married to a face that emerges from the study, arrives at the table and kills everything around it with apathy, coldness, indifference and boredom: an amusing husband, in short.

LISA. You make my flesh crawl. But what about Mr. Trueblood?

SYLVIA. Oh, yes, Mr. Trueblood. The other day when I called on the family, he had been quarreling with his wife. He greeted me with open arms, all cheerful and relaxed. You'd think he had just had a merry conversation—his mouth and eyes were still laughing. The hypocrite! That's what men are! Who'd believe that his wife is to be pitied? I found her depressed; her face was livid; her eyes were red. She looked as I may look one day. I pitied her. If I too needed your pity, Lisa—wouldn't it be terrible? Think what it means to have a husband.

LISA. A husband? A husband is a husband. You shouldn't have ended with that word. It reconciles me to everything.
(*Enter Mr. Humphrey.*)

MR. HUMPHREY. Good morning, my dear. Will my news make you happy? Your future husband is arriving today. Here's a letter from his father. Why don't you say something? You look unhappy. And Lisa is averting her eyes from me. What does it all mean? Tell me, what's the matter?

LISA. Sir, a face that makes you shudder, another that freezes the blood in your veins; an indifferent and solitary man; then the portrait of a woman depressed, her face livid, her eyes puffed up. That is what we have been concentrating on.

MR. HUMPHREY. What's all this gibberish? A face? A portrait? Explain, if you please; I don't understand a word of all this.

SYLVIA. I was telling Lisa about the unhappiness of a wife who is mistreated by her husband. I mentioned Mr. Trueblood's wife. The other day I found her despondent because her husband had been abusing her. And I was making a few comments about her plight.

LISA. Yes, we were talking about a face that comes and goes. A husband who wears a mask for the world and a grim look for his wife.

MR. HUMPHREY. I gather that marriage frightens you, my dear—especially since you don't know Dorian.

LISA. First, he is handsome and that's almost a pity.

MR. HUMPHREY. A pity! Are you mad? A pity, indeed!

LISA. I'm only repeating what I'm taught. It's your daughter's theory; I'm only her student.

MR. HUMPHREY. Come, come. That's neither here nor there. My dear girl, you know how much I love you. Dorian is coming here to marry you. On my last trip to the country, I arranged this marriage with his father, who is an old and close friend of mine.

But the condition is that you two must like each other and that both of you will be allowed to speak freely. I don't want you to marry him for my sake. If you don't like Dorian, say so and he'll leave. And he'll leave just as quickly if he doesn't take a fancy to you.

LISA. There'll be a tender love duet, like an opera: You want me, I want you. Quick, a notary! Or, do you love me? No! I don't love you either. Saddle my horse!

MR. HUMPHREY. I've never seen Dorian, you know. He was away when I visited his father. But with all the good things I've heard about him, I am not afraid of your dismissing each other.

SYLVIA. Father, I am deeply touched by your kindness. You forbid me to marry out of a sense of duty. And I promise to obey.

MR. HUMPHREY. I demand it.

SYLVIA. But if I dared, I would ask you—the thought just occurred to me—to grant me one favor that would set my mind at ease.

MR. HUMPHREY. Speak up. If it's something feasible, I'll grant it.

SYLVIA. It's quite feasible. But I'm afraid I would be taking advantage of your kindness.

MR. HUMPHREY. Well, take advantage. In this world a man has to be more than kind in order to be kind enough.

LISA. Only the kindest of men could say that.

MR. HUMPHREY. Let's hear your request.

SYLVIA. Dorian is arriving today. If only I could see him and study him a little without his knowing me! Lisa is clever. She could take my place for a while and I would take hers.

MR. HUMPHREY (*aside*). A charming idea! (*Aloud*) Let me think it over. (*Aside*) If I allow it, something very odd is going to happen, something she is far from expecting. (*Aloud*) Very well, my dear, you have my permission to disguise yourself. Lisa, are you sure you'll be up to your part?

LISA. You know me, sir. (*With a haughty air*) Sir, this is stuff and nonsense! Do you forget your place? And that's only a sample of the airs I'm going to give myself. What do you think? Do you recognize your Lisa?

MR. HUMPHREY. Why, I'm confused already. But we have no time to waste. Go dress for your part. Dorian might surprise us here. Hurry and tell all the servants.

SYLVIA. All I need is an apron.

LISA. And I'm going to dress. Come, help me comb my hair, Lisa. I want you to become accustomed to your duties. And take your work seriously, if you please.

SYLVIA. Madam will be satisfied. Let's go!
(*Exit Lisa. Enter Thomas Humphrey.*)

THOMAS. My congratulations, sister. I understand we're going to meet your suitor.

SYLVIA. Yes, brother, but I'm in a hurry—important business! Father will explain. (*Exit Sylvia.*)

MR. HUMPHREY. Don't take up her time, Thomas. Come, I'll tell you all about it.

THOMAS. Anything new?

MR. HUMPHREY. First I'll ask you to be discreet about what I'm going to tell you.

THOMAS. You can rely on me.

MR. HUMPHREY. We're going to meet Dorian today. But he's coming to us disguised.

THOMAS. Disguised? You mean in costume? Are you giving a masked ball in his honor?

MR. HUMPHREY. Nonsense. Listen to this part of his father's letter . . . "But I don't know what you will think of an idea that has struck my son. Even he agrees that it's unusual. But his motive makes it understandable and even delicate. He has asked me to allow him to come to your house dressed as his servant, who in turn will play the part of his master."

THOMAS. Ha, ha! Very good!

MR. HUMPHREY. Listen to the rest . . . "My son knows how serious a bond marriage is, and by means of this disguise he hopes to catch something of the character of his future bride, and to become better acquainted with her. Thereafter he can make his decision with the full liberty we have agreed to give our children. Though I have entire confidence in all you told me about your charming daughter, I have agreed to his plan; at the same time, however, I am taking the precaution of warning you, although he asked me to keep the secret from you. You may use your judgment in dealing with your daughter." But that's not the end of it. Your sister is also worried about Dorian. She knows nothing about his plan, but she asked me to let her play a part too, to observe Dorian—exactly as Dorian wants to observe her. Mistress and maid are busy disguising themselves this very moment. Well, Tom, what do you advise me to do? Shall I give your sister fair warning?

THOMAS. Heavens, no. I'd let things follow the course they're taking, and respect the idea which occurred to them both. Their disguise will throw them together much of the time. We'll see whether each will discover what the other is worth. Dorian might like my sister even as a maid; she'll be delighted if he does.

MR. HUMPHREY. I wonder how she'll manage.

THOMAS. In any case, this is going to be excellent sport for us. I want to enjoy this game from the start—and I intend to needle both of them.
(Enter Sylvia.)

SYLVIA. Here I am, sir. How do I strike you as a maid? Brother, you seem to know all about it. Well, what do you think of me?

THOMAS. On my soul, you'll catch the servant and even steal Dorian from your mistress.

SYLVIA. Actually, I wouldn't object if he found me attractive in this disguise. I'd even enjoy turning his head and leaving him perplexed because of the distance between us. If my charms achieve this much, I'll think the better of them. Besides, all this will help me understand Dorian. As for the servant, I'm not worried about his advances. He won't dare approach me. The scamp will be able to tell from my appearance that he owes me more respect than love.

THOMAS. Careful, sister. That scamp will be your equal.

MR. HUMPHREY. And will inevitably fall in love with you.

SYLVIA. Good; I'll put that honor to some use too. Servants are indiscreet by nature, and love is talkative. I'll make him the chronicler of his master.
(A servant enters.)

SERVANT. Sir, there's a man at the door asking to speak with you. He is followed by a porter carrying a suitcase.

MR. HUMPHREY. Let him in. It's probably Dorian's valet. His master must have been detained. Where is Lisa?

SYLVIA. She's dressing. Her mirror tells her we're being reckless in handing Dorian over to her. She'll be ready soon.

MR. HUMPHREY. Quiet, somebody is coming.
(Enter Dorian disguised as a valet.)

DORIAN. I am looking for Mr. Humphrey. Have I the honor of bowing to him?

MR. HUMPHREY. Yes, my friend, I am Mr. Humphrey.

DORIAN. Sir, you have undoubtedly received word about us. I serve Mr. Dorian, who will be here shortly. He sent me ahead to pay you his respects in anticipation of doing so himself.

MR. HUMPHREY. You have carried out your orders gracefully. Lisa, what do you think of this young man?

SYLVIA. Sir, I bid him welcome and I think he shows promise.

DORIAN. You are most kind. I do my best.

THOMAS. He is very handsome. Take care of your heart, Lisa.

SYLVIA. My heart! What a to-do about my heart!

DORIAN. Don't be angry, madam. I am not so vain as to take these remarks seriously.

SYLVIA. I like your modesty. Please preserve it.

THOMAS. Very good. But it seems to me that his calling you madam is rather too grave. Servants needn't be quite so formal among themselves, or on their toes all day about points of etiquette. Come, both of you, unbend a little. Your name is Lisa; what's yours, young man?

DORIAN. Trivet, at your service.

SYLVIA. Good, Trivet it shall be.

DORIAN. And I'll call you Lisa. But I'll be your obedient servant all the same.

THOMAS. Your obedient servant! Still on formal terms.[1]

MR. HUMPHREY. Ha, ha, ha, ha!

SYLVIA (aside to Thomas). You're making fun of me, brother.

DORIAN. I will speak in more familiar terms whenever Lisa orders it.

SYLVIA. As you like, Trivet. The ice is broken, since we're entertaining these gentlemen.

DORIAN. Thank you, Lisa.

MR. HUMPHREY. Courage, my children. If you're beginning to fall in love, you don't have to stand on ceremony.

THOMAS. Not so fast. Love is another matter. Apparently you don't know that I'm after Lisa's heart myself. True, she's been cruel to me, but still I forbid Trivet to cross my path.

[1] By "formal terms" it is meant that the two make-believe servants are addressing each other with the *vous* instead of the *tu* which would be expected between servants. [Tr.]

SYLVIA. You don't say! Well then, I insist that Trivet fall in love with me.

DORIAN. Beautiful Lisa, you wrong yourself when you say "I insist." A girl like you doesn't have to command in order to be served.

THOMAS. Mr. Trivet, you stole that compliment from somewhere.

DORIAN. You are right, sir. I took it from her eyes.

THOMAS. Worse and worse. Enough. I forbid you to be so witty.

SYLVIA. It doesn't cost *you* anything. And if he finds it in my eyes he is welcome to it.

MR. HUMPHREY. Let's go, son, you're losing the game. Dorian is coming soon. I want to announce his arrival to my daughter. And you, Lisa, show the fellow his master's rooms. Good-bye, Trivet.

DORIAN. Sir, you are too kind.
(*Exeunt Mr. Humphrey and Thomas.*)

SYLVIA (*aside*). They're laughing at my expense. No matter. I can turn everything to my advantage. This fellow is no fool, and I don't pity the maid who gets him. He is going to use his charm on me, but as long as I can learn something I'll let him talk.

DORIAN (*aside*). This girl astounds me. There isn't a woman in society who wouldn't be proud of such a face. I'll make friends with her. (*Aloud*) Since we have dropped all formalities in order to be friendly, tell me, Lisa, is your mistress worthy of you? She is very bold to have engaged a maid like you.

SYLVIA. Trivet, I can see that you are going to treat me to pretty speeches, as custom requires. Am I right?

DORIAN. I assure you I hadn't come with that intention. Although I am a valet, I have never carried on with maids. I don't enjoy the servant mind. But you're different. You subdue me, I'm almost shy, I don't dare become familiar with you. I want to keep taking my hat off to you. What kind of maid are you with that regal air of yours?

SYLVIA. Why, you're echoing all the servants who have seen me.

DORIAN. I shouldn't be surprised if I echoed the masters too.

SYLVIA. You're very clever. But I repeat I am not the sort who encourages the attentions of those who dress like you.

DORIAN. You don't like my livery?

SYLVIA. No, Trivet. Let's put love aside and be good friends.

DORIAN. Nothing more? You made two impossible stipulations.

SYLVIA (*aside*). An exceptional valet! (*Aloud*) Still, you'll have to resign yourself. I was told I would marry a gentleman. And I swore never to listen to anybody else.

DORIAN. How interesting! What you vowed concerning a husband, I have sworn in the matter of a wife. I have taken an oath to love none seriously but a gentlewoman.

SYLVIA. Well, don't forget your decision!

DORIAN. I'm not forgetting it as much as you think. You have such a distinguished air, you might be well-born without knowing it.

SYLVIA. Ha, ha, ha! I would thank you for the compliment if it weren't made at my mother's expense.

DORIAN. Well, take revenge on mine, if my looks warrant it.

SYLVIA (*aside*). They do warrant it. (*Aloud*) It's not a matter of looks. But enough of this foolishness. It was predicted that my husband would be a gentleman, and I'll take nothing less.

DORIAN. If I were such a man, I declare I would be endangered by this prophecy and afraid it was aimed at me. I have no faith in astrology, but I do in your beauty.

SYLVIA (*aside*). He is inexhaustible. (*Aloud*) Are you nearly done? This prediction is of no concern to you, since you're excluded from it.

DORIAN. It didn't say I wouldn't love you.

SYLVIA. No, but it said you'd leave empty-handed, and that much I can confirm!

DORIAN. You're right, Lisa, and I like you for your pride—even though it condemns me. From the moment I saw you I wanted you to be proud. Pride gives the final touch to your charms, and I'm resigned to my fate, because my loss is your gain.

SYLVIA (aside). I like him in spite of myself. (Aloud) Tell me—you who are so eloquent—who are you?

DORIAN. The son of poor but honest people.

SYLVIA. You deserve a better position in life. And I wish it for you with all my heart. I really would like to help you. Fate has been unjust to you.

DORIAN. Love is treating me worse. I'd prefer the right to love you to all the riches in the world.

SYLVIA. Trivet, I'm not angry with you, but you simply must change the subject. Let's turn to your master. You can stop talking about love, can't you?

DORIAN. Yes, but can I stop feeling it?

SYLVIA. I am losing my temper now! Once and for all, put your love aside.

DORIAN. First put your face away!

SYLVIA (aside). He's beginning to amuse me. (Aloud) Are you going to persist, Trivet? Shall I have to leave? (Aside) I should have left long ago.

DORIAN. Wait, Lisa, I wanted to talk to you about something else—but I've forgotten what it was.

SYLVIA. I too had something to tell you, but you've distracted me as well.

DORIAN. I remember asking whether your mistress deserved you.

Sylvia. We're back where we started. Good-bye.

Dorian. No, Lisa, wait, I was asking for my master's sake.

Sylvia. Good. I wanted to talk about him too, and I hope you'll tell me confidentially what he is like. Your devotion to him is a good sign. He must have some merit, if a man like you waits on him.

Dorian. Am I allowed to thank you for this remark?

Sylvia. Please don't pay any attention to it. You caught me off guard.

Dorian. Charming reply! Lisa, do with me anything you wish—I won't struggle, I promise. Poor Trivet! Your mouth is stopped by the most heavenly creature that ever breathed.

Sylvia. I'd like to know why I'm so good-natured as to listen to you. It's incredible.

Dorian. You're right. Ours is a unique experience.

Sylvia (aside). In spite of all he's said, I haven't left, I'm not leaving, I'm still here, and I'm even answering him! This has gone beyond a joke. (Aloud) I'm leaving.

Dorian. Let's finish what we wanted to say.

Sylvia. No, I'm leaving. That's my last word. I'll try to talk to your master when he comes—if he's worth the trouble. I'd like to observe him on behalf of my mistress. Meantime, do you see this room? It's yours.

Dorian. Wait, here is my master.
(Enter Trivet.)

Trivet. Oh, there you are, Trivet. Were you and my suitcase well received?

Dorian. Everybody has been most kind, sir.

Trivet. A servant below told me to wait here. He's going to announce me to my father-in-law and my wife.

SYLVIA. Do you mean Mr. Humphrey and his daughter?

TRIVET. Why yes, but I might as well say my father-in-law and my wife. They're waiting for me to bring off the marriage. It's all agreed. The only thing missing is the ceremony, and that's a detail.

SYLVIA. It's a detail worth thinking about.

TRIVET. Yes, but once you've thought about it you can forget it.

SYLVIA (*in a low voice, to Dorian*). It doesn't seem to take much to be a gentleman where you come from.

TRIVET. What are you saying to my valet, my pretty one?

SYLVIA. Nothing. I merely said I would ask Mr. Humphrey to come down.

TRIVET. Why don't you say father-in-law, like me?

SYLVIA. Because he's not your father-in-law yet.

DORIAN. She is right, sir. The wedding hasn't been performed.

TRIVET. Well, I'm here to perform it.

DORIAN. By and by.

TRIVET. Bless me! What difference does it make whether you call him father-in-law before or after the wedding?

SYLVIA. True—what difference is there between being married and not being married? Yes, sir, we are wrong, and I'm going at once to tell him you're here.

TRIVET. And let my wife know it too, if you please. But before you go, tell me something, you lovely girl: aren't you the maid here?

SYLVIA. I am, sir.

TRIVET. Good, I'm glad. Do you think they will like me? What do you think of me?

SYLVIA. I think you are . . . diverting.

TRIVET. Better still! Don't change your mind, and you won't regret it.

SYLVIA. You're easily satisfied, I see. By your leave, sir. Our people must have forgotten to tell your father-in-law that you had arrived, otherwise he would have been here by now. Let me look for him.

TRIVET. Say that I await him with affection.

SYLVIA (aside). How strange life is! Neither of these men is in his right place.
(Exit Sylvia.)

TRIVET. Well, sir, I'm doing well for a beginning. The maid likes me already.

DORIAN. You're a clown.

TRIVET. Why? I made quite a genteel entrance.

DORIAN. You promised me to give up your coarse and ridiculous manners. And what about my instructions? My one recommendation to you was that you must be serious. But I was a fool to trust you.

TRIVET. I'll improve from now on. And since it isn't enough to be serious, I'll throw in some melancholy. I'll cry if necessary.

DORIAN. I don't know what to think. This whole affair is making me dizzy. I wonder what I should do.

TRIVET. Why? Is the daughter a bore?

DORIAN. Quiet. I hear Mr. Humphrey.
(Enter Mr. Humphrey.)

MR. HUMPHREY. My dear sir, a thousand apologies for having made you wait. But I found out only a minute ago that you were here.

TRIVET. Sir, a thousand apologies are too many. One per mistake is enough. Moreover, all my pardons are at your service.

MR. HUMPHREY. Let me try not to need them.

TRIVET. You are the master and I am your servant.

MR. HUMPHREY. Well, I am delighted to see you. I have been anxiously waiting for you.

TRIVET. I would have come here directly with Trivet, but you know how worn out one is after a trip. I wanted to make a more appetizing appearance.

MR. HUMPHREY. And you have succeeded. My daughter is dressing. She has been a trifle indisposed. While we wait for her to come down, may I offer you something to drink?

TRIVET. I've never refused a drink yet.

MR. HUMPHREY. Trivet, take care of yourself, my boy.

TRIVET. The rascal is a connoisseur. He'll drink up your best wines.

MR. HUMPHREY. Let him have all he wants.

ACT TWO

(Enter Mr. Humphrey and Lisa.)

MR. HUMPHREY. What is it, Lisa?

LISA. I must have a word with you, sir.

MR. HUMPHREY. What about?

LISA. About the situation here. I want everything to be perfectly clear, so you'll have no cause for complaint against me.

MR. HUMPHREY. This sounds pretty serious.

LISA. It is. You gave your consent to Miss Sylvia's disguise, and I myself took it lightly at first; but I should have known better.

MR. HUMPHREY. What has happened, Lisa?

LISA. It's not easy to praise oneself. But rules of modesty aside, I must warn you that if you don't put an end to this game, your supposed son-in-law is lost. Your daughter had better unmask at once. This is urgent. Another day and I won't answer for him.

MR. HUMPHREY. Oh? Will he refuse my daughter even after he is told the truth? Don't you trust her charms?

LISA. Don't you distrust mine? I'm warning you that mine are doing their work, and I advise you to stop them while you can.

MR. HUMPHREY. Congratulations, my dear. Ha, ha, ha!

LISA. Very amusing. But you won't be laughing when you're left high and dry.

MR. HUMPHREY. Don't worry about that, my dear Lisa. Carry on as before.

LISA. Sir, let me repeat. Dorian is falling in love with me. Today he likes me very much; tonight he'll love me; tomorrow he'll worship me. It's more than I deserve; I grant you he's showing poor taste. But that's how it is. Believe me—tomorrow he'll be on his knees.

MR. HUMPHREY. What does it matter? If he loves you so violently, let him marry you.

LISA. What! You wouldn't interfere?

MR. HUMPHREY. On my honor, if you can bring him to it, I won't interfere.

LISA. Sir, be careful. Up to now I haven't enhanced my charms. I've left them alone in order to keep him from losing his head. But if I set my mind to it, he's my slave beyond rescue.

MR. HUMPHREY. Enslave, ravage, burn, marry him if you can. You have my permission.

LISA. Very well; my fortune is made.

MR. HUMPHREY. Tell me, what does my daughter report? What does she think of her suitor?

LISA. We haven't had a moment to talk because her suitor gives me no respite. But even from a distance I can see she's not at all happy. I expect she'll tell me to discourage him.

MR. HUMPHREY. And I forbid you to do anything of the sort. I'm avoiding an explanation with my daughter, but I've my reasons for continuing this masquerade. I want her to observe her future husband at leisure. But how is the valet behaving? Has he taken a fancy to my daughter?

LISA. He's a strange fellow. I noticed he plays the courtier with her because he's handsome. He looks at her and sighs.

MR. HUMPHREY. Does she mind?

LISA. Well . . . she blushes.

MR. HUMPHREY. You must be mistaken. She wouldn't let a servant embarrass her.

LISA. Sir, she blushes.

MR. HUMPHREY. In that case, she's indignant.

LISA. Have it your way!

MR. HUMPHREY. When you speak to her, tell her you suspect that the fellow is trying to prejudice her against his master. If she gets angry, don't worry. That's my business. Well, here is Dorian. He's obviously looking for you.
(*Enter Trivet.*)

TRIVET. I've found you at last, radiant Sylvia. I have been asking everyone I meet where you are. At your service, dear almost father-in-law.

MR. HUMPHREY. How do you do. I'll leave you together now, my children. I advise you to fall in love a little before the wedding day.

TRIVET. I'm willing to love and marry at the same time.

MR. HUMPHREY. Don't be too impatient. Good-bye.
(*Exit Mr. Humphrey.*)

TRIVET. Madam, he tells me not to be impatient. But that's more easily said than done.

LISA. I can't really believe it's all that difficult for you to wait. Your impatience is flattering, but we've barely met. Your love can't be very strong as yet. At most, it's just being born.

TRIVET. You're mistaken, celestial creature. The kind of love you beget does not linger in the cradle. Your first glance caused Cupid to be born; the second gave him strength, and the third made him a man. Let's provide for him as soon as possible. You're his mother, you must look after him.

LISA. Do you feel he's being mistreated? Is the poor boy neglected?

TRIVET. All I know is that he needs your beautiful white hand to distract him a little while he is still unsure of his future.

LISA. Take it, you tease. I'll have no peace unless I keep you amused.

TRIVET (*kissing her hand*). Fairest angel, this tickles me like a delicious wine. Alas, all you're allowing me is a mere drop or two.

LISA. Stop, you're too greedy.

TRIVET. I am only trying to remain alive.

LISA. Be reasonable.

TRIVET. Reasonable? Out of the question. Your beautiful eyes have robbed me of my reason.

LISA. Is it possible that you love me so much? I can't really believe it.

TRIVET. The devil take what is possible. I love you like a soul in torment. Your mirror will tell you why.

LISA. My mirror would only add to my doubts.

TRIVET. Sweet darling, in you humility is hypocrisy.

LISA. Someone is coming. It's your valet.
(*Enter Dorian.*)

DORIAN. Sir, may I have a word with you?

TRIVET. No; curse the flunkeys who don't leave us in peace.

LISA. See what he wants, sir.

DORIAN. I've only one word to say.

TRIVET. Madam, if he says two, his dismissal will be the third.

DORIAN (*in a low voice, to Trivet*). Come here, insolent rascal.

TRIVET (*in a low voice, to Dorian*). Those are insults, not words. (*To Lisa*) Excuse me, my queen.

LISA. Of course.

DORIAN. Everything's off, do you hear? Don't commit yourself. Look serious and pensive. Even dissatisfied. Do you understand?

TRIVET. Leave it to me, my friend, don't worry. You can go now. (*Exit Dorian.*)

TRIVET. Madam, I was about to utter the most beautiful speeches, when this fellow disturbed us, and now all I can think of is commonplaces. Only my love itself remains extraordinary. But apropos of my love, when will yours keep it company?

LISA. Let's hope it will sometime.

TRIVET. But do you *think* it will?

LISA. That's a pointed question. Are you aware that you're hardly allowing me to breathe?

TRIVET. What can I do? I'm burning and I'm crying for help.

LISA. If decency allowed me to declare myself . . .

TRIVET. In my opinion, it does.

LISA. A woman must be reserved.

TRIVET. But not old-fashioned. Nowadays reserve isn't so finicky.

LISA. But what do you want of me?

TRIVET. I want to hear a little word—that you love me. Look here—I love you. Be my echo. Repeat after me, my princess.

LISA. You're insatiable! Well, all right—I love you.

TRIVET. You love me! I'm delirious, I'm dying, this is too much happiness, I won't survive it.

LISA. I ought to be amazed by this sudden devotion. Perhaps you won't love me so much once we know each other better.

TRIVET. Madam, when we come to that, you are the one who will have to make large allowances.

LISA. You credit me with more qualities than I have.

TRIVET. And you, madam, you don't know mine. I ought to speak to you on my knees.

LISA. Remember, we are not the masters of our fate.

TRIVET. Fathers and mothers don't consult us, do they?

LISA. As far as I'm concerned, my heart would have chosen you no matter what your rank had been.

TRIVET. Your heart will be given that opportunity.

LISA. I do hope that you feel the same way about me.

TRIVET. If you were nothing but a farmgirl or a housemaid—if I saw you walking down to the cellar with a candlestick in your hand, I'd still choose you as my princess.

LISA. May your feelings last!

TRIVET. To strengthen them, let's both swear to love one another forever, even if a few irregularities show in the accounts.

LISA. This oath means more to me than to you, and I take it with all my heart.

TRIVET (*on his knees*). Your goodness dazzles me. I kneel to it.

LISA. Stop! I can't bear to see you on your knees. People would laugh at me. Get up. Here's somebody again.
(*Enter Sylvia.*)

LISA. What do you want, Lisa?

SYLVIA. A few words with you, madam.

TRIVET. You don't say! Come back in fifteen minutes, my pet. Go away. Where I live, chambermaids don't interrupt unless they are called.

SYLVIA. Sir, I wish to speak with my mistress.

TRIVET. Stubborn, too! Queen of my heart, do send her away.

Go back where you came from. We've been told to fall in love before we're married. You're interrupting our assignment.

LISA. Can't you come back in a little while, Lisa?

SYLVIA. Madam . . .

TRIVET. No madams, or I'll have a fit.

SYLVIA (*aside*). What a horrid man! (*Aloud*) Madam, it's urgent.

LISA. Sir, allow me. I'll soon be rid of her.

TRIVET. Since the devil's in her, I'll take a walk until she's had her say. God, the stupidity of these stupid servants!
(*Exit Trivet.*)

SYLVIA. Why didn't you throw him out when I came in? Why did you let that beast inflict his vulgarities on me?

LISA. Madam, I can't play two roles at the same time. I am either the mistress or the maid—the one who obeys or the one who gives orders.

SYLVIA. I agree, but now that he's out of the room, listen to me as my maid. You can see that this man is not for me.

LISA. You haven't had much time to observe him.

SYLVIA. There's no need for observation. Do I have to look twice to know that he's not for me? I don't want him; that's all there is to it. But I can see that my father doesn't approve; he says nothing and he avoids me. You must help me out of this predicament, Lisa. Tell the young man as tactfully as you can that I don't relish the thought of marrying him.

LISA. I can't do that, madam.

SYLVIA. You can't? Why not?

LISA. Mr. Humphrey has forbidden it.

SYLVIA. Forbidden it! That's not like my father at all.

LISA. Absolutely forbidden it.

SYLVIA. In that case you'll tell my father that I find this man invincibly disgusting. I hope he'll know better than to insist after that.

LISA. But madam, what is so disgusting about him?

SYLVIA. I don't like him; and by the way, I don't like your shilly-shallying either.

LISA. Give yourself more time. That's all we ask of you.

SYLVIA. I hate him enough right now. The more time I have, the more I'll hate him.

LISA. His man may have slandered him. Look at the airs he gives himself.

SYLVIA. What does the servant have to do with this, you fool?

LISA. I don't trust him. He likes to talk.

SYLVIA. Spare me your observations, will you? I see to it that he doesn't address me more than is necessary, but in the little he has said to me he has always made sense.

LISA. I think he is the sort of man who would tell you God knows what nonsense to show how brilliant he is.

SYLVIA. Well, what if my disguise forces me to listen to a few compliments? Why this grudge against him? And why do you foist evil intentions on him—hard feelings against his master and the like? You're forcing me to defend the man. I don't see the good of causing a quarrel between him and his master, or of making him out a rascal and myself a fool for listening to his stories.

LISA. Dear me, if you're going to defend him in that tone of voice! And with angry words! I won't open my mouth again.

SYLVIA. If I'm going to defend him in that tone of voice! What do you mean? Is this a hint of some kind?

LISA. I mean that I've never seen you in such a huff. I don't understand your excitement. If the man hasn't said anything, well and good. There's no need to fly off the handle to defend him. I believe you, and that's that. I wouldn't dream of contradicting your high opinion of him.

SYLVIA. What an evil mind! Look at her twisting my words about! I'm so indignant I could cry.

LISA. But why, madam? What double meanings do you find in my words?

SYLVIA. I find double meanings! I scold you for his sake! I have a high opinion of him! That's how far you presume to go with me. A high opinion! Heaven help me! A high opinion! What should I answer? What does it all mean? And to whom do you think you're speaking? Is there any protection left for me? What have we come to?

LISA. I've nothing more to say. But I won't recover from my surprise for many a day.

SYLVIA. Your way of putting things simply infuriates me. Go away—you're unbearable. Leave me alone. I'll have to take other measures.
(*Exit Lisa.*)

SYLVIA (*alone*). I'm still shaking from what I heard her say. The insolent thoughts these servants allow themselves! Always ready to degrade us! I can't get over it. I don't dare remember the things she said. It's frightening! And all this for a valet. How strange. I intend to drive all her ideas out of my mind. They're defiling my imagination. Ha! Here's Trivet, the cause of it all. Poor fellow, it's not his fault I lost my temper, and I'm not going to blame him.
(*Enter Dorian.*)

DORIAN. Sweet Lisa, no matter how much you dislike me, I really must talk to you and complain a little.

SYLVIA. Please don't be too familiar, Mr. Trivet.

DORIAN. I'll obey you, Lisa my dear.

SYLVIA. There you go again.[2]

DORIAN. Let's speak any way we can. We have so little time left together, it's useless to worry about formalities.

SYLVIA. Is your master leaving? He's no great loss.

DORIAN. That's your feeling about my leaving too, isn't it?

SYLVIA. I really wasn't thinking about you.

DORIAN. And I can think of nothing but you.

SYLVIA. Listen, Mr. Trivet, once and for all. You can stay, leave or come back—I mustn't care what you do, and in fact I don't. I wish you neither joy nor grief. I neither love you nor hate you. And I'll never love you, unless I lose my sanity. This is how I feel about you, and this is all that reason allows. I shouldn't even have to tell you all this.

DORIAN. I am infinitely unhappy. You've taken my peace of mind away forever.

SYLVIA. What absurdities have you put into your head? I feel sorry for you. Please come to your senses. You speak to me and I answer you. Believe me, this is much, even too much. If you knew the truth, you would praise me for my kindness. I'll go farther. My kindness is so extraordinary that I would criticize it in any other girl. However, I won't blame myself for it. In my heart of hearts I know that my actions are laudable, and that I converse with you out of pure generosity. But a touch of generosity is enough; one mustn't overdo it. I don't wish to trouble my head day and night about the innocence of my motives. A person gets confused in the end. So, Trivet, please let's stop all this. It's all perfectly meaningless, ludicrous, it mustn't be talked about any more.

DORIAN. How you make me suffer, dear Lisa.

---

[2] Again the question of the *tu* form is at stake. [Tr.]

SYLVIA. Come to the point. When you came in you were complaining about me. Tell me why.

DORIAN. For no reason at all; a trifle. I wanted to see you, and I needed an excuse.

SYLVIA (aside). What can I answer? Getting angry doesn't help.

DORIAN. Your mistress seems to think that I've been spreading tales about Mr. Dorian.

SYLVIA. So she believes. But if she brings it up again, deny it outright. I'll see to the rest.

DORIAN. Still, this is not what distresses me.

SYLVIA. But if it's all you have come to tell me, we can part.

DORIAN. Allow me at least the pleasure of looking at you.

SYLVIA. Here's a lovely reason for staying! My duty will be to nurse Trivet's passion. Some day I'll be able to laugh when I remember all this.

DORIAN. You're right to mock me. I don't know what I'm saying any more. Good-bye.

SYLVIA. Good-bye. Now you're sensible at last. But speaking of farewells—there's one more thing I'd like to know. You said you and your master were leaving. Is this definite?

DORIAN. As far as I'm concerned, either I leave or I go mad.

SYLVIA. That's not what I asked.

DORIAN. I made only one mistake. I should have left when I first saw you.

SYLVIA (aside). I have to keep forgetting that I'm listening to him.

DORIAN. Lisa, if you knew my condition . . .

SYLVIA. It's not as strange as mine, I assure you.

DORIAN. You have nothing to reproach me with. I don't intend to play on your feelings.

SYLVIA (*aside*). I wouldn't count on that.

DORIAN. And what could I hope to achieve by making you love me? Even if I had your heart . . .

SYLVIA. Heaven forbid! Even if you had it, you wouldn't know it. And I'd be so careful, I wouldn't know it myself. The very idea!

DORIAN. Is it true then that you are indifferent to me—that you can never love me?

SYLVIA. It is true.

DORIAN. What is so horrible about me?

SYLVIA. Nothing. That's not what counts against you.

DORIAN. Well then, Lisa, repeat to me a hundred times that you will never love me.

SYLVIA. I have said it often enough. Try to believe me.

DORIAN. I must believe you! Yes, Lisa, discourage to the uttermost this dangerous passion of mine. Save me from its consequences. You are indifferent to me! You will never love me! Pound this truth into my heart. I beg you on my knees, help me against myself! (*He falls to his knees. At this moment, enter Mr. Humphrey and Thomas. They remain concealed.*)

SYLVIA. That's all I needed! So it has come to that! Oh, I'm so unhappy! My weakness has put him there. Stand up, Trivet, I implore you. Somebody may come—I'll tell you whatever you like. What should I say? I don't hate you. Rise! I would love you if I could. I don't dislike you. That should be enough.

DORIAN. What are you saying, Lisa? If I were not what I am; if I were rich, if I were a gentleman, and if I loved you as much as I do now, would you tolerate me?

SYLVIA. Certainly.

DORIAN. You wouldn't hate me? You would find me bearable?

SYLVIA. I would. Please get up.

DORIAN. I think you mean it. And if you do—my sanity is gone.

SYLVIA. I've said what you wanted, and still you won't get up!

MR. HUMPHREY (*coming forward*). Excuse me for interrupting you. Good work, my dear children. Bravo!

SYLVIA. Sir, I couldn't keep this fellow from falling on his knees. I've no right to order him about, have I?

MR. HUMPHREY. You two are a perfect match. But there's something I want to tell you, Lisa. You can pursue your conversation afterwards. Would you mind, Trivet?

DORIAN. I'm leaving, sir.

MR. HUMPHREY. Go now, and try to speak of your master with a little more discretion.

DORIAN. I, sir?

MR. HUMPHREY. Yes, you, Trivet. You are not notorious for the respect you show your master.

DORIAN. I don't know what you mean.

MR. HUMPHREY. Good. You'll justify yourself another time. You can leave now. (*Exit Dorian.*) Well, Sylvia, won't you look at us? You seem embarrassed.

SYLVIA. Why should I seem embarrassed, father? Thank heaven, I am my usual self. I'm sorry to tell you that you're imagining things.

THOMAS. There *is* something, sister. Yes, there *is* something.

SYLVIA. Yes, there is something, namely in your head. The only thing in mine is surprise at your remarks.

MR. HUMPHREY. Is the fellow who just left responsible for your violent dislike of his master?

SYLVIA. Who? Dorian's servant?

MR. HUMPHREY. Yes, the gallant Trivet.

SYLVIA. The gallant Trivet—I hadn't heard that adjective before—doesn't talk to me about him.

MR. HUMPHREY. And yet, I am told he is ruining Dorian for you. And that's what I want to talk to you about.

SYLVIA. Don't worry, father. No one but the master himself is responsible for my natural aversion.

THOMAS. Say what you like, sister, but your aversion is too strong to be natural. Someone must have helped it grow.

SYLVIA (excitedly). You sound very mysterious, brother. Let's see, who do you suppose helped it grow?

THOMAS. You're in a strange mood, sister. Why are you so upset?

SYLVIA. Because I'm tired of the part I'm playing. I would have revealed my identity by now if I hadn't been afraid of annoying father.

MR. HUMPHREY. See that you don't, Sylvia. Since I was good enough to allow your disguise, you must suspend your judgment of Dorian long enough to see whether the dislike somebody taught you for him is legitimate.

SYLVIA. Won't you listen to me, father? I told you no one has taught it to me.

THOMAS. Come, now! You'll tell us that the babbler who just left hasn't incited you against him?

SYLVIA (heatedly). This conversation is really offensive. Incited me against him! Incited! I have to swallow very strange expressions. I look embarrassed. Something is going on. And then the gallant Trivet incited me. I don't care what you say—it's all utterly beyond me.

THOMAS. You're the one who is strange now. Why are you so touchy? Why so suspicious of us?

SYLVIA. Good work, brother. Why is it that every word you say today offends me? What suspicions could I have? You must be having visions.

MR. HUMPHREY. He's right, though. You're so perturbed, I hardly recognize you. Now I see what Lisa meant. She accused this man of having prejudiced you against his master. "Miss Sylvia," she told us, "defended him against me with so much anger that I'm still amazed." We scolded her for saying she was "amazed." But servants don't realize the consequences of a word.

SYLVIA. Is there anyone more odious and impudent than this girl? I admit I was angry, but only in justice to that poor fellow.

THOMAS. There's nothing wrong with that.

SYLVIA. Could anything be simpler? Because I love justice, because I want no one to suffer, because I try to protect a servant from malicious reports to his master, you say I have fits of anger which surprise everybody. A minute later, a vicious girl opens her mouth. Now you decide to object, to silence her, to take my side against her because of the importance of what she has said. Take my side! Do I need to be defended or justified? Can my actions be misinterpreted? What have I done? What are you accusing me of? I beg you to enlighten me. Are you serious? Are you making fun of me? My mind's in a whirl.

MR. HUMPHREY. Gently; calm yourself a little.

SYLVIA. No, I can't calm myself. You talk about surprises, consequences! What do you mean? Why do you raise false accusations against a servant? You are unjust, all of you. Lisa is out of her mind, Trivet is innocent, and let's not talk about it again. It's outrageous.

MR. HUMPHREY. You're trying to control yourself, but I can see you'd like to put me in my place too. However, we can do something better than that. The only one under suspicion here is the valet. Dorian can simply dismiss him.

SYLVIA. Oh, this wretched disguise! Above all, don't let me see Lisa. I hate her more than Dorian.

MR. HUMPHREY. You'll see her only if you wish. But you must

be delighted to have the fellow go. He is in love with you, and I daresay this must be annoying to you.

SYLVIA. I have no complaints. He thinks I'm a maid and speaks to me accordingly. But he doesn't tell me everything that enters his head, I see to that!

THOMAS. You're not as much in command as you think you are.

MR. HUMPHREY. Didn't we see him fall on his knees in spite of you? And, in order to make him get up, didn't you have to tell him that you don't dislike him?

SYLVIA (aside). I'm choking!

THOMAS. And when he asked you whether you could love him, didn't you have to answer, and tenderly too, "Oh, willingly"? Otherwise he'd still be there.

SYLVIA. Very witty! But as I didn't like his behavior, it's none too kind of you to bring it up again. Let's be serious now. When are you going to stop this game you're playing at my expense?

MR. HUMPHREY. The only thing I ask of you is not to refuse Dorian until you really know why. Wait a little longer. You'll thank me for the delay, believe me.

THOMAS. You will marry Dorian, and even for love. Take my word for it. But, father, I'm going to ask you to forgive the servant.

SYLVIA. Why forgive him? I want him to leave.

MR. HUMPHREY. Let his master decide. Come along, Thomas.

THOMAS. Good-bye, sister. No hard feelings.
(Exeunt Mr. Humphrey and Thomas.)

SYLVIA. I feel so oppressed! I'm troubled and I don't know what else besides. Wretched masquerade! I distrust everybody, even myself.
(Enter Dorian.)

DORIAN. I was looking for you, Lisa.

SYLVIA. It's no use your having found me. I'm trying to keep away from you.

DORIAN (*detaining her*). Stay, Lisa. I must speak to you for the last time. It's about something very important which concerns your masters.

SYLVIA. Go tell it to them, not to me. Every time I see you, you add to my troubles. Let me go.

DORIAN. And don't you add to mine? But listen to me. You'll see that what I'm about to say will change things completely.

SYLVIA. Very well; it seems I'm condemned to be eternally obliging to you.

DORIAN. Can I confide in you?

SYLVIA. I have never betrayed anyone.

DORIAN. I am telling you my secret only because of my admiration for you.

SYLVIA. I believe you. But try to admire me without saying so; I smell a pretext.

DORIAN. You're mistaken, Lisa. But you promised to keep the secret; let me finish, therefore. You have seen me deeply moved, unable to suppress my love for you.

SYLVIA. Here we go again! I refuse to listen to you. Good-bye.

DORIAN. Don't go. This is no longer Trivet speaking.

SYLVIA. Ha! Who *are* you?

DORIAN. Lisa, now you'll be able to understand my grief.

SYLVIA. I'm not speaking to your grief but to you.

DORIAN. Is anybody coming?

SYLVIA. No.

DORIAN. Matters have gone so far—it would be dishonorable of me not to stop them.

SYLVIA. Very good.

DORIAN. The man who is with your mistress is not the man people think he is.

SYLVIA (*quickly*). Who is he?

DORIAN. A servant.

SYLVIA. And?

DORIAN. I am Dorian.

SYLVIA (*aside*). Now I understand my heart!

DORIAN. I wanted to know something about your mistress before marrying her. With my father's permission I took this livery. The whole undertaking seems like a dream. I hate the mistress and I love the maid. What am I to do? I blush for her as I say it, but your mistress has so little sense that she dotes on my man and is ready to marry him. What next, Lisa, what next?

SYLVIA (*aside*). I'll conceal who I am. (*Aloud*) This is a strange predicament for you. But, sir, before anything else I want to apologize for being too free in our conversations.

DORIAN (*quickly*). Hush, Lisa. Your apology hurts me. It reminds me of the distance which separates us, and which breaks my heart.

SYLVIA. Are you seriously drawn to me? Do you love me to that extent?

DORIAN. To the extent of giving up all thoughts of marriage, since a union between us is impossible. The only happiness I am able to look forward to is not to be hated by you.

SYLVIA. A man whose heart went out to me in my humble situation deserves to be accepted; and I would grant you my love if I didn't fear I would injure your prospects in life.

DORIAN. Aren't you lovely enough as it is? Must you add a noble mind to all your charms?

SYLVIA. I hear someone. As far as your servant is concerned, have a little patience. We'll meet again and think of a way out.

DORIAN. I'll follow your advice. (*Exit Dorian.*)

SYLVIA. Merciful heavens, he turned into Dorian not a moment too soon.
(*Enter Thomas.*)

THOMAS. I wanted to see you, Sylvia. We left you so worried that I decided to come to your rescue. Listen to me.

SYLVIA (*quickly*). Don't worry, brother, I've quite different news for you!

THOMAS. Namely?

SYLVIA. He's not Trivet at all; he's Dorian.

THOMAS. Which one are you talking about?

SYLVIA. About him, I tell you. I found out a minute ago. He told me himself.

THOMAS. Who told you?

SYLVIA. Don't you understand me?

THOMAS. On my life, I don't understand a word.

SYLVIA. Never mind; let's find father and tell him. I'll need you too, brother. I've just had an idea. You'll pretend you're in love with me. You've already said something about it as a joke. But above all, please keep it a secret.

THOMAS. Of course, I'll have to keep it a secret; I don't know what it is.

SYLVIA. Come with me, Thomas. Let's not waste any time. Oh, this is the most amazing thing ever!

THOMAS. Heaven grant she hasn't gone mad!

ACT THREE

(Enter Dorian and Trivet.)

TRIVET. Sir, most honored master, I beg of you—

DORIAN. Again?

TRIVET. Be kind to my good luck. Don't put the jinx on my happiness now that it's blossoming. Don't blast the little bud.

DORIAN. Hang the clown! A hundred lashes on your back is what you deserve.

TRIVET. I agree. Give them to me. But when you're done, allow me to deserve a few more. Shall I go for the whip?

DORIAN. Villain!

TRIVET. Present! But being a villain doesn't prevent a man from striking gold.

DORIAN. What in heaven's name has gotten into you, you good-for-nothing?

TRIVET. Good-for-nothing suits me too. A villain is not disgraced by being called a good-for-nothing. And a good-for-nothing can still make a good marriage.

DORIAN. So, you rascal, you think I'm going to allow you to trick a gentleman and use my name to marry his daughter. If you ever mention this plot again, not only will I expose you to Mr. Humphrey, but I'll turn you out naked into the street. Is that clear?

TRIVET. May I suggest a compromise? The young lady worships me. She idolizes me. Suppose I tell her I am a servant, and suppose she is still hungry for me, will you let me call the fiddlers?

DORIAN. As soon as it's known who you are, I wash my hands of the whole business.

TRIVET. Good! I'm off to tell my angel the truth about me. I hope the little detail of a livery won't stand between us. May her love elevate me from my place at the sideboard to a seat at the table. (*Exit Trivet.*)

DORIAN. What has happened here—what has happened to me—is unbelievable. Still, I want to ask Lisa whether she has had any success with her mistress. She promised to help me out of this quandary. Perhaps I can find her alone.
(*Enter Thomas.*)

THOMAS. Stay, Trivet. I have something to tell you.

DORIAN. What can I do for you, sir?

THOMAS. Have you been flirting with Lisa?

DORIAN. She is so lovely—it's difficult not to talk about love with her.

THOMAS. And how does she respond?

DORIAN. She makes a joke of it.

THOMAS. You're clever, but aren't you playing the hypocrite with me?

DORIAN. No, I'm not. But why do you care? Suppose Lisa finds me appealing . . .

THOMAS. Finds you appealing? Where do you take these expressions? You know—your speech is rather too flowery for a lad of your class.

DORIAN. Sir, I know no other speech.

THOMAS. You're obviously using these refinements, these imitations of the gentleman, to turn Lisa's head.

DORIAN. I assure you, sir, that I am not imitating anyone. However, I can't believe that you came here to ridicule me. Was there something else? We were speaking about Lisa, about my feelings for her, and about the interest you take in the matter.

THOMAS. I detect a note of jealousy in your answer. A little moderation, if you please. You were saying that if Lisa finds you appealing . . . What then?

DORIAN. Why should you know anything about it, sir?

THOMAS. Because, even though I've bantered about this up to now, I won't stand for anything serious between you and her. Therefore I place you under orders to leave her alone—and no arguments, please. Not that I suspect her of being partial to you—she is too high-minded for that. But I wouldn't like to have Trivet for a rival.

DORIAN. I can believe you; because Trivet himself, though he is only Trivet, is not happy either to have you for a rival.

THOMAS. He'll have to get used to it.

DORIAN. He will. But, sir, how devoted are you to her?

THOMAS. Enough to engage myself seriously to her as soon as I've taken certain steps. Do you understand what that means?

DORIAN. Yes, I believe I do. And on these terms I daresay you've won her love.

THOMAS. Why not? Don't you think I'm a good catch?

DORIAN. You don't expect praise from your own rivals, I hope.

THOMAS. Your answer makes sense, and as such I excuse it. For the rest, I admit, reluctantly enough, that I can't boast of being loved. I'm not saying this because I owe you an explanation, far from it, but simply because a man ought to be truthful.

DORIAN. You surprise me, sir. Doesn't Lisa know your intentions?

THOMAS. Lisa knows all the good I mean to do her, and yet she seems indifferent to it. But I hope her common sense will bring her round. I advise a graceful retreat, my friend. Let her coolness to me console you when she becomes mine. Your livery can't possibly tip the scale in your favor; and, in short, you're not the man to contend with me.
(*Enter Sylvia.*)

THOMAS. Lisa!

SYLVIA. What has happened, sir? You seem vexed about something.

THOMAS. Nothing has happened. I was having a word with Trivet.

SYLVIA. He looks downcast. Were you abusing him?

DORIAN. This gentleman tells me that he loves you, Lisa.

SYLVIA. That's not my fault.

DORIAN. And he forbids me to love you.

SYLVIA. Does he also forbid me to seem lovable to you?

THOMAS. I can't stop him from loving you, my beautiful Lisa—only I won't allow him to tell you so.

SYLVIA. He doesn't tell me any more. He only repeats it.

THOMAS. At least he won't repeat it in my presence. Leave us now, Trivet.

DORIAN. I am waiting for her to give the order.

THOMAS. What?

SYLVIA. He says he's waiting, so be patient. . . .

DORIAN. Do you have a warm feeling for this gentleman, Lisa?

SYLVIA. You mean, do I love him? I won't require any prohibitions against *that!*

DORIAN. Is this the truth?

THOMAS. I'm playing a pretty part here! Away with him! Who does the fellow think he is?

DORIAN. He is simply Trivet.

THOMAS. Well, let him get out.

DORIAN (*aside*). What agony.

SYLVIA. Give way, Trivet, since he's angry.

DORIAN (*low, to Sylvia*). Perhaps you're happy to see me go.

THOMAS. That's enough. Out, out.

DORIAN. You hadn't told me about his love, Lisa. (*Exit Dorian.*)

SYLVIA. I would be an ingrate if I didn't love that man. Admit it.

THOMAS. Ha, ha, ha, ha!
(*Enter Mr. Humphrey.*)

MR. HUMPHREY. What are you laughing at, Tom?

THOMAS. At Dorian's anger. I forced him to leave Lisa.

SYLVIA. But what did he tell you during the tête-à-tête you had with him?

THOMAS. I never saw a man more baffled or in a worse temper.

MR. HUMPHREY. I'm not sorry to see him caught in his own trap. And all things considered, nothing could be more flattering for him than what you have done till now. But you've gone far enough.

THOMAS. Where exactly does he stand, sister?

SYLVIA. I don't know, my dear brother, but I have grounds for satisfaction.

THOMAS. "My dear brother," she says to me! And did you notice how sweet and pacified her voice has become?

Mr. Humphrey. Do you really expect him to propose marriage to you as a housemaid?

Sylvia. Yes, dear father, I expect it.

Thomas. "Dear father"! I don't believe it! And how she used to scold us! But suddenly we're all sugar.

Sylvia. I see you're determined not to overlook a word I say.

Thomas (*laughing*). You were quibbling over my words before, and I'm teasing you about yours now; it's my little revenge. Besides, I'm enjoying your happinesss as much as I did your misery.

Mr. Humphrey. Well, I'm going to be kinder to you than your brother. I give you a free hand in everything.

Sylvia. Father, if you knew how grateful I am! Dorian and I were made for each other. He *must* marry me. And I'll never forget what he is doing for me today—the amazing tenderness he has shown me. What a blessing this will be for our marriage! And I'll have you to thank for it, dear father, because you allowed me to have my way. He and I will love each other anew every time we remember our strange meeting. Our marriage will be unique. People will be touched when they hear our story. Oh this has been the most extraordinary adventure, the happiest, the most—

Thomas. Babble, babble, babble! Ha, ha, ha, ha! Isn't she eloquent!

Mr. Humphrey. I agree, however, that you'll be offering yourself quite a treat—that is, if you succeed in bringing him down.

Sylvia. It's as good as done. Dorian is vanquished. I am waiting for my prisoner.

Thomas. His cage will be more gilded than he thinks. But for the moment, I know he's suffering, and I am sorry for him.

Sylvia. Because it costs him so much to overcome himself, he will be all the more precious to me. He thinks that by marrying me he will grieve his father, betray his birth and jeopardize his fortune. These are great obstacles—and I want the satisfaction of triumphing over them. I would hate a victory given to me as a present. I want him to struggle. I want to see a fight between passion and reason.

THOMAS. And let reason perish, what?

MR. HUMPHREY. Which means you want him to feel to the marrow the folly he'll think he is committing. What insatiable vanity!

THOMAS. The vanity of a woman: there's not a crease in it. (*Enter Lisa.*)

MR. HUMPHREY. Hush, here comes Lisa. Let's see what she wants.

LISA. Sir, you told me earlier that you'd leave Dorian to my mercy; I took you at your word, and I've seasoned him as if it were for myself. You'll see a sound piece of work. He is done to a turn. But what's my next step? Does Miss Sylvia yield him to me?

MR. HUMPHREY. Once more, Sylvia, do you give up your claim to him?

SYLVIA. I do, Lisa, I surrender him to you. I hand over all my rights, and, to use your jargon, I'll never take a man I didn't do to a turn myself.

LISA. You mean I can marry him? And you, sir, what do you say?

MR. HUMPHREY. Yes, I agree.

THOMAS. So do I.

LISA. I do too, and I thank you all.

MR. HUMPHREY. Wait. Just one stipulation. You must tell him a little something about who you are. This will relieve us of our responsibility.

LISA. A little something means everything.

Mr. Humphrey. Well, now that you have him on a spit, I'm sure he can take another roasting. I don't believe he is a man you can frighten with your news.

Lisa. Here he comes, looking for me. Please leave me to my own devices. My masterpiece is at stake.

Mr. Humphrey. Fair enough. Away, children.

Sylvia. With pleasure.

Thomas. Let's go.
(*Exeunt Mr. Humphrey, Thomas and Sylvia. Enter Trivet.*)

Trivet. At last, my queen. Now that I have found you I am determined never to leave you again. I've suffered too much in your absence. Have you been avoiding me?

Lisa. A little, perhaps.

Trivet. Dear soul, balm of my heart, have you undertaken to put an end to my life?

Lisa. No, my dear. Its continuation is too precious to me.

Trivet. Oh, your words revive me!

Lisa. And you mustn't doubt my affection.

Trivet. I wish I could kiss these sweet little words and pick them off your mouth with mine.

Lisa. I avoided you because you were so very persistent about marrying me, and my father hadn't allowed me to give you an answer. But now that I have spoken to him, you may ask him for my hand whenever you wish.

Trivet. Before I ask it of him, allow me to ask it of you. And I want to thank it for being so charitable as to place itself in mine, which is truly unworthy of it.

Lisa. I lend you my hand for a second, on condition that you keep it forever.

Trivet. Dear little hand, plump and chubby little hand, I take you without haggling. I'm content with the favor you're doing me. It's the favor I'm returning which worries me.

LISA. That favor is greater than any I require.

TRIVET. Oh, no! You don't know this arithmetic as well as I do.

LISA. I regard your love as a gift from heaven.

TRIVET. Heaven won't go broke on this miserly gift.

LISA. I think it only too magnificent.

TRIVET. That's because you're not seeing it in full daylight.

LISA. You don't know how your modesty embarrasses me.

TRIVET. Don't expend your embarrassment on me. If I weren't modest, I'd be pretty brazen.

LISA. Sir, must I insist that I am the one who is honored by your affection?

TRIVET. Merciful heavens, I don't know where to turn.

LISA. Let me repeat, I know who I am.

TRIVET. I too know who I am. I'm not a choice acquaintance, alas; neither for myself nor for you. There'll be the devil to pay when you know me. Wait until you see the bottom of the barrel.

LISA (aside). This self-abasement is unnatural. (Aloud) Why are you saying all this to me?

TRIVET. You're beginning to smoke out the fox.

LISA. Again! What do you mean? You worry me. Aren't you . . .

TRIVET. Ay, ay, now you're unwrapping me!

LISA. I want to know the facts.

TRIVET (aside). I'd better prepare her for this. (Aloud) Madam, does your love have a strong constitution? Can it stand a great strain? Does a poor shelter terrify it? Because it will be shabbily lodged with me.

Lisa. You must reassure me! Who are you?

Trivet. I am . . . Have you ever seen counterfeit money? Do you know what a false coin is? Well, between that false coin and myself there's a kind of family resemblance.

Lisa. Come to the point! What is your name?

Trivet. My name? (*Aside*) Should I tell her my name is Trivet? No, she'll tell me I'm a rogue.

Lisa. Well?

Trivet (*aside*). Let's try a roundabout way. (*Aloud*) Madam, do you despise the soldier's trade?

Lisa. What do you call a soldier?

Trivet. For example, a soldier of the wardrobe.

Lisa. A soldier of the wardrobe! I can't be speaking to Dorian.

Trivet. Dorian is my captain.

Lisa. Oh what a rogue!

Trivet (*aside*). I knew it!

Lisa. Look at the rascal!

Trivet. I've come down in the world!

Lisa. For a whole hour I've been begging him to forgive me. I've been humiliating myself before this clown.

Trivet. And yet, my dear lady, if you preferred love to pride, I could be as serviceable to you as any gentleman.

Lisa (*laughing*). Ha, ha, ha! I can't help laughing! Do I prefer love to pride! Well, I'd better come to terms with you—go on, my pride is good-natured and forgives you.

Trivet. Do you mean it, my generous lady? What gratitude I promise you!

Lisa. Let's shake hands on it, Trivet. I was duped. A soldier of the wardrobe deserves a lady's hairdresser!

TRIVET. A lady's hairdresser!

LISA. The lady is *my* captain.

TRIVET. You cheat!

LISA. Take your revenge.

TRIVET. And I've been abasing myself before this hussy!

LISA. Let's settle our question. Do you love me?

TRIVET. I do. You didn't change your face when you changed your name. You know we promised to be true to each other in spite of any little mistake.

LISA. No harm done, I suppose. Let's dry our tears, pretend nothing happened, and give no one a chance to laugh. It seems your master doesn't know the facts about my mistress yet. Don't tell him; leave things as they are. Wait—I hear him coming. Sir, I am your servant.

TRIVET. And I yours, madam. (*Laughs*) Ha, ha, ha!
(*Exit Lisa. Enter Dorian.*)

DORIAN. That was Mr. Humphrey's daughter, wasn't it? Did you tell her who you are?

TRIVET. I did. Poor child. I found her as soft as a lamb; she didn't let out a whimper. When I told her that my name is Trivet and that I wear a servant's livery, she said to me, "Each one of us has his name in life, each one has his costume. Yours cost you nothing, but it is a pretty thing all the same."

DORIAN. What nonsense is this?

TRIVET. Nonsense that ends in a marriage proposal.

DORIAN. What! She agreed to marry you?

TRIVET. Poor girl . . . ruined for life. . . .

DORIAN. You're lying to me—she doesn't know who you are.

TRIVET. God in heaven! I'll marry her in my stable-coat if you provoke me! Let me tell you, sir, that the kind of love which I,

Trivet, inspire is unbreakable. Nor do I need silk embroidery to snare my game, as I'll prove to you if you'll kindly return my clothes.

DORIAN. You're an impostor. What you say is inconceivable. I see I'll have to warn Mr. Humphrey.

TRIVET. Who? Our father? The dear fellow! He's eating out of my hand. A jewel of a man. You'll be surprised.

DORIAN. You're mad. Have you seen Lisa?

TRIVET. Lisa? No. Maybe she crossed my path, but a gentleman pays no attention to a chambermaid. I leave that to you.

DORIAN. Go away. You're going berserk.

TRIVET. Your manners are improving, you know. That's what comes of keeping good company. Good-bye for now; once I'm married we'll live as equals. Your little maid is here. Good-day, Lisa. Take care of Trivet. He's not a bad sort.
(Enter Sylvia. Exit Trivet.)

DORIAN (aside). How she deserves to be loved! Why did Thomas have to forestall me?

SYLVIA. Where have you been, sir? I haven't been able to find you since I left Mr. Thomas. I want to give you an account of what I told Mr. Humphrey.

DORIAN (indifferently). I've been here all the time. You wish to tell me something?

SYLVIA (aside). How cold all of a sudden! (Aloud) I did the best I could to convince your valet of his unfitness. I tried as hard as possible to make him at least put off the wedding. He didn't even listen to me. I warn you, there is talk of sending for the notary. It's time for you to intervene.

DORIAN. I intend to. I have decided to leave incognito after writing a full explanation to Mr. Humphrey.

SYLVIA (aside). Leave? Oh, my God!

DORIAN. Don't you like my idea?

SYLVIA. Not much.

DORIAN. I can't think of anything better to do in my present situation, unless I speak out myself; and I can't bring myself to do that. Besides, I have other reasons for wanting to leave. I am no longer of any use here.

SYLVIA. Since I don't know your reasons, I can neither approve nor disapprove of them. And it's not my place to ask you.

DORIAN. It should be easy enough for you to guess, Lisa.

SYLVIA. Perhaps. For example, I think you rather like Mr. Humphrey's daughter.

DORIAN. Is that all you can see?

SYLVIA. There is something else I might suppose, but I am neither a fool nor vain enough even to think about it.

DORIAN. Nor courageous enough to speak of it. You wouldn't have anything obliging to tell me. Good-bye, Lisa.

SYLVIA. Take care! I don't think you understand me.

DORIAN. Thank you; but I'm sure the explanation wouldn't be flattering to me. Keep it secret until I'm gone.

SYLVIA. Are you serious about leaving?

DORIAN. You're afraid I'll change my mind.

SYLVIA. How kind of you to understand!

DORIAN. It's all very simple. Good-bye (*He moves away.*)

SYLVIA (*aside*). If he leaves now, my love is dead. I'll never marry him. (*She watches him out of a corner of her eye.*) He stopped. He is perplexed. He wants to see whether I'll turn around. But I won't call him back. And yet it would be strange if he left, after all I've done. Well, it's all finished. He is really going. I haven't as much influence over him as I thought. That clumsy brother of mine! He didn't really care, so he spoiled everything. And now I'm left empty-handed. What a sad conclusion! . . . Oh! There's Dorian again! I think he's coming back. I was wrong, I still love him. I'll pretend to leave and make him stop me. Our reconciliation ought to cost him a little anxiety.

DORIAN (*stopping her*). Please, Lisa, wait. There's something more I want to tell you.

SYLVIA. Tell me, sir?

DORIAN. I can't leave unless I convince you it's not wrong of me to go.

SYLVIA. There's no reason for you to explain. Why should you? I am only a servant; and how you've made me feel it!

DORIAN. I? Do you have the right to complain? You who saw me leave and said nothing?

SYLVIA. Hm! If I wanted to, I could answer that.

DORIAN. Answer, then. I ask nothing better than to be wrong. But what am I saying? Thomas loves you.

SYLVIA. That's true.

DORIAN. And you are responsive to his love. I knew it when I saw how anxious you were that I should go away. I understood then that I meant nothing to you.

SYLVIA. Responsive to his love! Who told you that? And how do you know that you mean nothing to me? You make up your mind too quickly.

DORIAN. Lisa, I beg of you, enlighten me in the name of everything that's dear to you!

SYLVIA. Enlighten a man who is leaving?

DORIAN. I'll stay.

SYLVIA. If you love me, please ask me no questions. You fear my indifference, but other than that, what do my feelings matter to you?

DORIAN. What do they matter to me, Lisa? Can you still doubt that I adore you?

SYLVIA. No, you've repeated it so often that I believe you. But why do you insist? What can I do with your love? This love is not serious for you. You'll find a thousand ways of forgetting it. The distance between us, distractions, the attempts of others to bring you to your senses, the pleasures of a man of your station—all this will drive your love out of your mind, though you urge it ever so ruthlessly on me. I think you'll be laughing at it, and rightly so, the moment you leave this house. But what if I can't forget it? What help will I find? Who will compensate me for having lost you? Do you understand that if I loved you, nothing else in this world would be capable of attracting me? Think in what state you'd be leaving me—be generous—conceal your love from me. I myself—seeing you as you are now—I wouldn't dare tell you that I loved you. If you knew my feelings, you might do—I don't know what, something senseless—and that is why I refuse to reveal them.

DORIAN. Lisa, dearest, your words are burning through me. I adore you. And I respect you. All rank, birth, and fortune vanish in the presense of a soul like yours. I would be ashamed if my pride held out against you. Take my heart and my hand.

SYLVIA. I should, but I am generous enough to suppress my joy; and yet, how long can I hold out?

DORIAN. You do love me?

SYLVIA. No, no. But if you ask me once more, beware.

DORIAN. Your threats don't frighten me any more!

SYLVIA. And what about Thomas? Have you forgotten him?

DORIAN. No, Lisa. Thomas no longer worries me. He is nothing to you. You can't deceive me any more. You do reciprocate my love, and you'll never rob me of that certainty.

SYLVIA. Oh, I wouldn't think of trying. Hold fast to your certainty. We'll see what you do with it.

DORIAN. Do you consent to be mine?

SYLVIA. What? You'd marry me in spite of your fortune and your rank, and you'd submit to your father's anger for my sake?

DORIAN. My father will forgive me as soon as he sees you. Besides, I have enough of my own for both of us. And your merit outweighs my birth. Don't argue, Lisa; I'll never change.

SYLVIA. You'll never change! Dorian, do you know that you enchant me?

DORIAN. Don't hold back your love. Let it answer my question. Will you be mine?

SYLVIA. I've worn him out at last! You will never, never change?

DORIAN. Never, dear Lisa.

SYLVIA. So much love!
(*Enter Mr. Humphrey, Thomas, Trivet, and Lisa.*)

SYLVIA. Father, you wanted your daughter to marry Dorian. Here she is, and she obeys you with unspeakable joy.

DORIAN. What are you saying? You her father, Mr. Humphrey?

SYLVIA. Yes, Dorian. We each had the same idea for making the other's acquaintance. Need I say more? I am sure that you love me; now it is your turn to know my feelings for you. Think of the refinements I used to win your heart, and then judge how important you are to me.

MR. HUMPHREY. Do you recognize this letter? Here's how I discovered your scheme. But Sylvia knew nothing about it until you told her yourself.

DORIAN. I can't find words to express my happiness. But what delights me most is the proof which I gave you of my love.

THOMAS. Will Dorian forgive me for making Trivet angry?

DORIAN. He not only forgives you. He is indebted to you.

TRIVET (*to Lisa*). Let me see you smile, madam! You've come down in the world, but you're not to be pitied. You still have your Trivet.

LISA. What a consolation. *You're* the one who drew the lucky prize.

TRIVET. I'm not complaining. Before I knew who you were, your dowry was worth more than you. Now you're worth more than your dowry. Three cheers for the happy groom!

THE END

The Wiles of Love
(L'Heureux stratagème)

Presented for the first time at
the Théâtre Italien on June 6, 1733

CHARACTERS

BELINDA
ARABELLA
DORIAN
CAPTAIN COXE
FANNY
PUFF
TRIVET
MR. NUBBINS
A LACKEY
A NOTARY

The action takes place in Belinda's country residence.

ACT ONE

(*Enter Dorian and Mr. Nubbins.*)

DORIAN. Come now, Mr. Nubbins, what do you want? Speak up; what can I do for you?

MR. NUBBINS. Well, you see, like the man said, you could do me a favor.

DORIAN. Tell me what it is.

MR. NUBBINS. Ain't that Mr. Dorian all over! A man what never argufies when it comes to doing his neighbor a good turn. I never did see the likes of him for a helpful deposition.

DORIAN. Out with it, man. I'll be delighted to be useful to you.

MR. NUBBINS. Oh, no, Mr. Dorian, it's all of us what's delighted with you.

DORIAN. Well, then—

MR. NUBBINS. First put your hat on your head, sir.

DORIAN. No, I never cover my head.

MR. NUBBINS. That's good; but I always cover mine, and that's good too.

DORIAN. To the point.

MR. NUBBINS (*expansively*). Yes, sir. How've you been, Mr. Dorian? You've put on flesh since I met you last. I remember the days when you was as thin as a bean, but God bless you, you've grown plump and you're looking fit.

195

DORIAN. Thank you for the compliment; but I seem to recall that you wanted to tell me something.

MR. NUBBINS. Well, I was only spooning out a few compliments between this and that, dutiful-like.

DORIAN. The trouble is that I've business to attend to.

MR. NUBBINS. Hang business! Nothing but one headache after the other.

DORIAN. I'll be gone in a moment. Finish what you came to say.

MR. NUBBINS. I'm beginning. It's about my daughter Fanny, and for love of her because she's a-going to be married up to Puff, your footman.

DORIAN. I know.

MR. NUBBINS. To which I know you've given your consent, being that Fanny is chambermaid to Miss Belinda, who's a-going to take you for her mate.

DORIAN. So?

MR. NUBBINS. So I come to ask you a favor, that's if you don't mind.

DORIAN. What is the favor?

MR. NUBBINS. Well, there's going to be the trousseau for Fanny; there's going to be a wedding, and then a shambles at the wedding, and then vittles to buy for the shambles, and cash to pitch in for the vittles. Nothing but cash anywhere a body looks, except that we haven't got none. So that if you, being on cozy terms with Miss Belinda, could ask her to loan me a little advance on my wages as gardener—

DORIAN. I understand you, Mr. Nubbins, but I'd rather give you the advance myself than ask it of Miss Belinda, who is not likely to heed any request of mine today. You're mistaken if you think that I am about to marry her. Captain Coxe seems to have supplanted me. Go to him; but if he won't listen to you, I'll give you the money myself.

Mr. Nubbins. You don't mean it! What you tell me stoopefies me so, I can't hardly find the words to thank you. A sweet gentleman like you, with the face of a prince and the heart to give me your own money, forsook by your lady-love! It can't be, Mr. Dorian, it can't be. Why, Miss Belinda is near being my own child; it was my wife, may she rest in peace, what gave her suck. She was a decent woman, was my wife, and surely her milk must have took after her. Cheer up, Mr. Dorian, and don't be worried; I tell you Captain Coxe is a pigment of your imagination.

Dorian. I'm sorry, but what I have told you is only too true.

Mr. Nubbins. By gad, if I believed you, I'm the man to tell her she's done you wrong. A lady I saw in her diapers! Do you want me to preach her a sermon, Mr. Dorian?

Dorian. And what would you tell her, my good fellow?

Mr. Nubbins. What wouldn't I tell her! "And what is the meaning of this, madam, what is the meaning of this?" That's what I would tell her, because God strike me if I didn't dandle her in my arms when she was a baby; which gives me the pervilege of speaking my mind.

Dorian. Meantime here's Puff, looking as glum as can be. I wonder what news he brings.
(Enter Puff.)

Puff. Uff!

Dorian. What's the matter?

Puff. Much trouble for you, and quantities of trouble for me as a result; because a good servant has to copy his master.

Dorian. Go on.

Mr. Nubbins. What's ailing you?

Puff. Prepare yourself for grief, dear master; and a great deal of it, I'm afraid.

Dorian. Tell me.

Puff. I'm crying in advance, so I can cheer up afterwards.

Mr. Nubbins. My eyes are beginning to itch too.

Dorian. Are you going to come to the point?

Puff. Alas, I've nothing to tell you, because I know you'll be unhappy; I'm prognosticating your sorrow.

Dorian. I can live without your prognostications.

Mr. Nubbins. Bad news can wait, better late than soon.

Puff. A while ago as I was finishing—but that's a detail.

Dorian. I want to know everything.

Puff. It's nothing. I was finishing a bottle of wine somebody had forgotten in the drawing room, when I thought I heard Miss Belinda coming with Captain Coxe.

Dorian (*sighing*). And then?

Puff. I was afraid she'd scold me for drinking on the sly, so I ran to the kitchen with my bottle; and first I drank it up in order to make it safe.

Mr. Nubbins. That's what I would have did.

Dorian. Will you drop your bottle and come to what concerns me?

Puff. I mentioned the bottle because it happened to be there; I didn't *want* to introduce it.

Mr. Nubbins. Anyway it's too late, he drunk it all up.

Puff. Now then, the bottle is empty, and I have put it down on the floor.

Dorian. Still at the bottle?

Puff. Next, without breathing a word, I looked through the keyhole.

Dorian. And you saw Belinda with Captain Coxe in the drawing room?

Puff. No. That dog of a locksmith had made the keyhole so small, I couldn't see a thing.

Mr. Nubbins. Damn.

Dorian. In other words, you couldn't be sure it was Belinda at all.

Puff. Yes, I could. Because my ears recognized her voice, and the voice couldn't be there without the person.

Mr. Nubbins. He's right, the voice and the person couldn't help being together.

Dorian. All right. What did they say?

Puff. I don't know. I only remember the idea, I've forgotten the words.

Dorian. So be it; tell me the idea.

Puff. I can't without the words. But, sir, they were together, they were laughing as hard as they could, that ugly Captain Coxe was opening a mouth wider than—anyway, nobody laughs like that without being in a good mood.

Mr. Nubbins. Well, it's a sign they're happy; but that's all.

Puff. True. But their happiness is going to bring us bad luck. When a man is that full of cheer, it's usually a bad omen for somebody else, and (*pointing to Dorian*) there's the somebody else for you.

Dorian. Bah. Leave me alone. Did you tell Miss Arabella that I wanted to speak with her?

Puff. I don't remember whether I told her; but I know I was supposed to.
(*Enter Fanny.*)

Fanny. Sir, I don't know what you're about, but your composure surprises me. If you're not careful, you're going to lose my mistress. I may be wrong, but I'm afraid I'm not.

Dorian. I agree with you, Fanny; but what can I do about it?

MR. NUBBINS. So it's all true, Fanny?

FANNY. It is. The captain never leaves her side; he makes her laugh, he gushes over her, he whispers to her; and she smiles. Her heart may join in the game, if it hasn't already. I'm worried, sir; first because I like you, but also because here's a lad who's supposed to marry me, and if you don't become master of the house, we'll be in trouble.

PUFF. Separate households, you know; very annoying.

DORIAN. What discourages me so is that I don't see any remedy. Belinda avoids me.

MR. NUBBINS. A bad sign, sure enough.

PUFF. And what does that dog Trivet say to you, Fanny?

FANNY. He's very sweet to me, and I'm very rude to him.

MR. NUBBINS. Well done, my girl; always rude to him, always a grouchy face when he comes by; shake your head when he talks to you, and tell him, "On your way, boy." Faithful from head to toe! That'll teach Miss Belinda, won't it, sir?

DORIAN. I could die, I'm so unhappy!

MR. NUBBINS. Don't die, sir, you'd spoil everything. Better set a snare to catch your bird again.

FANNY. Here comes Miss Belinda now, and alone, too. Let me talk to her, Mr. Dorian, and find out what's on her mind. When you come back, I'll repeat our conversation to you.

DORIAN. I'll leave you.

PUFF. Remember, always a grouchy face when he comes by, and shake your head when he talks to you.

FANNY. Don't worry. (*They leave.*)
(*Enter Belinda.*)

BELINDA. Fanny, I was looking for you. Who was here with you? I thought I saw somebody leaving as I came in.

FANNY. It was Mr. Dorian, madam.

BELINDA. Oh, I wanted to speak to you about him. What does he say, Fanny?

FANNY. He says he has cause to be dissatisfied; and I do believe he's right. What do you think, madam?

BELINDA. Does he still love me?

FANNY. How can you ask? Does he still love you! You know he hasn't changed. But you, madam, have you given up loving him?

BELINDA. What do you understand by "given up"? When did I ever love him? The truth is, I took notice of him, that's all; and to take notice of a man is not yet to love him. It may lead to love, but it is not love.

FANNY. And yet I have heard you call him a most attractive man.

BELINDA. That may be.

FANNY. I have seen you waiting impatiently for his arrival.

BELINDA. I have a nervous disposition.

FANNY. And unhappy when he didn't come.

BELINDA. You're perfectly right. I repeat, I took notice of him, and I still do. But I haven't engaged myself to him in any way; indeed, I came here to tell you that when he speaks to you again, you should skillfully turn him away from me.

FANNY. And all this in favor of Captain Coxe, because you admire his mustache.[1] How can a woman who is supposedly sensible be so fickle? People will talk, you know.

BELINDA. Very good, if you insist, I'm fickle. Do you think I can be frightened by a word? Fickle! What a dreadful insult! There are words, my dear, which people use to alarm cowards, words which carry a great deal of weight because nobody thinks about them, but which mean nothing in fact.

[1] In the original, Fanny refers to the Gascon accent of our Captain Coxe (the Chevalier Damis). The Gascons, it will be remembered, had the reputation of being braggarts. [Tr.]

FANNY. Goodness, madam, how hard-bitten you sound! I didn't know you were so far gone. You're ready, I see, to break your word.

BELINDA. Oh, well. Say I break my word—break it a thousand times, if you like—I am simply obeying orders from my heart. Say I betray a thousand men; I am still only obeying my heart, and my heart's inclinations are uncontrollable. What are you trying to prove to me? The truth is that in a woman unfaithfulness is no crime. On the contrary, I say that the moment she is tempted, a woman must never hesitate to exchange one man for another. Otherwise she is guilty of deception, which is a hideous sin.

FANNY. But, but . . . Well, the way you're turning everything around, I see you really have a point. Yes, I understand that unfaithfulness can be a duty sometimes. I never suspected it before!

BELINDA. And yet you see how obvious it is.

FANNY. So obvious that now I have to ask myself whether I shouldn't make a change of my own.

BELINDA. Dorian is ridiculous. Because he loves me, I'm not to dare digress with so much as a glance? Only *he* is to be allowed to think me young and charming? Must I be a hundred years old for everybody else, bury my attractions, and devote myself to all the austerities I can devise?

FANNY. This is apparently what he wants.

BELINDA. No doubt about it. That is how these gentlemen would like us to live. To listen to them, a woman's universe should consist in one man. All the others are crossed off, they might as well be dead. And if you miss them now and then, if your self-esteem hungers for a little attention, what of it? You've been dumb and faithful, and you should be satisfied. You have your man, enjoy him as best you can, and be still. Do you see how unjust this is, Fanny, how very unjust? Go now, go speak to Dorian, forget your scruples. Do men think twice when they want to leave us? Don't we see every day how unreliable they are? And have they privileges which are denied to us? Absurd! Captain Coxe likes me; I don't dislike him; and I refuse to punish my inclination.

FANNY. Bravo, madam; now that you've instructed me, let forsaken lovers take their complaints elsewhere; you've cured me of my compassion.

BELINDA. Mind you, I don't despise Dorian; but we are often bored by people we value. Here he is again. Let me escape from his groans; speak to him—rid me of him.
(*Dorian enters and stops Belinda. Puff is with him.*)

DORIAN. Are you running away from me, Belinda?

BELINDA. Oh, it's you, Dorian. No, I'm not running away; I was only leaving the room.

DORIAN. May I beg you for one second of your time?

BELINDA. One second, but literally; I'm expecting guests in the house.

DORIAN. They will be announced, madam. Allow me to speak to you about my love.

BELINDA. Is that all? I know your love by heart. What does your love want of me?

DORIAN. I can see that I am a nuisance to you.

BELINDA. To tell you the truth, your prelude is less than entertaining.

DORIAN. How unhappy I am! What have I become for you? You are driving me to despair.

BELINDA. My dear Dorian, when will you get rid of that lugubrious voice and that somber face of yours?

DORIAN. My love will not survive these cruel replies.

BELINDA. Cruel replies! Listen to him! You would have made a marvelous hero in a romance, Dorian; yes, you've missed your vocation.

DORIAN. Ungrateful woman!

BELINDA (*laughing*). This rhetoric isn't going to mend me, I'm afraid. (*Puff is groaning.*) Look! Your misery is so contagious that even your footman has caught it. Listen to him sighing his heart out!

PUFF. My master is suffering, so I'm suffering too.

DORIAN. I need all my respect for you to contain my anger.

BELINDA. Oh? And why are you angry, may I ask? Are you complaining because you care for me? I can't help that; I hope it's no crime to be attractive to you. Or are you unhappy because I have failed to return your love? But that's hardly my fault either. You can wish that love had come to me, but don't, I beg you, reproach me because it didn't. Be sensible, my dear Dorian. Your feelings are not law to me; I am not in your debt just because you love me. You're free to sigh, but don't expect me to keep you company. Accustom yourself to the thought that your tears needn't make me weep; they needn't even amuse me. There was a time, I confess, when I endured them more cheerfully, but I warn you that now they bore me. I advise you to act accordingly. And with this, good day.

DORIAN. In plain words, you no longer love me.

BELINDA. Ha! Your "no longer" is really bizarre. I don't recollect ever having loved you.

DORIAN. Don't you? Good. I swear to you that I shall forget it too.

BELINDA. Believe me, you will have forgotten what was only a dream. (*She leaves.*)

DORIAN (*stopping Fanny, who is leaving too*). Unprincipled woman . . . Fanny, wait!

PUFF. What a lesson Miss Belinda has taught us!

DORIAN (*to Fanny*). You've spoken to her about me. I know only too well what she thinks, and yet—what has she told you in private?

FANNY. I'm sorry, sir, but I can't stop. Miss Belinda is expecting guests, and she may need me.

PUFF. Ho, ho, listen to her!

DORIAN. Have we lost you too, Fanny?

PUFF. Are you another fraud?

DORIAN. Speak up; what reasons does she give for her behavior?

FANNY. Excellent reasons, Mr. Dorian. To be faithful is a waste of time; and furthermore it's wrong; what's the good of being pretty, only one man has the advantage of it, the others are dead; one mustn't deceive anybody; and besides, a woman is buried, her self-esteem lies neglected; it's as though she were a hundred years old. Not that she doesn't appreciate you, but then boredom sets in; she might as well be an old woman; and all this works to your detriment.

DORIAN. That was a very strange speech.

PUFF. Those are the foulest-looking words I ever saw.

DORIAN. Make yourself a little clearer, Fanny.

FANNY. What, didn't you understand me? Well, sir, we have taken notice of you.

DORIAN. Do you mean she loves me after all?

FANNY. No. Taking notice may lead to love, but it is not love.

DORIAN. I'm at sea. How does Captain Coxe stand with her?

FANNY. He's a very attractive man.

DORIAN. And what about myself?

FANNY. You were very attractive too. Do you understand me now?

DORIAN. This is outrageous.

PUFF. And what do you think of me, housemaid of my soul?

FANNY. Of you? I take notice of you.

PUFF. And I curse you, charwoman of the devil! (*Fanny leaves.*)
Pretty people we're dealing with, sir.

DORIAN. My heart has stopped beating.

PUFF. My lungs won't breathe.
(*Enter Arabella.*)

ARABELLA. You are hanging your head, Dorian; what's the matter?

DORIAN. Oh, Arabella, I am betrayed, I am murdered, the dagger
has been plunged into my bosom.

PUFF. Madam, I've been strangled, my throat has been cut, I've
been taken notice of!

ARABELLA. I suppose that Belinda is somehow involved in this.

DORIAN. She is, she is.

ARABELLA. Let me have a word with you.

DORIAN. By all means. I myself wanted to speak with you.

ARABELLA. Tell your man to keep watch at the door, in case
somebody comes.

DORIAN. Do so, Puff, and give us a sign the moment you see
anyone.

PUFF. Heaven help us! Here we are cast out onto the pavement,
all three of us; yes, you too, madam; because your Captain is no
better than our Belinda and our Fanny. Here are three hearts in
the gutter. (*He goes out.*)

ARABELLA. Well, it seems we are both jilted.

DORIAN. As you can see, madam.

ARABELLA. And you don't mean to take any action?

DORIAN. What action can I take? Our dismissal is final. To think how badly we were all matched! Why am I not in love with you?

ARABELLA. Well, Dorian, I suggest you try to fall in love with me now.

DORIAN. Ah, I do wish I could succeed.

ARABELLA. The answer is not flattering, but your state of mind justifies it.

DORIAN. My dear madam, I beg your forgiveness. I am so distracted, I don't know what I'm saying.

ARABELLA. Oh, nothing I didn't expect; don't trouble to explain.

DORIAN. Your charms are evident to all, Arabella, and I have lamented my negligence a hundred times; a hundred times I have told myself—

ARABELLA. Stop! The more you try to compliment me, the more you really abuse me.

DORIAN. And yet, madam, you are the only person I can turn to. I agree: I must fall in love with you; how else can I punish the woman I hate and adore?

ARABELLA. No, Dorian, I know a pleasanter way of avenging ourselves. I am willing enough to punish Belinda, but I intend to punish and restore her to you with a single blow.

DORIAN. What! restore Belinda to me?

ARABELLA. More loving than ever.

DORIAN. Is it possible?

ARABELLA. Possible even without the trouble of falling in love with me.

DORIAN. Do as you wish, madam.

ARABELLA. My wish is this: don't love me, but make believe you do.

DORIAN. With all my heart. I accept any condition you set.

ARABELLA. Tell me; was Belinda deeply in love with you?

DORIAN. So I believed.

ARABELLA. Was she convinced that you loved her as much?

DORIAN. I adore her, and she knows it.

ARABELLA. That's in our favor.

DORIAN. But what do you propose to do about the Captain, who abandoned you and who loves her now? Shall we give him time to win Belinda?

ARABELLA. If Belinda thinks she cares for him, she is mistaken; she only wanted to take him away from me. And if she thinks she is no longer in love with you, she is mistaken again: only her vanity is neglecting you.

DORIAN. That's possible, of course.

ARABELLA. I know what women are. Leave her to me. Here is what I intend to do. Wait—somebody is coming.
(*Enter Puff.*)

PUFF. Oh, what misery!

DORIAN. Are you interrupting us only to sigh under our noses?

PUFF. I'm done, sir. But I wanted to tell Miss Arabella that there's a rascal outside who wishes to speak with her. Should I let him in, or may I thrash him?

ARABELLA. Who is it?

PUFF. A scoundrel who made off with the girl I loved, and whose name is Trivet.

ARABELLA. The Captain's valet. Show him in; I want to talk to him.

PUFF. Oh, the rabble you're acquainted with, madam! (*He goes.*)

ARABELLA. This Trivet is a subtle and clever fellow, in spite of his livery. I've set him to spy for me on his own master and on Belinda. Let's hear what he reports. I want to make sure that they are really falling in love with each other. But if you're not strong enough to listen with indifference to whatever he may tell us, you ought to leave.

DORIAN. I'm outraged, but you can count on me.
(*Enter Puff and Trivet.*)

PUFF. You can go in, Mr. Ruffian.

TRIVET. I'll answer you when I leave.

PUFF. And I'm getting a reply ready that won't cost me a syllable. (*He leaves.*)

ARABELLA. Come here, Trivet, come here; what news for me?

TRIVET. Shall I speak in this gentleman's presence, madam?

ARABELLA. Yes, it's quite safe.

DORIAN (*pretending ignorance*). Who is in question here?

ARABELLA. Belinda and Captain Coxe. Do stay; I think you will be amused.

DORIAN. Gladly, then.

TRIVET. Mr. Dorian might even be fascinated.

DORIAN. We'll see.

TRIVET. As soon as I had promised you, madam, to keep my master and Miss Belinda under observation, I placed myself in ambush—

ARABELLA. To the point, Mr. Trivet; abbreviate.

TRIVET. Excuse me, madam, when I abbreviate I never finish.

ARABELLA. Does the Captain still love me?

TRIVET. Not a vestige of love, he doesn't know who you are.

ARABELLA. And does he love Belinda?

TRIVET. Does he love her! He is wounded to the core. And you're making a molehill out of a mountain. His heart is on fire, madam; love has utterly consumed him.

DORIAN (*putting on a cheerful air*). And I don't suppose Miss Belinda hates him in return.

TRIVET. By no means. The truth of the matter lies a thousand miles the other way.

DORIAN. I mean, she responds to his love, I suppose.

TRIVET. Tut, tut. She doesn't respond; the responses are done with; or rather, in this business there was never time for demand and response. Imagine two hearts dashing off together; never was there such speed; and quite impossible to tell who emitted the first sigh; it was a regular duet.

DORIAN. Ha, ha, ha! . . . (*Aside*) I'm dying!

ARABELLA (*aside*). Be careful. (*Aloud*) But can you prove any of this?

TRIVET. I have infallible witnesses: my eyes and my ears. Yesterday Miss Belinda—

DORIAN. That's enough. They love each other; the story ends. What can he possibly add?

ARABELLA. Still, I'd like him to finish.

TRIVET. Thank you, madam. Yesterday Miss Belinda and my master were strolling about the grounds. Picture me following them at a distance. They enter the wood; so do I; they turn into an alley; I conceal myself in the thickets. They speak to each other, but I catch only a confusion of voices. I slither, I slide, and between bush and shrub I manage to hear, and even to see them. "Bully, bully," Captain Coxe is saying, holding a portrait in one hand, and Miss Belinda's hand in the other. "Bully!" says he. For, as he is a military man, at this point I become one too in my zeal to serve you and to be exact.[2]

[2] Here and throughout, I have replaced the "Chevalier gascon" by the military man. [Tr.]

ARABELLA. Very good.

DORIAN (*aside*). Very bad.

TRIVET. Now this portrait, madam, though I could see only a chin and an earlobe, was a portrait of Miss Belinda. "Yes," says she, "I'm told that it is a fair resemblance." "A bull's eye," says my master; "couldn't be more accurate, except for a thousand attractions I adore in you, which the painter could only look at; his art gave up; only the brush of nature itself was able to paint them."—"Come, come," says Miss Belinda, "you flatter me"—her eyes sparkling with vanity—"you flatter me." "No, madam, or else strike off my head; I myself demote you when I talk about your charms; no words can reach them; you get your due only in my heart."—"But aren't we both dwelling there—Arabella and I?" asks Miss Belinda. "Arabella and you!" cries my master; "and where would I billet *her*? You would be quartered in a thousand hearts of mine, if I had them; my love doesn't know where to stop, it gallops all over my words, my feelings, my thoughts, my soul!" And all the time, he was kissing, now Miss Belinda's hand, and now the portrait. Each time Miss Belinda took her hand away, he flung himself on the picture; when she asked for the picture back, he would catch her hand again; and right and left and right and left it went; very entertaining to watch.

DORIAN. Oh, madam, what a story.
(*Arabella makes a sign to Dorian to be still.*)

TRIVET. Did you say something, sir?

DORIAN. No, I was only telling Miss Arabella that it was a comical scene.

TRIVET. I should say so. Whereupon: "Give me my picture again"—"Oh, Belinda"—"Oh, Captain"—"But, madam, if I return the copy, let the original grant me compensation"—"I really can't"—"You really must." And then Captain Coxe fell on his knees. "Madam, in the name of your innumerable attractions, deliver up the resemblance, while I bide my time for the original; my devotion requires a hostage!"—"But, Captain Coxe, to give one's portrait is to give one's heart away."—"What of it, madam, I can bear to have them both!"—"But—"—"No more buts; my life is yours, the portrait is mine; let each keep his share."—"Well, you are taking it, Captain, I am not giving it."—"Agreed! the responsibility's mine; I've captured it, and you've only allowed me to keep what I seize."—"You abuse my kindness, alas." That sigh belongs to Miss Belinda. The next one comes from the Captain: "Ah, I am happy . . ."

DORIAN. Oh . . .

TRIVET. And Mr. Dorian supplies the third.

DORIAN. Only because these two sighs were so amusing; I was imitating them. Miss Arabella, do imitate them too.

ARABELLA. No, not I, I understand nothing about sighs, but I can imagine them. Oh, ah, oh. (*She laughs.*)

TRIVET. This morning in the gallery—

DORIAN (*aside to Arabella*). Stop him; I can't hold out.

ARABELLA. That will do, Trivet.

TRIVET. I have a few fragments left, each of the choicest quality.

ARABELLA. But I won't need them. I know enough.

TRIVET. Am I still to enjoy the emoluments of this assignment, madam?

ARABELLA. No, your work is done.

TRIVET. Would Mr. Dorian care to lodge me in his service?

DORIAN. No.

TRIVETT. This no, if I am not mistaken, discharges me without reply; and so I take my humble leave. (*He goes out.*)

ARABELLA. Their secret understanding is now beyond all doubt; but we shall fail if you continue to play your role as badly as you did just now.

DORIAN. I confess that the story he told made me suffer; but I'll control myself better in the future. Oh, wretched girl! Never would she give me her portrait.
(*Enter Puff.*)

PUFF. Sir, your pickpocket is coming this way.

DORIAN. Who?

PUFF. One of our two thieves, the master of mine.

DORIAN. That will do. (*Puff leaves.*)

ARABELLA. I'll leave you too. We've had no time to elaborate our plan; but in the meantime, remember: you are in love with me; this must be believed. Your rival is coming, and you must pretend to be indifferent. That is all I have time to tell you.

DORIAN. Trust me, I'll play my part.
(*Arabella leaves, and Captain Coxe appears.*)

CAPTAIN COXE. You're just the man I'm looking for, Dorian; I want a word with you.

DORIAN. With pleasure, Captain; but quickly; I have letters to write, and I want to catch the post.

CAPTAIN COXE. I'll be as quick as a trigger. Dorian, I'm your friend, and I'm asking you to relieve me of a scruple.

DORIAN. You?

CAPTAIN COXE. Yes; you could rid me of a quibble which my honor has raised against me. Tell me whether my honor is right or wrong. There's a rumor going about that you love Belinda. I don't credit it. But the case of conscience I'm placing before you depends on the yes or no in reply to this question.

DORIAN. I understand you, Captain. You would like me no longer to care.

CAPTAIN COXE. That's it. I love the lady; and my ticklish conscience requires your indifference.

DORIAN. Does she favor you?

CAPTAIN COXE. I don't need any favors. She does me justice.

DORIAN. That is to say, she likes you.

CAPTAIN COXE. The moment I loved her, all was said. Spare my modesty.

DORIAN. Modesty aside, I ask you in plain language: does she love you?

CAPTAIN COXE. The answer is yes. Her eyes have sent out probes; they've fired on my heart; they're demanding a surrender. Do I negotiate for terms? I want a safe-conduct from you.

DORIAN. You have it, provided you give me one in return.

CAPTAIN COXE. To go where?

DORIAN. To a pair of beautiful eyes of your acquaintance.

CAPTAIN COXE. The beautiful eyes of Arabella?

DORIAN. Yes.

CAPTAIN COXE. And you're holding your fire because of me?

DORIAN. I am.

CAPTAIN COXE. Attack; she's yours.

DORIAN. I warn you I mean to marry her.

CAPTAIN COXE. And I inform you there'll be a wedding in our camp as well.

DORIAN. You'll marry Belinda?

CAPTAIN COXE. My posterity hopes so.

DORIAN. Soon?

CAPTAIN COXE. Tomorrow our celibacy may expire.

DORIAN (troubled). Good-bye, Captain; I'm delighted.

CAPTAIN COXE. Let's shake hands. Are we friends?

DORIAN. Oh, yes . . .

CAPTAIN COXE. You're mine, I tell you, and I'm yours for a century; after that, we'll renew the pact.

DORIAN. Yes, of course. Tomorrow? . . .

CAPTAIN COXE. What do you mean, tomorrow? You're my friend past, present, and future. The feeling is mutual, I hope.

DORIAN. Of course. Good-bye . . . (*He leaves.*)
(*Enter Trivet.*)

TRIVET. I was waiting for him to leave, sir, before coming in.

CAPTAIN COXE. What do you want? I'm in a hurry to see Belinda again.

TRIVET. Wait; by God, this is serious. I saw Miss Arabella and gave her my report.

CAPTAIN COXE. You confided in her that I love Belinda and that Belinda loves me? What was her answer? Quick!

TRIVET. Her answer was that you're doing a good thing.

CAPTAIN COXE. Which I intend to keep doing. I'll see you later.

TRIVET. Stop, sir! You can't be serious. You must see Miss Arabella again and fan her love a little, otherwise you're a dead man, you're carried off the battlefield, you're wiped out of her memory. (*Captain Coxe laughs.*) I don't see anything to laugh at.

CAPTAIN COXE. Wiped out or not—what does it matter? I die in one memory, I revive in the next. Doesn't Belinda resurrect me?

TRIVET. To be sure; but I'm afraid you'll be meeting there with sudden death again. She killed Mr. Dorian with a single flip of whimsy.

CAPTAIN COXE. No, Trivet; the whimsy that killed him stands before you; I dispatched him; and he's not the first man I've brought low. Don't fret, my boy; I've battled my way to her heart, and there I'll stay.

TRIVET. You'll pitch your tent in it for twenty-four hours; nobody settles in Miss Belinda's heart.

CAPTAIN COXE. Stuff! This is a love Captain Coxe has lit, and it will live as long as she does. Chin up, and trust your master. I never retreat. Kick your doubts out of your mind.

TRIVET. I've tried, but I haven't succeeded. However, here's Fanny. I wish you could ask Miss Belinda to make her love me. (*Enter Fanny.*)

FANNY. Sir, Miss Belinda wants to see you.

CAPTAIN COXE. I'm flying to her, Fanny. Meantime you can mend this fool's wits; you've run off with his brains—he tells me he loves you.

FANNY. Why doesn't he confide in me?

TRIVET. Very well, my pigeon; I love you; and now you know as much as I do.

FANNY. I see. Try me, why don't you? What can you lose? And now you know more than you did before. I'm off to announce you to my mistress, sir. Good-bye, Trivet.

TRIVET. Good-bye, my beauty. (*Fanny leaves.*) You were right, sir, by God you were right! Our prospects are excellent. We seem to be marked for success.

CAPTAIN COXE. I'll vouch for yours, Trivet.

TRIVET. Your word will have to do, sir—pending a better guarantee.

ACT TWO

(Enter Dorian and Puff.)

DORIAN. Come here, I want a word with you.

PUFF. A dozen, if you like.

DORIAN. Puff, I notice you haven't stopped running after Fanny.

PUFF. That's because I can't catch her unless I run; she takes to her heels every time she sees me.

DORIAN. Tell me, in whose service do you prefer to be, mine or someone else's?

PUFF. Yours, sir. Naturally, I'd rather be in my own. First me, then you. That's how things are arranged in my mind. And let the rest of the world go whistle.

DORIAN. If that's how you feel, you must think again about your relationship with Fanny.

PUFF. But, sir, is Fanny any concern of yours? I'm in love with her, whereas you've washed your hands of love once and for all.

DORIAN. Nevertheless, I want you to stop courting her; I even want you to avoid her; to be perfectly plain, I want you to break with her.

PUFF. Bless my soul, sir, your wants and mine don't seem to resemble each other. Why can't we get along today as well as we did yesterday?

DORIAN. Because things have changed. Belinda might suspect that I am using you to spy on her movements. In short—leave

Fanny alone. I'll compensate you for the sacrifice you're making.

PUFF. Sir, the sacrifice will kill me before the compensation arrives.

DORIAN. That will do. Miss Arabella's girl, Betty, is as good as Fanny. You can marry her.

PUFF. If you threw in Miss Arabella herself, you'd still be robbing me.

DORIAN. Say what you like, you'll have to make a choice. Which do you prefer: your dismissal, or Betty?

PUFF. I couldn't say. I'm not acquainted with either.

DORIAN. You'll be acquainted with your dismissal, as of today, if you don't obey my orders. On the other hand, obey them and you'll see how terribly Fanny will miss you.

PUFF. Fanny will miss me! Why didn't you say so before, sir?

DORIAN. Off with you. Miss Arabella is coming.

PUFF. I'll obey you, sir, provided I'm going to be missed.

DORIAN. By the way, say nothing about my commands to you. Since you were marrying Fanny with my consent, I don't want to shock Belinda by seeming to forbid you now. I allow you only to say that you prefer Betty, who is Miss Arabella's choice for you.

PUFF. Don't worry. The only villains will be Miss Arabella and myself. Miss Arabella gives me Betty. I take her. And you're only an innocent bystander.

DORIAN. Very good. Go now.

PUFF (coming back). But I'll be missed? (He goes.)
(Enter Arabella.)

ARABELLA. Have you given your man his instructions, Dorian?

DORIAN. Yes, madam, I have.

ARABELLA. This little action may be useful to us. If Belinda hears of it, she'll be uneasy.

DORIAN. I'm beginning to believe in our success. Already I have seen her surprised at my behavior. She was expecting me to upbraid her, and now she is ready to ask me why I don't.

ARABELLA. Hold fast, Dorian, and you'll have her weeping yet.

DORIAN. I'll hold fast until the tears begin to fall. Are you satisfied?

ARABELLA. I answer for nothing if you break down.

DORIAN. But what about Captain Coxe?

ARABELLA. Don't mention him. We'll crush him, and then let him take his remains where he pleases. Now—I've asked one of Belinda's servants whether I could speak with her. I believe the answer is coming. (*Enter a lackey.*) Well, shall I see your mistress?

LACKEY. Yes, madam, here she comes.

ARABELLA (*to Dorian*). Leave me. She mustn't see us together; it would look contrived.

DORIAN. And I have a little plan of my own after you are done with her.

ARABELLA. Don't spoil anything.

DORIAN. Trust me. (*He leaves.*)
(*Enter Belinda.*)

BELINDA. I have come to look for you myself, Arabella. You were asking to see me in private. Apparently it's something important.

ARABELLA. Oh, it's only a question I would like to ask you; and since you are truthfulness, candor, and sincerity personified, it will take but a moment.

BELINDA. I understand. You don't believe in my frankness, but you hope to induce it by praising me for it. Am I right?

ARABELLA. Well, then, *are* you frank?

BELINDA. I will make a start by telling you that I don't know.

ARABELLA. If I asked you, "Does Captain Coxe love you?", would you tell me the truth?

BELINDA. No, my dear, I don't want to spoil our friendship, and you would hate me if I told you the truth.

ARABELLA. I promise not to.

BELINDA. You couldn't keep your promise. I myself would absolve you of it. Some feelings are simply too strong for us.

ARABELLA. But why should I hate you?

BELINDA. Is it not rumored that the Captain was in love with you?

ARABELLA. The rumor was well founded.

BELINDA. There we are. And now I am to tell you that he is in love with me! Not for the world!

ARABELLA. Is that all? Believe me, I hope I have lost him. With all my heart, I want him to love you.

BELINDA. Well, then, you can thank heaven; your wishes are fulfilled.

ARABELLA. I assure you that I'm delighted.

BELINDA. And my own mind is at rest. He is misguided, of course. You are so very charming that he ought to have paid attention to no one else. But perhaps he was less attached to you than people have supposed.

ARABELLA. No; he was sincerely attached to me. But I forgive him. I may be charming, but you excel me; you know the game better than most women.

BELINDA. Indeed! Now, Arabella, you are not so delighted as I thought. I warned you that would fail to keep your promise. Already your compliments are faltering. But I am still satisfied; I detect a tiny barb of spite that rather pleases me. I am being praised by your jealousy.

ARABELLA. My jealousy?

BELINDA. A compliment whose conclusion is that I am a coquette—in this not jealousy? My dear, I know it when I see it.

ARABELLA. I wouldn't dream of calling you a coquette.

BELINDA. Sometimes a thing is said before it is dreamed.

ARABELLA. But tell me frankly now, are you not actually a little bit of a coquette?

BELINDA. Yes, I am. But don't say a little bit. Help yourself, tell me I am a great coquette. It won't prevent you from being one yourself.

ARABELLA. I don't exhibit quite the same evidence, my dear.

BELINDA. That is because the only evidence is success. Failure sends all these pretty lures into retirement. A person withdraws in silence, a little humiliated perhaps, but undetected; which is an advantage.

ARABELLA. I shall succeed whenever I want to, madam, and easily too. As for the Captain, he might not have turned to you, had I given him a little more encouragement.

BELINDA. You were aloof; have it your way. That's how pride speaks when it tries to save itself.

ARABELLA. Shall I prove to you that my pride doesn't need saving?

BELINDA. Oh, are you hoping to reconquer Captain Coxe? If you can, you're welcome to him.

ARABELLA. You are fond of him, I suppose.

BELINDA. So-so. But I will be fonder now, to make him resist you better. A woman needs all her resources to contend with you.

ARABELLA. Never fear, I leave him to your care. Good-bye for now.

BELINDA. Why? Let's fight over him, and let's take an oath to forgive the one who gets him. I insist on that clause because I do so want you to remain on good terms with me.

ARABELLA. Remain on good terms with you! In other words, you're sure of victory.

BELINDA. I hold the better hand of cards.

ARABELLA. My cards were as good as yours when you took him from me; our luck might shift again.

BELINDA. Very good, go for your revenge.

ARABELLA. I don't want to. I have a more pleasant occupation.

BELINDA. May one ask what it is?

ARABELLA. Of course. Dorian is as good as the Captain, Belinda. Good-bye. (*She leaves.*)

BELINDA (*alone*). Dorian! Take Dorian away from me! The woman is mad. Her jealousy has addled her brains. I'm really sorry for her. (*Enter Dorian. He approaches Belinda hurriedly, pretending to mistake her for Arabella.*)

DORIAN. Still raising questions in your mind, my dear Arabella? Oh! Excuse me! I thought I saw Arabella here, and I was so absorbed that I mistook you for her.

BELINDA. No harm done, Dorian. But what questions were you referring to? What did you mean?

DORIAN. Oh, nothing. I was about to remind her of a conversation we had.

BELINDA. But why the complaint about her raising questions? I insist on your telling me.

DORIAN. Really, madam, it was so trifling a point that I can hardly recollect it. There was something—I think—about her wondering how I used to fare in your heart.

BELINDA. I hope you were discreet enough to say nothing about it.

DORIAN. I am not vain.

BELINDA. Truth is sometimes as bad as vanity. And why did she want this information?

DORIAN. Sheer curiosity, I assure you.

BELINDA. And yet this curiosity was raising questions! I'm lost.

DORIAN. It was I who used the expression when I thought I was approaching her. Quite at random—I hardly know why.

BELINDA. At random! For an intelligent man, Dorian, you're rather bungling your explanation. There's a mystery somewhere in this.

DORIAN. I see I won't be able to dissuade you, madam, and so I suggest we talk about something else. Speaking of curiosity, have you had news from Paris recently? Arabella is expecting some; she adores news, and I know her friends will not disappoint her if anything has happened.

BELINDA. Your embarrassment is pitiful.

DORIAN. What, madam, are you harping on this nonsense again?

BELINDA. I thought I had a certain power over you.

DORIAN. You will always have a great deal of power over me. If there has been a small decline lately, I am not to blame for it. But so much is left that, in order not to succumb to it, I had better leave you at once. (*He goes.*)

BELINDA (*alone*). I don't recognize Dorian in this tirade. (*She is in a brown study.*)
(*Enter Captain Coxe.*)

CAPTAIN COXE. My Belinda is dreaming; she has fallen into a contemplation.

BELINDA. Yes . . . I have found Arabella and Dorian in a state of affliction which grieves me. You and I were speaking of marriage a while ago. We must absolutely postpone it.

CAPTAIN COXE. Postpone it!

BELINDA. Yes; for a fortnight or so.

CAPTAIN COXE. Ha! that's a century. Why the delay?

BELINDA. You haven't noticed their behavior as I have.

CAPTAIN COXE. Why should I notice behaviors?

BELINDA. Let me tell you, our friends are in a passion. Do you want to drive them over the brink? We're not as impatient as all that.

CAPTAIN COXE. I'm dying with impatience, confound it! If the case requires a victim, why select me?

BELINDA. I can't bring myself to reduce them to despair, Captain Coxe. Let us be honest. Our relationship does look a little like unfaithfulness. These two had a right to believe that they meant something to us. We must handle them tenderly. I don't like to hurt anyone, and neither, I am sure, do you. You are not hard-hearted, are you? They are your friends as much as mine. Let them at least get accustomed to the idea that we might be married.

CAPTAIN COXE. But to get them accustomed I would have to be alive; and I defy you to keep me breathing; I cannot survive that long. Why not try to accustom them at a smaller cost? It isn't the fashion yet to die in order to comfort one's friends. Besides, we don't need their blessing. Do you know that rumor has it they are making their own arrangements?

BELINDA. Arrangements! What arrangements are you talking about?

CAPTAIN COXE. Why, arrangements of the heart.

BELINDA. Your ways of expressing yourself are sometimes quite beyond me. Do you suggest that they are in love with each other? Speak clearly, will you?

CAPTAIN COXE. The talk is not quite of love, but I hear they are fond of each other.

BELINDA. Fond of each other! What nonsense! How do people get these ideas? Well, sir, if you can prove to me that they are in love—that they are fond of each other—if you can prove it to me, I shall marry you tomorrow; I shall marry you tonight. Take advantage of my offer and show me the proof.

CAPTAIN COXE. I can't vouch for their being in love.

BELINDA. Very well. Then prove that they are comforting each other; that's all I demand.

CAPTAIN COXE. And if I do, you'll take the plunge?

BELINDA. Yes; if I know they are content. But who will tell us the truth?

CAPTAIN COXE. You're caught! Let me inform you that Arabella has charged Trivet to examine us, and to report on the condition of our two hearts. I had forgotten to tell you.

BELINDA. There's nothing in her charge that supports you. If they had forgotten us, they would scarcely be troubling themselves about our hearts.

CAPTAIN COXE. Trivet may have spoken to her already; I haven't seen him yet. Let's hear his account and act accordingly.

BELINDA. Agreed.
(*Enter Trivet.*)

CAPTAIN COXE. Come here, Trivet. Have you seen Miss Arabella?

TRIVET. Yes, sir, I have, and in Mr. Dorian's company at that; I saw them both a little while ago.

CAPTAIN COXE. Tell us how they are behaving. Miss Belinda is so kind, she is afraid of driving them to despair. I, on the other hand, assert that they are recuperating together. Which of us two is right? Her concern for them is all that stands in her way. You understand me, I hope.

TRIVET. Perfectly. Madam can marry you in all safety. I haven't noticed so much as the shadow of despair.

CAPTAIN COXE. The battle is won. Tonight you are mine.

BELINDA. Hm! I'm not so sure; Trivet doesn't seem to have observed them too well.

TRIVET. With your permission, madam, despair is easy to recognize. I might be led astray by flimsy or unsteady feelings, but despair is massive, it moves and it occupies space. Desperate people fidget and fret, they make noise, they gesticulate; whereas I saw nothing of all that.

CAPTAIN COXE. The man is right. I met Dorian an hour ago; I told him: "I love Belinda, I'm mad about her."—"Well, keep her," says he calmly to me.

BELINDA. My dear Captain, you are his rival; do you expect him to confide his grief to you?

CAPTAIN COXE. I tell you he was smiling, and his soul was at peace.

BELINDA. Peace in the soul of a man who loved me with more passion than the world has ever known!

CAPTAIN COXE. Except for mine.

BELINDA. If you insist. And yet he has more tenderness than you. I say it incidentally. It isn't your fault. Every man loves as much as he can, and nobody loves as deeply as Dorian. That is why I'm sorry for him. Besides, on what evidence does Trivet conclude that Dorian is happy? Look—isn't it true that you're paid by Arabella, and perhaps by Dorian as well, to observe us both? And does one pay a spy to discover things one isn't interested in?

TRIVET. You're right; but I'm paid very badly; Miss Arabella is in arrears.

BELINDA. Well, because she is not liberal with her money, she must be indifferent! What kind of reasoning is that?

TRIVET. And Mr. Dorian has discharged me, and owes me my wages.

BELINDA. Never mind your wages. What did you see? What did you learn?

CAPTAIN COXE (*aside to Trivet*). Gently . . .

TRIVET. "Tell us, Trivet," they asked me, "are they a little in love perhaps?"—"Oh, very much," said I; "extremely, sir; extremely, madam." I was categorical.

BELINDA. And then?

TRIVET. Nothing stirs. Miss Arabella yawns in my face, Mr. Dorian opens his snuff-box nonchalantly, and that's all I can draw from them.

BELINDA. Come, come, my lad, leave us alone, you're all thumbs. Captain, your servant is a fool, and his observations are pitiful. All he noticed was the surface.

TRIVET. You may hack me to pieces if I'm wrong. Do you want to hear more? I'll inform you that they are in love, and that they themselves told me to let you know it.

BELINDA (*laughing*). They themselves told you! You simpleton, why didn't you say so at once? Open your eyes, Captain—they are perfectly comforted, and yet they want to arouse our jealousy! Well, they are doing it with a clumsiness that's worthy of their spite. Wasn't I right about them?

CAPTAIN COXE. They do seem to be displaying some anger.

BELINDA. Grossly displaying it.

TRIVET. I see it now. They are trying to vex you. Now I understand why, when Mr. Dorian was looking at his watch, he was not looking straight at it, and why he almost made a face.

BELINDA. That was because his soul is *not* at peace.

CAPTAIN COXE. That face he was making is significant.

TRIVET. Furthermore, after opening his snuff-box, he took snuff with two trembling fingers. And I noticed that his mouth was laughing against the grain; the rest of his face was going its own way.

BELINDA. Because his heart wasn't laughing.

CAPTAIN COXE. I give up. Dorian sighed, he made a face, and my wedding is retreating. Hang the fool who has thrown Belinda into a compassion that's going to be fatal to me.

BELINDA. Not at all. Don't worry, Captain; Dorian has behaved too badly to deserve my consideration. But isn't this Arabella coming our way?

TRIVET. It is.

BELINDA. I know her. You'll see that she is coming here to insinuate in her usual sly way that she and Dorian are in love. Let's listen to her.
(*Enter Arabella.*)

ARABELLA. Do forgive me, Belinda, if I am interrupting an interesting conversation. I was only passing by. I have been told that you are postponing your marriage with Captain Coxe only out of consideration for me. I'm obliged to you, but there's no need, I assure you. I urge you to proceed, and better today than tomorrow. Excuse me—I'm expected elsewhere.

BELINDA. Wait a moment, Arabella. Tell me, is it true that you and Dorian are in love? Tell me, so that I can rejoice with you.

ARABELLA. Rejoice; the news is good.

BELINDA (*laughing*). Really?

ARABELLA. Really. Proceed with your wedding, Belinda. (*She leaves.*)

BELINDA (*laughing*). She's running away. All this mockery is too much for her. What a woman won't do for her vanity! The girl is choking with resentment.

CAPTAIN COXE. I could see she was in a turmoil.

TRIVET. She was making the same face that I saw on Mr. Dorian before. But now, sir, will you say something to Miss Belinda on my behalf with reference to Fanny?

BELINDA. What's this about Fanny?

TRIVET. It's a little request I am submitting to you, madam; I beg you to be so kind as to take Fanny away from Puff, and to transfer her to me.

CAPTAIN COXE. Exactly.

BELINDA. Is Fanny willing?

TRIVET. Oh, yes. The transfer is all to her liking.

BELINDA. You've given me an idea. Arabella's little tricks ought to be punished. Let's see whether Dorian is indifferent to what I am about to do. If she is telling the truth, he won't care, and I'll be satisfied. Here, at any rate, is an infallible means of finding out the truth. I'll tell Fanny to marry Trivet. Dorian and I had agreed that Puff would have her. If Dorian doesn't complain, Arabella is right, he has forgotten me, and my mind will be at rest. Trivet, go look for Fanny and her father, I want to question both of them.

TRIVET. They'll be easy to find, because here they are.
(*Enter Mr. Nubbins and Fanny.*)

BELINDA. Come nearer, Fanny, and you too, Mr. Nubbins. Your daughter was supposed to be married to Puff; but if you want to do me a great pleasure, you'll give her to Trivet instead; do you hear me, Mr. Nubbins?

MR. NUBBINS. Yes, I hear you, ma'am. But there's another story going around the world that's been tormenting us, and that's why I'm here to get your help.

BELINDA. What now? And why is Fanny crying?

FANNY. My father will tell you, Miss Belinda.

MR. NUBBINS. The fact, ma'am, is that Puff is no better than a snake, by your leave. But the worst snake of them all is Mr.

Dorian and Miss Arabella, for hyppotizing Puff so's he'd turn up his nose at Fanny, even though she's still longing after him, and I'm guessing that he's still sweet on her too, if only they'd let him be wanting what he's really wanting without putting no sticks in his wheel.

BELINDA. What sticks?

MR. NUBBINS. A stick of a girl they call Betty, which Miss Arabella has thought up and promised to Puff.

BELINDA. Very curious.

MR. NUBBINS. And saying, just like that, that they're to be wedded in town, the hussy and him, meaning to make trouble for my child, that's going to be crying her eyes out over this trick. 'Cause a trick it is, ma'am, and it's meant to spoil our good repetition and yours, so they can snigger at the threes of us. And that's why she and me is here to cry for justice.

BELINDA. And we'll try to get justice done. Captain Coxe, this alters my plans. Trivet will have to forget Fanny. Come, Fanny, wipe your tears; let Arabella propose all the Bettys she has; leave her to me. This woman, to whom I was showing so much consideration, has found a new weapon against me. Dorian, I am sure, is simply standing out of her way; but I hope I have more credit left with him than she imagines. Calm yourself, Fanny.

FANNY. Puff has been treating me so coldly, I can't bear it. He acts as though he'd never seen me. And it's all Miss Arabella's doing.

MR. NUBBINS. Keeping a girl from being a body's wife!

BELINDA. I'll find a remedy, trust me.

TRIVET. Yes, but the remedy isn't going to help me, is it?

CAPTAIN COXE. Madam, I have been listening to you all this time. My ear catches you, but the mind is at sea. Speak up, Fanny: let me hear a clear report. Weren't you infatuated with Trivet?

FANNY. No, sir. To be sure, I thought so as long as Puff was in love with me; but now that he turns his back on me, I see I was mistaken.

CAPTAIN COXE. How does one answer a woman?

BELINDA. I happen to think that this woman is right and doesn't deserve your sarcasm. A man who was in love with her tells her that he no longer cares; this is not pleasant, and she can't help feeling the wound. Were you and I in her place, we should certainly feel it too. Enough. Go your ways, all of you, and let me take the situation in hand.

MR. NUBBINS. I've already complained to Mr. Dorian and Miss Arabella, ma'am.

BELINDA. Let me handle everything. Here is Dorian. I'm going to speak to him at once.
(*All leave except Belinda and Captain Coxe. Enter Dorian.*)

BELINDA. Come here, Dorian, and first of all let us talk a little about Arabella.

DORIAN. With all my heart, madam.

BELINDA. Tell me then, with all your heart, what mischief she is contriving today.

DORIAN. What has she done? I can't conceive of anyone finding fault with her.

BELINDA. Oh, I'll make it easy for you to conceive it.

DORIAN. You know how careful she is—

BELINDA. You are a stubborn eulogizer, my friend! Well, then, the woman you are praising, who is jealous of me because Captain Coxe has left her—as though I were to blame for that—goes looking now for trifles by means of which she can avenge herself, trifles which are really unworthy of the paragon you make of her. She does not think it beneath herself to keep a footman from being in love with a maid. Because she knows that you and I have worked together to see them married, and because she knows of my interest in this marriage, in her rage she dreams up some miserable Betty to throw in my path. And what I marvel at most in all this, is to see you of all people lending a hand in this shabby enterprise.

DORIAN. Do you really think that Arabella meant to offend you? And that I imagined for a moment that you were still concerned about Puff and Fanny? No, Belinda, Puff was complaining about Fanny's unfaithfulness; he was, he said, losing his prize. People like us are sometimes sorry for our servants; and that is why, out of sheer kindness, and to compensate him a little, Arabella proposed that he should marry her own maid, Betty. He accepted the girl, said thank you, and that is the whole story.

CAPTAIN COXE. Dorian makes sense. I see no malice anywhere. Let the great powers make peace on this point, and let the small fry fight it out by themselves.

BELINDA. Be still, Captain Coxe. You will give us your opinion when we ask it of you. Dorian, please drop this silly intrigue. It annoys me. I hope that this is all I need to say.

DORIAN. Wait—let's call someone; Puff may be near. Puff!

BELINDA. What are you doing?

DORIAN. Arabella is not far from here. I suggest you send for her and talk things over together.

BELINDA. Arabella! Why Arabella? Do you have to consult *her* about this? I'm not looking for her approval, I'm speaking to you, I'm telling you, Dorian, that I want to hear no more of this Betty; and all this, without troubling over Arabella's opinion.

DORIAN. Yes, but remember, if you please, that I must trouble about it. I couldn't make a decision without consulting her. Can you see me forcing my footman to reject her favor after accepting it? This is not my way of dealing with Arabella—far from it.

BELINDA. In short, you're hesitating between her and me. Do you understand what you are doing?

DORIAN. I hesitate precisely because I understand.

CAPTAIN COXE. Let's forget this trio of valets and maids, shall we, eh?

BELINDA. I suppose it is I who should apologize for my unlady-like words.

DORIAN. Your words always honor me, whatever they are, and I would obey them if I could.

BELINDA (*laughing*). We have nothing more to say to each other, I see. Come, Captain Coxe, give me your hand.

CAPTAIN COXE. Take it, and don't return it, madam.

DORIAN. Before you go, may I ask you a question, Belinda?

BELINDA (*turning around*). I know nothing, sir.

DORIAN. Yes, you do, madam. For example: will you be united to Captain Coxe in the near future? When shall we have the pleasure of seeing you joined?

BELINDA. The pleasure may come to you this very evening, sir.

CAPTAIN COXE. Gently, divine Belinda, I am shot through the heart, I can't breathe for joy.

DORIAN. Delighted! Captain Coxe, let me congratulate you.

BELINDA (*aside*). The wretch!

DORIAN (*aside*). Her face is red!

BELINDA. Is that all, sir?

DORIAN. Yes, madam.

BELINDA (*to the Captain*). Come away.
(*Enter Arabella and Puff.*)

ARABELLA. Belinda, your gardener tells me that you are angry with me. I've come to ask your forgiveness; I was at fault without meaning to be; but now I've brought you the lad in order to make amends. Puff, when I promised Betty to you, I was not aware that I might be irritating Miss Belinda. Now, however, you must put Betty out of your mind.

PUFF. I won't sue for damages, madam. As a matter of fact, I hear that Mr. Nubbins has been calling for justice against me. Well, I'm ready to make restitution. Send for the notary, and if he's not in, his clerk will do, I'm satisfied.

BELINDA. Just one moment. (*To Dorian*) Send your man away, if you please; as for you, madam, I invite you to keep your promise to him. More than that: I'll pay the expenses of his wedding. Let's say no more about it.

DORIAN (*to Puff*). You'd better go.

PUFF (*going*). So there's no escape from Betty! You, Captain Coxe, all this uproar is your fault; all our loves are topsy-turvy because of you. If you hadn't been here, me and my master would have been neatly married to our Belinda and our Fanny, without any Arabellas and Bettys on our backs. (*He sniffles. Arabella and Captain Coxe laugh.*)

BELINDA (*also laughing*). If his extravagances entertain you so much, don't let him leave. Such a pretty scene!

CAPTAIN COXE. He's berserk with love.

DORIAN (*to Puff*). Off with you, you rascal! (*Puff leaves.*)

ARABELLA. Well now, Belinda, are we friends again?

BELINDA. The best friends in the world. You're an angel.

DORIAN. Arabella, I have news: Belinda and Captain Coxe may be married this very evening.

ARABELLA. Really?

CAPTAIN COXE. The evening is still far off.

DORIAN. Your impatience is natural. Now, with the sweet event so close at hand, there must be a thousand things you want to talk over. Let's leave them alone, Arabella, and attend to our own concerns.

ARABELLA. Come, Belinda, let me kiss you before going. Farewell, Captain Coxe, and my best wishes; we shall meet again. (*Arabella and Dorian leave.*)

BELINDA. You've really broken her heart, I see. Oh, she must have worshiped you.

CAPTAIN COXE. I'll do without her worship. Especially tonight.

BELINDA. Ha! This is too much.

CAPTAIN COXE. How is that? Are you changing your mind again?

BELINDA. A little.

CAPTAIN COXE. What now?

BELINDA. I have a plan . . . and you must help me with it. I shall tell you about it by and by. Let me go mull it over for a while . . . Don't worry . . . and don't follow me. (*False exit.*) Now that I think of it, you and I had better not meet for the time being. The moment I need you, I shall send for you. (*She leaves.*)

CAPTAIN COXE. I'm speechless. And I seem to be losing ground. This woman is more woman than any woman I have ever known.

ACT THREE

(Enter Captain Coxe, Fanny, and Trivet.)

CAPTAIN COXE. Do me a favor, Fanny, tell her that I beg to see her for one moment.

FANNY. I can't talk to her, Captain Coxe; she is resting.

CAPTAIN COXE. Resting! Does she rest on her two feet?

TRIVET. She does; I just saw her walking about the gallery.

FANNY. What of it? Everybody rests in his own way. What is *your* way, Captain?

CAPTAIN COXE. You're taunting me, Fanny.

TRIVET. I think so too.

FANNY. Not at all. It's a question which sprang up as we were chatting.

CAPTAIN COXE. I've even a tiny suspicion that you don't like me.

TRIVET. I had the same tiny suspicion, but I've exchanged it for a large certainty.

FANNY. The exchange speaks well for your intelligence.

CAPTAIN COXE. Didn't I say so? Why in the devil's name am I on your side when you won't be on mine? How is it I have friendly feelings for you which you don't reciprocate? Why can't we see eye to eye, Fanny?

FANNY. I don't know. Maybe because people need variety in life.

TRIVET. It seems to me there's some variety between the two of us as well.

FANNY. There is if you still love me; otherwise we're even.

CAPTAIN COXE. Tell me the truth: do you recommend me to your mistress?

FANNY. I recommend you to her indifference.

TRIVET. A touching service!

CAPTAIN COXE. You're trying to prejudice her against me.

FANNY. Oh, as much as I can. But only by maligning you. I want her to dislike you, and I admit it, you see. I don't ever deceive people.

TRIVET. This is downright cordial.

CAPTAIN COXE. Look here, Fanny, let's be friends.

FANNY. No. Follow my example, sir, and like me as little as I like you.

CAPTAIN COXE. I want you to like me, and you *will* like me, by God, I'll take an oath on it.

FANNY. I'll break it for you.

TRIVET. May I remind you, sir, that some aversions have to be paid to go away?

CAPTAIN COXE. How much do I pay for yours to vanish?

FANNY. Not a penny. It's not for sale.

CAPTAIN COXE (*offering his purse*). Take this, and keep it.

FANNY. No, thank you. I'd be robbing you.

CAPTAIN COXE. Take it, I say, and tell me one thing: what does your mistress intend to do? Tell me.

FANNY. I won't; but I'm willing to tell you what I *want* her to do; that's all I know. Shall I?

TRIVET. You've told us already in ten different ways, my beauty.

CAPTAIN COXE. Doesn't she have a design of some sort?

FANNY. Who doesn't? Everyone has a design of some sort. For instance, my design is to leave you, unless yours is to leave me first.

CAPTAIN COXE. Let's withdraw, Trivet; I feel I'm going to fume. We'll be back to tell her mistress what a courteous maid she has.

TRIVET. Farewell, unfriendly maid; farewell, capricious lass of my heart; farewell, most lovable of weathervanes.

FANNY. Farewell, most banished of men.
(*Captain Coxe and Trivet leave. Enter Puff.*)

PUFF. My pigeon, I keep making signs to my master; but he won't come over to find out what I want him to do.

FANNY. I'm afraid you'll have to speak to him in front of Miss Arabella.

PUFF. Hang Miss Arabella! (*He sighs.*) My chuck, the favor I did you when I gave you my heart again won't help either one of us. I've forgiven your insults in vain. The devil himself has set his mind on marrying me off to Betty.

FANNY. Go back to your master. Tell him that I'm waiting for him here.

PUFF. He doesn't care about your waiting.

FANNY. Go anyway; we've no time to waste.

PUFF. I'm frozen with unhappiness.

FANNY. Unfreeze yourself, if you love me. Wait, here come your master and Arabella. Pull him aside while I step out. (*She leaves.*)
(*Enter Arabella and Dorian.*)

PUFF. Sir, come here so I can talk to you.

DORIAN. What do you want?

PUFF. Not before the lady.

DORIAN. I have no secrets for her.

PUFF. But I have one which doesn't want to be known to her.

ARABELLA. Is it such a great mystery?

PUFF. It is; namely that Fanny wants to speak with Mr. Dorian; but this is not meant for your ears, madam.

ARABELLA. Your discretion is admirable! See what she wants, Dorian; but first I must tell you something myself. You, go call the girl. (*Exit Puff.*) I daresay it's on behalf of Belinda.

DORIAN. Undoubtedly. You can see how troubled she is.

ARABELLA. And you—ready to yield!

DORIAN. Why should I play at being cruel?

ARABELLA. Because we've almost reached the goal. But all's lost if you hurry too much. Believe me, the symptoms are still equivocal. I am not convinced it's love; perhaps she is more jealous of me than eager for you; and, for all we know, she may be plotting a victory over both of us which will expose us to her laughter. Our measures are all taken. We'll draw up the marriage contract. Then and only then will we know whether she cares for you. Love speaks one language, pride speaks another. Love weeps over what it loses; pride snubs what it cannot obtain. We must wait for either the tears or the snub. Until then, hold fast in the interest of your own affection. Go; be brief with Fanny, and return to me.

DORIAN. You put me to a difficult test, Arabella. I'm trembling! But reason is on your side, and I won't flinch, I promise you.

ARABELLA. Remember, my part is not a pleasant one either; and it will grow less pleasant the nearer we draw to the end, because I must become stronger as you become weaker. But what won't a woman do to be avenged? (*She leaves.*)
(*Enter Fanny and Puff.*)

DORIAN. What do you want of me, Fanny? I've only a moment to give you. You know I've just left Miss Arabella; and in my situation a conversation between us might arouse suspicion.

FANNY. What situation is there between you and Miss Arabella, sir?

DORIAN. A simple one. I am going to marry her.

PUFF. Oh, no, sir, no, no.

FANNY. You, marry her?

PUFF. Never.

DORIAN. Be quiet. Don't keep me waiting, Fanny; what do you want?

FANNY. Gently, if you please! Give yourself a chance to breathe. Oh, how you have changed!

PUFF. He is angry because he has been wronged, but it will all come right in the end.

FANNY. Do you remember that I am Miss Belinda's maid, sir? Or have you quite forgotten her?

DORIAN. No; I still honor and respect her. But I'm going, unless you finish your story.

FANNY. Very well, I'll finish it. Ye gods, behold these men!

DORIAN (going). Good-bye.

PUFF. Run after him.

FANNY. Wait, sir, wait!

DORIAN. Why? To listen to these shocking outbursts?

PUFF. The outburst was downright impudent; you'd better take it back.

FANNY. Well, be that as it may, my mistress has sent me to tell you she wants to speak with you.

DORIAN. What! At this moment?

FANNY. Yes, sir.

PUFF. The sooner the better.

DORIAN. Will you be still? You haven't by any chance made up with Fanny, have you?

PUFF. Alas, dear sir, love desired it, and he's the master, you know; myself, I was against it, I was.

DORIAN. That's your business. As for me, Fanny, tell Miss Belinda that I beg her to postpone our interview. Say that I ask her in all humility to forgive me, but that I have reasons for the delay which she herself will approve when I impart them to her.

FANNY. Mr. Dorian, she *must* speak with you. She insists.

PUFF (*on his knees*). And here I am begging you on my two knees. Please go, Mr. Dorian; the good lady has learned her lesson; I'm sure she will tell you beautiful things to renew your love.

DORIAN. I think you've lost your wits. Fanny, in a word, I can't; and you know why. An interview of this sort would alarm Arabella. Miss Belinda is sensible enough to understand this. Besides, I am sure that she has nothing urgent to tell me.

FANNY. Nothing, except that she still loves you, I think.

PUFF. And very tenderly, in spite of the little parentheses.

DORIAN. Except that she still loves me! Has she sent you to say this to me? Unbearable! Her request to see me would be sheer malice. She has deserted me; she no longer loves me—you told me so yourself. So be it; I was unworthy of her. But now—to seek an interview with me—to involve me frivolously in a quarrel with Arabella—no, this is too much. From now on, if I see Miss Belinda again, it will be with Arabella at my side. (*He leaves.*)

PUFF (*going after him*). No, no, sir, my dear master, turn to the right, don't turn to the left. Never mind; I'll shout until he hears me. (*He leaves.*)

FANNY (*alone*). The fact is that Miss Belinda is getting what she deserves.
(*Enter Belinda.*)

BELINDA. Well, Fanny, is he coming?

FANNY. No, madam.

BELINDA. No!

FANNY. No. He asks you to excuse him, but this interview would upset Miss Arabella, whom he is going to marry.

BELINDA. What's that? What did you say? Marry Arabella—Dorian?

FANNY. Yes, madam, and he is sure you yourself will approve of him.

BELINDA. What you tell me is unbelievable, Fanny; this cannot have come from Dorian; you're speaking of someone else.

FANNY. I'm speaking of Mr. Dorian, madam; but of a Mr. Dorian who no longer loves you.

BELINDA. It's not true. No one will make me believe it. My heart and mind tell me it's impossible, absolutely impossible.

FANNY. Your heart and mind are mistaken. Mr. Dorian suspects that the only reason you want to see him is to worry Miss Arabella and create a rift between them.

BELINDA. Stop bringing up this everlasting Arabella! Pretend she doesn't exist. Enough of her. Never! This woman was not made to thrust me out of Dorian's heart.

FANNY. Excuse me, madam, but she is most attractive.

BELINDA. Most, most? Are you mad?

FANNY. At least she is capable of pleasing a man. Add your own unfaithfulness, and that's enough to have brought Mr. Dorian to his senses.

BELINDA. But where is my unfaithfulness? Strike me dead if I have ever felt it!

FANNY. And yet I learned all about it from your own lips. First you denied that it was unfaithfulness because, you said, you didn't love Mr. Dorian to begin with. Then you proved to me that your infidelity was innocent. Finally you sang its praises to me, and praised so well that I copied you, and have been very sorry since that I did.

BELINDA. Well, then, I was wrong, my poor child. I was talking about unfaithfulness without knowing anything about it.

FANNY. Then why did you use every possible cruel device to get rid of Mr. Dorian?

BELINDA. I don't know. But I love him, while you're taunting and tormenting me. Yes, I mistreated him, I admit it—I have been wrong, miserably wrong; I'll never forgive myself, and I don't deserve ever to be forgiven! What more shall I say? I condemn myself, I confess my wrongs.

FANNY. I told you so, before you misled me.

BELINDA. Miserable female vanity! Miserable urge to be admired! This is what you have brought down on me. I wanted to attract the Captain, as though he were worth attracting; I wanted this proof of my merits, I wanted this victory for my charms. And look at my glory now! I have conquered the Captain, and I have lost Dorian.

FANNY. And what a difference.

BELINDA. Worse; the Captain is a man my whole nature detests when I truly listen to myself; a man I have always thought ridiculous, a man I have mocked a hundred times; and now I am left with him, and I have lost the most lovable of all men!

FANNY. Don't waste your time crying, madam. Mr. Dorian doesn't know that you still love him. Surely you're not going to leave him to Miss Arabella! Do something, take steps, since you admit that you were in the wrong, and that he is right to be angry.

BELINDA. But what do you advise me to do for an ingrate who

refuses to speak to me? I must quite give it up. Is this commend-
able of him? You say he is right to be angry, but did I dream I
was going to lose him? Did I suspect that he would be weak
enough to discard me? And has any woman ever counted on a
man's heart as much as I counted on his? Mine was an infinite
regard, a blind confidence, and yet you tell me I am to blame.
No, when a woman distinguishes a man with feelings like mine,
he is a villain to betray them.

FANNY. I've lost you completely.

BELINDA. And so deep were my feelings that I paid no attention
to his complaints or his jealousies; I laughed at his reproaches; I
defied him ever to grow cold to me. I liked to plague him with
impunity; to drive him consciously to the edge. Never did a
woman live in a more gratifying security than I; and I congratu-
lated myself on it, because it spoke so well for his devotion. And
after all this, he dares toss me aside! Can such a man be forgiven?

FANNY. Calm yourself, madam. Your grief is pitiful to see, but
let's try to bring him back; denouncing him is useless. First of all,
break with Captain Coxe; he has asked to see you twice already,
and I've sent him packing both times.

BELINDA. Didn't I tell that oaf not to appear until I called for
him?

FANNY. What do you propose to do with him?

BELINDA. To hate him as much as he deserves to be hated. Wait;
I'd better see him after all; he'll be useful to me. Let him come.
Better still, bring him to me.

FANNY. Here comes my father. Let's first find out what he wants.
(*Enter Mr. Nubbins.*)

MR. NUBBINS. Ten thousand devils! Do you know what's going
on, ma'am? Have they told you there's a notary walking in the
garden with Mr. Dorian, Miss Arabella, and a scrap of a con-
track they made him bring along? And they're ready to clap their

names to it. What do you say, ma'am? Because my girl says to me, she says, madam's love for Mr. Dorian has growed back again; and as for the notary, says I, let him milk his own cows and leave ours be.

BELINDA. A notary on my grounds! Fanny! Are they thinking of being married here?

MR. NUBBINS. Yes, they are. They're writing out papers for all fours of you. One on yon side for your old flame and Miss Arabella, and one on this side for yourself and your new spark, Captain Coxe. I can almost hear 'em laughing, and, by thunder, it makes my hackles rise. What about yours, ma'am?

BELINDA. I'm dizzy. This is unbelievable.

FANNY. It's revolting.

MR. NUBBINS. Miss Arabella is a blueblooded lady of the world, but she's not acted aboveboard, says I. Is it right, I ask, to diddle a lady of your kind out of her beaux? But I'm a-waiting for your word, ma'am, one word from you, my hoe is ready, and, by gad, I'll clean out the notary with his scribbles like a heap o' weeds.

BELINDA. Fanny, say something! Give me some advice. I'm at my wits' end. Unless I act at once, they'll be married under my own roof. This has nothing to do with Dorian. You realize that I hate him. But this is an insult.

FANNY. So it is, madam, this news makes me angry too. If I were you, I'd stop caring and let him go.

BELINDA. Let him go! And what if you loved him?

FANNY. You just said you hated him!

BELINDA. But I love him too. One doesn't prevent the other. Besides, why should I hate him? He believes me to be in the wrong—you said so yourself, and you were right. I jilted him first. I must find him at once and tell him the truth.

MR. NUBBINS. He used to swear by me, ma'am; why don't you send me to palaver with him?

BELINDA. What I'll do, I think, is write him a note. Your father can slip it into Dorian's hand while Arabella isn't looking.

FANNY. A good idea, madam.

BELINDA. Come to think of it, I happen to have a letter on me which I wrote him a while ago. I had quite forgotten it! Here, Mr. Nubbins, take it, and try to slip it to him in secret.

MR. NUBBINS. Nobody won't know beans about it. And whilst he reads your letter, I'll pepper it with a few discriminations of my own. (*He leaves.*)
(*Enter Captain Coxe and Trivet.*)

CAPTAIN COXE. What has happened to our love, my Belinda? Where is your heart? Is this your way of summoning me? And what was your reason for ordering me to fall back? You kept me waiting so long that I decided at last to issue my own command to appear before you.

BELINDA. I was about to have you called, Captain.

CAPTAIN COXE. By a slow messenger, it seems. Make up your mind, madam. Our friends are getting married, and the contract is being dispatched this moment. Why don't we take advantage of the notary? They have delegated me to invite you. Ratify my impatience. Remember, love groans when it is kept waiting; a lover's needs are urgent; every second you withhold from me is precious and irreplaceable. To make a long story short: I am dying. To arms, madam, to arms!

BELINDA. No, Captain Coxe; I have changed my mind.

CAPTAIN COXE. No marriage?

BELINDA. No.

CAPTAIN COXE. What do you mean—no?

BELINDA. No means—no. I want to reconcile you to Arabella.

CAPTAIN COXE. To Arabella? You are the one I love, Belinda!

BELINDA. But I am the one who does not love you, Captain. I am sorry to say it so bluntly. But I must let you know it somehow.

CAPTAIN COXE. You're playing with me, by Jove.

BELINDA. No; I mean it very seriously.

CAPTAIN COXE. Don't jest, Belinda; I'm perishing with terror.

BELINDA. Surely you must have been aware of my feelings. You know I have always delayed this marriage. How could you fail to understand that I didn't wish to consummate it?

CAPTAIN COXE. But what about the bliss you promised me for this very night?

BELINDA. It's yours for the asking—with Arabella. Did you speak with her, as I recommended you should a little while ago?

CAPTAIN COXE. Recommended? When did you recommend it? Never, on my oath.

BELINDA. I'm sure you must be wrong. I did tell you, I think.

CAPTAIN COXE. But what have Captain Coxe and Arabella to do with each other?

BELINDA. They have to love each other, just as they did before. That is all I am in a position to offer you; I undertake to bring you two together again.

CAPTAIN COXE. This is a passing whim.

BELINDA. No; my mind is made up forever.

FANNY. For all eternity—take it from me.

CAPTAIN COXE. Trivet, where do we stand?

TRIVET. By the looks of the land, nowhere. I don't think we'll find lodgings on this road.

FANNY. Yes, you will; because it's taking you straight home.

CAPTAIN COXE. Your orders are to march, Belinda?

BELINDA. I'm waiting for the answer to a letter. You'll know the rest when I receive it. Don't go till then.
(*Enter Puff.*)

PUFF. Madam, my master and Miss Arabella have sent me to ask if they may see you. They are going to pass sentence on you—and on me too, because as far as I'm concerned, since Mr. Dorian won't have you, I'm not going to marry Fanny.

BELINDA. Let them come. (*Aside to Fanny*) He hasn't received my letter, Fanny . . .

PUFF. Here they are.

BELINDA. What I am about to tell them will enlighten you, Captain; and it won't be my fault if you're not happy.

CAPTAIN COXE. I was duped. I'm enlightened already.
(*Enter Arabella and Dorian, with the Notary.*)

ARABELLA. Well, now, Belinda, I don't see any trace of marriage between you and Captain Coxe. When do you intend to make him a happy man?

BELINDA. Whenever you wish, Arabella. Decide for him: his happiness is in your hands.

ARABELLA. Very well; you will marry him today, and allow us to celebrate our marriage together with yours.

BELINDA. Your marriage! May I ask to whom? Is someone arriving to marry you?

ARABELLA. Yes, and he's not far. (*Pointing to Dorian*) Here he is.

DORIAN. It's true, Belinda, Arabella is honoring me with her hand. And as we are already in your house, will you allow us to be married here?

BELINDA. No, my dear sir. I am deeply flattered, but I have reason to believe that heaven has another fate in store for you.

CAPTAIN COXE (*to Dorian*). We're exchanging booty, it seems; Arabella falls to me, and Belinda goes to you.

ARABELLA. Oh, no; we'll remain just as we are.

BELINDA. Let me speak now; may I, Arabella? Listen to me. Captain Coxe, the time has come to undeceive you. You thought I was in love with you; something in my ways with you may have caused you to believe it; but you were making a mistake. I have never stopped loving Dorian, and I endured you only to test him. I am sorry you expended your feelings on me, but I needed your love for my design. As for you, Arabella, I admit that you have grounds for complaint against him. The Captain's heart has strayed a little from you, but when all is said and done, his fault is forgivable, and I am far from gloating because I stole him from you for a while. He did not yield to my charms, but to my skill. I was not more attractive than you in his eyes, but I seemed better disposed toward him, and that is a very strong lure. However, you Dorian did not meet my tender challenge altogether brilliantly. The delicate feelings which prompted me to put you to the proof are less than satisfied. But perhaps your decision was due to your resentment more than to imperfect love. I went rather far, I confess; and I must not judge too harshly. I am willing to close my eyes to your conduct, and I forgive you.

ARABELLA (*laughing*). Ha, ha, ha! You are a little late, Belinda; at least I am vain enough to think you are. Or else—yes, here is a thought—why not be even more generous; forgive him for taking me as his wife.

BELINDA. Dorian, if you hesitate one moment, you lose me forever.

CAPTAIN COXE. It's my turn to speak! I demand to be heard. I have lost Arabella, but I'm not complaining. I was unfaithful— God knows why, because she deserved better; it's a disaster I don't understand. In a word, I'm fickle, I confess it; but I'm also truthful, and I boast of it. I could take reprisals and say to Belinda, you were tricking me, I was tricking you, tit for tat. But that's too involved for me; I'm a plain soldier. The truth is this: You, Belinda, you say you were only pretending love. Well, that's all I was worth; granted; but as a matter of fact you loved me better than I was worth. Don't underrate it now. I loved you, but you gave as good as you took.

BELINDA. So you thought.

CAPTAIN COXE. Let me finish. I loved you, though a little less than I loved Arabella. I'll explain. She had full possession of me, I adored her; but I loved you well enough, hang it, with a bit of her still on my mind. The truth, Dorian, is that Belinda and I had come to terms. Don't believe her story, my friend. She's in a rage because you're deserting her, because her beauty came in second. Her pride is crying out, demanding you back, crooning like a siren; but don't listen to the song. (*Pointing to Arabella*) These beautiful eyes will keep you from harm; stay with her; it's Love's revenge against me. I say it with a groan; I'd fight for Arabella with my last drop of blood, if I had the right. Take her, Dorian, and thank heaven for your luck. Of all wives, yours is the best. Of all losses, mine is the heaviest. And of all ungrateful, disloyal, and stupid men, the worst is the wretch who is speaking to you.

ARABELLA. Well said; I've nothing to add.

BELINDA. I won't stoop to answer you, Captain; you are venting your spite on me. Dorian, I have told you my intentions. If you're not worthy of them, all's finished.

ARABELLA. There is no remedy, Belinda; we two are really in love. Two jilted lovers have the right to look elsewhere. Try, both of you, to forget us once more. You know already how it is done; and the second time round it should be easier. (*To the Notary*) Sir, will you come here? We are ready to sign the contract. Dorian, ask Belinda to honor it with her signature.

BELINDA. Now? So soon?

ARABELLA. Yes, if you will be so kind.

BELINDA. I'm speaking to Dorian, madam.

DORIAN. Yes, Belinda.

BELINDA. Your contract with Arabella?

DORIAN. Yes, madam.

BELINDA. I wouldn't have believed it!

ARABELLA. And we hope that yours will come next. And you, Captain Coxe, won't you sign?

CAPTAIN COXE. I've forgotten how to write.

ARABELLA (*to the Notary*). Give this lady the pen, sir.

BELINDA (*quickly*). Give it . . . (*She signs and then throws the pen away.*) Ah! traitor! (*She swoons in Fanny's arms.*)

DORIAN (*falling at her feet*). Oh, my Belinda!

ARABELLA. Surrender, Dorian; she loves you.

PUFF. Fanny, I'm happy.

FANNY. And so am I.

BELINDA. What! Dorian—at my feet!

DORIAN. And more in love with you than ever.

BELINDA. Rise. Does my Dorian love me still?

DORIAN. He never did otherwise.

BELINDA. And Arabella?

DORIAN. I shall owe your love to her, if you give it to me again. The whole design was hers.

BELINDA. I'm breathing again. But how much sorrow you have caused me! And how could you wear a mask so long?

DORIAN. Love gave me the strength. I wanted to reconquer the woman I love.

BELINDA (*with vehemence*). Where is Arabella? I want to kiss her. (*Arabella draws near, and they embrace.*)

ARABELLA. Here she is. Are we friends again?

BELINDA. Because of you, I am happy—and sensible again. (*Dorian kisses Belinda's hand.*)

ARABELLA. As for you, Captain Coxe, I advise you to take *your* hand elsewhere. I don't know of anyone who longs for it here.

BELINDA. No, Arabella, in my gratitude I will plead for him and obtain his pardon. I wish it to complete my happiness.

ARABELLA. We shall see six months from now.

CAPTAIN COXE. A term is all I wanted; leave the rest to me.
(*Arabella, Belinda, Dorian, Captain Coxe and the Notary leave.*)

TRIVET. Are you marrying Puff, Fanny?

FANNY. My heart says yes.

PUFF. Mine agrees.

MR. NUBBINS (*entering*). And old Nubbins says bless you both.

TRIVET. Well, Fanny, I give you six months to come back to me.

THE END

Sylvia Hears a Secret (Les Fausses confidences)

Presented for the first time at
the Théâtre Italien on March 16, 1737

CHARACTERS

Sylvia, *daughter to Mrs. Grumby*
Dorian, *nephew to Mr. Rooney*
Mr. Rooney, *solicitor*
Mrs. Grumby
Puff, *servant to Sylvia*
Trivet, *formerly in Dorian's service*
Alice, *maid to Sylvia*
Lord Dorimont
A Servant
An Apprentice to a Jeweler

The action takes place in Sylvia's house.

ACT ONE

(*Enter Dorian and Puff.*)

Puff. Please, sir, be good enough to sit down in this room for a moment. Miss Alice is busy with madam, but she'll be down soon.

Dorian. I'm obliged to you.

Puff. If you like, I'll stay here to keep you entertained. We can chat while you wait.

Dorian. Thank you, but that won't be necessary; don't let me disturb you.

Puff. It's no disturbance, sir. Miss Sylvia has given us orders to be civil. Now you can be my witness that I've been polite.

Dorian. And yet I'd be very glad to be left alone a moment.

Puff. As you wish, sir. Thank you.
(*He leaves. After a while, Trivet enters with a mysterious air.*)

Dorian. Oh. There you are.

Trivet. Yes, I was looking out for you.

Dorian. I couldn't get rid of a servant who insisted on entertaining me. Tell me, hasn't Mr. Rooney come yet?

Trivet. Not yet, but he's due here any moment. (*Looking around*) Can anybody see us together? None of the servants must know that we are acquainted.

Dorian. I don't see anyone.

TRIVET. And you haven't said a word to your uncle, Mr. Rooney?

DORIAN. Not a word. As far as he is concerned, he is recommending me as steward to a lady I simply happened to mention to him, and whose solicitor he happens to be. He doesn't know that I went to him on your advice. In any case, he wasted no time; he talked to her about me yesterday, and ordered me to be here this morning. He expected to arrive in time to perform the introductions, but if he was detained, my instructions were to ask for a certain Miss Alice. And that was all. Believe me, I'm not in the least tempted to confide in him or in anyone else. I've agreed to play my part in your scheme, Trivet, but it still looks like madness to me. Don't misunderstand me—I'm exceedingly grateful to you. You were in my service once; I wasn't able to keep you, or even to pay you what you deserved. And yet you decided to make me rich. I'm more grateful than I can say.

TRIVET. Don't mention it, Mr. Dorian. It's really very simple. I like you, and I've always liked you. If I had any money of my own, I'd put it all at your disposal.

DORIAN. And I'd give you half my fortune, Trivet. I wish I could show you my appreciation. But frankly, I expect nothing from our enterprise, aside from the shame of being turned away tomorrow.

TRIVET. If so, you'll go back where you came from and no harm done.

DORIAN. Here is a woman who holds a high place in society, and who enjoys the best connections as the widow of an important official in the Treasury. Can you imagine her taking notice of me, or myself marrying her—I, a nobody without a penny to my name?

TRIVET. Nonsense; your appearance is your Eldorado. Turn around, let me look at you again. Never mind, there's not a lord in town who can beat you. Look at that build! That shape of yours is worth more than any title you may care to mention. Our plan is infallible, I tell you. I already see you at home here, and wearing slippers in Miss Sylvia's bedroom.

DORIAN. A mirage!

TRIVET. No, take my word for it. You're as good as under your own roof, and your carriages are waiting for you in the coach-house.

DORIAN. Trivet, she has over ten thousand a year . . .

TRIVET (*tapping him*). And you have at least fifteen thousand right there.

DORIAN. . . . And you tell me that she is very sensible.

TRIVET. So much the better for you, and so much the worse for her. If she likes you, she'll be so embarrassed, she'll struggle so hard, she'll become so weak, that her only prop will be a husband. The rest is up to you. You have seen her, you say, and you're in love with her?

DORIAN. Passionately. That's why I'm so worried.

TRIVET. Don't come to me with your worries! Let me see a little confidence, by God. You'll succeed, I tell you; I'm in charge, and I've decided it. Here, it's written in my head. All our measures are taken. I'm familiar with my lady's character, your merits, and my talents. You're in good hands. Is she sensible? She'll fall in love with you anyway. Is she proud? Still she'll marry you. And are you penniless? Very good; she'll make you rich. Pride, reason, and wealth, all will have to surrender. When Love speaks, Love is the master. And speak he will. I'm going now—somebody is coming—it may be Mr. Rooney. The vessel is launched; sail on. (*False exit.*) I almost forgot. See to it that Alice takes a liking to you. Venus and I will do the rest. (*He leaves.*)
(*Enter Mr. Rooney.*)

MR. ROONEY. How do you do, nephew; I'm glad to see you so punctual. Miss Alice will be down in a minute—they've gone to call her. Do you know her at all?

DORIAN. No, sir. Why do you ask?

MR. ROONEY. Because, as I was on my way here, certain thoughts came to me. . . . She is a pretty girl.

DORIAN. So I hear.

MR. ROONEY. And comes from a good family. I inherited her father's clients. Your father and he were good friends, by the way. But the man was a little disturbed in his mind and made no provision for his daughter. After his death she became Miss Sylvia's housekeeper. Miss Sylvia loves her; she treats her more like a companion than a servant; she is generous to her now and will be even more so, she says, when Alice takes a husband. Besides, there is an old asthmatic relation in the picture, well-to-do, who'll leave her all she has. Both of you are going to be living in the same house. Take my advice and marry her. What do you say?

DORIAN. Well—I wasn't really thinking of her.

MR. ROONEY. I advise you to think of her from now on. Try to make her like you. You own nothing, nephew—nothing, that is, except a bit of hope, because you're my heir. But I'm in good health, and I mean to make it last as long as I can. Not to mention that I might get married myself. I don't intend to, mind you, but intentions have a way of springing on a man when he least expects them. Think of all the pretty dimpled faces in this world! Comes a wife, come children, such is the custom. Where-upon, farewell nephews. So take your little precautions, my boy, and put yourself in a position where you can do without my money, which is yours today, but which I might take away from you tomorrow.

DORIAN. You are right, dear uncle, and I'll set to work at once.

MR. ROONEY. Do so. Here is Miss Alice. Step aside a little; I want to ask her what she thinks of you.
(Dorian obeys as Alice enters.)

ALICE. I'm sorry, sir, to have made you wait; but Miss Sylvia kept me occupied.

MR. ROONEY. That's quite all right, Miss Alice; I've just arrived. Tell me, what do you think of that tall young man in the corner?

ALICE (*laughing*). And why should I answer you, Mr. Rooney?

MR. ROONEY. Because he is my nephew.

ALICE. Well, you've a nephew worth exhibiting; he's no disgrace to your family.

MR. ROONEY. Do you mean it? He's the lad I'm giving Miss Sylvia for a steward, and I'm glad you like his looks. He has seen you several times in my chambers. Do you remember his gazing at you?

ALICE. No. Not in the least.

MR. ROONEY. Well, a person can't notice everything. Do you know what he said to me the first time he saw you? "Who," he asked, "is that lovely girl?" (*Alice smiles.*) Come here, nephew. Miss Alice, your father and his were dear friends; why shouldn't their children take a fancy to each other as well? Here's one of them, at any rate, who is more than willing; he loves you already.

DORIAN (*embarrassed*). It's not surprising, I'm sure.

MR. ROONEY. See how he stares at you! Not a bad purchase, is he?

ALICE. If you say so, Mr. Rooney. I trust you; we'll have to see.

MR. ROONEY. We'll have to see! We'll have to see! I won't leave until the seeing is done.

ALICE (*laughing*). I don't want to go too fast.

DORIAN. Dear uncle, you're really imposing on Miss Alice.

ALICE (*laughing*). On the other hand, I'm not unmanageable either.

MR. ROONEY. Perfect—you're both agreed! Here, my children. (*He takes their hands.*) I betroth you until further notice. But I can't stay any longer. (*To Alice*) You can introduce your fiancé to Miss Sylvia yourself. Farewell, dear niece.

ALICE (*laughing*). Farewell, dear uncle. (*Mr. Rooney leaves.*) This is all like a dream. How Mr. Rooney rushes things! But will your love be as lasting as it is sudden?

DORIAN. As much the one as the other, Miss Alice.

ALICE. Mr. Rooney left too quickly. Ah, here comes Miss Sylvia. Now that your interests are almost the same as mine—thanks to Mr. Rooney's arrangements—do step out on the terrace for a moment, and let me tell her you've arrived.

DORIAN. With pleasure. (*He leaves.*)

ALICE (*looking after him*). Amazing how sudden a thing love is. (*Enter Sylvia.*)

SYLVIA. Alice, who is the man who bowed so gracefully to me just now, and then went on to the terrace? Did he come for you?

ALICE. No, madam, for you.

SYLVIA. Well, let him come in. Why is he going away?

ALICE. Because he wanted me to speak to you first. He is Mr. Rooney's nephew—the young man who has been suggested as your business agent.

SYLVIA. Is that the man? You don't say. He seems quite well-bred.

ALICE. I know he's well thought of in town.

SYLVIA. I don't doubt it; he seems to deserve it. And yet—Alice—isn't he too handsome for a steward? What will people say?

ALICE. What *should* people say? Are stewards supposed to be brutes?

SYLVIA. You're right. Tell him to come in again. These preliminaries are quite unnecessary. Mr. Rooney's recommendation is enough; I'll engage him.

ALICE. You couldn't make a better choice. (*Leaving, and then coming back.*) Have you decided what consideration he is to have? Mr. Rooney asked me to mention the matter to you.

SYLVIA. Why? We'll have no quarrel on this point. If the man is honest, I will look after him. Go, call him.

ALICE (*hesitating*). You will give him the little cottage that looks out over the garden, won't you?

SYLVIA. Yes, anything he wishes. Go call him, Alice.

ALICE (*calling Dorian from the terrace*). Mr. Dorian, Miss Sylvia is waiting for you.
(*Enter Dorian.*)

SYLVIA. Sir, I am obliged to Mr. Rooney for having thought of me. As he is recommending his own nephew, I feel he is doing me a distinct favor. One of my friends was mentioning another steward he wanted to send me today; but I intend to look no further.

DORIAN. I hope, madam, that my zeal will justify your preference, which, indeed, I hope to preserve. I should be most unhappy if I lost it.

ALICE. Miss Sylvia does not take back her word.

SYLVIA. No, sir, I do not; the matter is settled; all other candidates will be turned away. You are familiar and experienced in business matters, I take it.

DORIAN. Yes, madam; my father was a barrister, and I could be one myself.

SYLVIA. Which is to say that you are a man of condition; in fact, above what you are doing here.

DORIAN. I feel no indignity in my position, madam. To serve you would be an honor for any man, however exalted his rank.

SYLVIA. Well, I will see to it that you keep thinking so. You'll be treated here with all the respect you deserve; and if I can be of service to you in the future, please count on me.

ALICE. This is the true Miss Sylvia speaking; I know her.

SYLVIA. I confess I am angry when I see true gentlemen without means of support while countless nobodies welter in money. It hurts me—especially in young men like yourself. Surely you're not over thirty years old, Mr. Dorian?

DORIAN. I am not quite thirty, madam.

SYLVIA. What must comfort you is that you have ever so much time before you to become happy.

DORIAN. My happiness begins today.

SYLVIA. You'll be shown the rooms I have prepared for you. If they don't suit you, please choose some others. But now we must find somebody to wait on you. Let me see. Alice, whom shall we give him?

ALICE. I suggest Puff. Wait, there he is; let me call him. Puff, come here, Miss Sylvia wants to speak with you.
(*Enter Puff.*)

PUFF. Here I am, Miss Sylvia.

SYLVIA. Puff, this is your new master; I am giving you to Mr. Dorian.

PUFF. What's that, ma'am? You're giving me to Mr. Dorian? Won't I belong to myself any more?

ALICE. What a ninny!

SYLVIA. I only meant that instead of serving me, you will be serving Mr. Dorian.

PUFF (*tearfully*). I don't know why Miss Sylvia is sending me away. I don't deserve to be treated like this after being so faithful to her.

SYLVIA. I'm not sending you away at all, Puff; I'm going to pay you for taking care of Mr. Dorian.

PUFF. But that isn't right. I don't want to toil on one side, while my money comes from another. If I'm going to have your wages, you ought to get my services. Otherwise I'd be robbing you, Miss Sylvia.

SYLVIA. I give up!

ALICE. You're a clown, so help me God. When I send you somewhere or when I tell you to do this or that, don't you obey me?

PUFF. Always.

ALICE. So now it's Mr. Dorian who will be ordering you about instead of me, and it will always be under instructions from Miss Sylvia.

PUFF. Well, that's different. Miss Sylvia will order Mr. Dorian to submit to the service which I will give him by command of Miss Sylvia.

ALICE. Exactly.

PUFF. You see, it had to be explained.
(*Enter a servant.*)

SERVANT. Excuse me, madam; the woman with the new fabrics has arrived.

SYLVIA. I'm going to take a look, but I'll be back presently. Please wait for me, Mr. Dorian; I want to discuss a business matter with you. (*She leaves.*)

PUFF. Well, well, so now we belong one to the other, eh? And you've got precedence over me. I'll be the valet who serves, and you the valet who is told to be served.

ALICE. The booby with his comparisons! Get away from here.

PUFF. Just a moment. With your permission, sir, won't you be paying me at all? Are you told to be served gratis?
(*Dorian laughs.*)

ALICE. That's enough. Leave us alone. Miss Sylvia is going to pay you. Doesn't that satisfy you?

PUFF. Bless me, won't I cost you anything at all? I'll be the cheapest servant anybody ever had.

DORIAN. Puff is right. Here's a little advance of my own.

PUFF. Now you're behaving like an employer. The rest at your convenience.

DORIAN. Go drink to my health.

PUFF. If drinking is all your health needs, I can promise you'll be blooming as long as I live. (*Aside*) A sweet partner the wind has blown my way. (*He leaves.*)

ALICE. Well, congratulations on your reception. Miss Sylvia seems to be making much of you. I'm glad, because we both stand to gain by her favor. Ay! Here comes Mrs. Grumby now; that's her mother, I warn you, and I'll wager I know what brings her our way.
(*Enter Mrs. Grumby.*)

MRS. GRUMBY. Alice, my daughter tells me she has a new steward, courtesy of her solicitor; and frankly I'm not happy about it. She is simply being rude to Lord Dorimont, who had a man of his own selected for her. It seems to me she might at least have waited to see them both. What made her prefer this one? What kind of fellow is he?

ALICE. Here he is, madam.

MRS. GRUMBY. So he's the one, is he? I wouldn't have guessed it; he looks a bit young to me.

ALICE. At thirty, a man is old enough to be steward of a property, madam.

MRS. GRUMBY. That depends. Are you definitely engaged, young man?

DORIAN. I am, madam.

MRS. GRUMBY. And where was your last position?

DORIAN. At home, madam; this is my first employment.

Mrs. Grumby. Indeed! You're going to serve your apprenticeship here, in other words.

Alice. Not at all. Mr. Dorian understands business matters. He is the son of an exceedingly clever man.

Mrs. Grumby (*aside to Alice*). I don't like the fellow. Is that the face of a steward? Or the bearing?

Alice (*aside to Mrs. Grumby*). Bearing doesn't mean a thing. I'll answer for him. He's the very man we need.

Mrs. Grumby. Actually, as long as the gentleman adheres to our intentions, I don't care whether we have him or anyone else.

Dorian. May I ask what these intentions are, madam?

Mrs. Grumby. By all means. Are you acquainted with Lord Dorimont? A name to conjure with in the world. My daughter and he were about to go to law over a considerable piece of land; whereupon the suggestion was made that they marry rather than litigate. My daughter's husband was a man of some standing in society, and he left her a fortune. But as Countess Dorimont her rank would be so high, her connections so distinguished, that I can hardly wait to see the marriage concluded. Naturally, for myself, I am not unwilling to be the mother of a countess, and perhaps—who knows?—even something higher, because his lordship may rise to anything he wishes.

Dorian. Is the marriage quite settled?

Mrs. Grumby. More or less; not quite; my daughter is on the verge. She wants to make sure that her claim to the land is better than his lordship's—so that, if she marries him, he will be all the more beholden to her. But sometimes I am afraid that this is only a pretense on her part. Sylvia has one fault: too little elevation of mind. The name of Dorimont and the rank of countess do not touch her closely enough. She fails to understand how dreary it is to belong to the middle classes. In spite of her wealth, she slumbers in mediocrity.

DORIAN (*softly*). Perhaps she will be no happier for rising above it.

MRS. GRUMBY (*sharply*). Your opinion hardly matters, my dear sir. Please keep your plebeian reflections to yourself, and help our side if you want our friendship.

ALICE. It was only a small moral observation, madam, really harmless.

MRS. GRUMBY. I don't like a base-minded morality.

DORIAN. What help were you referring to, madam?

MRS. GRUMBY. Tell my daughter, after looking at the papers, that her claim is the weaker of the two, and that if she presses the suit, she will lose it.

DORIAN. If her claim is really the weaker, I will not fail to warn her, madam.

MRS. GRUMBY (*aside to Alice*). The man's a fool.—You don't seem to understand. You are being told to inform her that her case is weak, whether it is or not.

DORIAN. Excuse me, Mrs. Grumby, but misleading her sounds a little like dishonesty to me.

MRS. GRUMBY. Dishonesty? Am I by any chance dishonest? What sort of argument is that? I am her mother, sir, and I order you to mislead her for her own good. I, her mother, give the order.

DORIAN. Still, the bad faith will be mine.

MRS. GRUMBY (*aside to Alice*). This blockhead will have to go.—Good day, Mr. Steward. We'll see you soon stewing in another place. (*She leaves.*)

DORIAN. What a difference between mother and daughter!

ALICE. Yes, I suppose so. I'm sorry I didn't have time to warn you about her temper. Anyway, you can see that her mind is set on this marriage. And why should you care what you tell her daughter, as long as the mother stands behind you? I see no need to pester your conscience about this.

DORIAN. I'm sorry; but I'd be encouraging her to take an action she might not have taken without me. However, tell me this: since I'm being asked to persuade her, am I to understand that she is resisting?

ALICE. Only out of laziness.

DORIAN. Let's put our cards on the table, Miss Alice.

ALICE. Well, then, you'll see things in a new light if I tell you that Lord Dorimont is giving me a thousand crowns the day the marriage contract is signed. With reference to Mr. Rooney's project, this money concerns you as much as myself.

DORIAN. Miss Alice, you are a wonderful girl, but you're letting these thousand crowns seduce you, and all for lack of a little thought.

ALICE. On the contrary, it's because of a little thought that I am seduced. In fact, the more thought I give those thousand crowns, the better I like them.

DORIAN. But you love your mistress; and if she were unhappy with this man, wouldn't you blame yourself for having played your part for the sake of this miserable money?

ALICE. Words, words! Lord Dorimont is a good man, so there's no malice on my side. Wait—I see Miss Sylvia coming this way. She wants to talk to you—I'd better go. Ponder the thousand crowns; you'll get to relish them too. (*She leaves.*)

DORIAN (*alone*). I'm not so sorry to be duping her.
(*Enter Sylvia.*)

SYLVIA. You've seen my mother.

DORIAN. Yes, madam, I saw her a moment ago.

SYLVIA. So she told me; she wishes I had taken another steward.

DORIAN. That was indeed my impression.

SYLVIA. Don't let it disturb you. I find you suitable.

DORIAN. And there my ambition ends.

SYLVIA. Let's talk about what is on my mind; but in the strictest confidence, if you please.

DORIAN. I would rather betray my own self.

SYLVIA. That's why I trust you, Dorian. Here is the point: attempts are being made to marry me off to Lord Dorimont in order to prevent litigation over a piece of land which I own.

DORIAN. I know; I had the misfortune of crossing Mrs. Grumby on this very subject a few minutes ago.

SYLVIA. Really? And why?

DORIAN. Because, even if your cause is just, I am requested to tell you the contrary, so as to hasten your marriage; and I begged to be relieved of this task.

SYLVIA. My mother is a frivolous woman. But your good faith doesn't surprise me; I was counting on it. Continue as you are, and don't let my mother's words trouble you. I've no patience with her. Was she disagreeable to you?

DORIAN. It doesn't matter, madam. My readiness and my devotion to you have only increased, and that is all.

SYLVIA. And that is why I *will* not have you plagued. I'll show my own temper if this continues. Really! Not to be left in peace; to be mistreated because of your good intentions; that would be the limit!

DORIAN. By all the gratitude I owe you, madam, I ask you to forget this little incident. I am overcome by your kindness, and only too happy to have been upbraided.

SYLVIA. Thank you. But to return to the lawsuit: if I do not marry his lordship—
(*Enter Trivet.*)

TRIVET. My Lady Fleetwell is feeling better, madam—(*He pre-*

tends surprise at seeing Dorian.) And thanks you—thanks you for your inquiry. (*Dorian pretends to turn away to conceal himself from Trivet.*)

SYLVIA. I'm pleased to hear it.

TRIVET (*still staring at Dorian*). I am also requested, madam, to give you some urgent news.

SYLVIA. What is it?

TRIVET. I have been told to speak only if you were alone.

SYLVIA (*to Dorian*). I haven't finished with you, but will you kindly excuse me for a moment, and then come back again? (*Dorian leaves.*) Now; explain the look of surprise that came over you when you saw Mr. Dorian. Why were you staring at him?

TRIVET. For no particular reason, except that I am no longer able to remain in your service, madam; I take my leave of you as of today.

SYLVIA (*astonished*). What! Because you saw Mr. Dorian here?

TRIVET. Do you know with whom you are dealing?

SYLVIA. Why, with my solicitor's nephew.

TRIVET. Ha! And by what sleight-of-hand did he become known to you? What did he do to gain entrance here?

SYLVIA. Mr. Rooney simply sent him to me to be my steward.

TRIVET. He, your steward? And Mr. Rooney sent him to you? The poor man doesn't know what he is giving you. This boy is a devil!

SYLVIA. What do you mean? Explain yourself; do you know Mr. Dorian?

TRIVET. Do I know him! Do I know him! Yes, I know him; and he knows me too. I hope you saw him hide his head for fear I should see him.

SYLVIA. You're right. Now is my turn to be surprised. Is he up to some wickedness that you know of? Is he dishonest?

TRIVET. Far from it! He is more honorable than fifty gentlemen put together. Oh, his honesty is the eighth wonder of the world.

SYLVIA. Well then, what *is* the matter with him? Why do you frighten me? I'm in a daze . . .

TRIVET. His fault is here (*he touches his forehead*)—here in the head; that's where he ails.

SYLVIA. In the head?

TRIVET. Unhinged. Fit for the padded cell.

SYLVIA. Dorian? He looks quite rational to me. What proof have you got that he is mad?

TRIVET. What proof? He lost his wits six months ago. For six months he has been a lunatic of love, love has parched his brain, he is beyond salvation. I ought to know, he was my employer; and his lunacy forced me to leave him, precisely as it's forcing me to leave you now. Aside from that, there's not another man like him on earth.

SYLVIA (*a little peevishly*). Oh, well, let him go his way—he won't stay here. The last thing I want about me is an addled brain; and addled, I suppose, over some worthless jade. I know the whims men are capable of!

TRIVET. As for that, I beg to differ. Nobody can object to the lady. He is mad, but mad in good taste.

SYLVIA. All the same, I intend to send him away. Do you happen to know the person?

TRIVET. It is my good fortune to see her every day; the person is you, madam.

SYLVIA. Me, you say?

TRIVET. He worships you. For six months he has been more

dead than alive. He'd give his life to look at you for a second. You must have noticed that he seems bewitched when he addresses you.

SYLVIA. I did feel there was something unusual . . . Heaven help him! Poor boy, what has gotten into his head?

TRIVET. Oh, you can't conceive the extent of his madness; it has ruined him, murdered him. He is well built, his face is not bad—good family, good education; not rich, of course. Let me tell you, however, that as for riches, he could have married women—women of quality—who had plenty, and who wanted nothing better than to give him their all, if he'd make them happy. I know of one who can't forget him even now; looks for him every day. I know, because I've met her.

SYLVIA (casually). Even now?

TRIVET. Yes, even now. A tall brunette, very spicy. He runs away from her. Out of the question; Mr. Dorian rebuffs them all. "I'd be deceiving them," he told me; "I cannot love them; my heart is taken." He used to say it with a tear in the corner of his eye; he knows he is to blame.

SYLVIA. This is really too bad. But where did he see me before he came here?

TRIVET. He lost his mind one day as you were leaving the Opera. It was on a Friday; yes, a Friday, I remember now; he told me he saw you come down the stairway, and followed you to your carriage. He had asked your name of someone; and I found him like a man in a trance, absolutely motionless.

SYLVIA. Amazing!

TRIVET. And cry as I would, "Mr. Dorian!"—not a word, nobody upstairs. Finally, however, he came to again with a dazed look on his face. I pushed him into a carriage, and we drove home. I hoped it would all go away, because I liked him; never had a better employer. But he was incurable. You killed his good sense, his jolly temper, his happy mind; from that day on, all he did was dream of you and love you, and all I did was spy on you from morning to night.

Sylvia. I'm utterly speechless . . .

Trivet. I even befriended one of your footmen, who is no longer with you. He gave me news, and drank at my expense. "We're at the playhouse today," he would tell me, and I'd run home with my report; after which, on the stroke of four, my gentleman was standing at the entrance. Or he'd say, "We're calling on Lady this or Lady that," which made us take our stand in the street all night to watch Miss Sylvia going in and coming out, he in a hired coach, and myself behind, both frozen into blocks, because it was winter time. He didn't feel it, but I did; my only relief was cursing my heart out.

Sylvia. Is it possible?

Trivet. Yes, madam. In the end, I had enough. My health was deteriorating, and so was his. I told him that you had gone to the country. He believed me, and I was able to rest—for a day, that is, because on the second day he caught sight of you in the Park, where he had gone to mope over your absence. God help me—he was so angry that, kind as he is, he was going to thrash me. I objected, and gave notice. I was lucky enough to land in your household, madam, where, heaven knows by what twisting and turning, he appears in the figure of a steward—a position, I might add, he would not exchange for that of an emperor.

Sylvia. How very strange. So many of my people cheat me, I was happy to have an honest man in my house at last. Not that I am the least bit angry; I am above that sort of thing.

Trivet. To dismiss him will be a kindness. The more he sees you, madam, the more he perishes.

Sylvia. Actually, I'd be glad to send him away; but that's not the way to cure him, is it? Nor would I know what to tell Mr. Rooney, who recommended him to me. I don't see how I can decently rid myself of him.

TRIVET. Very well; but he'll become incurable.

SYLVIA. I can't help that. My situation is such that I simply cannot do without a steward. Besides, the risk is not as great as you think. On the contrary, if there is anything that can bring the man back to his senses, it's seeing me more often than before; I consider I shall be doing him a favor.

TRIVET. So be it. The favor will do you no harm, at any rate. He won't breathe a word to you about his love.

SYLVIA. Are you sure?

TRIVET. Never fear. He'd rather die. His respect, his adoration, his humility are unbelievable. Do you think he so much as dreams of being loved in return? Never. He says there isn't a man in the universe who deserves you. He only wants to see you, to contemplate you, to gaze at your eyes, your lovely shape, your graceful bearing; nothing more; so he has told me a thousand times.

SYLVIA (shrugging her shoulders). This is really pitiful. Well now, I'll be patient for a few days, until I find a replacement. As for you, don't be afraid; I am satisfied with you; I'll reward you for your loyalty, and I absolutely want you to remain with me. Do you hear, Trivet?

TRIVET. Madam, I am yours for life.

SYLVIA. You won't regret it. Above all, he must not know that I know. Keep our secret, Trivet. No one, not even Alice, must have the least inkling.

TRIVET. You are the only one who knows, madam.

SYLVIA. Here he is again. Go away now. (Trivet leaves. Sylvia is alone.) The truth is, I've heard a secret I would gladly have done without.
(Enter Dorian.)

DORIAN. I am at your disposal, madam.

SYLVIA. Ah, yes. Where was I? I've forgotten.

DORIAN. You were speaking of a lawsuit against Lord Dorimont.

SYLVIA. Yes—that was it. I was mentioning our marriage.

DORIAN. Yes; and I believe you were about to add that you had no taste for it.

SYLVIA. True. I was going to ask you to examine the case and to let me know the risks of going to law. But I don't know. I may not be able to keep you on.

DORIAN. Oh! And yet, a moment ago—

SYLVIA. Yes, you are right. But I should have remembered that I promised Lord Dorimont to take a steward upon his recommendation. I mustn't break my word to him. At the very least I ought to speak to his man.

DORIAN. Nothing, nothing succeeds for an unhappy man like me! And now I am dismissed.

SYLVIA (*weakly*). I didn't say that. I haven't really decided.

DORIAN. I beg you not to leave me in this uncertainty.

SYLVIA. What shall I say? I'll try to keep you. I'll try.

DORIAN. And—the case—shall I proceed with it?

SYLVIA. Let's wait. If I marry his lordship, your time will have been wasted.

DORIAN. It seemed to me—you were saying you felt nothing for him.

SYLVIA. Nothing yet.

DORIAN. Besides, your present situation is so untroubled, so free of care.

SYLVIA (*aside*). I can't bear to hurt him.—Very well, examine the case, examine as much as you like. The papers are in the library, I'll gather them together and place them in your hands. (*Aside*). I haven't the courage to look at him. (*She goes.*)
(*Enter Trivet.*)

TRIVET. Miss Alice wants to show you to your rooms. Puff is enjoying a bottle, so I said I would look for you. Well, how are you being treated?

DORIAN. Lovely lovely girl! I'm in paradise! How did she take what you told her about me?

TRIVET. Her gentle opinion is that she had better keep you—out of compassion; she hopes that the habit of seeing her will cure you.

DORIAN (delighted). Really?

TRIVET. She can't escape; she's in the net. Well, I'm going back.

DORIAN. No, stay; here's Alice now. Tell her that Miss Sylvia wants to give me certain documents, and that I'll be with her as soon as I have them.

TRIVET. Very good. Besides, I've a bit of news of my own for Alice. We have to create a few suspicions where we need them. (Dorian leaves. Enter Alice.)

ALICE. Where's Mr. Dorian? I thought I saw him here with you.

TRIVET (brusquely). He says Miss Sylvia wants to give him some documents. Is it necessary for him to inspect his rooms? He'd be pretty squeamish if he didn't like them. Damn it, I'd advise him—

ALICE. Mind your own business. I'm just obeying Miss Sylvia's orders.

TRIVET. Miss Sylvia is a well-behaved, kind lady. But I'm warning you about our little upstart. Have you noticed him ogling her with his soft brown eyes?

ALICE. He ogles her with the eyes nature gave him.

TRIVET. As you wish. But I'm much mistaken if I haven't seen this puppy before, I don't remember where, staring hungrily at Miss Sylvia.

ALICE. Well, does it upset you if men admire her?

TRIVET. No; but I'm thinking that he came here for only one reason: to get a closer view of her.

ALICE (*laughing*). Ha, ha, the idea! Go on, you're a blockhead, an ignoramus.

TRIVET (*laughing too*). Well, I suppose I *am* a fool.

ALICE. Ha, ha, ha, the genius and his observations! (*She leaves, still laughing.*)

TRIVET (*alone*). Take root, little seed. She'll appreciate my observations better by and by. So. Every piece in my battery is loaded—and now: fire!

ACT TWO

(Enter Sylvia and Dorian.)

DORIAN. You'll incur no risk whatever if you press your suit, madam. I have gone so far as to consult several persons; your case is excellent; and if your only reason for marrying Lord Dorimont is the one you have mentioned, I hope I have removed it.

SYLVIA. I am also reluctant to distress the poor Count.

DORIAN. Still, it wouldn't be right to sacrifice yourself for fear of distressing him.

SYLVIA. Have you examined the case fairly? You were saying before that my present situation is untroubled and carefree. Aren't you interested in keeping it so? And aren't you a little too prejudiced against this marriage, and consequently against the Count?

DORIAN. I merely consider your interests above his, and above anyone else's in the world.

SYLVIA. I can't object to that! Well, be that as it may, if I do marry him, and if he wants to place his own steward here, you won't suffer for it. I promise to find you a position superior to this one.

DORIAN *(dejected)*. No, Miss Sylvia. If I am unlucky enough to lose my situation here, I'll look for no other. And I do expect to lose it.

SYLVIA. Oh, I don't know. I might take the case to court after all. We'll see.

DORIAN. There was something else I meant to tell you, madam. The overseer of one of your estates has died. I suggest that we send someone from here to step into his shoes; Trivet for instance; I'll replace him with a man I can vouch for.

SYLVIA. Why not send your man instead? I want to keep Trivet here; he is a man I trust. By the way, I think I heard him say that he was in your service for a short time.

DORIAN (*pretending embarrassment*). Yes, he was. He is a faithful servant, but not altogether punctilious. I'm afraid these people don't often speak well of their employers. Perhaps he will set your mind against me.

SYLVIA (*nonchalant*). No; Trivet speaks very highly of you. (*Enter Mr. Rooney.*) Mr. Rooney, what can I do for you?

MR. ROONEY. Miss Sylvia, I am your humble servant. I have come to thank you for engaging my nephew on my recommendation.

SYLVIA. I didn't hesitate a moment, as you can see.

MR. ROONEY. You're most obliging. Didn't you tell me that another man had been proposed to you?

SYLVIA. I did.

MR. ROONEY. Splendid. Because I have come to take this lad away for an important matter.

DORIAN (*bridling*). How is that?

MR. ROONEY. You'll see.

SYLVIA. But my dear Mr. Rooney, this is rather sudden, and very ill-timed, because I have already refused the other person.

DORIAN. As for myself, I'll never leave Miss Sylvia unless she discharges me.

MR. ROONEY. You don't know what you're saying, my boy. You'll see in a minute that you've got to pack your trunks. Miss Sylvia, I appeal to you. Picture a lady, thirty-five years old, said to be pretty, a worthy soul, and quality. She won't reveal her name, but says I have been her solicitor. Her income amounts to fifteen thousand a year at the lowest. She intends to show me her books. She has seen Dorian in my chambers, has spoken with him, knows he hasn't a penny, and offers to marry him on the spot. (*To Dorian*) The messenger she sent me is coming back in a short time for an answer. He has orders to take you directly to her. And that is why I want you home two hours from now. What is your opinion, madam? Am I acting right or wrong?

SYLVIA (*coldly*). Mr. Dorian must answer for himself.

MR. ROONEY. Well? What is he dreaming about? Sir, will you come?

DORIAN. No, I will not.

MR. ROONEY. What? What's that? Did you hear what I said? Fifteen thousand at the lowest!

DORIAN. If she had twenty times more, I still wouldn't marry her. Neither of us would be happy. My heart is pledged. I am in love with someone else.

MR. ROONEY (*mocking*). My heart is pledged! Isn't that a pity now! "My heart"—beautifully said! I didn't know you were a romantic puppy. So you want to manage somebody else's house instead of your own. Is this your last word, my faithful swain?

DORIAN. I'll never change my mind.

MR. ROONEY. My dear nephew, you are an ass, and as far as I am concerned, the woman you've "pledged your heart" to is a she-ass if she doesn't agree with me. What is your opinion, madam?

SYLVIA (*softly*). Don't scold him. He seems to be in the wrong, I admit—

MR. ROONEY. Seems! Excuse me, Miss Sylvia, but he's about—

SYLVIA. I don't know; his feelings are forgivable. And yet, Mr. Dorian, you must try to conquer this inclination, if you can. I know it is hard.

DORIAN. Impossible, madam; my love is dearer to me than my life.

MR. ROONEY. Those who enjoy romantic moonshine must be happy to hear you; you're a prize specimen, my nephew. Madam, I appeal to you; does this make sense?

SYLVIA. I'll leave you; speak to him alone. (*Aside*) I'm so shaken, I'd better go. (*She leaves.*)

DORIAN (*aside*). If he knew how helpful he has been!

MR. ROONEY. Dorian, do you know that people like you are bundled up in straitjackets? Come here, Miss Alice.
(*Enter Alice.*)

ALICE. I've just been told you were here, Mr. Rooney.

MR. ROONEY. We need your opinion, my dear. What do you think of a penniless man who refuses a respectable and good-looking woman with a steady income of fifteen thousand a year?

ALICE. The answer is easy: the man's a fool.

MR. ROONEY. Well, here is your fool; and his excuse is that you've stolen his heart away. Since, however, I suppose he hasn't won yours as yet, and since I think you've still got your wits about you, considering how recently you met him, I ask you very humbly to help me bring him back to his senses. You're a pretty girl, nobody can deny it; but you don't want to compete against fifteen thousand a year, I'm sure; that's more than the most beautiful eyes in the world are worth.

ALICE. Dorian is refusing all this wealth for me?

MR. ROONEY. Exactly; but you're too generous to let him.

ALICE (*passionately*). You're wrong, Mr. Rooney, I love him too much to set him free. This is heavenly. Oh, Dorian, how noble you are! I never thought I was so dear to you.

MR. ROONEY. Congratulations! I've hardly shown him to you, and already you're mad about him. Aren't women amazing! It didn't take you long to catch fire.

ALICE. Now, Mr. Rooney! Does anyone need so much money to be happy? Miss Sylvia likes me, and she'll make up in part for Dorian's sacrifice. Oh, Dorian, how grateful I will be!

DORIAN. Oh, no, Miss Alice, you've no reason to be grateful. I'm yielding to my own wishes, and I'm considering only myself. You owe me nothing; I wouldn't dream of claiming your gratitude.

ALICE. How considerate you are! This is the tenderest thing anyone ever said to a girl.

MR. ROONEY. Really? I suppose I'm no connoisseur, because it strikes me as downright stupid. Good-bye, my young beauty; I wouldn't have paid the amount *he* is choosing to spend on you. And good-bye to you, my idiot nephew; keep your tenderness, and I'll keep my legacy. (*He leaves.*)

ALICE. He's furious, but we'll bring him round, my dear.

DORIAN. I hope so. Here comes somebody else.

ALICE. Oh, it's the Count, the one I told you about, who is supposed to marry Miss Sylvia.

DORIAN. I'll leave you. He might speak to me about the lawsuit. You know what I've said on that subject. There's no point in my meeting him. (*He leaves.*)
(*Enter Lord Dorimont.*)

LORD DORIMONT. How d'you do, Alice.

ALICE. You're back, my lord.

LORD DORIMONT. Yes. I'm told that Sylvia is strolling in the garden; and I've heard something from her mother that I do not like at all. I had proposed a steward to her; he was to come here today; and now she has retained another man, a person whom her mother dislikes and who will obviously do little to help us.

ALICE. At the same time, my lord, he will do nothing to harm us. Come, set your mind at ease. He is a man of the world, and if Mrs. Grumby dislikes him, the fault is a little on her side. She began so roughly with him a while ago, she treated him so rudely, that it's no wonder she didn't make friends with him. She even took him to task for being handsome, believe it or not.

LORD DORIMONT. Isn't he the man I saw go out through this door a moment ago?

ALICE. Yes, my lord.

LORD DORIMONT. He is good-looking, to be sure; better than I would expect of a businessman.

ALICE. Excuse me, my lord; he is a man of excellent breeding.

LORD DORIMONT. There may be a way out. Sylvia is fond of me, but she is slow in making up her mind. She must be told that the outcome of her lawsuit is in doubt, and that marriage is the only solution. Let's take this steward into our confidence. If money will win him over to our side, I'll be generous with him.

ALICE. Impossible. He can't be bought. He's the most disinterested man in the realm.

LORD DORIMONT. I'm sorry to hear it. Disinterested people are good for nothing.

ALICE. Leave him to me, my lord.
(Enter Puff.)

PUFF. Miss Alice, here's a man who is looking for another man. Do you know who it would be?

ALICE. And who is the other man? Whom does he want?

PUFF. That's what I don't know; I came to ask you.

ALICE. Have him come in.

PUFF (calling). Hey, boy, come and tell your story here. (He leaves.)
(Enter the Apprentice, a young man.)

ALICE. What is it you want, my boy?

APPRENTICE. I'm looking for a gentleman to give him a portrait with a case he ordered for it. He told us to give it to no man but himself, and said he would come for it in person. But my father is going on a little trip tomorrow, so he sent me to return the case and portrait to the gentleman. I was told I could find him here. I know him by sight, but I don't know his name.

ALICE. Aren't you the man he means, my lord?

LORD DORIMONT. No, not I.

APPRENTICE. No, miss, he's not the man; it's somebody else.

ALICE. And where were you told that you could find him here?

APPRENTICE. In the rooms of a solicitor by the name of Rooney.

LORD DORIMONT. Isn't that Miss Sylvia's solicitor? Let me see the case.

APPRENTICE. You mustn't, sir; I'm supposed to give it only to its owner. The lady's picture is inside.

LORD DORIMONT. A lady's picture! What does this mean? Is it Sylvia's picture? I'm going to ask a few questions. (*He leaves.*)

ALICE. You did wrong to talk about the picture in front of this gentleman. I know the man you're looking for; he's Mr. Rooney's nephew—the solicitor to whose chambers you went.

APPRENTICE. Maybe.

ALICE. A tall man, whose name is Dorian.

APPRENTICE. Yes, I think that's his name.

ALICE. He told me about the portrait; I'm his trusted friend. Did you see the picture?

APPRENTICE. No, I didn't.

ALICE. Well, the picture is of me. Mr. Dorian will be away all day. You'd better give me the case; don't be afraid; he'll be obliged to you, as a matter of fact. You see I know all about it.

APPRENTICE. I suppose so. Here it is, miss. Please give it to him when he comes back.

ALICE. I certainly will.

APPRENTICE. He still owes us a little something for it, but I'll stop in again, and if he's still away, I'm sure you'll pay for him, won't you?

ALICE. Of course I will. You can go now. (*Aside*) Here's Dorian.—Go, go, my boy. (*The Apprentice leaves.*)

ALICE (*alone and happy*). It must be my picture. Isn't he wonderful! Mr. Rooney was right—Dorian *has* known me for some time.
(*Enter Dorian.*)

DORIAN. Miss Alice, has someone asked for me? Puff tells me he thinks somebody was looking for me.

ALICE (*looking at him tenderly*). You're ever so charming, Dorian. I'd be heartless if I didn't love you. Yes, you can be easy, the apprentice came, I talked to him, the case is in my possession, and I am keeping it.

DORIAN. I don't know—

ALICE. Don't pretend! I have it, I tell you, and I'm not angry with you. I'll return it to you as soon as I have peeked at it. Go now. Here comes Miss Sylvia with her mother and the Count; they must be talking about the picture. Don't wait for them; I'll explain everything.

DORIAN (*Chuckling, aside, on his way out*). She snapped at the bait. (*He leaves.*)
(*Enter Sylvia, Lord Dorimont, and Mrs. Grumby.*)

SYLVIA. Alice, what is this portrait his lordship has been telling me about—a mysterious portrait brought here no one knows to whom, and apparently a portrait of myself. Tell me about it.

ALICE (*dreamily*). Oh, it's nothing, Miss Sylvia; I unraveled the mystery after Lord Dorimont left—he needn't be alarmed at all. The portrait has nothing to do with you.

LORD DORIMONT. And how do you know that, my dear? You haven't looked at it, have you?

ALICE. No, but it's just as if I had. I know whom it concerns; I beg you not to trouble yourself about it.

LORD DORIMONT. All we know is that the portrait represents a woman, and that it was commissioned by someone in this house, who is not me.

ALICE. Quite; but I repeat, the picture concerns neither Miss Sylvia nor yourself.

SYLVIA. Well, if you are so well informed, share your knowledge with us; I insist. Rumors not at all to my liking are beginning to spread. Speak up, Alice.

MRS. GRUMBY. Yes, there's an unpleasant cloud of mystery hanging over all this; and yet you needn't upset yourself, my dear. Lord Dorimont is your suitor, and a little jealousy, even a little unjustified jealousy, is rather becoming in a lover.

LORD DORIMONT. I'm jealous only of the anonymous gentleman who dares to indulge in the pleasure of owning Sylvia's picture.

SYLVIA. As you please, my lord; I understand your hint, but I don't relish this kind of banter. Well, Alice?

ALICE. Well, madam, here's a great to-do about nothing. The picture is of me.

LORD DORIMONT. Of you?

ALICE. Yes, of me. And why not, if you please? Is this so inconceivable?

MRS. GRUMBY. I'm like Lord Dorimont; I think it's very strange.

ALICE. With all due modesty, Mrs. Grumby, I am better than a good many fashionable ladies who have their portraits painted every day.

SYLVIA. And who has gone to this expense for you?

ALICE. A very charming man who loves me, who is refined, who knows what tenderness is, and who wants to marry me; and since you force me to tell you who he is, his name is Dorian.

SYLVIA. My steward?

ALICE. Yes.

MRS. GRUMBY. The fop, with his tenderness!

SYLVIA (*angrily*). You're not telling us the truth; how has he had time to have you painted since he came to my house?

ALICE. Very simple; he knew me before.

SYLVIA. Give me the picture.

ALICE. I haven't opened the case yet, but here I am.
(*Sylvia opens the case; all look at the picture.*)

LORD DORIMONT. I knew it! I knew it! It's Sylvia.

ALICE. Miss Sylvia! I was wrong! (*Aside*) And Trivet was right.

SYLVIA (*aside*). I see it all. (*To Alice*) What made you believe it was your picture, Alice?

ALICE. Anybody would have made the same mistake, Miss Sylvia. Mr. Rooney tells me his nephew is in love with me; Dorian listens and doesn't say no. When he rejects a rich lady in my presence, the uncle reproaches me and says I am to blame. Then comes a man with a portrait, looking for its owner; I question him and I gather that he is talking about Dorian. He tells me the picture is of a woman. What was I to think? Dorian loves me so much he has refused a fortune for my sake. I could only conclude that I was the person in the painting. And yet I was mistaken. The honor turned out to be too great for me. I think I see where the truth lies, and I won't say another word.

SYLVIA. Well, the rest is not difficult to guess. My lord, you act surprised and angry; no doubt the orders you gave led to some confusion; but you can impose on me no longer. The unknown man is none other than yourself. I'm sure of it.

ALICE. I don't think so, madam.

MRS. GRUMBY. Yes, it must be, it is; my lord, why deny it? Considering on what footing you are with my daughter, the present of a portrait is no great crime. Confess, my lord.

LORD DORIMONT (*coldly*). No, madam, on my honor, I am not the man. I am not acquainted with Mr. Rooney. How could anyone say in his chambers that I could be found here? Impossible.

MRS. GRUMBY. This *is* a curious circumstance.

SYLVIA. What is a circumstance more or less? My opinion stands. Moreover, I am keeping the picture; no one else shall have it. But what's that noise? See what it is, Alice.
(*Enter Trivet and Puff.*)

PUFF. And you're a baboon!

ALICE. What's the matter, you two?

TRIVET. One word from me, and your master would be kicked out of here.

PUFF. From you! Ha, ha. If rabble like you hanged themselves, nobody would notice you were missing.

TRIVET. Damnation, I'd let you feel the end of my stick, if I didn't have too much respect for Miss Sylvia.

PUFF. Try, try if you dare. Here she is.

SYLVIA. Why are you two quarreling? What's the matter?

MRS. GRUMBY. Come here, Trivet. Tell us what's the one word you might say against Mr. Dorian; I think we ought to know it.

PUFF. That's right; let's hear the one word.

SYLVIA. You be still. Let him speak.

TRIVET. Madam, he has been belaboring me with insults for over an hour.

PUFF. I'm supporting my master's cause, that's what I get paid for, and I won't stand for a word against him from this vandal; I appeal to Miss Sylvia.

MRS. GRUMBY. Meantime, let's hear what the word is. First things first.

PUFF. I dare him to utter one letter of it.

TRIVET. I was carried away by my anger, madam. As I was tidying up Mr. Dorian's room, I noticed a painting of Miss Sylvia hanging on the wall. I wanted to remove it; it had no business being there, I thought; I thought it was indecent to have it on that wall. This lumphead tried to stop me, and we almost came to blows.

PUFF. And why were you trying to take it down? It's a pretty picture; and my master was staring at it so happily, it was a joy to watch him and see the satisfaction he was getting. Then comes this baboon and tries to take it away from the poor man. Oh, the wicked deed! Remove some other piece of furniture, you clown, and leave this one alone.

TRIVET. And I tell you it won't be left hanging, I'll remove it, and Miss Sylvia herself will give the order and put you in your place.

SYLVIA. Why? What does all this matter to me? Really! Brawling over an old portrait somebody happened to hang there a long time ago. Is this a thing worth talking about?

MRS. GRUMBY (*sourly*). Excuse me, my love, but that is no place for your picture, and it should be removed. Your steward will survive without his contemplations.

SYLVIA (*ironically*). You're right, dear mother, he won't miss the portrait. (*To Puff and Trivet*) Leave us, both of you. (*They go.*)

LORD DORIMONT (*sarcastically*). One point is established; your business manager has excellent taste.

SYLVIA (*likewise*). Oh, no doubt about it. It's absolutely fantastic that he should have glanced at that picture.

MRS. GRUMBY. I never liked the man, Sylvia. I'm a good judge of character, as you know, and I don't like him. Take it from me. You heard what Trivet said about his word. I come back to that. He must know something. Question him and try to discover what it is. I simply know that this young upstart is not for you. We all know it—all except you.

ALICE (*casually*). I certainly have my doubts about him.

SYLVIA. What is it you all see that I don't see? Of course I'm not very perceptive; I fail to grasp, for instance, why I should discharge a man who comes to me with the best recommendation, a valuable person who serves me well—and even too well, perhaps. This much, at any rate, has not escaped me.

MRS. GRUMBY. You're blind, my girl.

SYLVIA. Not so blind; to each her own light. But I'm quite willing to listen to Trivet. Your advice is good. Alice, will you call him, please? (*Alice leaves.*) If he gives me good reasons for dismissing the man—who was impudent enough to look at a painting—he won't be long with me. Otherwise, you must allow me to keep him until I dislike him, not you.

MRS. GRUMBY. Well, dislike him you will. I won't say anything else until I'm proved right.

LORD DORIMONT. As for me, Sylvia, I admit I have been afraid the man would urge you to go to law against me. Because you are dear to me, I wished him to discourage you. But no matter what he does, I declare here and now that I will not stand up in court against you; you and your agents are free to decide the case as you see fit; I'd rather lose all than contend with you.

MRS. GRUMBY. What contention? The marriage would settle everything. It is all decided, isn't it?

LORD DORIMONT. I'll keep my counsel about Mr. Dorian. But I will return to see what you think of him; and if you dismiss him, as I daresay you will, I shall offer you once more the steward I have retained for you.

MRS. GRUMBY. I'll do likewise; my mouth is shut; otherwise

you'd accuse me of having hallucinations. You'll change your mind without our help. I'm relying on Trivet for that, and here he is. Come away, my dear Count. (*They leave.*)
(*Enter Trivet.*)

TRIVET. You wished to speak with me, madam?

SYLVIA. Come here, Trivet. You're careless and indiscreet, and you'll be spoiling my good opinion of you. I asked you to keep what you knew about Mr. Dorian to yourself. Why, then, do you start quarreling over a wretched painting with a fool who raises a horrid clamor here, and who is capable of putting ideas into people's heads which I would rather die than see spread about?

TRIVET. Heaven forbid, madam; I saw no harm; I was only showing my respect and my zeal.

SYLVIA. Leave your zeal alone, I don't want it and I don't need it; what I need is your silence while I search for a way out of the muddle you've made for me. Without you I wouldn't know that the man is in love with me, and I wouldn't need to pry and investigate.

TRIVET. I realize now that I was wrong.

SYLVIA. That brawl was bad enough, but then to cry out "One word from me"! Can anything be more thoughtless?

TRIVET. Too zealous again.

SYLVIA. Don't babble—for heaven's sake, hold your tongue! I wish I could make you forget everything you told me.

TRIVET. I stand corrected, Miss Sylvia.

SYLVIA. Now, because of your thoughtlessness, I'm obliged to pretend that I'm interrogating you about Mr. Dorian. My mother and Lord Dorimont are expecting revelations from you. What am I to report to them?

TRIVET. Oh, as for that, nothing is easier. You can report that people who know him have told me he is a clever man, but incapable of doing the work you have laid out for him.

SYLVIA. Wonderful! There's only one drawback to your suggestion, namely that I will be told to discharge him; and the time for
that hasn't come. I have given the matter some thought. Caution
requires that I deal indirectly with this passion of his. Who
knows? If he is pushed too far, it may burst into the open. I can't
trust a desperate man. What holds me back is no longer my need
of him, but a care for my reputation—(*more softly*) unless what
Alice has said is true; and then I have nothing to fear. According
to her, Dorian saw her some time ago. It seems that Mr. Rooney
speaks openly of their love, in Dorian's very presence, and that
the two are going to be married. If this is true, I'm happy.

TRIVET. Stuff! Mr. Dorian has never seen Alice, near or far. The
old solicitor reeled off this fable because he wants to see them
married. "I didn't dare contradict him," says Mr. Dorian to me,
"because I would have set the girl against me, and I know she
has Miss Sylvia's ear. Now she thinks it was for her sake I
refused the fortune I was offered."

SYLVIA (*nonchalant*). Oh, he told you the whole story?

TRIVET. Yes, and only a moment ago, down in the garden, he
almost threw himself at my feet. Why? To beg me not to reveal
his passion and to forget his violence when I left his service. I
told him I would hold my tongue, provided he quits your house;
and this started him groaning and weeping. Oh, it was pitiful.

SYLVIA. Dear me, don't torment him, Trivet. You see how right I
was—we must be gentle with him. I placed my hopes in his
marriage to Alice; I thought surely he would forget me; and now
that's all gone up in smoke.

TRIVET. Pure fantasy. Does madam have any commands for me?

SYLVIA. Wait! What shall I do? If only he offended me when he
speaks to me; but not a word escapes him. All I know of his love
is what you report, and that, after all, is not grounds for dismissing him. Of course, he would provoke me if he revealed himself;
but I rather wish he would.

TRIVET. A good point. The truth is, Mr. Dorian isn't worthy of you. I wouldn't say it if he had a better income, because no one can find fault with his birth. But he is rich only in his soul, and that's not enough.

SYLVIA (*dejected*). No, it isn't; such is the custom. I don't know how to treat him. I really don't know. We shall see. . . .

TRIVET. Of course, there *is* an excellent pretext we could use. The picture—the one Alice thought was of herself—

SYLVIA. Oh, no; I can't accuse him of that; the Count had it painted.

TRIVET. Not at all. Mr. Dorian painted it with his own hand. He told me so himself. He was at work on it when I left him two months ago.

SYLVIA. Well, you'd better go. We've been chatting too long. If I am asked what I found out from you, I'll say what we agreed on. Here he comes. I want to set a little trap for him.

TRIVET. Very good, madam. If you're lucky, he'll make a declaration, and then, "Out you go!"

SYLVIA. Leave us.

TRIVET (*aside, as he is leaving*). I can't tell him what happened; but all's well whether he declares himself or not. (*He leaves.*) (*Enter Dorian.*)

DORIAN. I beg for your protection, madam. You see me utterly distraught. I gave up everything for the honor of entering your service; I am more attached to you than I can say; no one could be more loyal and disinterested; and yet my position here is in doubt. Everybody in this house resents me, persecutes me, plots my downfall. I don't know what to think. I live in dread that you will yield to all this hostility. Oh, I couldn't bear it. . . .

SYLVIA (*softly*). Calm yourself. You are not in the hands of those who are trying to harm you. They have made no impression on my mind, and their little plots will fail. I am the mistress here.

DORIAN. Yours is my only support, madam.

SYLVIA. It will not be withdrawn. But let me give you a piece of advice: don't look so perturbed in front of them; they'll doubt your competence, and it will seem as if I kept you out of mere kindness.

DORIAN. They wouldn't be far from wrong; your kindness fills me with gratitude.

SYLVIA. Very well; but they needn't know it. I am thankful for your devotion, but you ought to conceal it a little, because it is making enemies for you. Take the lawsuit, for instance; you refused to deceive me about it. But here's your opportunity of winning them over. Advise me as they wish; I give you my permission. They will feel that you served their interests, since, on further thought, I have decided to marry the Count.

DORIAN. Decided, madam?

SYLVIA. Yes, positively. His lordship will think that you contributed to my decision; I will even tell him so; and I can assure you that you'll remain in our service. (*Aside*) He's turning pale.

DORIAN. What a difference for me, madam. . . .

SYLVIA. None whatsoever. Set your mind at rest, and write a note I want to dictate to you. Pen and paper are on the table.

DORIAN. A note to whom, madam?

SYLVIA. To the Count, whom I left deeply alarmed. I shall give him a pretty surprise in the note you're about to write. (*Dorian doesn't move.*) There's the table, sir. You're dreaming!

DORIAN. Yes, madam.

SYLVIA (*aside*). He doesn't know what he's doing. Let's see how long this will last.

DORIAN (*at the table, looking for paper; aside*). Trivet duped me.

SYLVIA. Are you ready to write?

DORIAN. I can't find any paper, madam.

SYLVIA. Really! Here, under your nose.

DORIAN. So it is.

SYLVIA. Ready? "Come at once, my lord, your marriage is settled." Have you got that written down?

DORIAN. Excuse me?

SYLVIA. Aren't you listening? "Your marriage is settled. Miss Sylvia has asked me to write to you, and will confirm this letter in person." (*Aside*) He is suffering, but he is suffering in silence. Isn't he going to speak?—"Do not attribute this decision to any fear Miss Sylvia might be entertaining concerning the outcome of a dubious lawsuit."

DORIAN. Not dubious at all, madam; I have assured you that you would win it.

SYLVIA. No matter. Continue. "No, my lord. I am instructed by her to say that her determination rests entirely upon her recognition of your deserts."

DORIAN (*aside*). God almighty, I'm lost.—Madam, you felt nothing for him!

SYLVIA. Please finish the note. "Upon her recognition of your deserts." Your hand is trembling; and how strange you look! Are you ill?

DORIAN. I am not well, madam.

SYLVIA. What, so suddenly? How odd. Address the note, if you please, to Lord Dorimont, and have Trivet carry it to him. (*Aside*) My heart is drumming.—Dear heavens, this is a mere scribble! The name is almost illegible. (*Aside*) He's not entirely convinced.

DORIAN (*aside*). Is she testing me, by any chance? Trivet, why didn't you warn me?
(*Enter Alice.*)

ALICE. I am very glad to find Mr. Dorian here, madam. He'll confirm what I have come to say. You have offered several times to find a husband for me. I didn't take advantage of your kindness before today; but now Mr. Dorian has followed me to this house; he has even refused a lady of great means for my sake, or so at least he has led me to believe. The time has come for him to declare himself openly; but I want to obtain him only with your consent, madam. Now, sir, is the time to ask Miss Sylvia for my hand. If she gives her approval, I will not deny you. (*She leaves.*)

SYLVIA (*aside*). The silly girl!—I am delighted, Dorian; you have made an excellent choice. Here is a good, lovely young girl.

DORIAN (*dejected*). No, madam, I don't give her a thought.

SYLVIA. Don't you? She says that you are in love with her, and that you saw her before coming to this house.

DORIAN (*sadly*). It isn't true. My uncle told her this lie without consulting me, and I was afraid of contradicting him, because Alice might have turned you against me. And she was mistaken, too, about the rich marriage she thought I had refused on her account. I never encouraged her. I am in no condition to give my heart to anyone. It is given away already, and forever. The most brilliant fortune can no longer tempt me.

SYLVIA. You should have enlightened poor Alice.

DORIAN. She might have kept you from admitting me to your house. Besides, my indifference should have been obvious to her.

SYLVIA. But in your condition, what difference did it make to you whether you were employed in my house or in another?

DORIAN. It is happiness for me to be here, madam.

SYLVIA. There's something unintelligible in all this! And this person you love—do you see her often?

DORIAN. Not often enough, madam; to see her every moment of the day would not be often enough for me.

SYLVIA (*aside*). How sweetly he said that!—Is she young? Has she ever been married?

DORIAN. She is a widow, madam.

SYLVIA. Why don't you marry her? Surely she loves you too.

DORIAN. She knows nothing of my adoration. Forgive me for using such a word; I can't speak of her except with passion.

SYLVIA. I question you only because you amaze me. She knows nothing of your love, and yet you sacrifice a fortune for her sake! Incredible! How do you manage to keep such deep feelings silent? A man tries to obtain a woman's love, it seems to me; what is more natural and forgivable?

DORIAN. Heaven forbid that I should entertain the slightest hope! I obtain her love? Never; she is too far above me; my respect condemns me to silence, and I shall die at least without arousing her displeasure.

SYLVIA. I can't conceive of a woman who deserves this fabulous devotion. Is she so very wonderful?

DORIAN. I must not praise her, madam; I would lose my way if I tried to describe her. No woman equals her in beauty and charm; she never speaks to me, never looks at me, but my love for her increases.

SYLVIA (*lowering her eyes*). Your behavior offends good sense. A woman who will never know that you love her! How bizarre! What are you hoping for?

DORIAN. The pleasure of seeing her now and then, and of being in her presence.

SYLVIA. In her presence! Are you forgetting where you are?

DORIAN. I meant in the presence of her portrait, whenever I am away from her.

SYLVIA. Indeed! You have had her portrait painted?

DORIAN. No, I learned to paint and I painted it myself. I would rather have been without her portrait than owe it to another hand.

SYLVIA (aside). I'll push him to the breaking point.—Let me see the picture.

DORIAN. Excuse me, madam; my love is hopeless, but I must keep it inviolably secret.

SYLVIA. I have a picture which happened to fall into my hands. Somebody found it in the house. (She shows the case.) Is it hers, by any chance?

DORIAN. It can't be.

SYLVIA. And yet, wouldn't it be odd if it were? Look. (She opens the case.)

DORIAN (pretending to be abashed). I would have died a thousand deaths to prevent this accident. . . . How can I atone . . . Oh! (He falls to his knees.)

SYLVIA. I'm not angry, Dorian. I pity you for having gone astray. But don't persist. I forgive you.
(Alice appears at the door.)

ALICE. Ah! (She vanishes. Dorian leaps to his feet.)

SYLVIA. Oh, God, that was Alice! She saw you!

DORIAN (pretending to be upset). No—she didn't—I don't think so; she didn't actually come in.

SYLVIA. I say she saw you. Leave me; go away; I hate you. Give me the letter. (Dorian leaves.) This is what comes of having kept him here!
(Enter Trivet.)

TRIVET. Did Mr. Dorian make a declaration, madam? Shall I give him notice?

SYLVIA. No! He didn't say a thing. I saw no hint of anything you mentioned. Let me hear no more about it, and stop meddling. (She leaves.)

TRIVET (*alone*). This is the critical moment.
(*Enter Dorian.*)

DORIAN. Trivet, here you are!

TRIVET. Keep away!

DORIAN. I don't know what to think of her words.

TRIVET. Are you mad? She's not ten steps away. Do you want to ruin my work?

DORIAN. You must clear up—

TRIVET. In the garden!

DORIAN. . . . . a doubt—

TRIVET. In the garden—I'll join you there.

DORIAN. But—

TRIVET. I'm not listening.

DORIAN. I fear the worst!

ACT THREE

(Enter Dorian and Trivet.)

TRIVET. And I say no; let's not waste any time. Is the letter ready?

DORIAN. Yes, here it is. I've written the address on it: Broad Street.

TRIVET. Are you sure Puff doesn't know the neighborhood?

DORIAN. He says he doesn't.

TRIVET. And did you tell him to ask Alice or myself where it is?

DORIAN. I told him, and I'll tell him again.

TRIVET. Good. Go give it to him. I'll take care of Alice.

DORIAN. I'm still hesitant. Aren't we hurrying Sylvia too much? She is distraught enough as it is. Do you want to confound her now by suddenly exposing her to the world?

TRIVET. Absolutely. Let the ax fall. We'll finish her off while she's reeling. She doesn't know what she is doing any more. Don't you see—she's cheating with me and pretending you said nothing to her. I'll teach her to fool her own confidant and love you behind my back!

DORIAN. Oh, how I suffered during that last conversation! Since you knew that she wanted me to declare myself, why didn't you give me a sign?

TRIVET. Ridiculous; she would have noticed it at once. Besides, your ignorance made your grief look more real. Don't tell me you're sorry about the results! Our gentleman suffered! Well, by God, it's only right you should suffer a little.

DORIAN. Do you know what is going to happen? She'll suddenly decide to drive me out.

TRIVET. I dare her! No, it's too late for that. The time for courage is gone, she has to marry you.

DORIAN. Watch out. Her mother gives her no peace.

TRIVET. I'd be sorry if she did.

DORIAN. Sylvia herself is embarrassed because Alice discovered me at her feet.

TRIVET. Good. Let her wait a little. We'll embarrass her with embarrassments she hasn't thought of yet! It was I who sent Alice into the room just as you went down on your knees.

DORIAN. But she says she hates me.

TRIVET. Can you blame her? Do you expect her to be cheerful when she's in love against her own will? You're running away with her feelings and her property—the least she can do is make a little outcry. Enough arguments; I'm the man at the helm.

DORIAN. But remember that I love her; and if all this hurry leads to disaster, I'll be in despair.

TRIVET. I know you love her; that's precisely why I won't listen to you. You're in no condition to judge anything. Be sensible and trust a man who is acting in cold blood. Here comes Alice; away! I'll keep her here until Puff arrives.
(*Dorian leaves. Enter Alice.*)

ALICE (*gloomily*). I was looking for you.

TRIVET. What can I do for you, Miss Alice?

ALICE. You were right, Trivet.

TRIVET. About what? I don't seem to remember.

ALICE. About this steward—saying he dared lift his eyes to Miss Sylvia.

TRIVET. Oh, yes; you're referring to that glance I saw him give her; I'm not likely to forget it; that ogle boded no good; there was something irregular about it.

ALICE. Trivet, that man must go.

TRIVET. I agree, and I'm moving heaven and earth to ruin him. I've already told Miss Sylvia that persons who know him say he can't manage an estate.

ALICE. But is that all you know about him? Speak up, Trivet. I urge you on behalf of Mrs. Grumby and Lord Dorimont. Have you concealed something from Miss Sylvia? Or is there something she is keeping back from us? Tell us all; you won't regret it.

TRIVET. All I know about is his incompetence, which I have reported to Miss Sylvia.

ALICE. Don't dissemble.

TRIVET. I, dissemble? Or keep a secret? Of all people! I'm about as discreet as a woman. Excuse me for the comparison; I am drawing it to set your mind at rest.

ALICE. One thing is sure: he is in love with Miss Sylvia.

TRIVET. Beyond a doubt. And I have told her so.

ALICE. What did she answer?

TRIVET. That I was a fool. She's blinded—blinded, I tell you—

ALICE. Blinded to the point—I daren't say to what point, Trivet.

TRIVET. The devil understands mischief, and so do I. I know what you mean.

ALICE. I can read in your face that you know more about it than I do.

TRIVET. Not at all, I swear I don't. But since we're on the

subject—a little while ago he called Puff aside to give him a letter. If we could spirit that letter away, we might make some interesting discoveries.

ALICE. A letter! I should say so. Everything must be looked into. I'll go find Puff—I hope he hasn't left yet.

TRIVET. You don't have to go far; here he comes.
(*Enter Puff.*)

PUFF. There you are, eyesore.

TRIVET. Look who's calling me an eyesore!

ALICE. What is it you want, Puff, my boy?

PUFF. Do you know where Broad Street is lodged, Miss Alice?

ALICE. I do.

PUFF. The dear man I'm serving has asked me to take this letter to somebody who lives there. He said I should ask either you or this dog where it is, but the dog doesn't deserve to be talked to except to bawl him out. I'd rather the devil carried off every street in town than know my way thanks to a boor like him.

TRIVET (*aside to Alice*). Get the letter.—Miss Alice, don't tell him a thing; let him trot all over town on his own.

PUFF. Silence!

ALICE. Don't interrupt him, Trivet. Just give me the letter, my dear Puff; I'll send somebody to Broad Street with it.

PUFF. Oh, I like that. Thank you for your kindness, Miss Alice.

TRIVET (*going*). You're too good to this lump of idleness. (*He leaves.*)

PUFF. Worm! Go look at the painting and see how it's laughing at you!

ALICE. Don't answer him. Here, give me the letter.

PUFF. Here it is. You're very sweet. If you ever need anyone to run an errand for your obliging person, I'll be your messenger.

ALICE. The letter will go where it belongs.

PUFF. Oh, yes, please be careful with it for Mr. Dorian's sake; he deserves all kinds of loyalty.

ALICE (*aside*). The wretch!

PUFF. I am yours for all eternity.

ALICE. Good-bye.

PUFF (*coming back*). If you meet him, don't tell him somebody else is doing my work. (*He leaves.*)

ALICE (*alone*). Not a word until I've read the letter.
(*Enter Mrs. Grumby and Lord Dorimont.*)

MRS. GRUMBY. Well, Alice, what did you learn from Trivet?

ALICE. Nothing except what you already knew, Mrs. Grumby; and that is not enough.

MRS. GRUMBY. The rascal is throwing dust in our eyes.

LORD DORIMONT. True; his threat meant something more.

MRS. GRUMBY. Be that as it may, I've sent for Mr. Rooney; let's wait for him; and if he doesn't take his nephew off our hands, my daughter will be told that the young upstart dares to be in love with her. My mind is made up. The evidence is so strong that she must dismiss him, if only from a sense of propriety. At the same time, I've sent for the man my Lord Dorimont has recommended; he is in the house, and I mean to introduce him to Sylvia at once.

ALICE. I don't think you'll succeed, madam, unless you discover something new. I, on the other hand, may be able to drive him out. However, here comes Mr. Rooney; I can't tell you anything else at this point; but I'll know more in a little while. (*She goes.*)
(*Mr. Rooney enters and stops Alice.*)

MR. ROONEY. How do you do, my future niece. Do you know why I am wanted here?

ALICE (*rudely*). Go look for your niece elsewhere, Mr. Rooney; I don't like your jokes. (*She leaves.*)

MR. ROONEY. The little cat! (*To Mrs. Grumby*) Here I am, Mrs. Grumby; what can I do for you?

MRS. GRUMBY (*peevishly*). So it's you, solicitor.

MR. ROONEY. Yes, madam, in person.

MRS. GRUMBY. Why, I'd like to ask, have you burdened us with a steward out of your shop?

MR. ROONEY. And why, I'd like to ask, does Mrs. Grumby object to him?

MRS. GRUMBY. Because, Mr. Rooney, we could have survived without your gift.

MR. ROONEY. Could you now? If the gift is not to your liking, you are a little too fastidious, Mrs. Grumby.

MRS. GRUMBY. He is your nephew, I believe?

MR. ROONEY. He is.

MRS. GRUMBY. Well, nephew or whatever, you will be good enough to remove him.

MR. ROONEY. I didn't give him to you.

MRS. GRUMBY. No; but it's us he annoys, myself and Lord Dorimont, who is going to marry my daughter.

MR. ROONEY. This is unheard of! My dear lady, inasmuch as my nephew is not in *your* service, he is hardly required to appeal to you. His contract doesn't stipulate that you must like him; this never occurred to anyone; and as long as Miss Sylvia is satisfied with him, everybody else must comply. Whoever is unhappy has our sincere regrets.

MRS. GRUMBY. These are sour words, Mr. Rooney.

MR. ROONEY. Your compliments are not calculated to sweeten them, Mrs. Grumby.

LORD DORIMONT. Softly, Mr. Rooney, softly; it seems to me that you're in the wrong.

MR. ROONEY. As you wish, my lord, as you wish; but this is no concern of yours. Let me remind you that we are not acquainted, and that there isn't a pin's worth of connection between us.

LORD DORIMONT. Our acquaintance aside, it is not as irrelevant as you think that Mrs. Grumby should approve of your nephew; she is no stranger to this house.

MR. ROONEY. She is a perfect stranger to this particular matter, my lord; it would be impossible to be more of a stranger than she is. For the rest, Dorian is known as a man of honor—I have vouched for him, and will continue to vouch for him—and Mrs. Grumby's remarks about him are nothing less than libelous.

MRS. GRUMBY. Your Dorian is an impertinent puppy.

MR. ROONEY. Piffle. Coming from you, this means nothing.

MRS. GRUMBY. Coming from me! My lord, will you let this low scribbler insult me? Will you not force him to keep silent?

MR. ROONEY. Force me to be silent—me, a solicitor? Let me tell you that I have been talking for fifty years, Mrs. Grumby.

MRS. GRUMBY. Well then, for fifty years you have been talking nonsense.
(*Enter Sylvia.*)

SYLVIA. What's the matter here? Are you quarreling?

MR. ROONEY. We are not exactly at peace; I'm glad you've come, Miss Sylvia. We are talking about Dorian. Do you have any complaints against him?

SYLVIA. Not so far as I know.

MR. ROONEY. Have you noticed any signs of dishonesty in him?

SYLVIA. No; I know him only as an honorable man.

MR. ROONEY. And yet, according to Mrs. Grumby, he is a rascal and you must be rescued from his clutches. He is an impertinent puppy who annoys Mrs. Grumby, and who also annoys Lord Dorimont, speaking as your future husband; and I am accused of driveling because I defend him.

SYLVIA. This is really excessive. Believe me, Mr. Rooney, I've had no part in this. As far as Dorian is concerned, I am keeping him in my service; let that be his best defense. But I came here to inquire about something else. My lord, I am told that you have brought me your business agent after all; surely this is a mistake?

LORD DORIMONT. Ahem—he did come here with me, my dear Sylvia, but it was Mrs. Grumby who—

MRS. GRUMBY. Wait, let me answer. Yes, it was I who asked Lord Dorimont to bring him here to replace the man you're about to discharge. I know what I'm doing. I allowed Mr. Rooney to have his say; but he embroiders a little.

MR. ROONEY. Thank you.

MRS. GRUMBY. Peace; you've said enough. I did not suggest that his nephew is a thief. He may be one, for all I know; it's not an impossibility, and I wouldn't be surprised—

MR. ROONEY. This is a malicious parenthesis, if I may say so; an offensive and irrelevant supposition.

MRS. GRUMBY. Very well; he is an honest man. At least we have no proof as yet to the contrary. As for being impertinent, even very impertinent, I say he is, and I know I'm right. You say you are going to keep him; and I say you are not.

SYLVIA. I assure you I *am* keeping him.

MRS. GRUMBY. You are not, and you can't; will you keep a steward who loves you?

MR. ROONEY. Whom else should he love? You, madam?

SYLVIA. Should I have a steward who hates me?

MRS. GRUMBY. You're equivocating, my girl. When I say that

he loves you, I mean he is in love with you; is this plain English? In love, and pining for you in secret.

Mr. Rooney. Dorian?

Sylvia (*laughing*). Pining for me in secret! It must be in deep secret. Ha, ha, ha, I didn't know I was so alluring. Well, now that you've begun to spy out such wonderful secrets, why haven't you discovered that all my people are in love with me? Who knows? And what about Mr. Rooney? Mr. Rooney, you see me often enough; I am in a mood to guess that you are in love with me, too.

Mr. Rooney. My dear lady, were I as young as my nephew, I would feel exactly what he is accused of.

Mrs. Grumby. This is no joking matter, Sylvia. We're not talking about Mr. Rooney; leave the little man alone; and let's be serious. Your people don't get your picture painted, and they don't fall in a trance before your portrait, and they don't put on tender amorous airs in your presence.

Mr. Rooney. I let the "little man" go for your sake, Miss Sylvia; but the little man can be tough at times.

Sylvia. Really, mother, if I took your so-called discovery seriously, you'd be the first to laugh at me. To dismiss him for a suspicion of this kind would be childish. Is it impossible to set eyes on me without falling in love? If so, I can't help it, and I'll learn to live with it. You think he has an amorous air; I hadn't noticed, but say he has, I won't take it amiss. Nor am I so eccentric as to object to his good looks. I am no different from other girls: I rather like handsome men.
(*Enter Dorian.*)

Dorian. Please forgive me if I am interrupting you, Miss Sylvia. I have reasons to think that you are no longer satisfied with me; and, as matters stand, it is only natural for me to ask what is to be my fate.

Mrs. Grumby. His fate! A steward's fate! Isn't that beautiful!

MR. ROONEY. And why shouldn't he have a fate?

SYLVIA. Mother, if anyone is going to make a scene, I'll do it. (*To Dorian*) What are these "matters," Dorian, and why this alarm?

DORIAN. You know why, madam. You have called for a man to take my place.

SYLVIA. The man has been ill-advised. Please understand: I didn't call him.

DORIAN. Perhaps I was mistaken; but Miss Alice even told me that in an hour I'd be gone.

SYLVIA. Miss Alice spoke like a fool.

MRS. GRUMBY. An hour is too long. This minute would be better.

MR. ROONEY (*aside*). Let's see how all this will end.

SYLVIA. Don't be anxious, Dorian. I would keep you even if you were the least suitable of all men. I owe this to myself. Shocking procedures have been used against me. And to begin with, I intend to inform the gentleman below that he can go home. Let those who brought him without consulting me take him away, and I don't want to hear him mentioned again.
(*Enter Alice.*)

ALICE. Don't be too much in a hurry to dismiss him, madam. Here is a letter which recommends him. It was written by Mr. Dorian.

SYLVIA. What's that?

ALICE (*giving the letter to Lord Dorimont*). One moment, madam; it deserves to be read aloud. It comes, as I said, from Mr. Dorian.

LORD DORIMONT. "I beg you, my dear friend, to be at home tomorrow morning at nine o'clock. I have many things to tell you. I believe I shall be leaving the lady's house which you know of. She is no longer in the dark concerning the unhappy passion I have conceived for her, and of which I can never be cured."

MRS. GRUMBY. Passion! Did you hear that, Sylvia?

LORD DORIMONT. "A miserable messenger-boy came here unexpectedly to bring me the case for the portrait I had painted of her."

MRS. GRUMBY. So the fellow can paint.

LORD DORIMONT. "I was away, and he left it with one of the girls in the house."

MRS. GRUMBY (to Alice). That's you, my dear.

LORD DORIMONT. "I am suspected of being the owner of the portrait. All will be discovered, I fear; and along with the misery of being discharged and no longer beholding every day the woman whom I adore—"

MRS. GRUMBY. Whom I adore! Oh, whom I adore!

LORD DORIMONT. "I shall be the object of her contempt."

MRS. GRUMBY. For once he has guessed right.

LORD DORIMONT. "Not because of the narrowness of my means, for I cannot believe her to be capable of scorning me for that—"

MRS. GRUMBY. Ha, and why not?

LORD DORIMONT. "But only because I am unworthy of her, notwithstanding the high regard I enjoy in good society."

MRS. GRUMBY. And on what grounds is he highly regarded?

LORD DORIMONT. "This being the case, nothing holds me here. You are about to sail for America, and I am determined to join you."

MRS. GRUMBY. Enjoy your trip, lover.

MR. ROONEY. What a reason for going to America!

MRS. GRUMBY. Well, my dear daughter, is this clear enough?

LORD DORIMONT. I don't think anything could be clearer.

SYLVIA (*to Dorian*). This letter, Dorian—it is not a counterfeit? You don't disown it?

DORIAN. Madam . . .

SYLVIA. Please go. (*Dorian leaves.*)

MR. ROONEY. Well, what of it? He is in love. It isn't the first time a pretty woman has made a man fall in love with her. Besides, he has snubbed a dozen women who've thrown themselves at him. This love is costing him fifteen thousand a year, not to mention what it takes to sail the seven seas; and that's where the real evil lies. Because if he were rich, the boy would be as good as anyone else; he could even say he *adores* a certain person, and nobody would laugh. But do as you please, madam; I am your humble servant. (*He leaves.*)

ALICE. Shall I bring up Lord Dorimont's steward, Miss Sylvia?

SYLVIA. Still harping on that steward? There's the door, Alice; take your inane questions out with you. (*Alice leaves.*)

MRS. GRUMBY. But my dear girl, Alice is right. His lordship vouches for the man; do take him on.

SYLVIA. I don't want to.

LORD DORIMONT. Is it because he comes with my recommendation, madam?

SYLVIA. Interpret as you please, my lord; I don't want him.

LORD DORIMONT. Your tone is so biting—I am amazed.

MRS. GRUMBY. And I don't recognize you either. What is the matter?

SYLVIA. Everything. The way this was done—the rude manners, the offensive devices—everything shocks me.

MRS. GRUMBY. We don't understand you.

LORD DORIMONT. I am innocent of what has just happened,

Sylvia, but it's plain that I've incurred your anger, too. I don't wish to increase it by remaining.

MRS. GRUMBY. Wait, my lord, I am coming with you. Sylvia, I am going to detain his lordship, and I expect you to join us soon. Really! A person doesn't know *what* to think. (*She leaves with Lord Dorimont.*)
(*Enter Trivet.*)

TRIVET. At last, madam, I see that you are rid of him. Let him go to the devil now. The whole world has witnessed his extravagance, and his grief can no longer harm you; his mouth is shut. I met him just now more dead than alive. You would have laughed if you had heard him groan. And yet I must say I felt sorry for him. To see him so haggard, so pale, so unhappy, I was afraid he was going to be taken ill.

SYLVIA (*coming alive at these last words*). Why didn't you help him? Let somebody look after him, for heaven's sake! Must we kill the poor man?

TRIVET. I've already seen to him, madam. I called Puff and told him not to leave Mr. Dorian's side. But I doubt that anything will happen. It's all finished. I came only to warn you that he'll ask to see you again; and I want to advise you, if I may, against admitting him.

SYLVIA (*dryly*). That is my business; let me handle it as I please.

TRIVET. At any rate, he is off your hands. The letter which Miss Alice read to you she obtained from Puff at my urging; I rather thought it might be useful to you. I hope you approve of my device, madam.

SYLVIA. What! Are you responsible for the scene which took place here?

TRIVET. Yes, madam.

SYLVIA. Mischief-maker! Let me never set eyes on you again!

TRIVET (*as if surprised*). What is this? I thought I was doing you a favor.

SYLVIA. I hate you! I told you not to meddle any more. You're responsible for all the troubles I wanted to avoid. It was you who spread these suspicions against him. It was you who tattled to me about his love. And why? Because of your devotion to me? Not at all. Simply because you enjoy doing harm. What was the use of this revelation? Without you, I would have been happily unaware of his love. Oh, I pity him for having fallen into your hands—a man who was your master, who treated you kindly, and who begged you on his knees a while ago to keep his secret. You murder him, and you betray me at the same time. You're a man who will stop at nothing. Out of my house—and don't answer!

TRIVET (*aside, laughing*). Perfect, perfect. (*He leaves.*)
(*Enter Alice, dejected.*)

ALICE. From the way you sent me out of the room just now, I know I've become a nuisance to you. I shall make you happy, I think, if I give you notice.

SYLVIA (*coldly*). You may go.

ALICE. Do you wish me to leave today?

SYLVIA. Whatever suits you.

ALICE. This is a sad blow for me.

SYLVIA. No explanations, if you please.

ALICE. I'm in despair.

SYLVIA (*impatient*). Are you sorry to go? All right then, stay; you have my consent; stay, but let's hear no more about it.

ALICE. But, after all your kindnesses to me, what shall I do here? You have lost your confidence in me.

SYLVIA. And what do you want me to confide in you? Shall I invent secrets that I can tell you?

ALICE. You *are* sending me away, I see. But why? What have I done?

SYLVIA. Who is sending you away? You're imagining things. You gave me notice, and I accepted it.

ALICE. Oh, Miss Sylvia, why did you allow me to cross you? In my ignorance I persecuted the most wonderful man who ever lived, and who loves you as no one has ever loved before.

SYLVIA (aside). Oh, God!

ALICE. And a man whom I cannot blame for any fault. Just now he spoke to me. I had been his enemy, but I am now his friend. He had never seen me. Mr. Rooney invented that story.

SYLVIA. Very good.

ALICE. It was cruel of you to let me fall in love with him. I'm not good enough for him; it's you he deserves; and now I've made him miserable forever.

SYLVIA (softly). You loved him, Alice?

ALICE. My feelings are of no importance. Give me your own love again, and I will be happy.

SYLVIA. You have it all again.

ALICE (kissing her hand). Thank you, thank you.

SYLVIA. You're crying, and you'll make me cry too.

ALICE. Pay no attention to me. Your affection is all that matters to me.

SYLVIA. Come, I promise to make you forget your tears. Isn't this Puff? Puff, what's the matter with you?
(Enter Puff.)

PUFF (groaning and weeping). I can't tell you, Miss Sylvia; I'm speechless, I can't say a word, that's how unhappy I am about your traitress here, Miss Alice. Oh, the ungrateful perfidy!

ALICE. Don't talk about perfidy, and tell us what you want.

PUFF. Oh, that poor letter, and oh, what a swindle!

SYLVIA. What is it, Puff?

PUFF. Mr. Dorian begs on his knees to give you an accounting of the papers he has in hand. He is waiting at the door with tears in his eyes.

ALICE. Tell him to come in.

PUFF. Do you want me to, madam? I don't trust her. Once I've been wronged, I don't get over it.

ALICE (*sadly*). Do speak to him, madam. I'll go now. (*She leaves.*)

PUFF. Aren't you going to say something, Miss Sylvia?

SYLVIA. He can come.
(*Puff leaves; Dorian enters.*)

SYLVIA. Come nearer, Dorian.

DORIAN. I am afraid to show myself at all.

SYLVIA (*aside*). If he knew how I felt!—Why give me an accounting of these papers? I trust you implicitly—with this.

DORIAN. Madam—I have something else to report—but I'm so confused—so shaken—I can't bring out a single word.

SYLVIA (*aside*). How will this end? I'm trembling.

DORIAN. One of your—tenants—arrived—a short time ago.

SYLVIA. One of—my tenants? I see . . .

DORIAN. Yes, madam—he—the tenant—came to me.

SYLVIA. Really?

DORIAN. And he gave me—money—for you.

SYLVIA. Ah, money—we'll see . . .

DORIAN. I will bring it to you—whenever—you wish to have it.

SYLVIA. Yes—I wish—I'll take it—you'll give it to me. (*Aside*) I don't know what I'm answering.

DORIAN. Shall I bring it tonight—or tomorrow?

SYLVIA. Tomorrow? How can you stay till tomorrow, after what has happened?

DORIAN (*plaintively*). Think of all the years of my life I shall be spending far away from you. This would be my last precious day.

SYLVIA. No, Dorian; we must separate. Everybody knows that you are in love with me; people would think I didn't disapprove.

DORIAN. I am so unhappy.

SYLVIA. Everybody to his own sorrows, Dorian.

DORIAN. I have lost everything. I had a portrait, and even that is gone.

SYLVIA. Why do you need it? You know how to paint.

DORIAN. No, it can never be replaced. And it would have been so dear to me. You held it in your hands.

SYLVIA. This is unreasonable.

DORIAN. I'll be parted from you; what other revenge do you want? Don't add to my misery.

SYLVIA. But to give you my portrait! Think of it! This would be admitting that I loved you.

DORIAN. That you loved me! What an idea! Who could ever imagine it?

SYLVIA. And yet it's happening to me.

DORIAN (*at her feet*). I'll die of joy!

SYLVIA. I don't know where I am. Dorian, get up. This is too wild.

DORIAN (*rising*). Oh, this happiness—Sylvia—I don't deserve it, I don't deserve it. You'll take it from me again; but no matter; you must be told.

SYLVIA. Told? What do you mean?

DORIAN. All you have seen here, all is a sham, Sylvia, except the portrait I painted of you, and my infinite passion. All that happened here was plotted by a servant who knew of my love and who pitied me. I allowed him to scheme because he gave me hope, and because of my delight in being near you. He contrived to raise me in your esteem. I can no longer conceal it from you. I would rather give up your love than owe it to cunning, and I prefer your hatred to my remorse, knowing that I deceived the woman I worship.

SYLVIA (*after looking at him without speaking*). I should have hated you if someone else had told me all this. But your confession—now of all times—changes everything. So much sincerity overwhelms me. Dorian, you are honest, I know it. You loved me and used your cunning to win me; can I find fault with that? All means are fair to a lover. If he succeeds, he must be forgiven.

DORIAN. What! Is my lovely Sylvia willing to plead for me?

SYLVIA. Hush; here come my mother and his lordship; say nothing, and let me speak.
(*Enter Mrs. Grumby, Lord Dorimont, Trivet, and Puff.*)

MRS. GRUMBY. Oho! Is he still here?

SYLVIA. Yes, mother. (*To Lord Dorimont*) My lord, there was talk of a marriage beween us; but we must put it out of our minds. You deserve to be loved, but my affections are unable to do you justice; nor is my rank high enough to suit you.

MRS. GRUMBY. What, what? What's that?

LORD DORIMONT. I understand you, madam; and I was about to withdraw without informing your mother. I had already guessed that Mr. Dorian came here only in the service of his love; that he met with your favor; and that you wished to bestow your fortune on him. That is what you wanted to tell me.

SYLVIA. And I have nothing to add.

MRS. GRUMBY (*furious*). Your fortune on *him*?

LORD DORIMONT. As for our dispute, we will settle it out of court, as I promised.

SYLVIA. You are generous, my lord. Send me an arbiter; we shall let him decide.

MRS. GRUMBY. Oh, what a downfall, and oh, the damnable steward! He'll be your husband as much as you like, but my son-in-law, never.

SYLVIA (*to Dorian*). Let her indulge her anger; it will pass. Come away, my Dorian.
(*All leave except Trivet and Puff.*)

TRIVET. Oof! I stagger under my glory. I have a right to call this lady my daughter-in-law.

PUFF. As for your painting, who cares about it now? The original is going to be delivering copies before very long.

THE END

The Test
(L'Épreuve)

Presented for the first time at
the Théâtre Italien on November 19, 1740

CHARACTERS

Mrs. Grumby
Angela, *her daughter*
Jenny, *the maid*
Dorian, *in love with Angela*
Trivet, *Dorian's servant*
Mr. Lubbock, *a farmer*

The action takes place on Dorian's country estate.

(*Enter Dorian and Trivet, the latter dressed as a gentleman and wearing riding boots.*)

DORIAN. Let's go into this room. Have you just arrived?

TRIVET. Yes; I stopped off at the first inn. I asked the way to the manor—just as you ordered in your letter. And here I am dressed in accordance with your commands. Well, how do I look? (*He turns around.*) Would you recognize your own servant? Or do I look too much like a lord?

DORIAN. You look perfect. Did you speak to anyone as you came in?

TRIVET. No, I didn't. I saw only a little boy in the courtyard. But now tell me—what do you intend to do with me and my finery?

DORIAN. Propose you as a match for a very lovable girl.

TRIVET. Really? Sir, I'm ready to swear that you're twice as lovable as she.

DORIAN. Well, you're mistaken. I'm looking after my own interests.

TRIVET. In that case, I swear to nothing.

DORIAN. As you know, I came here almost two months ago to look at the manor my business agent had bought for me. I found a Mrs. Grumby looking after the estate, a woman who comes of a respectable local family. The good lady has a daughter; I've fallen in love with her, and I want to propose you as a match for her.

TRIVET (*laughing*). Propose me for the girl *you* love? Thank you for telling me! In other words, we're to make a threesome at the breakfast table.

DORIAN. Will you listen to me? I intend to marry the girl myself.

TRIVET. I understand; after *I*'ve married her.

DORIAN. Let me finish! I'm going to introduce you as a rich friend of mine in order to find out whether she loves me enough to refuse you.

TRIVET. Well, that's another story. There's something that worries me, though.

DORIAN. What's that?

TRIVET. On my way here, I noticed near the inn a girl chatting with someone on a doorstep. I don't think she saw me, but she looks like a certain Jenny I met in town four or five years ago. She was working for a lady my master used to call on. I saw this Jenny only two or three times; but as she was pretty, I rattled off the usual sweet nothings to her. I'm afraid this sort of thing sticks in a girl's memory.

DORIAN. As a matter of fact, there is a girl by that name working for Mrs. Grumby. She grew up in the village, but she spent some time in town working for a lady from these parts.

TRIVET. I'm afraid, sir, the little hussy will recognize me. There's a kind of man women don't forget.

DORIAN. The only solution is to be brazen and insist she is mistaken.

TRIVET. Good. When it comes to being brazen, I require no lessons.

DORIAN. After all, there are some amazing resemblances in this world.

TRIVET. There are, and I'll be one of them. But if you would allow me to make a comment—

DORIAN. Speak up.

TRIVET. For a young man, you're remarkably wise and reasonable. But this particular scheme of yours strikes me as childish.

DORIAN (*angry*). What?

TRIVET. Gently! Your father was a rich merchant who left you with an income of more than thirty thousand a year. With that you can aspire to a duchess. Now—is the little minx you've been telling me about fit to be your legitimate wife? For a man of your wealth there are, I believe, less expensive arrangements.

DORIAN. That's enough! You don't even know her. Though Angela is only a simple country girl, still, her family is as good as mine, and it so happens that I'm not aiming at an ambitious marriage. Besides, she is so lovely, and I detect, in the midst of her innocence, such a high sense of honor and virtue, and furthermore she has so much natural refinement, that if she loves me as I think she does, I will be hers for life and no one else's.

TRIVET. Did you say, "*if* she loves me"? You mean that isn't settled yet?

DORIAN. No. The word *love* has never been mentioned between us. I have never told her that I care for her, but all my actions have proved it, while hers too betray the most tender and sincere affection for me. Three days after I arrived, I became so ill that my life was in danger. I saw her worried, frightened, more alarmed for me than I was for myself. I saw tears in her eyes which she concealed from her mother. And since my recovery we have continued as before. I still love her without telling her so. She loves me too, confesses nothing, and yet, simple and honest girl that she is, doesn't try to make a secret of it.

TRIVET. But since you're more experienced in these matters than she is, why don't you help things along with a little word of love? It wouldn't hurt.

DORIAN. It's too soon. I'm sure of her feelings, but I want to know exactly to what I should attribute them. Does she love the rich man in me, or simply myself? I'll find the answer by putting her to the test. I'm going to take advantage of the fact that what exists between us has only been called friendship so far.

TRIVET. That's all very well, but I'm not the man you should choose for this.

DORIAN. Why not?

TRIVET. Why not? Put yourself in the girl's place for a moment, open your eyes—and you'll see why not. It's a hundred to one she'll be attracted to me.

DORIAN. Blockhead! If she is, I'll reveal who you are. That will cure her. Now then, did you bring the jewels?

TRIVET (*rummaging in his pocket*). Here they are.

DORIAN. Somebody is coming from the garden. Quick, go back to the inn, prepare yourself for your entrance, and report here in an hour.

TRIVET. If your plot miscarries, remember I warned you. (*He leaves.*)
(*Enter cautiously Mr. Lubbock, dressed as a rich farmer.*)

DORIAN (*aside*). He's coming toward me. He seems to have something to tell me.

MR. LUBBOCK. How do you do, sir. How is your health? You look in the pink today.

DORIAN. Yes, I'm quite well, Mr. Lubbock.

MR. LUBBOCK. No doubt about it, your sickness done wonders for you. Lord, look at you! Red as beets your cheeks is, regular tomatoes they are. It does me good to see you up and about again.

DORIAN. I'm much obliged.

MR. LUBBOCK. When I like a man I like to see him feeling good. Nothing beats health in this world, especially your health, sir, which is worth more than anybody else's.

DORIAN. You're right to take some interest in it, because I'd like to be of help to you sometime.

MR. LUBBOCK. Help is well and good; and as luck would have it, I've just come to ax for some.

DORIAN. What can I do for you?

MR. LUBBOCK. Well, you know, sir, now and then I pays my respects to Mrs. Grumby. And her daughter Angela's a sweet morsel, right enough.

DORIAN. She is indeed.

MR. LUBBOCK. Well, I hope it's all the same to you, but I want to marry the sweet morsel.

DORIAN. You mean you're in love with Angela.

MR. LUBBOCK. I'm nigh out o' my mind with love of her. I'm losing the two straws of sense I had. Come daytime, I think about her, come nighttime, I dream about her. A sickness is what it is, and that's why I've come to you. I thought what with the honor and respeck they pay you hereabout, and if it didn't bother you any, you could put in a few good words to her mother, because I need the mother likewise on my side.

DORIAN. I see. You want me to get Mrs. Grumby's consent. And what about Angela? Does the girl love you?

MR. LUBBOCK. Does she! Every time I tell her my condition, she laughs like she might split and turns her back on me. Don't you think that's a good sign?

DORIAN. Neither good nor bad. But anyway, since I believe that Mrs. Grumby is not exactly well off, whereas you're a landowner and son of a farmer . . .

MR. LUBBOCK. And young into the bargain, don't forget; I've only thirty years on my back, and I'm known as Good-time Jack, the village sport.

DORIAN. You'd be a good match except for one thing.

MR. LUBBOCK. What thing?

DORIAN. In return for the care Mrs. Grumby and her household took of me during my illness, I have proposed to marry Angela to a rich young man who is arriving here any moment. He is interested in settling down with a country girl of good family, and doesn't care whether she has a penny to her name.

MR. LUBBOCK. What the devil! With these projectings of yours you're playing me a dirty trick, Mr. Dorian. Christ, this is a jolt. I don't care if you oblige your friends, shake hands on that, but you needn't step on somebody else to do it. I'm your fellow man as good as the lad next door, don't knock me down while you're helping *him* up. And to think I was worried you was going to die! A lot of good it did me to come and ax twenty times, "Is he better?" "Is he worse?" Now you're healthy again you want to ruin me. And me running twice after the barber what bled you, my own cousin he is, my first cousin, my mother was his aunt; all I can say is, you've hit below the belt, by God.

DORIAN. Your relationship to the barber is one thing, my obligation to you another.

MR. LUBBOCK. And that's not counting the good fifteen hundred crowns you're taking away from me like it was air; the money I would have got when she married me.

DORIAN. Don't get excited. Is that how much you expected? Well, then, I'll give you three thousand crowns to marry someone else, and to make up for the grief I've caused you.

MR. LUBBOCK (*surprised*). What? Three thousand in hard cash?

DORIAN. Yes, it's a promise, and yet you may feel free to ask for Angela's hand at the same time. Wait; I *insist* that you ask her of Mrs. Grumby. I insist, is that clear? Because if Angela is fond of you, I shouldn't want to deprive her of the man she loves.

MR. LUBBOCK (*rubbing his eyes in surprise*). Angels in heaven! A prince is talking to me! Three thousand crowns! My head is spinning. Stand off a bit, sir, I want to prostrate myself before you no more and no less than I would before a projidy.

DORIAN. That won't be necessary. No need for compliments either. I'll keep my word.

MR. LUBBOCK. After I've bullied you like a boor! But tell me, being the king you are, if I'm in luck and Angela loves me, do I get the girl and the three thousand on top of her?

DORIAN. Not exactly. I told you I want you to ask for Angela's hand, independently of the suitor I'm going to propose. If she accepts you, I will have done you no harm and I'll give you nothing. If she refuses you, the money is yours.

MR. LUBBOCK. She'll refuse me, sir, she'll refuse me! Heaven will grant it to me because it's you that want to see it happen.

DORIAN. Careful! I can see that because of the three thousand crowns, you're already hoping to be rejected.

MR. LUBBOCK. Well, maybe it's true the money has struck me a blow. Between you and I, I like the feel of it. There's nothing like it to cheer you up.

DORIAN. Mr. Lubbock, I must add another stipulation to our agreement; to wit, that you appear really anxious to have Angela and that you continue to behave as though you were in love with her.

MR. LUBBOCK. You can count on me. But I'm hoping as I won't be worthy of her. Fact is, if you ask me, that if she was to dare, she'd love you, Mr. Dorian, more than anybody hereabout.

DORIAN. Me, Mr. Lubbock? Why, you surprise me. I hadn't noticed. You must be mistaken. However, if she doesn't want you, remember to mention this as a reproach to her. I'd be curious to know what she would say.

MR. LUBBOCK. Don't worry. I'll say it to her smack in your presence.

DORIAN. And since you're vain—justifiably so, of course—I wish you'd give a thought to Jenny. Quite aside from the three thousand crowns, you won't be sorry if you choose her.

MR. LUBBOCK. Just say the word and I'll about face into her arms, just to mortify myself.

DORIAN. I'll grant you she is Mrs. Grumby's maid, but she comes from as good a stock as any girl in the village.

MR. LUBBOCK. You're right. She was born native right here.

DORIAN. Besides, she's young and has a good figure.

MR. LUBBOCK. A very good figure. My mouth is beginning to water.

DORIAN. But I must warn you. Don't tell her you love her until Angela has given you her answer. Jenny must not know your intentions before that.

MR. LUBBOCK. Leave it to young Lubbock. When I talk to her, I'll be so muddled she won't understand nothing. Here she comes. Should I leave?

DORIAN. No reason why you shouldn't stay.
(Enter Jenny.)

JENNY. I've just heard from the winegrower's son that you have a visitor from town, sir.

DORIAN. Yes, a friend of mine has come to see me.

JENNY. What rooms shall we give him, sir?

DORIAN. We'll decide when he returns from the inn. Tell me, Jenny, where is Angela?

JENNY. I think I saw her in the garden picking flowers.

DORIAN (pointing to Mr. Lubbock). Here's a man who is disposed to marry her. I was asking how she feels about him. What is your opinion?

MR. LUBBOCK. Yes, what's your opinion, my lovely, my sweetheart?

JENNY. Well, as far as I can judge, she feels nothing for you.

MR. LUBBOCK. Nothing at all? That's just what I was saying. Miss Jenny has a head on her shoulders.

JENNY. I know my answer isn't very flattering, but it's the only one I can give.

MR. LUBBOCK (*gallantly*). It's a good one and I'll abide by it. I like people to speak their minds, and in fact what could a girl like her see in me?

JENNY. Oh, I wouldn't underestimate you, Mr. Lubbock. Only, I'm afraid Mrs. Grumby doesn't think you're rich enough for her daughter.

MR. LUBBOCK (*laughing*). That's true. I ain't rich enough. The more you talk, the better it sounds.

JENNY. Strange how cheerfully you take it.

DORIAN. It's because he wasn't too hopeful to begin with.

MR. LUBBOCK. Yes, that's the way it is. And rain or shine I'm always thankful. (*To Jenny*) You're a fine figure of a girl, Jenny.

JENNY. Either he's losing his mind or I don't understand what's happening here.

MR. LUBBOCK. Still an' all, I wouldn't mind suffering the pains of hell for Angela. And maybe it'll come out that I'll have her, or maybe it'll come out that I won't. You've got to consider both sides to guess right.

JENNY (*laughing*). You're a great fortune-teller, you are!

DORIAN. Be that as it may, I also have a match for her, and a very good one it is: a true man of the world. And that's why I wanted to know whether she is in love with anyone.

JENNY. I think she'll be happy with any man you choose for her.

DORIAN. Well, now, I'm going for a walk in the garden; will you please call me when Angela comes? And, Jenny, you may be sure that before I return to town I'll reward you for your good offices.

JENNY. You're very kind, sir.

DORIAN (*aside to Lubbock*). Watch what you say to Jenny.

MR. LUBBOCK. I'll be so careful I won't even make sense. (*Dorian leaves.*)

JENNY. Mr. Dorian has a heart of gold.

MR. LUBBOCK. Oh yes, solid gold. How is your health these days, my dear Miss Jenny?

JENNY. Why these courtesies, Mr. Lubbock? You've been speaking very strangely.

MR. LUBBOCK. Well, I suppose I've got some queer ways about me and they surprise you. Yes, I suppose they do. (*Musing*) You're the prettiest kitten.

JENNY. And you're the oddest bird! The way you look at me! Watch out, your wits are running wild.

MR. LUBBOCK. On the contrary, it's my foresight what's contemplating you.

JENNY. Very well, contemplate away. Is my face different today from what it was yesterday?

MR. LUBBOCK. No, it's just that today I see it clearer than before. It's all new to me.

JENNY (*starting to leave*). Well, God bless you.

MR. LUBBOCK. Wait!

JENNY. What do you want? I'm making a fool of myself listening to you. Are you trying to flirt with me? I know that you're a well-to-do farmer and that I'm not the girl for you. What does it all mean?

MR. LUBBOCK. I want you to listen to me careful-like and not understand a word I'm saying. I want you to tell yourself, "There must be a secret in it somehow."

JENNY. A secret in what? You're talking in riddles.

MR. LUBBOCK. I do it on purpose. It's all carefully thought out.

JENNY. What's all carefully thought out? Weren't you interested in Angela?

MR. LUBBOCK. That's been carefully thought out too.

JENNY. The more I try to understand you, the more confused I get.

MR. LUBBOCK. You're supposed to get confused.

JENNY. What makes you like me all of a sudden? And why today more than before? You've never shown me any particular attention up to now. Am I to suppose that you've suddenly fallen in love with me? If that's the case, I'm not going to stop you.

MR. LUBBOCK (*hastily and emphatically*). I didn't say I love you.

JENNY. Then what *did* you say?

MR. LUBBOCK. I didn't say I don't love you neither. Neither the one nor t'other. You're my witness. I've given my word, and I'm doing my duty straight. Nothing to laugh about either. I didn't say nothing. But I keep thinking to myself and repeating that you're the prettiest kitten.

JENNY (*looking at him in astonishment*). Now I'm looking at you, and if I didn't think your brain was addled I would suspect you didn't exactly hate me.

MR. LUBBOCK. Suspect, imagine, talk yourself into it. No harm in that—so long as I have nothing to do with it and it comes to you all by itself, without any help from me.

JENNY. What do you mean?

MR. LUBBOCK. Why, you're even allowed to fall in love with me. I give my consent. If your heart's set on it, don't hold back. I'm willing to hand over the reins. You won't break your neck.

JENNY. A charming compliment! But what good would it do me?

MR. LUBBOCK. My tongue is tied; I can't speak no clearer than that. Well, here comes Angela. I must coax her along with a few sweet flimflams—without meaning to cool your feelings of affection.

JENNY. I swear, you're far gone, Mr. Lubbock, and no mistake. (*Enter Angela, with a bouquet in her hand.*)

ANGELA. Good day, Mr. Lubbock. Is it true, Jenny, that Mr. Dorian has a visitor from town?

JENNY. Yes, so I hear.

ANGELA. Did he come to take Mr. Dorian back with him?

JENNY. I don't know. Mr. Dorian didn't say.

MR. LUBBOCK. It don't look that way. Mr. Dorian is minded to marry you off to the lap of luxury.

ANGELA. Marry me off, Mr. Lubbock? And to whom, if you please?

MR. LUBBOCK. The man ain't got a name yet.

JENNY. It's true, he has talked about a very good marriage to a man of the world, but he hasn't mentioned who he is or where he comes from.

ANGELA (*with a pleased and reserved look*). A man of the world whom he hasn't named . . .

JENNY. I'm repeating his own words.

ANGELA. I'm not worried. We'll know sooner or later who he is.

MR. LUBBOCK. Anyway, it ain't me.

ANGELA. Oh, I know that. What a fine mystery *that* would be! Besides, you're only a farmer.

MR. LUBBOCK. Which don't keep me from having aspirations of my own. But I don't keep myself under lock and key, I tell you my name, I show myself to the world and I scatter the news that I'm a-courting you. And you know it.
(*Jenny shrugs her shoulders.*)

ANGELA. I had forgotten it.

MR. LUBBOCK. Well, I'm here to remind you. Don't you care a little bit for me, Miss Angela?
(*Jenny pouts.*)

ANGELA. Oh, hardly.

MR. LUBBOCK. Hardly! That's still something. Better be careful, otherwise I'll get to thinking maybe you do like me.

ANGELA. I wouldn't advise you to do that, Mr. Lubbock, because I really don't.

MR. LUBBOCK. Well, now at least we've got things straight. It's a nuisance and I'm bothered something awful, but never mind, don't be worriting yourself about me. I'll come back in a little bit to ask if I should talk about it to Mrs. Grumby or shut my mouth. Turn it over in your head and do what you like with it. (*To Jenny*) Mmm, you beautiful girl!

JENNY (*angrily*). Fool!
(*Mr. Lubbock leaves.*)

ANGELA. Thank goodness his love doesn't worry me. If he decides to ask my mother, he won't get very far with her either.

JENNY. He's nothing but a tattler, not fit for a girl like you.

ANGELA. I don't pay any attention to him. But tell me, Jenny, was Mr. Dorian really talking about a husband for me?

JENNY. He was. About a distinguished husband, with a considerable fortune.

ANGELA. Very considerable, if it's what I suspect.

JENNY. And what do you suspect?

ANGELA. I can't say; I'd be too ashamed if I were wrong.

JENNY. Are you thinking that Mr. Dorian himself might be the man, riches, power, and all?

ANGELA. Oh, I don't know *what* I think. A girl dreams, she lets her fancy stray here and there, that's all. We'll see who this husband is—I'm not going to marry him sight unseen.

JENNY. Even if it were only a friend of his, he'd still be a good catch. Which reminds me, he wanted me to tell him when you came back. He's waiting for me in the garden.

ANGELA. Well, hurry! Why are you wasting time? Is that how you carry out his orders? Perhaps he's gone by now!

JENNY. Never mind, here he comes.
(*Enter Dorian.*)

DORIAN. Angela! Have you been here long?

ANGELA. No, sir. I heard just now that you wanted to see me, and I was scolding Jenny for not telling me sooner.

DORIAN. Well, I have something rather important to tell you.

JENNY. Is it a secret? Should I leave?

DORIAN. I don't want to detain you.

ANGELA. Besides, I think my mother needs her.

JENNY. All right, I'm going. (*Exit Jenny.*)

ANGELA. You're staring at me—what are you thinking about?

DORIAN. I was thinking that you're growing more beautiful every day.

ANGELA. That wasn't true when you were sick. By the way, knowing how much you like flowers, I picked these for you. Please take them.

DORIAN. I'll take them only to give them back to you. They're lovelier in your hands.

ANGELA (*taking the bouquet*). And I like them better now because they came from you.

DORIAN. Always kind!

ANGELA. It's easy to be kind with certain persons. What was it you had to tell me?

DORIAN. I've decided to give you a proof of my deep friendship. But first you must tell me whether your affections are engaged.

ANGELA. The answer is very simple, and you know it already. Take away our friendship and there's nothing left in my heart. It is all I have.

DORIAN. Your words make me so happy, I forget what I was going to say.

ANGELA. What shall I do? I'll be silent so you'll remember. I know no other way.

DORIAN. A painful solution for me! But let me continue. I have been here about seven weeks.

ANGELA. Has it been so long? How times flies! And so?

DORIAN. I've noticed that a number of young men are courting you. Which one of them would you choose? Tell me as you would your own best friend.

ANGELA. Why do you think I would choose any one of them? Courting me indeed! Do I pay any attention to them? Do I even see them? They're wasting their time.

DORIAN. I believe you, Angela.

ANGELA. I didn't notice them before you came, and I notice them even less now that you're here.

DORIAN. And are you also indifferent toward Mr. Lubbock? He tells me he wants to ask for your hand.

ANGELA. He can ask all he wants, but I dislike all these people from first to last, and him especially. Why, the other day he was scolding me for talking to you so often. Imagine that! As if it weren't natural that I should prefer your company to his! The fool!

DORIAN. I'm delighted you like my company, my dear Angela; I like yours more than I can say. I miss you when you're away, I look for you when I don't see you.

ANGELA. You don't have to look very long. I hardly ever go out, and when I do I come back as quickly as I can.

DORIAN. And when you come back I'm happy.

ANGELA. And I'm not unhappy.

DORIAN. I know. Your friendship is a wonderful echo to my own.

ANGELA. Yes, but unfortunately you're not from this village and perhaps you'll soon go back to that town of yours which I detest. If I were you, it would have to come here looking for me, because I wouldn't go looking for it.

DORIAN. Well, it doesn't matter whether I return to town or not; because you've only to say the word and both of us will be there.

ANGELA. Both of us, Mr. Dorian! Tell me, how can that possibly be?

DORIAN. It's very simple. I've found a husband for you who lives there.

ANGELA. Are you serious? Don't deceive me; my heart is pounding. Does he live near you?

DORIAN. Yes, Angela, we live in the same house.

ANGELA. That's not enough; I'm still uneasy. What sort of man is he?

DORIAN. A very rich man.

ANGELA. That's not what matters most. What else?

DORIAN. He's exactly my age and height.

ANGELA. Good. That's what I wanted to know.

DORIAN. We're very much alike. We even think the same way.

ANGELA. He sounds better and better. Oh, I'm going to love him!

DORIAN. He's as even-tempered and unpretentious as I am.

ANGELA. I don't want any other sort.

DORIAN. He's neither ambitious nor vain, and he asks nothing of the woman he marries except her love.

ANGELA. He'll have it, Mr. Dorian, he'll have it. He has it already. I love him as much as I love you, no more and no less.

DORIAN. And you can count on his devotion, Angela. I know him so well, it's as if he himself were talking to you now.

ANGELA. Of course; and I'm answering as if he were here.

DORIAN. You're going to make him very happy.

ANGELA. And I can promise you he won't be alone in that either!

DORIAN. I'll be going now, my dear Angela. I'm anxious to secure your mother's consent. This marriage delights me so much that I want it settled as soon as possible. But first, please accept this little wedding gift as a token of our friendship. They are jewels—trifles—which I had sent to me here.

ANGELA. I accept them, because they'll return to town with you and because we'll all be there together. Otherwise I don't care for them; your friendship is the only jewel I want.

DORIAN. Good-bye for now, my dear Angela; your husband will arrive before very long.

ANGELA. The more you hurry, the sooner I'll see him.
(*Exit Dorian; enter Jenny.*)

JENNY. Well, now! Did you find out who is going to be your husband?

ANGELA. He is, my dear Jenny, he is himself; and I'm waiting for him.

JENNY. Himself, did you say? Who is this wonderful "himself"? Is he in the house?

ANGELA. You must have run into him. He was on his way to see my mother.

JENNY. I only saw Mr. Dorian, but surely he's not the man you're going to marry.

ANGELA. Of course he is. I've told you twenty times! If you knew how we spoke together, how we both understood everything without his ever saying, "I'm the one." But it was all so clear, so delightful, so tender.

JENNY. Fancy that! I'd never have suspected it. Wait, here he is again.
(*Enter Dorian and Trivet.*)

DORIAN. I'm back, my dear Angela. I met my friend while I was hurrying to your mother. He had just arrived, and of course my most urgent duty was to introduce him to you at once. Here he is—the husband who already has your heart, and who is so much like me that he's practically my double. And by the way, he has also brought me the portrait of a pretty young lady in town whom my relatives would like me to marry. (*He shows it to her.*) Have a look; what do you think of her?

ANGELA (*pushing it away in anguish*). I don't know . . . Don't ask *me* . . .

DORIAN. Well now, I'm off again; I'll leave you two together while I see Mrs. Grumby. (*He approaches her.*) Are you happy? (*Angela does not reply, but takes the box of jewels and without looking at him puts it into his hand. Dorian appears surprised, but keeps the box and goes out. Angela stands motionless. Jenny walks around Trivet and examines him with wonder; he appears uneasy.*)

TRIVET. Madam, your amazing immobility intimidates the birth of my inclination for you. I'm altogether discouraged by your silence, and I feel that I am going to be speechless.

JENNY. Miss Angela stands still, you're struck dumb, and I'm stupefied. I open my eyes, I look, but I can't make head or tail of anything.

ANGELA (*sadly*). Jenny, who would have believed it?

JENNY. I don't, though here he stands before me.

TRIVET. If the charming Angela would only deign to glance my way, I daresay I would no longer frighten her, and she might even be tempted to offer me a second look. Most people grow accustomed to the sight of me. Believe me, such has been my experience, and I beg you to try.

ANGELA (*without looking at him*). I can't. Perhaps another time. Jenny, entertain the gentleman. Forgive me. I'm not well. Something is choking me. I'm going to my room. (*She leaves.*)

TRIVET (*aside*). For once my charms have missed their target.

JENNY (*aside*). It's Trivet, I recognize him.

TRIVET (*aside*). Now comes the real test. (*To Jenny*) Well, my dear, what conjecture am I to shape after this faint reception? (*Jenny stares at him.*) Well, can't you answer? Or are you about to say "Perhaps another time," too?

JENNY. Excuse me, sir, but haven't I seen your mug somewhere before?

TRIVET. What's that? "Haven't I seen your mug somewhere before?" You provincials don't stand on ceremony, I see.

JENNY (*aside*). Could I be making a mistake? (*Aloud*) Sir, I beg your pardon, but were you ever a visitor at a Mrs. Dorman's in town? I lived there at one time.

TRIVET. A Mrs. Dorman? In what part of the city does she live?

JENNY. In Birch Lane, on the second floor, over the Sword-Blade coffeehouse.

TRIVET. A Birch Lane, a Mrs. Dorman, a second floor! I know nothing about it, my dear. Besides, I always take my coffee at home.

JENNY. I'll say no more, but I confess I mistook you for Trivet. And it's all I can do to convince myself that you're somebody else.

TRIVET. Trivet! Why, that would be the name of a servant!

JENNY. I know, and I thought he was you, I mean you're his spitting image.[1]

TRIVET. Spitting image! Your familiarity is intolerable.

JENNY. I'm sorry, sir, but you do look so much like him, I can't get over it. Come on, Trivet, say it's you.

TRIVET (laughing). I suppose I had better laugh this off as a joke. Only a coarse-grained, low-born fool would be ruffled by your mistake. I find all this amusing, except for the unpleasantness of having a face in common with the rascal you mention. Mother Nature might have thought twice before making him my double. I take it as an insult from her. However, you're not to blame, and so let's talk about your mistress.

JENNY. Please don't be offended, sir. The man I mistook you for is likable, droll, very witty, and extremely handsome.

TRIVET. I see, and I'm his replica.

JENNY. So much so, I can't believe it. Look here, you'd be the lowest—oh, sir, I'm confused again—the resemblance—

TRIVET. Never mind. I'm getting used to it. You're not addressing *me*.

JENNY. Of course not, sir. I'm talking to your double. And he'd be a fool to play such a trick on me. Oh, I wish with all my heart that you were he. I think he loved me, and I miss him.

TRIVET. So you should, he was obviously worth it. (*Aside*) Very flattering, all this.

JENNY. Strange, I seem to hear him every time you say something.

TRIVET. That shouldn't really surprise you. People who look alike usually sound alike; they may even share the same interests. For instance, you mentioned that this Trivet liked you; and so

---

[1] In the following lines, Jenny keeps falling into the familiar *tu* and catching herself again. [Tr.]

would I, if I weren't conscious of the social abyss which yawns between us.

JENNY. And I was so happy thinking I had found him again!

TRIVET (*aside*). Ha!—So much love, my dear, is bound to be rewarded. All is not lost. I have taken an interest in you, and I place you under my protection. Don't choose a husband without consulting me first.

JENNY. Look, I can keep a secret. Tell me, sir, isn't it you, Trivet, my boy?

TRIVET. Come, come, you're taking advantage of my good nature. It's time for me to go. (*Aside*) Uff! What a close scrape that was! (*He leaves.*)

JENNY (*alone*). Well, I tried everything; I suppose he's not the man. Incredible! Still, even if he *is* Trivet, Mr. Lubbock has much more to offer—that is, *if* he loves me.
(*Enter Mr. Lubbock.*)

MR. LUBBOCK. Well, sweetie, where do I stand with Angela?

JENNY. Just where you stood before.

MR. LUBBOCK (*laughing*). I'm heart-broken, I am.

JENNY. How can you say you're heart-broken and laugh your head off at the same time?

MR. LUBBOCK. Oh, I laugh at anything, my pigeon.

JENNY. Anyway, I have a piece of information for you. Miss Angela doesn't seem to care for the man Mr. Dorian chose for her, and I fancy you can catch her yet if you go on courting her.

MR. LUBBOCK (*glumly*). Do you think so? That's good.

JENNY. You're provoking me with your glum "That's good" and your gay "I'm heart-broken," and calling me your pigeon and all. Let me understand you once and for all, Mr. Lubbock. Do you love me?

MR. LUBBOCK. Can't tell you that just yet.

JENNY. You're making fun of me, then?

MR. LUBBOCK. Hoo, that's an ugly thought.

JENNY. Do you still intend to marry Miss Angela?

MR. LUBBOCK. The plot demands it.

JENNY. The plot! And if she refuses you, will you be disappointed?

MR. LUBBOCK (*laughing*). Oh, sure enough!

JENNY. I don't know what to think. You've got me so confused, I don't know how to take your compliments. Put yourself in my place.

MR. LUBBOCK. Put yourself in mine.

JENNY. But where do you stand? Because if you honestly meant it, if you really loved me . . .

MR. LUBBOCK (*laughing*). If I did . . .

JENNY. I wouldn't be ungrateful.

MR. LUBBOCK (*laughing*). Look into my eyes. Let's see if you mean it.

JENNY. What will you do with my heart?

MR. LUBBOCK. I'll lock it up. Pretty, pretty baby, I'm so sorry to see it suffer.

JENNY. I still don't understand. Oh well, here come Mrs. Grumby and Mr. Dorian. They must be talking about marrying Miss Angela to their guest. Her mother will want her to accept him, and if she obeys, as I think she'll have to, you will be a free man, Mr. Lubbock. So now I think you'd better step out of the way.

MR. LUBBOCK. I will; but I'll be a-coming back to see whether I'm to blow hot or cold.

JENNY (*angrily*). Those conundrums again! I've had about enough.

MR. LUBBOCK (*laughing, on his way out*). That's three thousand crowns you've had enough of! (*He leaves.*)

JENNY. Three thousand crowns! Where did *they* come from? I'm beginning to think there's something behind all this.
(*Enter Mrs. Grumby, Dorian, and Trivet.*)

MRS. GRUMBY (*to Trivet*). Don't be discouraged, sir. Angela will yield, I'm sure of it. She *must* yield. Jenny, were you present when this gentleman saw my daughter? Is it true she received him coolly? Tell me, has he any grounds for complaining?

JENNY. None, madam. I didn't notice any coolness. Miss Angela was merely taken aback, as is normal for a girl who's to be married on the spur of the moment, so to speak. All she wants, I'm sure, is a trifle of encouragement from you.

DORIAN. I agree with Jenny.

MRS. GRUMBY. You may be right. She's so young, so innocent.

TRIVET. An impromptu marriage astonishes an innocent girl, but it cannot distress her. Your daughter, however, was taken ill and went up to her room.

MRS. GRUMBY. No, no, dear sir, you'll see, you'll see. Jenny, go tell her to come down immediately. Bring her to me, and I mean at once. (*To Trivet*) Sir, be good enough to forgive her for a moment of thoughtlessness. It will pass, believe me.
(*Jenny leaves.*)

TRIVET. Say what you like, but I ought to have been spared this episode. It is most disconcerting for a man of the world like myself, who has had every eligible girl in the capital thrown at him, and who breaks some twenty hearts a day, to appear in his own person in a remote village, only to be snubbed by a country girl with nothing more than a pretty face to recommend her. Your daughter suits me, I don't deny it! And I thank my friend for having set her aside for me; but I ought to have found her hand extended to me upon my arrival, ready for mine to take it without further commotion.

DORIAN. I could hardly have foreseen all these problems.

MRS. GRUMBY. Gentlemen, gentlemen, a little patience! Look upon her—on this occasion, at any rate—as no more than a child.
(*Enter Angela and Jenny.*)

MRS. GRUMBY. Come here, young lady. Here is a gentleman who wants to marry you in spite of your reduced circumstances. Doesn't this honor mean anything to you?

TRIVET. Delete the word *honor!* My love and my gallantry forbid it.

MRS. GRUMBY. We must face the facts, dear sir. Answer, Angela.

ANGELA. Mother—

MRS. GRUMBY. At once.

TRIVET. Gently, madam, or else I'll call for my boots and leap to my horse again. (*To Angela*) Delicious child, you still haven't looked at me. You haven't seen the man I am. You scorn me without knowing me. Look first, and trust your eyes.

ANGELA. Sir—

MRS. GRUMBY. Raise your head!

TRIVET. Silence, madam. She said "Sir." Here's a beginning at least.

JENNY. You're luckier than you deserve, Miss Angela. You were born with a silver spoon in your mouth.

ANGELA (*sharply*). At least I wasn't born a chatterbox.

TRIVET. That makes you a rarity among women. Come, dear young lady, take a deep breath and declare yourself.

MRS. GRUMBY. I'm trying to swallow my anger.

DORIAN. All this is most distressing to me.

TRIVET (*to Angela*). Don't be afraid; one more effort.

ANGELA. Sir—I don't know you.

TRIVET. You shall know me once we are married. Marriage is a wonderful spur to familiarity.

MRS. GRUMBY. Well? Ungrateful goose!

TRIVET. Mrs. Grumby! Your conversation is unbearably coarse.

MRS. GRUMBY. Very well, I'll leave. I can't control myself any longer. Mark my words, gentlemen, I'll disinherit her if she doesn't return kindness for kindness. Mr. Dorian has showered us with favors; and now, to cap them off, he brings my daughter a husband who surpasses all our hopes, either for wealth, rank, or merit . . .

JENNY. I wouldn't stress that last item.

MRS. GRUMBY. As heaven is my witness, either she accepts him or I disown her. (*She leaves.*)

JENNY. Really, Miss Angela, I don't know what to say. You must be waiting for Prince Charming to appear.

TRIVET. I don't mean to boast, but this marks my initiation as a rejected suitor.

DORIAN. You know, my dear Angela, that I discussed this marriage with you. You seemed to be happy with it. As for me, I had only your interest in mind.

ANGELA. Your interest is admirable; it's one of the seven wonders of the world. And I am a fool, I know. But let me say something too. Now that my mother is gone, I feel a little bolder, and it's only right that I should take my turn. I'll begin with you, Jenny. Kindly keep your thoughts to yourself. Nothing that has happened here concerns you in the least. When a proposal comes your way, you can do whatever you like with it. I won't be asking you to account to me, nor will I make stupid remarks, like "You were born with a silver spoon in your mouth," or "You don't know how lucky you are," or "You must be waiting for Prince Charming to appear," or the rest of your nonsense.

TRIVET. After this, I can guess what's in store for me.

ANGELA. A great deal, sir. You're a gentleman, are you not?

TRIVET. It is my chief distinction.

ANGELA. Then you can't wish to make a girl unhappy who never did you any harm. That would be cruel and inhuman.

TRIVET. Oh, I'm the most human creature alive, as I have proved to the fair sex a thousand times.

ANGELA. I'm so glad to hear it. Because I must tell you, sir, that I would perish if I were compelled to love you. My instinct tells me so. I am willing to admit that you are a lovable man, so long as it isn't I who must love you; and I would sing your praises to any girl you might choose, other than myself. Please don't take my words amiss; they are spoken straight from the heart. Remember, it wasn't I who went looking for you. I didn't know you existed, and if I had known you did, I would have said to you, "Don't come" exactly as I am now telling you, "Go away."

TRIVET. "Go away"?

ANGELA. Yes, and the sooner the better. But this shouldn't trouble you; you'll find plenty of other girls. Don't they all flock to rich men? Only it so happens that I am not interested in money. I'd rather give it away than receive it. That's how I am.

TRIVET. And that's how I am not. What time do I leave?

ANGELA. You're very kind. Whenever you like. I won't detain you. It's too late now, but tomorrow promises to be a sunny day.

TRIVET (to Dorian). My dear friend, that is what I call a flat refusal. Though I yield to it, I shall want your advice before I go. And so, my heartless beauty, I'll put off my last farewell for a while longer.

ANGELA. What? Not leaving after all? That's what I call persistence! (*Trivet goes out.*) Your friend has no backbone. He asks me at what time he should leave, and then he stays.

DORIAN. It isn't easy to leave you, Angela. But don't worry, I'll take him off your hands.

JENNY. What a pity! A man who offered her a fortune!

DORIAN. There are such things as insurmountable dislikes. If that is what troubled Angela, I'm not surprised at her refusing him. But I still intend to arrange a good match for her.

ANGELA. Please don't interfere again. Some people bring nothing but trouble.

DORIAN. I bring trouble? With my good intentions? Haven't I been a friend to you?

ANGELA (*aside*). A friend! Wicked man!

DORIAN. Where have I failed you?

ANGELA. Failed me, sir? It never occurred to me to say that you failed me. Do I blame you for anything you have done? Do I look angry? No, I am not complaining. I'm perfectly satisfied. You've done everything a girl could ask for. Why, you offer me as many husbands as I could wish. You have them shipped from the city without my asking you. I've never met anyone more thoughtful and obliging. True, I refuse them all. But even though you are full of consideration for me, I am not required to throw myself at the first man who arrives in his riding boots from God knows where, and who offers to carry me off on your say-so. No, thank you. I'm very grateful to you, but I'm not an idiot.

DORIAN. Say what you like, but these are bitter words. I see no reason why I deserve them.

JENNY. I could tell you the reason if I wanted to.

ANGELA. Ha! Listen to the little know-it-all! What can she be thinking of? Look, Jenny, you know I am usually good-natured—a baby is more vicious than I—but if you provoke me—I think you know what I mean—I'll bear you a grudge for a thousand years.

DORIAN. If you are really not angry with me, please take back the little present I made you, which you returned to me for no reason at all.

ANGELA. My reason is, it wouldn't be proper for me to take it. The jewels were meant to go with the husband, and in returning the one, I am returning the other. What can you answer to *that*? Keep them for that dazzling creature in the portrait you carry about.

DORIAN. I'll find other jewels for her. These are meant for you.

ANGELA. Let her have them all. I'd throw them away.

JENNY. And I'd pick them up.

DORIAN. In short, you don't really want me to find you a husband. I do believe you must be concealing some secret love from me.

ANGELA. That may be. Yes, that's it. I'm in love with a man who lives near here. And if I weren't, I'd fall in love tomorrow for the sheer pleasure of choosing a husband all by myself.
(*Enter Mr. Lubbock.*)

MR. LUBBOCK. I'm asking kindly for permission to interrupt. Miss Angela, what's the declaration of your last decision? Are you going to keep your new wooer that came a-wooing here a while ago?

ANGELA. No; leave me alone.

MR. LUBBOCK. And are you a-going to keep me?

ANGELA. No.

MR. LUBBOCK. Once and once makes twice: will you have me?

ANGELA. He's unbearable!

JENNY. Are you deaf, Mr. Lubbock? She said no.

MR. LUBBOCK. So she did, dearie. Now, sir, you're my witness as how I love her and how she don't want no part of me. And since she don't, it's her fault and I mustn't get blamed for it. (*Aside to Jenny*) Hey ho, my pigeon. (*Aloud*) Besides, I ain't surprised. Miss Angela has showed the door to two lads, and she'd show the door to three, five, and a bushel of them. There's only one man she wants. The rest is weed and stubble for her—all except Mr. Dorian, just like I guessed from the start.

ANGELA (*furious*). Mr. Dorian!

MR. LUBBOCK. Mr. Dorian hisself. Oh, I seen you crying when he was sick, thinking as he was going to die.

DORIAN. I'll never believe that. Angela, crying out of affection for me?

ANGELA. Don't believe it! No—you can't be so rude as to believe it. Imagine accusing me of being in love because I cry and because I'm kind! Why, I cry for anyone who is sick, I cry for anything whose life is in danger! I'd cry for my canary if it were to die. Does that mean I'm in love with my canary?

JENNY. Well, let it go, let it go. And yet, to be perfectly honest, I had the same thoughts as Mr. Lubbock.

ANGELA. What, Jenny—you too? Are you going to tear me to pieces? What have I done to you? Oh, God, you think me capable of loving a man who is indifferent to me, who wants to marry me off to half the world! I tell you that I love someone else; I'd have no room for *him* even if he wanted me. You must think me vile and base to taunt me like this.

DORIAN. Really, Angela, you're not being reasonable. Don't you see that our little conversations are responsible for this extraordinary idea? You mustn't pay any attention to it.

ANGELA. I suppose I have been too discreet to explain my true feelings toward you, Mr. Dorian. I like you so little that if I didn't constrain myself, I could easily hate you, now that you have brought me your friend. Yes, I could hate you; I'm not sure that I don't hate you already. I can't swear that I don't. The feeling of friendship I once had for you is gone. Well, then, is that a symptom of love?

DORIAN. Your unhappiness makes me blush for myself. Please don't defend yourself. Since you're in love with someone else, what else is there to say?

MR. LUBBOCK. In love with someone else! Pah! Let her show who; I dare her.

ANGELA. You do, do you? Well, since you all insist—there he is: Mr. Lubbock, the beast!

DORIAN. I thought as much.

MR. LUBBOCK. Me?

JENNY. Bosh! It's not true.

ANGELA. What's that? Don't I know my own feelings? I assure you he's the one.

MR. LUBBOCK. Now, missy, let's not have no more jokes out o' season. Honest now, is it me or ain't it?

ANGELA. Haven't I said it often enough? Yes, it's you, you ill-mannered clown; believe me or don't, it's all one to me.

MR. LUBBOCK. Your mother won't never approve.

ANGELA. I know.

MR. LUBBOCK. What's more, you flunged me aside once, and I was counting on that. I've made other arrangements.

ANGELA. That's your business.

MR. LUBBOCK. My mind don't turn thither and fro like a weathervane or a woman. I put my faith in the snub you gave me.

ANGELA. Suit yourself, you nitwit.

MR. LUBBOCK. Besides, I ain't rich.

DORIAN. Don't let that worry you, I'll take care of everything.

Since you're lucky enough to be favored by Angela, I'll give you five thousand crowns as a wedding present. Now I'm going to carry the news to Mrs. Grumby. I'll be back in no time with her answer.

ANGELA. How they all persecute me!

DORIAN. And then I shall have the satisfaction of seeing you married to the man you love, cost what it may.

ANGELA (*aside*). Oh, he's going to be the death of me.
(*Dorian leaves.*)

JENNY. Mr. Dorian is a great marriage-broker! What have you decided to do, Mr. Lubbock?

MR. LUBBOCK (*after a moment's thought*). I still think you're a beauty, but them five thousand crowns is doing you powerful harm.

JENNY. There's a rascal for you.

ANGELA (*gloomily*). Did you have some design on her?

MR. LUBBOCK. I won't say as I didn't.

ANGELA. In other words, you don't love me.

MR. LUBBOCK. Yes, I do. It went away for a while, but now I re-love you again.

ANGELA (*gloomier than ever*). Because of the five thousand crowns?

MR. LUBBOCK. Because of you, and them too.

ANGELA. Do I understand that you intend to take the money?

MR. LUBBOCK. Don't I though! And don't you want me to?

ANGELA. If you accept the money, you must give me up.

MR. LUBBOCK. Did I hear what I just heard?

ANGELA. It wouldn't be gentlemanly of you to accept money from a man who wanted me to marry somebody else. Not only that; he insulted me by supposing that I care for him, and people are saying that I'm in love with him. You can't take money from such a man, Mr. Lubbock.

JENNY. Miss Angela is right. I agree with every word she says.

MR. LUBBOCK. Let's keep our heads, in the name o' God! If I don't take the money, I can't take you neither. Your mother won't never allow you to marry without it.

ANGELA. Well, if she won't allow it, I'll have to give you up.

MR. LUBBOCK (*worried*). Is that your last word?

ANGELA. My very last word.

MR. LUBBOCK. Here's a kettle of fish!
(*Enter Dorian.*)

DORIAN. Your mother has given her consent, my pretty Angela. Your marriage to Mr. Lubbock is settled by virtue of the five thousand crowns I'm giving him. You must both go and thank her.

MR. LUBBOCK. Not yet. She's put another extramaganza into her head. Now she's acting pernickety about the five thousand, because it's you what's giving it to me. She won't have me if I take the money, and I won't take her without it.

ANGELA (*going*). And I don't want anybody, and I don't care who it is.

DORIAN. Wait, please, dear Angela. You two, leave us alone.

MR. LUBBOCK (*to Dorian, aside, and taking Jenny by the arm*). Are you sticking to our first bargain?

DORIAN. I certainly am.

MR. LUBBOCK (*to Jenny*). Heaven bless you, my pigeon. I'm betrothing you on the spot. (*They leave.*)

DORIAN. Angela, you're crying.

ANGELA. Because my mother will be angry. And also because I've suffered enough to make anybody cry.

DORIAN. Leave your mother to me. But for yourself—must I give up all hopes of making you happy?

ANGELA. Enough! I want no favors from a man who let it be known that I was in love with him all by myself.

DORIAN. It wasn't I who created the impression, my dear.

ANGELA. You didn't hear *me* boasting that you loved me, did you? Even though I had good reasons to believe it; as good as yours. I never took advantage of your compliments and attentions, but you did take advantage of mine. I was a fool to trust you.

DORIAN. And yet, if ever you thought that I loved you, and that my heart was overflowing with tenderness for you, you were not mistaken. (*Angela breaks into sobs.*) Angela! Now at last I can open my heart and confess that I adore you.

ANGELA. I don't know. But if I ever love a man, I won't go hunting up girls for him to marry. I'd see him die a bachelor first!

DORIAN. Heaven help me! If it hadn't been for your aversion to me, which seems so genuine and natural, I would have said to you, "Angela, take me." Why are you crying now?

ANGELA. You talk about aversion; am I not right to hate you? And what about that portrait you are carrying in your pocket?

DORIAN. Pure pretense. It's a picture of my sister.

ANGELA. I couldn't guess that, could I?

DORIAN. Here it is: let me give it to you.

ANGELA. What am I to do with it, once you're gone? A picture is no remedy for anything.

DORIAN. What if I stay? What if I ask you to marry me? And what if we never separate again?

ANGELA. That's a little better.

DORIAN. Then do you love me?

ANGELA. Have I ever done anything but love you?

DORIAN (*falling on his knees*). Oh, Angela, I'm the happiest man alive!
(*All the actors come in.*)

MRS. GRUMBY. What now, sir! On your knees before my daughter?

DORIAN. Yes, madam, and with your consent, I'll marry her today.

MRS. GRUMBY (*delighted*). My consent! Sir, this is too great an honor for us. But you will make us still happier by asking this gentleman, who is your friend, to remain ours as well.

TRIVET. I'm so well-disposed toward you, madam, that I'll even fill your glass at table. (*To Jenny*) My queen, since you're mad about Trivet, and since I resemble Trivet, I've decided, why not, to *be* Trivet.

JENNY. I understand you well enough, you rascal, but you're too late.

MR. LUBBOCK. Me and she is one for life, and three thousand crowns is coming along to keep us company.

MRS. GRUMBY. What does all this mean?

DORIAN. I'll explain everything later. But first, send for the village fiddlers, and let's end the day with a dance.

THE END

Appendixes

Table of Characters in the English Versions and in the Originals

Robin, Bachelor of Love
(*Arlequin poli par l'amour*)

Lucinda	La Fée
Trivet	Trivelin
Robin	Arlequin
Sylvia	Silvia

Double Infidelity
(*La Double inconstance*)

The Prince	Le Prince
Lord Lumley	Un Seigneur
Flaminia	Flaminia
Lisa	Lisette
Sylvia	Silvia
Robin	Arlequin
Trivet	Trivelin

Money Makes the World Go Round
(*Le Triomphe de Plutus*)

Apollo, as Dulcimer	Apollon, as Ergaste
Plutus, as Richard	Plutus, as Richard
Mr. Grangewell	Armidas
Lydia	Aminte
Puff	Arlequin
Spinetta	Spinette

The Game of Love and Chance
(Le Jeu de l'amour et du hasard)

Mr. Humphrey	Monsieur Orgon
Thomas Humphrey	Mario
Sylvia	Silvia
Dorian	Dorante
Lisa	Lisette
Trivet	Arlequin

The Wiles of Love
(L'Heureux stratagème)

Belinda	La Comtesse
Arabella	La Marquise
Dorian	Dorante
Captain Coxe	Le Chevalier
Fanny	Lisette
Puff	Arlequin
Trivet	Frontin
Mr. Nubbins	Blaise

Sylvia Hears a Secret
(Les Fausses confidences)

Sylvia	Araminte
Dorian	Dorante
Mr. Rooney	Monsieur Remy
Mrs. Grumby	Madame Argante
Puff	Arlequin
Trivet	Dubois
Alice	Marton
Lord Dorimont	Le Comte

The Test
(L'Épreuve)

Mrs. Grumby	Madame Argante
Angela	Angélique
Jenny	Lisette
Dorian	Lucidor
Trivet	Frontin
Mr. Lubbock	Maître Blaise

Published English Translations
of Marivaux's Plays

LE JEU DE L'AMOUR ET DU HASARD

George Colman: TIT FOR TAT (London, 1786), an alteration of Joseph Atkinson's *Mutual Deception* (1785, never printed). This is a free adaptation of Marivaux.

Harriet Ford and Marie Louise le Verrier: LOVE IN LIVERY (New York, Samuel French, 1907).

Richard Aldington: THE GAME OF LOVE AND CHANCE; in *French Comedies of the 18th Century* (London, Routledge, 1923).

Wallace Fowlie: THE GAME OF LOVE AND CHANCE; in *Classical French Drama* (New York, Bantam, 1962).

LES FAUSSES CONFIDENCES

W. S. Merwin: THE FALSE CONFESSIONS; in *The Classic Theatre*, vol. 4, ed. Eric Bentley (New York, Anchor, 1961).

LE LEGS

Barrett H. Clark: THE LEGACY (New York, Samuel French, 1915).

L'ÉPREUVE

Willis K. Jones: THE TEST; in *Poet Lore*, Boston, vol. 35, no. 4 (1924).

LA JOIE IMPRÉVUE

> THE AGREEABLE SURPRISE; in *Poetical Blossoms: or, The Sports of Genius,* "by the young gentlemen of Mr. Rule's Academy at Islington" (London, 1766).

LA DOUBLE INCONSTANCE

> Cosmos G. Lennox: SYLVIA's LOVERS, "a light opera" (London, 1921); a libretto based on Marivaux's play.

Chronological List of All the Known Plays of Marivaux

1706. *Le Père prudent et équitable, ou Crispin l'heureux fourbe*
One act. Written and published in Limoges, and never performed in Paris.

1720. *L'Amour et la vérité*
Three acts. In collaboration with the chevalier de Saint-Jory. Performed at the Théâtre Italien.

1720. *Arlequin poli par l'amour*
One act. Théâtre Italien.

1720. *Annibal*
Five acts. Marivaux's only tragedy. Comédie-Française.

1722. *La Surprise de l'amour*
Three acts. Théâtre Italien.

1722. *La Double inconstance*
Three acts. Théâtre Italien.

1724. *Le Prince travesti, ou L'Illustre aventurier*
Three acts. Théâtre Italien.

1724. *La Fausse suivante, ou Le Fourbe puni*
Three acts. Théâtre Italien.

1724. *Le Dénouement imprévu*
One act. Comédie-Française.

1725. *L'Ile des esclaves*
One act. Théâtre Italien.

1725. *L'Héritier de village*
One act. Théâtre Italien.

1727. *L'Ile de la raison, ou Les Petits hommes*
Three acts. Comédie-Française.

1727. *La Seconde surprise de l'amour*
Three acts. Comédie-Française.

1728. *Le Triomphe de Plutus*
One act. Théâtre Italien.

1729. *La Colonie*
One act. Théâtre Italien.

1730. *Le Jeu de l'amour et du hasard*
Three acts. Théâtre Italien.

1731. *La Réunion des amours*
One act. Comédie-Française.

1732. *Le Triomphe de l'amour*
Three acts. Théâtre Italien.

1732. *Les Serments indiscrets*
Five acts. Comédie-Française.

1732. *L'École des mères*
One act. Théâtre Italien.

1733. *L'Heureux stratagème*
Three acts. Théâtre Italien.

1734. *La Méprise*
One act. Théâtre Italien.

1734. *Le Petit-Maître corrigé*
Three acts. Comédie-Française.

1734. *Le Chemin de la fortune, ou Le Saut du fossé*
One act. Published but never performed.

1735. *Le Mère confidente*
Three acts. Théâtre Italien.

1736. *Le Legs*
One act. Comédie-Française.

1737. *Les Fausses confidences*
Three acts. Théâtre Italien.

1738. *La Joie imprévue*
One act. Théâtre Italien.

1739. *Les Sincères*
One act. Théâtre Italien.

1740.   *L'Épreuve*
        One act. Théâtre Italien.

1741.   *La Commère*
        One act. Never published or performed, this play was
        discovered in the archives of the Comédie-Française in
        1965.[1]

1744.   *La Dispute*
        One act. Comédie-Française.

1746.   *Le Préjugé vaincu*
        One act. Comédie-Française.

1755.   *La Femme fidèle*
        One act. Performed in the theatre of the comte de Cler-
        mont's chateau of Berny. Only fragments survive.

1757.   *Félicie*
        One act. Never performed. Published in the *Mercure
        de France.*

1757.   *Les Acteurs de bonne foi*
        One act. Never performed. Published in the *Conser-
        vateur.*

[1] Excerpts appeared in the *Figaro Littéraire,* January 13, 1966, and
the premiere of the play took place at the Comédie-Française on April 26,
1967. However, Marivaux's authorship is open to question.

Bibliographical Note

For these translations I have used Marcel Arland's edition of the complete dramatic works in the Bibliothèque de la Pléiade (1961). Marivaux's texts present no significant problems.

STUDIES IN ENGLISH. E. J. H. Greene's exhaustive *Marivaux* (University of Toronto, 1965) is highly recommended. Most readers will have to go no further. Kenneth McKee's *Theatre of Marivaux* (New York University, 1958) is a useful handbook. Several essays should be mentioned: T. S. Eliot's "Marivaux" in *Art and Letters* (Spring 1919), a perceptive fragment; A. A. Tilley, in *Three French Dramatists* (Cambridge, 1933); and a brilliant, all too brief discussion by F. C. Green, in *Minuet: A Critical Survey of French and English Literary Ideas in the Eighteenth Century* (Dent, 1935). Georges Poulet's chapter on Marivaux in *La Distance intérieure* (1952) can be read in Elliott Coleman's translation: *The Interior Distance* (Johns Hopkins, 1959), but it is little more than a recondite oddity.

Clarence D. Brenner, in *The Théâtre Italien: Its Repertory 1716–1793* (UCLA, 1961) has an authoritative introductory history of this theatre. For personages of the *commedia dell'arte*, Allardyce Nicoll's *The World of Harlequin* (Cambridge, 1963) may be consulted.

Ruth K. Jamieson's excellent *Marivaux, a Study in Sensibility* (King's Crown, 1941) is a specialized thesis dealing almost exclusively with the novels.

STUDIES IN FRENCH. A brief but basic list must begin with Gustave Larroumet's pioneering work, *Marivaux, sa vie et ses oeuvres* (1882). This should be supplemented and corrected by Marie-Jeanne Durry's *A Propos de Marivaux* (1960). Frédéric Deloffre's *Marivaux et le marivaudage* (1955) is standard for Marivaux's language and dialogue. Two studies of the theatre are indispensable in connection with Marivaux: Xavier de Courville's *Un Apôtre de l'art du théâtre au XVIIIᵉ siècle, Luigi Riccoboni dit Lélio,* volume II (1945), and Gustave Attinger's *L'Esprit de la Commedia dell'Arte dans le théâtre français* (1950). A fine earlier work is N.-M. Bernardin, *La Comédie italienne en France et les Théâtres de la Foire et du boulevard* (1570-1791) (1902). For adequate recent presentations of Marivaux, the following can be consulted: Claude Roy, *Lire Marivaux* (1947); Marcel Arland, *Marivaux* (1950), as well as his introduction to the Pléiade edition; and Paul Gazagne, *Marivaux par lui-même* (1954). I have not seen Bernard Dort's introductory essay to a limited edition of Marivaux (1961: Le Club français du livre), which is praised by Professor Greene.

An excellent work on the French salons is *Salons du XVIIIᵉ siècle* by M. Glotz and M. Maire (1949).

The works by Jamieson, Deloffre, and Greene cited here include long and useful bibliographies.